# PRAISE FOR
## THEA HARRISON AND HER NOVELS

"Black Dagger Brotherhood readers will love [this]! . . . A smart heroine, a sexy alpha hero and a dark, compelling world. I'm hooked!"

—J. R. Ward, #1 *New York Times* bestselling author of *The Bourbon Kings*

"Thea Harrison is a master storyteller, and she transported me to a fascinating world I want to visit again and again. It's a fabulous, exciting read that paranormal romance readers will love."

—Christine Feehan, #1 *New York Times* bestselling author of *Dark Blood*

"Smoldering sensuality, fascinating characters and an intriguing world . . . Thea Harrison has a new fan in me!"

—Nalini Singh, *New York Times* bestselling author of *Archangel's Enigma*

"A truly original urban fantasy romance."

—Angela Knight, *New York Times* bestselling author of *Love Bites*

"Sexy and action-packed . . . Held me transfixed from beginning to end!"

—Anya Bast, *New York Times* bestselling author of *Capturing Caroline*

"A colorful, compelling world with magic so real, the reader can feel it."

—Shannon K. Butcher, national bestselling author of *Edge of Betrayal*

"Fun, feral and fiercely exciting—I can't get enough! Thea Harrison supplies deliciously addictive paranormal romance."

—Ann Aguirre, national bestselling author of *Breakout*

"Sexy and romantic and refreshingly different."     —Dear Author

"An epic story of myth, ma⎯⎯⎯⎯⎯⎯⎯⎯⎯⎯⎯⎯
readers satisfied and breathi⎯⎯

D0188538

*Berkley Sensation Titles by Thea Harrison*

*Novels of the Elder Races*

DRAGON BOUND
STORM'S HEART
SERPENT'S KISS
ORACLE'S MOON
LORD'S FALL
KINKED
NIGHT'S HONOR
MIDNIGHT'S KISS
SHADOW'S END

*Game of Shadows Novels*

RISING DARKNESS
FALLING LIGHT

WITHDRAWN

# SHADOW'S END

## Thea Harrison

BERKLEY SENSATION, NEW YORK

## BERKLEY
## SENSATION

**An imprint of Penguin Random House LLC**
**375 Hudson Street, New York, New York 10014**

SHADOW'S END

A Berkley Sensation Book / published by arrangement with the author

ISBN: 978-0-425-27439-2

PUBLISHING HISTORY
Berkley Sensation mass-market edition / December 2015

PRINTED IN THE UNITED STATES OF AMERICA

10  9  8  7  6  5  4  3  2  1

Cover design by Adam Auerbach.
Interior text design by Tiffany Estreicher.

Penguin
Random
House

# ⇒ ONE ⇐

W ith one blunt forefinger, Graydon tapped out a text on his smartphone.

We can't put off meeting any longer. I can't explain why in a text, but we're running out of time. I need . . .

He paused as an onslaught of emotion cascaded through him.
I need to see you.
I need to touch your cheek, clasp your hand.
I need to look into your eyes, your beautiful eyes.
I need to know the precious light inside you has not died.
That was when the vision hit him.

He was used to having visions. He'd had them his entire, very long life. The Gaelic had many words and terms for such a thing. *An Da Shealladh* or "the two sights" was one of the most famous of them.

When he was tired to the point of distraction, or hungry to the point of feeling hollow, he saw images of places he had not yet seen or things he had not yet done, and he knew he would see those places, and he would do those things. Eventually.

The vision rolled over him as inescapably as if he had plunged into a vast ocean and water had closed over his head.

Over the last two hundred years, the scene had become familiar. He had seen it so many times. It held a scent of danger, smoky like gunpowder and sharp as a stiletto.

White, like snow, blanketed the ground near a dark, tempestuous shore. The white was broken by rocks as black as midnight. Nearby, a behemoth of a building crouched atop a sprawling bluff like a huge predator. When he looked down, he saw bright scarlet blooming on the white ground, like roses opening to the sun.

Only the scarlet wasn't flowers, but blood.

His blood, dripping between his fingers.

"Uncle Gray?"

The boy's voice penetrated the images, and the vision snapped.

It didn't fully dissipate but lingered at the edge of his mind, ready to surge back the moment he became too tired, hungry or careless.

Frustrated, he shoved it aside through sheer force of will. He was on the clock and didn't have time for this shit. He didn't care if the vision returned later, just as long as he could focus on his real surroundings for now. He could wrestle with his inner demons when he was on his own time.

As he fought to clear his head, a solid, prosaic reality settled into place around him.

He wore combat boots, jeans and a leather jacket, and he had an assault rifle slung over one shoulder. Beside him stood a young, curious dragon in human form.

Graydon's assault rifle was a just-in-case accessory, since the most important duty he had that night was watching the boy. If something outlandish did occur, any action he took would be purely defensive.

They stood at the top of Cuelebre Tower at night. The Tower was in the heart of the Wyr demesne, eighty stories of financial and political dominance stamped onto the New

York landscape. The air felt frigid and bracing, and fluffy white snowflakes were beginning to drift and eddy on a fitful breeze.

No other building in the immediate vicinity was as tall as Cuelebre Tower. Some people claimed that was the hubris of Dragos Cuelebre, the Lord of the Wyr, multibillionaire and head of Cuelebre Enterprises.

Along with the other six sentinels, Graydon knew better. While Dragos had pride enough in spades, the relative height of his Tower didn't have anything to do with it.

Between avian Wyr and the occasional helicopter, the Tower rooftop saw a lot of traffic. Dragos's decision to bribe the city council into keeping the surrounding buildings shorter had been based on security considerations, pure and simple.

As Liam Cuelebre, Dragos's son and Prince of the Wyr, stared up at Graydon, he realized he hadn't responded to the boy. He cleared his throat. "Yeah, what is it, sport?"

The wind ruffled Liam's dark blond hair. His wide, dark violet gaze was so like his mother's. "Is everything okay?"

Graydon had been standing frozen for too long, and while Liam might appear to be a sunny-natured, ordinary boy, he had been born a mere nine months ago and there was nothing ordinary about him.

Physically he appeared to be a tall, handsome twelve-year-old, but that was the result of the Powerful dragon in him straining to become fully grown.

In his human form, Liam was bigger and stronger than any normal twelve-year-old. In his Wyr form, his dragon was already twice the size of any of the gryphons—and the gryphons were some of the largest Wyr in the world. Graydon's Wyr form was easily the size of an SUV, a massive, muscled blend of eagle and lion.

In terms of sheer strength, Liam could also overpower any of the sentinels, although that didn't mean the boy could take any of them in a fight, since the sentinels had age, cunning and experience on their side. Not that any of them fought Liam in anything other than a carefully controlled training exercise.

Intellectually, the boy's reading was at college level, his math skills were off the charts, and the gods only knew how good his truthsense was, or any of his other senses, for that matter. Sweet-natured as he was, much of him remained a mystery.

So Graydon ruffled Liam's hair affectionately and told him a version of the truth. "Sorry, I got lost in thought. Everything's as normal as can be. Wanna listen in for a minute?"

The boy's gaze sparked with interest. "Sure."

Graydon said into his mic, "Watch your language, folks. I'm putting a guest on the line for a few minutes."

Even though the security detail's channel was encrypted, hackers were a constant concern, and nobody used real names over the comm link. Still, everyone knew the identity of Graydon's visitor.

Alexander, the pegasus, was the other sentinel on duty that night. His rich, warm voice came down the comm link. He sounded amused. "Roger that."

Graydon removed his headset and handed it to Liam. "If you just hold it up to your ear, I'll be able to hear it too."

His eyes wide with fascination, Liam nodded. He held the headset up to listen to the security detail.

Propping one booted foot on a railing, Graydon crossed his arms over his knee and surveyed the surrounding area as events unfolded like clockwork. He nodded to himself in satisfaction. He liked an evening that held no surprises.

All the rooftops of the neighboring buildings had been checked and cleared, and the last team member had settled into place. Eighty stories below, on the ground, a crowd of paparazzi had formed along the sidewalk that bordered the front steps of the Tower. Legally, the sidewalk was as close to Cuelebre Towers as the paparazzi were allowed to get without an express invitation to a press conference.

Graydon's smartphone buzzed in the front pocket of his jeans, a short vibration that indicated he had received a text message or an email. He ignored it for the moment, as he gave the rooftops of the surrounding buildings one last, narrow-eyed check.

Three blocks away a sleek, black limousine turned a corner. Dragos and Pia were arriving right on time. The limo pulled to a smooth stop at the front steps of the Tower.

Hugh, a gargoyle Wyr who alternated between acting as Liam's bodyguard and a member of Pia's personal security team, stepped forward to open the rear door. Bending slightly, he held out a hand in invitation.

Slender female fingers grasped Hugh's. Graydon might be eighty stories away, but his sharp gryphon's eyes picked up the brilliant flash of diamond on the woman's ring finger.

First Pia's long slender legs emerged, then the woman herself appeared as she climbed out of the car, her gleaming pale blond hair piled high on her head. She wore a silver sequined dress and a luxurious-looking white faux fur stole, and she shone like a slender pillar of white fire in the night.

Immediately following Pia's exit, her husband Dragos poured out of the limo, nearly seven feet tall and three hundred pounds of hard, muscled male, the most lethal Wyr predator in the world.

The white shirt of his tux emphasized his dark bronze skin, straight black hair and piercing gold eyes. Several of the paparazzi took a step back, their instincts telling them that danger walked in their midst. They were the smart ones of the bunch.

Their instinctive caution didn't stop them from doing their jobs. Lights exploded from cameras all around the couple, and Dragos turned his face away. His expression looked hard and bored. He hated having his picture taken.

Pia and Dragos climbed the steps and disappeared from Graydon's sight as they stepped into the building. The paparazzi's attention splintered. Individuals wandered in different directions, several talking on cell phones. With a near silent, collective sigh, the security detail outside relaxed.

Alexander said, "Stand down. That's a wrap for the night."

Graydon held out his hand for the headset, and Liam handed it over.

"Nice work, everybody," Graydon said into the mic. "The

kitchen will be serving a late supper for the next hour. Chef said there would be prime rib in the cafeteria for people who pulled security duty tonight."

A flurry of *good nights* came down the link.

Liam grinned at him. "One of these days I'm gonna be on one of those details."

"Yeah?" Graydon returned his grin. "One of these days, you might be leading one."

"Cool." Liam fell into step beside him as he strode across the rooftop, heading for the staircase. "Can I have some prime rib too?"

Earlier that evening, the two of them had polished off an extra-large pepperoni pizza while watching old *Hammer House of Horror* episodes, but the boy was a bottomless pit.

"Of course you can," Graydon said. The cafeteria was located just one story below the penthouse. The upper stories of Cuelebre Tower were secure, so he told Liam, "You go on to the cafeteria."

Liam paused on the steps to look back at him. "Aren't you coming?"

"I'm gonna check in with your mom and dad," he told the boy. "Come back up to the penthouse when you're done eating."

"Okay," said Liam. He gave Graydon a hug and a quick smile. "Thanks for letting me hang out with you this evening."

His expression softened, and he returned the hug. "My pleasure, sport."

He watched as Liam ran ahead, then he continued on his way to the penthouse.

That evening, Dragos and Pia had attended one of the major political functions of the year, a kick-off event that started two weeks of meetings, suppers and balls that surrounded the winter holiday celebrations.

For the Elder Races, the time around the summer solstice was the main political season. Winter solstice marked a smaller, secondary season. Some politics were involved, but those meetings tended to be quieter and smaller.

Much of the focus of the winter season was social, as it was the time to celebrate the Masque of the Gods. Every year in New York, the numbers of the Elder Races swelled as Dragos hosted one of the biggest, most elaborate masques in the world, and dignitaries and celebrities came from all the other demesnes to attend.

Once Graydon stepped inside the penthouse, he set his rifle aside gently. His cell phone vibrated again, and he pulled it out of his pocket to check his messages.

The messages app was still open to his unsent text.

He gazed down at it. He hadn't typed, "I need to see you," as he had intended.

Instead, his screen read: I need you.

The cool silence in the spacious, luxurious apartment pressed against his ears. Gently, he tapped the erase button until the text disappeared.

Pia appeared in the doorway. She had slipped off her faux fur stole and carried it slung over one shoulder. Up close, she was even more eye catching, as the sequins in her dress picked up every fraction of light and magnified it.

She and Dragos had not yet made a formal announcement about the fact that she was pregnant again. So far, only their inner circle knew. While she hadn't yet begun to show, the pregnancy suited her. Her skin and hair looked more lustrous than ever.

She gave him a tired, cheerful smile. "Everything go all right?"

"Of course," he told her. "I love spending time with Liam. He's gone to get a second supper in the cafeteria."

She shook her head. "Why does that not surprise me?"

"He'll be up in a half an hour or so."

Dragos entered the room, his tuxedo tie loosened. He had shrugged out of his jacket and rolled up his sleeves. He nodded a greeting to Graydon.

Even though Graydon had already heard a preliminary report, he asked, "How did the evening go?"

With a cynical twist of his lips, Dragos replied, "Same old, same old."

Pia rolled her eyes. Leaning against the end of the couch, she slipped off her sparkly high heeled pumps.

"There was plenty of ammunition for the gossip magazines. The Light Fae ambassador from Brazil got drunk, took off all his clothes and went for a swim in the big fountain in the hotel lobby, and the heir to the Algerian witches demesne vomited all over the Demonkind prime minister's Stuart Weitzman diamond stiletto shoes." She paused thoughtfully. "If you ask me, I think he did that on purpose. The prime minister was being very snippy."

Graydon gave her a brief smile, then turned to Dragos. "I know it's late, but I need a few moments."

Dragos and Pia exchanged a glance. Bending to scoop up her shoes in one hand, she said, "I'm headed for a shower and bed."

"I'll wait for Liam to get back and join you later," Dragos told her.

She nodded and padded over to kiss Graydon on the cheek. "Goodnight, Gray."

A rush of affection hit him. Pia had only come into their lives a year and a half ago, but now he couldn't imagine life without her.

"Goodnight, cupcake," he replied, patting her back.

Both men watched her disappear down the hall. She closed the door to their master suite and a few moments later, Graydon heard a faint, distinct sound of water running.

Only then did Dragos move. He strolled to the bar located at one end of the spacious living room, sloshed brandy into two snifters and returned to hand one of the glasses to Graydon.

"Step out onto the balcony with me," Dragos said. "I could use some fresh air."

Graydon blew out a breath. "Sure."

Outside, the wind was knifelike, but both Wyr males generated enough body heat that the cold felt refreshing. Dragos lifted his face and took a deep breath, the line of his wide shoulders easing.

Graydon couldn't join him in relaxing. The vision pushed along the edges of his awareness, seeking to take over his mind again. His muscles tightened against the instinctive urge to shift and launch into the night.

Dragos took a mouthful of his brandy. "What's on your mind?"

Walking to the edge of the balcony, Graydon looked down at the incandescent ribbon of traffic below. "I told you once, a long time ago, that I might have to take a leave of absence. Do you remember?"

His question wasn't just a conversational prompt. Over the summer, Dragos had sustained a traumatic brain injury that had resulted in odd gaps in his memory.

Dragos joined him at the balcony. Graydon was a big guy, the largest of the sentinels, but even he had to look up a few inches as he glanced at the new pale scar that slashed down the other male's temple.

None of the Wyr lord's incisive intelligence or aggressive personality had been affected by his injury. After a few tense days of suffering total post-traumatic amnesia, he had recalled the most vital parts of his life—his mate and family, and those in his closest circle.

Even so, Pia and his seven sentinels kept a sharp watch at public events, so they could help fill in any unexpected blanks Dragos might encounter. In the months that had followed the accident, Dragos had collected countless history books and read through corporate files obsessively in order to recover as much as he possibly could, as quickly as possible.

Graydon thought of all the secrets the Cuelebres were keeping. Pia's Wyr form. Her new pregnancy. Dragos's accident, and the fact that he might have recovered most of his memory, but he hadn't regained all of it.

So far, they'd been damn lucky that none of their secrets had come out.

At least as far as he knew. Blowing out a breath, he rubbed the back of his head and let the thought go. No sense in getting himself riled up until he had reason to.

At Graydon's question, Dragos's dark, sleek brows had drawn together. The expression in his fierce gold gaze grew intent.

"Yes, I remember," he said. "You had talked about taking a leave of absence—what, nearly two hundred years ago?"

"That's right. Two hundred years, almost to the day." With a quick flick of his wrist, Graydon tossed back the contents of his brandy glass. The liquor was smooth on his tongue, warm like liquid sunshine, and fiery on the way down. He welcomed the burn.

Dragos's gaze turned uncomfortably sharp. "I also remember you'd said that if you ever needed to ask for the leave of absence, you might not be able to tell me why. Is that still the case?"

"Yeah. And you promised I could have the time if and when I needed it." Graydon met the other male's gaze. "I need to hold you to that promise now."

Dragos's frown deepened. He turned to face Graydon fully, and Graydon braced his wide shoulders in response. To get the full focus of the Lord of the Wyr's attention could sometimes be an unsettling experience.

"I don't like it," growled the dragon. "It smells like trouble. Like *you're* in trouble. Tell me what's going on."

Slowly, he replied, "I can't. I made a promise, too, and it's not my secret to tell."

The moment stretched tight, straining the air between them.

"What if I say no?" Fierce, gold eyes burned as hot as lava.

Unsurprised, Graydon nodded. The dragon disliked constraints of any kind, even those of his own devising. "That would be unfortunate, because I would have to go anyway."

"To keep that promise you made."

"Yes."

The pressure built, from the weight of Dragos's attention and the vision that pushed at Graydon from within, until he thought his skin might split open.

Breathing evenly, he stiffened his spine. Holding one's ground was not passivity. It took its own kind of strength. *She* had said that to him once, all those many years ago, and he had never forgotten it.

He would hold fast.

Muttering a curse, Dragos pivoted to scowl down at the traffic below. "I gave you my word, and I'll keep it," he said. "But now you have to promise me something in return."

Releasing his pent-up breath on a soundless sigh, Graydon pinched the bridge of his nose with thumb and forefinger. "What's that?"

Dragos stabbed him with a sharp look. "You're my First. The other sentinels rely on you. Hell—Pia, Liam and I rely on you. More than that, you're family."

Unexpectedly touched, he ducked his head. "You're mine too."

"So," Dragos said, "you go and take care of whatever you need to take care of, but you have to promise that you'll tell me what's going on the moment you can, and that you'll come to me for help if you need it—and you must promise to come back."

He understood exactly why Dragos pushed for that last part.

Wyr mated for life. Nobody fully understood the dynamic, which involved a complex combination of timing, circumstance, sex and personality.

A year and a half ago, Dragos had lost two of his sentinels, Rune and Tiago, because they had mated with women elsewhere. It had taken months to choose two new sentinels, and for the Wyr demesne to stabilize again from the change.

Graydon found he had room for a wry smile. If only Dragos knew how unlikely it was that he might run the risk of losing Graydon to mating.

"As soon as I can tell you anything, I promise I will. I'll ask for help too, if it becomes appropriate." He met Dragos's gaze steadily. "As long as I am alive and able to do so, I'll always come back. This is my home. I've made that commitment to you, and to here."

And besides, she wouldn't have me, anyway.

His jaw tightened. Like he had with the vision, he shoved the thought out of his head.

Managing to look curious, frustrated and mollified all at once, Dragos angled out his jaw. "Fine," he said. "Go."

Giving him a grateful nod, Graydon turned away.

A heavy hand fell on his shoulder, causing him to stop in his tracks. Dragos's grip clenched, almost to the point of pain.

Normally, Dragos was not demonstrative with anyone other than Pia and Liam. Moved, Graydon angled his face away. After a moment, he reached up to grip the other man's hand in return. Only then did Dragos's hold ease and allow him to continue on his way.

He strode out of the penthouse, pausing only to collect the rifle. He could go to his apartment, grab his pack, and if the goddamn vision would only loosen up so that he could see to fly, he could be in the air inside of fifteen minutes.

In just a few hours, he could see her again. His world ground to a halt as he finally allowed himself to think of it.

He could see for himself how she was healing. Life's cuts had wounded her deeply, but she had a strong, unique spirit, forged most elegantly and tempered by adversity and time.

After everything they had endured, he had grown a bone deep, unshakable faith in her. She was true, her spirit clean, straight and strong. She knew how to stand her ground and hold steady, no matter what the odds.

That much had become clear as he had watched her covertly over the centuries, knowing he could only ever catch glimpses of her, because anything else, *everything* else between them, had become far too dangerous.

Even though the evening had grown late, the elevators and hallways in the Tower were crowded with late-night revelers and the personnel that had pulled third-shift security. Several times, people stopped Graydon, either to ask him questions or exchange pleasantries.

He gave each of them his unhurried attention, while inside him everything strained to be on the move. His head was beginning to pound from the effort of maintaining control, but he would not be ruled by either his visions or his desires.

*She* had taught him that kind of iron, ruthless self-control. Sometimes he had hated her for it, with a private, passionate insincerity that disturbed him profoundly.

Once he finally reached the privacy of his apartment, he flipped on the lights. All of the sentinels had apartments in the Tower, although some, like Quentin and Aryal, only chose to use them sometimes.

Graydon was different. He chose to live full time in his Tower apartment. To a man of his simple tastes, it was more than luxurious and met all of his needs. While it was only a one bedroom, it had been built with such spacious dimensions, even someone his size could sprawl out and feel comfortable.

Floor-to-ceiling windows in the living room and bedroom gave him a panoramic view of the New York skyline, and he had a private balcony where he could enjoy quiet dinners or launch for a quick flight to clear his head after work.

A giant Jacuzzi tub in the bathroom could soak away most aches and pains after a brutal day at work, and a professional decorator had made sure the furniture was good and the colors didn't suck.

He had laundry service, housekeeping service, and the Tower cafeteria kept his fridge fully stocked with excellent cooked meals, freshly made, whole grain sandwiches stuffed with meats and cheese, and his favorite kind of beer.

It was a fine enough place, a good enough place, most of the time.

"This is my home," he whispered through clenched teeth. He could hear the desperation in his own voice. "This is where I belong. I will keep all of my promises. I will hold true."

Right now the apartment felt like a cage. He thought about smashing his fist into the plate-glass window, just to see it shatter and to feel the wild wind rush in.

He closed his eyes. Swiftly like a predator, the vision of his death struck. This time it would not be denied.

The white ground, black rocks, and red drops of his heart's blood growing on the ground like blooming roses. He lost himself in the sensation of liquid warmth flowing between his fingers.

When he could finally see again, he found himself

kneeling on the floor, shoulders hunched. That damned scene hung like an albatross around his neck, until he almost wished it would go ahead and happen, just so that he could get it the fuck over with.

He had carried that albatross for almost two hundred damn years—exactly from the moment when he had responded to a damsel in distress and had embroiled himself in another man's curse.

And wasn't that too much to swallow as a coinkydink.

It was all connected. He knew it.

Stiffly, he forced himself to his feet, walked to a cupboard and pulled out a bottle of Johnnie Walker Blue. After taking several deep pulls from the bottle, he scrolled quickly through the contacts on his phone until he found the right one.

He punched the call button.

Despite the late hour, the person on the other line answered almost immediately. "Hello?"

The feminine voice sounded cautious and guarded. In the background, he could hear sounds of Elven music, quick moving and passionate.

"Linwe," he said. He didn't bother to introduce himself. Linwe knew very well who had called her, even if she refused to say his name aloud.

Over the connection, he heard quick, light footsteps, and the music faded. His mind constructed an image from the sounds. She was walking out of the great hall in the Elven home.

"What do you want?" Linwe asked.

He drank scotch. "She doesn't answer my phone calls or texts."

"She doesn't answer anybody's phone calls or texts." The young Elven woman kept her voice low. "She doesn't carry her phone anymore, not since . . . not since what happened in March."

He held his phone tightly. "How is she?"

"She's recovering, like everybody else in the Elven demesne. Look, I shouldn't talk to you about her, or tell you things. It doesn't feel right. You need to stop calling me."

"You're right," he said. "I do need to stop."

When he closed his eyes, he saw the colors. White, and black, and red like roses. Those colors looked a lot like destiny.

"It's nothing personal," Linwe said, her voice softened. "You saved her life. All of us are grateful to you for what you did."

"Tell her I'm coming," Graydon said, keeping his voice as soft as Linwe's. Soft, courteous and inexorable. "I'll be there by morning. She and I have things to discuss."

And a demon to exorcise once and for all.

Her indrawn breath was audible. "I absolutely will not. She's gone to bed, and I'm going soon too. Graydon, you can't come into the Elven demesne without permission."

"Fine," he said. "Just whatever you do, don't tell Ferion."

He hung up, turned off his phone and went to stuff things into a backpack. Weapons, clothes, basic toiletries, cash and credit cards, and a couple sandwiches for the road. When he was finished, he jogged up the stairwell to the roof, shapeshifted into his gryphon form and launched.

Usually the city of New York shone with panoramic brilliance, but the snowfall had grown thicker and obscured much of its brightness. As he flew through the keen sharp night, his obligations to the Tower fell from his shoulders, and in the silent, solitary space that remained, other images came in.

Only those images weren't of the future, but of the past. From two hundred years ago, when it had all begun.

# ⇒ TWO ⇐

**London, December 1815**

Nerves knotted Bel's stomach. Even though Ferion had promised to attend her at the masque, she couldn't find him anywhere.

At least, she noted, the Great Beast had not yet arrived. His absence might be the only bright spot in what was rapidly turning into a tense, wretched evening.

Flanked on either side by two attendants, she forced herself to take the path at a leisurely seeming stroll, while she searched the laughing crowd.

Blast Ferion. She shouldn't have taken him at his word.

Instead, she should have insisted he accompany her directly from their rented house in Grosvenor Square. But she had wanted so much to trust him. She had wanted to believe he had finally gotten through the worst.

As she searched for her stepson, huge snowflakes wafted through the air, each one sparkling with magic. No matter what the weather was like throughout the rest of England, for the last several years on winter solstice, snow always fell in the Vauxhall Pleasure Gardens.

The enchantment was courtesy of the Daoine Sidhe King

and his formidable wizard knights. The most mysterious and Powerful of all the Fae, the Daoine Sidhe were split into two distinct peoples—the Light Court, or the Seelie Fae, ruled by Queen Isabeau, and the Dark Court, or the Unseelie Fae, ruled by Oberon. Tonight, the gardens were closed to the public, as the King hosted his annual Masque of the Gods.

Eerie, fantastical ice sculptures decorated the paths, glittering from the light of white witch lights floating a few inches above the ground.

A Sidhe knight prowled along the path, dressed in black. Bel thought he might be Ashe, or Thorn, but she couldn't tell for sure. His face was obscured by a harlequin's mask, his long, dark hair bound back in a queue.

Black velvet bows and crystals adorned the trees, while invisible musicians played a sharp, tinkling music. Open flame from gigantic braziers lent a dash of heat and a feral quality to the scene.

Smiling jugglers performed for the crowd, and magicians pulled party favors made of paste and paint from behind onlookers' ears. Occasionally, a delighted scream pierced the air as a magician revealed the gleam of a real jewel nestled in a painted robin's egg.

The refreshments were equally fantastical, served by Dark Court attendants dressed in spotless white, intricately embroidered uniforms.

Baked cockatrices, a classic medieval dish created from half pig, half rooster, and cooked with saffron and ginger and gilded with edible gold, steamed in the chill night air. Strange, delicate meringue structures, sprinkled with sugar, tilted and swirled on glass plates. Savory jellies of lamb, lavender and lemon had been set in molds shaped like roses, the dishes interspersed with bowls of cherries, oranges, nuts, and sausages. A cocktail of brandy and champagne bubbled in ice fountains.

Everybody who was anybody traveled from all over the world and swathed themselves in wool, furs and jewels to attend the King's masque.

Eventually, Bel knew, the fashion would change. It always

did. Some other spectacle would become de rigueur, but in this age and place, Oberon and his strange, elegant Dark Court held sway. Despite the history of enmity between the two Courts, even the Seelie Queen Isabeau put in an appearance for a short while.

In order to attend without squandering months on travel, those who lived in faroff lands, such as the Elves in the South Carolina demesne, often bargained for transportation from the Djinn, to which the Djinn comfortably agreed.

Quick transportation was an easy task for the Djinn to perform, and in return they collected a fortune in favors. The winged Wyr smiled in pity at such pedestrian arrangements, and generally almost everyone found a way to feel superior.

Very few humans were invited to attend the King's masque, although Bel noticed one or two in the crowd. Usually they were fantastically rich or well favored in Power or political standing. Oberon liked to cultivate opportunity wherever he might find it.

Worry nipped at her heels as she approached the dance floor and walked along the border, her gaze darting over the dancers.

The evening was young, well before midnight, so everyone went masked. Some wore plain dominoes, while others wore masks as fantastical as their surroundings, along with costumes of brilliant color that stood out against the black-and-white background.

The masks made it difficult to identify anybody at a distance with any surety. Magic swirled and eddied, dizzying the senses. Her attention caught on a trio of males, standing beside one of the brandy and champagne fountains.

The Great Beast might not have arrived, but two of his sentinels had. Over the millennia, the Beast had acquired a name, Dragos Cuelebre. Then he had become a Lord and ruled over his own demesne of Wyr, an event the Elves considered an act of outrageous ill fortune.

Of the Beast's seven sentinels, those attending the masque were two of his most Powerful—gryphons Constantine and Graydon. They stood talking with another Wyr, the ever-courteous and enigmatic Francis Shaw, the Earl of Weston.

Despite her preoccupation, Bel paused to consider the men. No matter how she felt about Dragos personally, overall she enjoyed the Wyr. They had a sense of wildness and a connection with nature that appealed enormously to her.

Reputably, Weston was the one Wyr whom Dragos could not persuade to join him in governing the Wyr demesne in New York. Nicknamed the Eighth Sentinel, Weston had chosen instead to remain loyal to England, and to the family title which he had inherited many years ago. In recent years, he had worked tirelessly in the War Office against Napoleon.

Whatever truth was behind the story, there did not appear to be any ill feeling between the earl and the gryphons. As she watched, Constantine threw back his head and guffawed at something Weston said, his handsome face creased with laughter.

Beside him, his fellow sentinel Graydon grinned as well, his rugged features creased with good humor. While Weston's slim height hinted at a falcon's grace, the gryphons were heavier and taller, the rangy bulk of their muscles indicative of their Wyr form's lion bodies.

Of the three men, Graydon was the biggest. He towered over the other two like a lazy-seeming, good-natured mountain, his masculine form broad and powerful. In defiance of the masque's tradition to go masked until midnight, he had pushed his plain, black domino down so that it hung loosely around his neck like an extra cravat.

Caught by Graydon's easy, relaxed demeanor, Bel's gaze lingered on his face.

There was something about his expression, a kindness perhaps, that touched a place inside of her that had gone cold and quiet a very long time ago. Troubled at the deep, distant ache, she frowned and pressed a hand to her chest.

Unexpectedly, Graydon's gaze shifted. He looked directly at her. In contrast to his relaxed demeanor, his eyes were sharp and alert.

Caught off balance, she felt stabbed by his scrutiny. She heard herself suck in a breath.

The humor faded from his expression. Subtly his posture shifted, until he looked intent, tense.

Even . . . concerned.

That was totally unacceptable. Forcing her spine ramrod straight, she schooled her features so that nothing of her inner turmoil showed. Giving him a polite nod, she turned away to focus on the two young Elven women hovering at her elbow.

"Damn Oberon's need for ostentatious display," she muttered. "Do either of you see Ferion anywhere?"

In defiance of convention for the chilly masque, Bel's attendants, Alanna and Lianne, eschewed the warm woven brocades and thick furs. Like Bel, they wore light, silk gowns with short, bell-capped sleeves, the delicate blue and green colors evocative of a brighter, warmer season.

The King's wintry magic had no power over Bel. As long as the two younger women remained with her, they stayed as comfortably warm as they would if they were in the Elven great hall. All three wore delicate dominoes made of transparent silk that did nothing to mask their identities and everything to enhance the feminine shape of their faces.

In answer to her question, both Alanna and Lianne shook their heads wordlessly.

The sharpness of Bel's anxiety dulled to a leaden disappointment.

She said, "Retrieve your cloaks and weapons, and go search for him. Be careful if you go off the main paths. The dark places here are kept so intentionally. If you find him, tell him I need to see him immediately."

"My lady, I don't think we should leave you," Lianne replied.

While Bel's attendants had young-looking faces and slender figures that gave the impression of gentle, wide-eyed innocence—and they were, in fact, youthful Elves—in reality they were several hundred years old and experienced members of the demesne's military guard.

Even though Lianne questioned her orders, Bel didn't waste energy on frustration or getting angry.

Instead she said in a gentle voice, "I'm in the heart of the masque. This area is well lit and populated, and I know the names of almost everyone present. Many are friends of mine. Besides, I can take care of myself. Do as you're told, and be discreet about it."

"Yes, ma'am," replied Alanna, bowing her head.

They had barely taken their leave, when a deep, masculine voice said from behind Bel, "It has been so very long since the Elven Lord and his Lady have arrived together at a function that almost no one remarks upon it any longer."

Briefly, her mouth tightened in annoyance, before she made her expression ease. She turned to face the Daoine Sidhe King.

Whatever else one might say about Oberon, he certainly made a compelling figure.

Bel was tall, but he was taller still. His tailored evening coat and waistcoat fit his powerful frame like a second skin, the cloth made of an intricate, silver brocade. His mask was also silver and just as elaborate, with a sharp pointed nose and an outward flare like wings at the temples.

The outfit provided a striking contrast to his dark, glittering eyes. Light from a nearby bonfire shimmered over his raven hair, giving it a blue-black sheen.

Raising one eyebrow, she replied coolly, "Indeed, the subject of how my husband and I choose to attend parties is so boring, the only thing remarkable is that anyone would wish to discuss it at all." She waited a heartbeat to let whatever small sting from her words sink in. Then she offered her hand to him in greeting. "Oberon."

Gracefully, he bowed. Instead of brushing the air over her fingers, he touched her skin with his lips. At the same moment, his cold Power brushed alongside hers, like a massive snow cat sliding along her legs, its fur chilled from the winter's night.

"Beluviel," he murmured against her fingers in a deliberate caress. "As always, your radiance is nonpareil. No matter how I might try to outdo myself at these masques, you remain the brightest star in my night. How your husband can dance with others without giving you so much as a single glance is quite beyond me."

She flicked her forefinger against his full lower lip in rebuke for his forwardness. "You pay far too much attention to that which does not concern you."

His mouth compressed in a smile as he straightened. "I disagree. The whereabouts of every beautiful woman's husband is of immense concern to me. My darling radiance, this year, please say you'll be mine."

He was so outrageous, despite herself, she felt her lips pull into a responding smile. "You only want what you can't have."

"You never know," he said, with dangerous gentleness. "Eternity might be captured in a single kiss."

"Not your eternity," she told him dryly. "And not my kiss."

"If I still had a heart, it would be broken at how you spurn me," he murmured. "I could give you so much pleasure, more than you have ever dreamed of, if only you would let me."

Her eyes narrowed. She remembered Oberon when he was much younger, but something had happened to him over the course of the centuries. Perhaps it was an event, or maybe it was just the inevitable march of time.

Whatever had caused the change, the young, smiling Fae King that he had once been was gone. He had grown icy and distant, and his dark eyes glittered like hard onyx. She had heard whispers that his cold, compelling Power could bring his lovers to a screaming ecstasy, only to leave them at dawn, shattered and weeping in desolation at his absence.

She had been shattered enough in her time. She had no intention of deliberately choosing to experience that again.

Easing her fingers out of his grip, she glanced sidelong across the dance floor at the stern profile of her husband, Calondir, High Lord of the Elven demesne, as he talked with a couple wearing matching satyrs' costumes. As Oberon had observed, Calondir did not glance once in her direction.

She was quite content that it remain that way.

"Don't worry," said Oberon, catching the direction of her attention. "He has displayed a perfectly perplexing indifference to my flirtation with you."

Calondir wasn't the only one who was displaying a perfectly perplexing indifference to Oberon, who was tantalizing and goading in return. Again, she was reminded of a snow cat, batting at her in frustration with one paw. It wanted to play with prey.

But she was not, nor would she ever be, Oberon's prey.

"I can't think of a single reason why either Calondir or I should be troubled by your flirtations." She gave the Unseelie King a bland look. "Your party is beautiful as always, Oberon. You should go enjoy it while you can."

His nostrils flared, and he exhaled with some leisurely force, emitting a barely audible growl. "Before I go, tell me—what would it take to win you?"

For a brief moment, her troubles fell to the side, and her smile widened into real amusement. "My dear winter's night, you ask an impossible question that cannot be answered. There's nothing that could win me."

Behind the silver mask, his deadly gaze narrowed. "We'll see, my darling radiance. Eternity gains more answers from us than we might wish."

Despite her best effort at maintaining appearances, her smile slipped. She knew the worn anxiety she felt showed in her expression, but as luck would have it, Oberon's attention had moved on.

As he stepped away, she moved also, picking up her pace as she strode along the edge of the dancing crowd.

Magic sparked and eddied, so thick and plentiful from the many types of Power present, that no matter how she tried, she couldn't sort through it to find the one life spark she sought.

Certainty chilled her veins. She didn't need Alanna or Lianne's return to confirm what she already knew.

Ferion hadn't come. He had broken his promise, and she knew where he had gone—to the one place he had sworn he wouldn't. The place that would destroy him, if she could not find a way to stop him.

Determination hardened her jaw. If he couldn't keep his promise to show up, why then, she would go to fetch him, by force if necessary.

She would need Alanna and Lianne in order to pull it off. Calondir mustn't discover what was happening.

He might ignore Bel all he wished—and, the gods only knew, she welcomed his neglect—but she had said she would attend the masque, and if he realized she had gone missing, he might start asking questions that nobody wanted him to ask.

Intent on finding her attendants, she pivoted to go in the direction of the paths they had gone to search.

A lazy-seeming, good-natured mountain stepped in front of her. The wintry, elaborate masque disappeared from her sight, to be replaced by a waistcoat that covered a broad expanse of powerful chest. At the same moment, she was enfolded by a golden warmth.

All of the first generation of the Elder Races carried something of creation's first fire. Graydon was no exception, and his Power rippled around his body in an invisible corona.

While Oberon's chill Power might have no hold over Bel, stepping within the radius of Graydon's warm aura was like coming close to the comfort of a warm, bright fire, and she felt her breath leave her in an involuntary sigh.

To be honest, the tailoring was rather indifferent on that very large waistcoat of his. It was so unlike Oberon's or Calondir's glittering elegance, she felt the most ridiculous desire to pat it.

She lifted her gaze to Graydon's face. Smooth, classic handsomeness had passed him by. He had rough features, with a strong bone structure.

Eschewing the current fashion maintaining a pale, indoors complexion, he was clearly a man who relished the outdoors. The fact was stamped in the athletic shape of his muscular body and deeply suntanned skin. The sun had also lightened his short, tawny hair, and faint lines fanned out from the corners of his eyes.

It was a good face, she thought, in somewhat of a daze. A kind face that liked to smile often. Masked by a relaxed demeanor, his dark gray eyes looked sharp and intent, and she felt stabbed all over again.

She could tell he knew something was deeply wrong.

"Good evening, my lady Beluviel," Graydon said. The rumble of his deep voice was quiet and gentle. "It's a pleasure to see you, as always."

A wild upsurge of emotion shocked her. It poured out of her chest, from the deep, distant ache of the place that had gone cold and quiet so long ago. She felt a sudden urge to fling herself against his chest and huddle close.

The urge wasn't to fling her problems at him in the hopes that he might fix them. She always fixed her own problems. The urge was for the simple comfort of that warm, companionable blaze.

Of all the impulses she could possibly experience, this had to be the most inappropriate. Appalled, she nearly recoiled but caught herself in time.

"Graydon," she said stiffly. Hearing how that sounded, she reached for more warmth. "It's always good to see you too. I'm very sorry, but I'm afraid I don't have—"

As she spoke, he held out one large hand. Automatically, she curled her fingers around his in greeting. Instead of bowing, he turned and tucked her hand into the crook of his elbow.

While keeping a strong, steady grip on it.

She had room inside for one more flicker of amusement that lived the life of a moment before it died. "I believe you've absconded with my hand," she told him. "Perhaps you've retained it by mistake."

"Walk with me," he said. His easygoing smile had disappeared.

"I don't have time to visit right now." As she spoke, she glanced around.

Calondir had escorted a woman dressed in a Grecian

costume onto the dance floor. Smiling at each other, they swirled with the other dancers. Weston and Constantine had busied themselves at the refreshments table. Virtually no one paid attention to Graydon and her.

Underneath the cloth of his coat, the massive arm muscle underneath her fingers bunched. He began to stroll away from the main crowd on the dance floor.

Due to the strong grip he maintained on her hand, she either had to fall in step beside him or cause a stir.

And since calling attention to herself was the very last thing she wanted, she went with him.

At least that was why she told herself she went with him.

"I know you're distressed, and something is wrong," he said quietly. "It's clear that Calondir either has no knowledge of it, or the issue doesn't concern him."

Possible responses flitted through her mind.

*I'm sure I have no idea what you're talking about.* But the companionship of his presence was too warm and alluring, and the memory of that one shared glance between them still stabbed at her. And she couldn't bring herself to utter such an untruth.

*You are too forward, sir.* But while she would not have hesitated to say such a thing to Oberon, the power of Graydon's simple kindness was such she could not find it in her heart to rebuke him.

The tension in her throat muscles made it difficult to swallow. "I don't suppose it would do any good to deny it."

He had dropped all pretense of lightheartedness, and the glance he gave her was both piercing and troubled at once. Gently, he brought them to a halt and turned so that he faced her.

"I'm well aware that I'm crossing boundaries, and my overtures might be unwelcome," he said quietly. "You're the Lady of the Elven demesne. I'm just a Wyr sentinel in the demesne that borders yours, and the Wyr and the Elves aren't always on the friendliest of terms."

"That's never personal, Graydon," she said quickly.

He nodded. He had stopped gripping her fingers, yet

somehow her hand still remained in the crook of his arm. She regarded her offending limb with some annoyance. While she felt she should do something to rectify the situation, she couldn't seem to make herself withdraw.

"I know it's not personal." Graydon patted her hand. "But historically, the Elves and Dragos have been enemies before, so you can deny that anything's wrong, and you can send me away with a word—and if you do, I will respect your wishes and never speak of this again. I just couldn't stand back and say nothing, not when you're under such distress. Is there anything I can do for you?"

She averted her gaze as she tried to decide how to respond. As she looked around, she saw that he had chosen the spot with care.

They now stood some distance away from the dancers and the densest part of the crowd, but they were still well visible, just not in the thick of things. It was a good choice for a sensitive conversation, offering both privacy and respectability at once.

She glanced back up at him. "What gave me away?"

He lifted one massive shoulder in a shrug. "I thought there seemed to be some tension as you talked with your ladies, but I only really knew for sure when I walked up and could sense the stress in your scent."

The Wyr and their sensitive senses. She paused while the part of her that relished the companionable warmth of the fire actually considered taking him up on his offer.

She shouldn't. There were so many reasons why she shouldn't. Not least among them was the one he had brought up—they were from different demesnes, and they had different responsibilities and commitments. They had different governments, with different, often conflicting, agendas.

Without realizing it, her fingers had tightened on his coat sleeve. When he shifted subtly to draw closer to her, his large body taking a protective stance, she realized what she was doing and made her grip relax.

Then she heard the exact wrong thing come out of her mouth. "Can I rely upon your discretion?"

He bent his head, studying the ground at their feet. She felt warmed all over again as she saw how carefully he considered her question.

He looked up at her again. "As long as you can say it has nothing to do with the workings of either demesne?"

"It doesn't," she said as she met his gaze. With those two simple words, she set them both on a path to disaster.

"Then you absolutely can," he told her, dark gray eyes unwavering. "You have my word on it."

Even as he spoke, she sensed a presence enter the Gardens, fierce and lava hot.

The Great Beast had arrived at the masque at last.

Inside, she completely fell apart. At the best of times, she had to brace herself to endure Dragos's presence. To have him come so close now, when she was off balance anyway, abraded her nerves until she felt raw inside.

"Good, thank you, yes." The words tumbled rapidly out of her mouth. "I must leave. I mean, in that case, if you would join me, we need to go. Only first, I must speak with one of my attendants."

"Of course," said Graydon immediately. "Let's find one."

As she fell into step beside him, she glanced over her shoulder.

Even in his human form, Dragos looked like a killer. The battles the Elves had fought against the dragon had burned the landscape and literally reshaped large tracts of the world. Many Elves had died, and several of them had been Beluviel's friends.

The war had occurred so very long ago, but that was the thing about the Elves.

And the dragon.

None of them ever forgot.

# ≡ THREE ≡

Graydon's assignment in attending the masque was a simple one.

Dragos wanted him and Constantine to show up, make nice, and demonstrate to people that they were friendly, domesticated creatures and not the wild, vicious animals that the Wyr were often reputed as being.

While the Wyr were very well aware that one thing did not necessarily preclude the other, putting a friendly face to their demesne did seem to help the rest of the world relax whenever they were present.

Graydon figured the parameters of the assignment meant he could enjoy himself as well, and Oberon's cocktail fountains never did seem to run dry. The food was pretty decent too, except those gold cockatrices were frankly odd. He much preferred the plainer sausages.

One of the advantages of attending the masque meant a rare opportunity to visit with Francis, which was how Graydon came to be standing with Weston and Constantine when Beluviel and her two attendants appeared.

As always, whenever Graydon saw Beluviel, he had to

pause what he was doing to take in the pleasure of her presence.

The three women made a uniquely powerful statement that had nothing to do with swords, armor, or anything else overtly warlike. In direct contrast to everyone else, they wore thin, colorful gowns, with short puffy sleeves.

While Graydon didn't know the first thing about female fashion, he thought the dresses were lovely in their simplicity. Their bare, slender arms, and lack of jewelry or warm, thick clothing made everyone else seem lumbering and overdressed, the lavish decorations and refreshments garish and overdone.

Smiling, his gaze passed over the two other pretty Elven women to concentrate on Bel.

The Lady of the South Carolina Elven demesne was beautiful, of course. All the normal requisites for a face were arranged in the most pleasing proportions imaginable. She had a wide, dark gaze filled with calm intelligence, and her long, shining dark hair, also unadorned, cascaded down, like a silken waterfall, to her hips.

Beluviel's beauty was the first thing anybody seemed to notice. Graydon thought it was the least important thing about her.

As one of the eldest of the Elven race, her Power had grown with age. It manifested as a brightness of spirit that lightened everything around her, gently transformative, like the first, tantalizing breath of spring when Graydon knew the season had changed, the cold of winter had fled, and life was beginning to burgeon once again.

That single breath was the rarest of delights. You could only take one breath like that in a year's time. Each successive breath might be pleasurable and refreshing, but none of them quite held the same power as the first epiphany of spring.

That was the essence of what Beluviel's presence brought to him. Also, like the first breath of spring, she was a rare, passing delight. She did not always attend public functions, preferring, or so he had heard, the peace and quiet of her Wood.

Except, this time was different. Graydon looked at her with every anticipation of the pleasure that the sight of her had always brought to him. What he saw instead made his fingers clench on his champagne glass.

She carried the same brightness of spirit. She couldn't help but do so; the quality was an intrinsic part of her and woven into the fabric of her being.

But his sharp eagle's eyes picked up a multitude of tiny fractures in her demeanor. The flex of tension in those long, graceful fingers. The rigid set to her shapely shoulders. The hooded quality to her gaze, and the tight line of her slender jaw.

Disappointment and concern welled up inside of him.

The disappointment was ludicrous and inappropriate. She was her own unique person. The purpose of her existence was not to bring him pleasure. He shoved the feeling aside and studied her more closely.

That was when the vision of the white ground, black rocks, and the red of his blood swept over him for the first time.

With an instinct born from long experience, he held still, enduring the image until it faded enough so that he could glance around surreptitiously to see if anyone had taken note of his odd stillness.

Neither Francis nor Constantine appeared to have noticed that anything was amiss. The two other men had turned their attention to the refreshments table and were piling plates high with food.

As they returned to his side, Francis asked, "Aren't you going to eat?"

Shaking his head, he put effort into making his voice sound normal. "I stole some sausages earlier off one of the tables. I might have more to eat in a bit."

As he spoke, he watched Bel send away her attendants, and her brief conversation with Oberon. How could Oberon flirt with her and not see that something was wrong? Was the Daoine Sidhe King that shallow and self-absorbed?

The taut, delicate set of her mouth, and the fist that she

made of one hand then pressed against her thigh, as if to hide it in her skirts . . .

Something about her distress—or what caused it— mattered so much that it had triggered an image of his heart's blood dripping between his fingers.

The second sight was a tricky bitch. If he chose to ignore Bel and turned away to focus on his own life and concerns, would that indifference trigger events that would lead to the vision coming true?

Or, if he stepped forward to involve himself in whatever troubled her, would that lead to the incident?

Action or nonaction—there was literally no way to be sure. He could waste his life trying to second-guess everything he did, but that was no way to live. A very long time ago, he had decided to set aside second-guessing for the useless endeavor that it was.

He had not become a sentinel by worrying about what he should or shouldn't do. He would live or die as he always had, by making decisions he knew to be right.

If Beluviel truly was in some kind of distress, there was no way in hell he could walk away from her. That would be like closing the door on spring to spend his life hiding indoors.

Graydon didn't hide from life. He flew at it with everything he had.

He glanced at Beluviel's husband. Lord Calondir looked like he was enjoying himself, as he bent his head close to his female companion.

The physical and psychic distance between the smiling Elven Lord and his tense wife couldn't have been more apparent. They existed in two completely separate realms.

*What's going on, Gray?* Constantine asked telepathically. Appearing to have not a care in the world, the other sentinel popped a fantastically shaped meringue into his mouth.

So his behavior had not gone unnoticed after all. He wasn't really surprised. Constantine was an observant son of a bitch. After working together for so long, he knew Graydon much better than Francis did.

*I don't know,* he said. Dismissing Calondir, he turned his attention back to Bel. *Something.*

Constantine glanced in the direction of his gaze then swiveled his whole body to face Graydon. His handsome face turned sober. *That, my friend, is the very definition of unobtainable.*

A rare surge of anger flashed through him. He bit out, *That's not what this is about.*

A pause. Graydon could almost see the other male's mental shift.

*Okay,* said Constantine. His mental voice remained neutral. *What is this about?*

It was about decency and concern for another being's welfare. It was about living his life to the fullest, and making the right decisions in defiance of any potential future harm that may or may not come to him.

He told Constantine, *I don't know, but I'm about to find out.*

He took his leave of the other two men and strode forward. Whatever this challenge was, and whether or not the vision came to fruition, he would approach this like he did the rest of his life—with everything he had.

If he was strong enough, smart enough, if he fought hard enough and tried long enough, he could win through.

Several minutes later, as he escorted Bel away from the dance floor and along a main path, a sense of rightness settled into his bones. They might be mere acquaintances—he had only ever exchanged pleasantries with her and they had never shared a tête-à-tête—but it felt delightful to have her hand tucked into the crook of his elbow, and to shorten his stride so that he matched hers.

His enjoyment of her company, in the face of whatever was causing her hardship, seemed as inappropriate as his earlier disappointment. Deliberately, he turned his attention away from the pleasure and focused on other details of his surroundings.

Nearby, a Daoine Sidhe knight stood in the middle of a group of inebriated partygoers. The knight's identity was cloaked behind a full mask with two faces, one facing front and the other facing backward. The forward-facing face was dark, while the backward-facing face was light.

Graydon recognized the costume. It was Janus, the Roman two-faced god, with one face looking forward into the future, and the other face looking backward into the past.

The mask mirrored too much of what Graydon was thinking and feeling. Unease tried to ripple through his body, but ruthlessly, he shoved it away. He had lived with the second sight for far too long to read omens into everything.

A light breeze brushed against his face, and he caught a hint of the knight's scent tangled with several others. It was Ashe, Oberon's oldest and strongest wizard knight. As he watched, Ashe pulled a delicate, fresh orchid out of a woman's hand muff and handed it to her with a silent bow. The woman squealed with delight.

"I would like to make one thing clear," Bel said suddenly.

Instantly, his attention snapped back to the pale, set features of her profile. He said, "By all means, please do."

Her large, dark eyes flashed at him and then away again. Some force of unknown emotion made them sparkle with reflected firelight. "I don't actually need your help."

Had she changed her mind? Bemused by another wave of inappropriate disappointment, he murmured, "I see."

Of course he didn't see. That was merely one of the things he said when he felt the need to say something instead of remaining silent. He had always found it to be one of the most useful phrases in his repertoire when speaking to members of the fairer sex, who, truthfully, were some of the most mysterious creatures ever created by the gods.

"You're a convenience," she whispered. "That's all. I can handle my issues by myself."

Ah. He thought he began to get a glimmer. That sounded like worried pride. Sometimes it could be hard to accept help.

"Bel," he said gently, giving her hand a squeeze. "I never

presumed anything different. You can send me away at any point you like, but if my help will halve your trouble or ease your path in any way, I'm honored to be of assistance. What *can* I do for you?"

She didn't appear to mind that he had dropped all formality. Her shoulders straightened as she took a deep breath and again gave him a sidelong look.

Then her telepathic voice sounded. *If you don't mind, I would rather not discuss such a sensitive subject aloud.*

Caught by surprise, he fell into enchantment. Carrying something of her physical demeanor, her mental voice sounded bright and silvery.

He felt almost as if he had looked up and caught an unexpected glimpse of sunlight flashing on a starling's wing as it flew overhead. Her telepathic voice was entirely and uniquely her, and she was inside his head.

She seemed to be waiting for something. With a start, he realized she was waiting for his response.

"Of course," he said. "Of course" belonged alongside "I see" in his repertoire of generic responses. Shaking his head, he amended that to something more meaningful as he switched to telepathy. *I mean, of course, telepathy is the best way to keep something private.*

*I need to go to some place called Malfeasance.* Her expression settled into lines of determination. *While I could do that on my own—and would, if I had to—it would be easier if I had a male to escort me. If we went together, I could hopefully do what I need to do with a minimum of fuss and attention.*

*Malfeasance,* he repeated. His own mood turned grim. *You mean the gaming hell.*

She jerked her head in a nod. *Yes.* Switching to verbal speech, she said, "There's one of my attendants. Lianne?"

While she had kept her voice quiet, the cloaked Elven woman several yards away turned toward them and approached with quick, light steps. "Yes, my lady."

Giving his arm a quick squeeze, Bel slipped from his

side and stepped forward to meet the other woman. They went silent, looking into each other's eyes.

Troubled, Graydon glanced around to make sure no one paid them any undue attention. When he was satisfied, he turned his attention back to the women while he considered what little Bel had revealed thus far.

London was littered with social clubs and houses of chance, but Malfeasance was not just any gaming hell. It was located in the most notorious part of London and, Graydon had heard, was run by a pariah Djinn named Malphas.

While the Djinn could take physical shape if they chose, at their essence, they were Powerful creatures of air and fire. Social by nature, they had an elaborate community structure and traded in favors as their form of commerce.

Because of that, keeping their word meant a great deal to the Djinn, except their pariahs were an entirely different kind of creature. As social outcasts, they were not to be trusted to keep their word, yet they were still extremely Powerful, which made them very dangerous.

Why did Bel feel the need to go there, of all places? Did she know that Malfeasance was run by a pariah Djinn?

The Elder Races weren't like human society, with its unfair and unrealistic restrictions on women. It would have been perfectly acceptable for Bel to walk into Malfeasance on her own, if she chose.

However, if she did so, as Lady of the South Carolina Elven demesne, she would draw all manner of attention to herself. If she was intent upon a mission of some privacy, she could potentially do more harm than good.

The two women appeared to be arguing. With a sharp downward slice of one hand, Bel brought the conversation to a close. "That's quite enough, Lianne," she said aloud. "You and Alana must do as you're told. I'll return as soon as I possibly can."

"Yes, ma'am," Lianne said. The younger Elven woman's frustration was evident in the glowering glance she gave Graydon. Lianne shrugged out of her cloak. "At least take this so you can try to be less conspicuous."

Bel attempted to refuse it. "You need the protection. It's too cold for you."

"Please, don't worry about me. I'll find another cloak."

Stepping forward, Graydon took the cloak from Lianne's grasp. As both women turned to him, he told Bel, "She's right. You need the anonymity the cloak will bring you. Let her help you by allowing her to look after herself."

Bel's mouth tightened, while Lianne's resentful frown turned into an expression of grudging approval.

After a moment, Bel gave a short nod. As Graydon held the cloak for her, she turned her back to him so he could settle it onto her shoulders.

She said to the other woman, "The sooner we leave, the sooner we can hopefully come back. Make sure Alanna knows what to do, should Calondir inquire as to my whereabouts. If my absence is discovered before I can return, tell people I felt unwell and had to leave."

Although Graydon could see acquiescence was difficult for Lianne, the younger woman nodded and turned to hurry away down the path.

Then he forgot about the other woman as Bel turned to face him.

Moving with care, he reached for the hood, pulled it over her head and ran his gaze down her slim figure. She asked, "What do you think? Will it do?"

The cloak was well made and warm. It was also a plain and discreet black, and it covered her face and form completely. With her face tilted up to his, he could make out her shadowed eyes, a hint of angled cheekbone, and the tilt to her nose, but someone standing a short distance to either side of him wouldn't be able to see anything.

But the cloak did absolutely nothing to disguise either her physical scent or her elegant, distinctive Power.

He told her in perfect honesty, "It might hide your identity from a casual observer, but it won't hide anything from someone who knows you, or who is sensitive to Power. And it won't do a thing to stop a Wyr who might catch your scent."

There was a slight pause, as she absorbed his words.

"Well," she said heavily, "it will have to do." From within the depth of the hood, she seemed to search his gaze. "Will you still accompany me?"

"Of course," he said. "I wouldn't leave you now for the world."

As he offered his arm to her again, she slipped her hand into the crook of his elbow. Together, they strode for the nearest exit.

She switched back to telepathy. *Perhaps once we're out of the Gardens, we'll be able to hire a hansom. I don't want to use any of our carriages.*

A medusa with an Orc guard approached. He waited until they had walked past the Demonkind pair before he replied, *If you think you can stomach a ride through the air, I can shapeshift and carry you. It would be more discreet than renting a hansom. It would also get us to Malfeasance much faster, but I'm told flying isn't to everybody's taste.*

The opening of her hood turned toward him, and her hand tightened. She replied, *I think that would be absolutely marvelous. Thank you.*

A glow of warmth spread through him. *I could shapeshift now and attempt to cloak it, but there are so many creatures present that have either a great deal of Power, or sensitivity to it. I would rather not risk exposing you.*

*No, you're quite right to be careful.* Her hood shifted as she turned to look ahead. Almost as if speaking to herself, she continued, *I would love to fly. I've always wondered what it would be like to have that sense of freedom.*

A wistful note in her voice tugged at something deep inside him. He replied, *I couldn't conceive of living without it. I can't imagine being forever grounded.*

*No, I don't suppose you can.*

They were almost at the gate.

He really didn't want to say what he was about to say. In fact, he had to fight himself to say anything at all.

Quietly, he told her, *If you could trust me enough with the reason why you need to go to Malfeasance, I could make*

*the trip on your behalf. It would save you the risk of possible
exposure. No one need ever know.*

Calondir, he meant. Calondir need never know.

Because, while Bel had not explicitly said so in his hearing,
it had become abundantly clear to Graydon that she didn't
want Calondir to know anything of what was happening.

Having once acknowledged that truth, he dug further
inside himself, trying to ascertain how he felt about keeping
a secret from Bel's husband.

All he could remember was the scene beside the dance
floor, with Calondir dancing and laughing with a costumed
woman while just a short distance away, Bel stood tight with
suppressed misery.

And, he realized, he was perfectly fine with keeping any
number of secrets from Calondir.

Any number of secrets at all.

There were implications in that thought, serious ones that
he needed to consider, but all his focus remained on her. He
would have time enough to think things over when he was
alone again.

She had paused for so long, he thought she might not
answer him.

Then she said softly, *Thank you so much for your generous offer, but it isn't a matter of whether or not I can trust
you. This is about someone else, and whether or not he
would listen to anything you had to say.*

The swiftness of Graydon's internal reaction was as wild
and vicious as any Wyr could turn. Who did she need to see
so badly, and why did it matter so that she had to hide it from
everybody?

Shocked at himself, he drew in a deep breath and forced
his reply to remain mild, without a hint of snarl. *Are you
sure? I can be persuasive when I put my mind to it.*

*I'm sure,* she told him. *I'm probably the only person he
will listen to, so I have to confront him in person. You see,
my son has developed a serious problem.*

As fast as he had reacted, his strange, unruly emotions

morphed into surprise. Whatever starburst of nonsense had just exploded in his brain, he hadn't considered anything like this.

Malfeasance did not just offer games of chance, which was part of its notoriety. Other vices could be purchased, including sex and drugs. If one had enough money, or so Graydon had heard, one could purchase anything one wanted, no matter how unsavory.

He could not imagine that Ferion would need to resort to a place like Malfeasance for sex. The handsome, charming Elven heir could have his pick of any number of sexual partners for free, yet there was no accounting for taste.

Another possibility occurred to him. He asked, *Don't tell me he's developed an opium addiction?*

*No,* she replied grimly. *Games of chance are his vice. No matter how many times he has promised that he will quit, he cannot seem to control himself.*

They had reached the gate. As they passed through to the London street outside, the frigid air caused by the Daoine Sidhe's magical influence warmed. The snowfall stopped, to be replaced by a steady, cold drizzle.

Falling silent, they picked their way through the crowds of people and carriages around the entryway.

Hoping to disguise Bel's presence, Graydon put his arm around her shoulders and drew her against his side. If anyone were paying attention, perhaps his Wyr scent and signature presence would confuse them enough they would not be able to identify her.

Bel neither objected nor questioned his move. Once away from the thick of the crowd, he picked up the pace until they were striding swiftly away.

Only then did he speak aloud. "An addiction to gambling can be every bit as serious as any other kind of addiction," he said. "How long has he been having the problem?"

"It began several years ago." Although she kept her tone low, Bel spoke aloud as well. She paused. "That's not exactly true. I'm not quite sure how long ago it might have started. It was several years ago when I first noticed how often he gambled, but he always seemed to be in control of it."

"People who have a problem with drinking spirits often disguise how much they drink," he said.

Under his arm, her shoulders lifted in a shrug. "And gaming is a pastime so many people indulge in, I didn't really think anything of it, until he came to me the first time with a debt he couldn't pay. He said he made a mistake and lost his head. He swore it would never happen again, so I paid the debt for him."

As he listened, he watched for a quiet side street or private park where he might be able to shapeshift hidden from casual sight. While the weather was inclement, it was still winter solstice, the night that masques were celebrated all throughout the Elder Races.

Not everyone was lucky enough to get an invitation to King Oberon's event, and the streets were busier than they might otherwise have been. Drunken, cheerful groups passed them more than once, and a solitary, cheap, gaudy mask lay abandoned on the cobblestones.

When she fell silent, he said, "I think I can see where this is going. Even though Ferion promised, he didn't really stop. Did he?"

He felt rather than saw her shake her head within the depths of the hood. "I thought he had. I truly didn't think any more of it. Mistakes happen, and in some ways, Ferion has had a more challenging life than most."

"What do you mean?" he asked.

She sighed. "He is his father's heir and expected to remain close and available, knowledgeable on demesne affairs but not too involved. Calondir guards his authority jealously, and he won't let Ferion assume too much responsibility."

He frowned. "That sounds frustrating."

"It is, and we are so long lived as a race, he won't ever inherit unless an accident takes his father's life. Every time he has tried to develop a sense of purpose for himself, it has become skewed and stunted by this very narrow role he's supposed to fulfill."

Graydon had never witnessed the complications of family life up close. Children were rare in the Elder Races. While he loved them, as an unmated sentinel, he didn't get much occasion to spend time with any. The situation Bel described had truly never occurred to him.

Shaking his head, he muttered, "I had no idea."

"Ferion lives in a particularly difficult cage. At times, he doesn't handle it well. He has bouts of drinking and melancholia too." She drew in a sharp breath. "It's too easy to confide in you. I know you've already promised you would be discreet, but please don't say anything."

"I won't," he said, tightening his arm in reassurance. "I wouldn't."

"Thank you," she told him. "So, yes, I thought everything was taken care of, but sometime later, he accumulated another debt he couldn't pay. That time, we argued about it. He promised it wouldn't happen again. Even though I had doubts, I paid the bill. Again."

"Let me guess," he said quietly. "Calondir doesn't know any of this."

She went silent again for a long moment. Through his arm still across her shoulders, he could feel the tension gripping her slender body.

"No," she responded at last. "Calondir doesn't know, and he can't know." When he didn't reply, she said stiffly, "There are reasons."

Why couldn't Calondir know? He wanted to ask, but it was evident she was already having difficulty with telling her story, and it wasn't his place to pry. He also didn't want to cause her any discomfort so that she shut down and possibly turned him away.

"I believe you," he told her. His truthsense was highly developed, and he could hear the truth in every word she spoke.

Finally, as they came to the mouth of an alleyway, he found what he was looking for. Pausing, he checked it. Save for a couple of cats rustling through some rubbish, the alley was empty. It was also large enough to accommodate him in his gryphon form.

After one quick glance around them, he let his arm slide from her shoulders, stepped into the alley and shapeshifted.

# ⸺ FOUR ⸺

When Graydon strode into the alley, Bel thought she knew what to expect. She had been around Wyr many times, and she had seen several in flight before. On occasion, ancient memories of Dragos flying overhead in his Wyr form still gave her nightmares.

None of that prepared her for the sheer physical impact of watching Graydon's human form flicker and change, to be replaced by an immense, majestic creature. With a panicked yowl, the two alley cats fled.

The gryphon standing in front of her melded eagle and lion together so seamlessly, she knew it was the most natural thing in the world, and yet it was so strange, she had to stare.

She had expected he would be large. She hadn't realized he would be quite so huge. His gigantic lion's body was heavy with powerful muscle, the feline shape both masculine and deadly. Immense bronze wings were folded tight against his back, the tips of the great feathers brushing against the brick wall at the end of the alley.

She glanced down at one of his paws. It was easily twice

the size of a large serving platter. The hidden claws sheathed by that paw had to be as long as her hand.

Lost in wonder, her feet began to move of their own volition and drew her closer to him. His sleek eagle's head bent, and he watched her with one immense golden eye. His beak had a deadly curve at the end, as sharp as a scimitar.

Even though his visage was naturally fierce, he seemed to be watching her with a mild, uncertain expression, almost as if he were . . . self-conscious?

For some reason, she thought of the indifferent cut of his waistcoat, and the arrangement of his cravat that had managed to achieve a state of adequacy. Again, she felt the urge to pat him.

Raising one hand, she hesitated. "Is it all right if I touch you?"

The gryphon nodded in silence.

Slowly, she let her hand trail along the sleek feathers that cloaked his neck. When she reached the area where the feathers turned to fur, she brushed the thick, tawny fur covering his powerful breastbone.

It was slightly damp from the light drizzle. Luxuriating in its richness, she sank her fingers into the fur until she touched his skin. His body threw off heat like a furnace.

"I wish I could see you in better lighting," she told him. "Even here in the shadows, you're one of the most beautiful creatures I've ever seen."

The gryphon bent its head even further, until it very gently touched its beak to her shoulder. He could decapitate her with a single snap, yet it never occurred to her to be afraid.

Graydon's deep, telepathic voice sounded in her head. *Thank you. Do you think you'll be able to climb onto my back?*

He was helping her out of the pure goodness of his big, generous heart. She would not scorn such kindness by snorting.

Instead, she retreated several yards, gathered the skirt of her cloak and gown in one hand, and raced toward him. Even though his shoulders were the same height as her head, she gathered her body into a gracefully powerful leap.

As she settled into place just behind his neck, he chuckled. *I expect you're a talented rider, but I need to warn you, this won't be the same as riding a horse. The beat of my wings has an entirely different rhythm than a horse's gait. When I launch, I'll do it from a standstill. Again, it won't be anything like jumping a fence. You also might experience vertigo, as we'll be high in the air. If you find you're having trouble for any reason, be sure to tell me.*

"I will." Her promise came out breathless.

She was worried about Ferion, and very angry at him, and she felt as if she had come to her wit's end in trying to figure out how to help him with his problem. Yet suddenly, in the midst of all that, she was more excited than she could remember being in a very long time.

And more than a little nervous too.

She thought she would be okay with flight. It seemed like something she might love desperately, but that was a created scenario in her head.

This was reality. For all she knew, she might be overcome with the vertigo he mentioned and not able to keep her seat. She gripped him tightly with her knees.

This was . . .

In a classic feline move she had seen before in hundreds of barn cats, the gryphon crouched, tail lashing. Then he *leapt*.

The surge of power between her legs was incredible. The world fell away.

He was too big, too heavy. He shouldn't have been able to do it, but as he cleared the restriction of the alleyway, his massive wings snapped open and hammered down, once, twice, and then again. Each time, he lunged higher.

Almost before she realized it, they were soaring over rooftops, and oh my gods, the view of London from the air was utterly breathtaking.

The sharp wind caught at the edges of her cloak, and moody clouds wreathed the pale smile of a new moon. Sparks of lights lit the night-darkened city. Even from where they were, she could feel the concentration of Power emanating from Vauxhall.

Incredulous laughter spilled out. She realized she was shaking like a leaf and clamped down harder on him.

*Are you all right?* the gryphon asked.

"I'm absolutely splendid!" she shouted.

There was a smile in his mental voice. *Not dizzy or nauseated?*

"Not in the slightest!" Overcome with delight, she pointed then realized he couldn't see her. "Look at the Thames. It looks like a huge shining ribbon, or maybe a snake. I wish we could see the stars. Graydon, this is *glorious*!"

He laughed gently and banked, and the entire panoramic landscape spun below her. *I'm not sure of the exact address, but Malfeasance is somewhere on the street below. We'll have to walk the length to find it.*

Disappointment pulsed. Their flight had only just begun, and the experience was so joyous, she didn't want it to end. "We can't be there already."

She had a sudden, passionate desire to forget about all her troubles and leave them behind.

To tell him to keep flying. Keep flying and never stop.

*Traveling by flight is quite a bit faster than it would be if we had to contend with the traffic in the streets,* he said. *It's also much more direct. Hold on.*

His prosaic words grounded her back into her body. He wheeled in great circles, so that they descended at a slow, careful pace. She sensed he did so for her sake, not for his. She had seen how eagles could plummet when they were in search of prey, and how cats could pounce with breathtaking speed. He embodied the best qualities of both creatures.

After coasting a short distance, he landed behind a derelict, dark building, in another alleyway. Her legs shook so badly when she slid to the ground, she had to lean against him before she could stand on her own. He held steady, with no sign of impatience, until she moved away.

When she turned to face him, he had already shape-shifted back into a man. Without a word, he offered his arm to her again. After pulling the hood over her head once more, she slipped her hand into the crook of his elbow. Together, they stepped onto the street.

Bel had never explored this part of the city. She saw that she hadn't missed much. An acrid stench came from piles of refuse, while prostitutes plied a busy trade and raucous laughter spilled from taverns. Street toughs watched passersby with sharp smiles and predatory eyes.

As she took in the scene from the fragile privacy within the cloak's hood, she had a sudden, deep pang of longing for the fresh, clean air and green scents of her Wood. Her Wood was wild and sentient, and while it wasn't always a safe place for strangers to wander, it was the child of her Power, her hearth and home.

She also noted how a few of the sharp, edgy men eyed her and Graydon. Their gazes lingered on Graydon's height and bulk, and the men left them alone.

They were fools to only take Graydon into consideration. If she had come here alone, she could have handled them, but that might have indeed brought her unwanted attention, so she was glad she didn't have to.

"There," Graydon said suddenly.

The sound of his voice made her jump. This place gnawed at her nerves. "What?"

He inclined his head. She looked in the direction of his nod to a plain building that was in much better repair than its neighbors. A single letter M hung above a doorway that was guarded by two hulking Orcs.

She sighed. She hated Orcs.

"I don't understand how he could stomach coming to such a place," she muttered as they strode toward the building.

Graydon sounded as grim as she felt. "If he's caught in the throes of a gambling addiction, then he may not have had much choice. This might be the only place that would run him a line of credit."

A combination of anger and despair made her clench her teeth. As they grew closer to the building, she switched to telepathy. *I don't know how to help him, and I can't keep bailing him out. Each time the debt grows higher and higher. Sooner or later, he's going to come to his father's attention.*

If that happened, Calondir would react as he always did when he was confronted with a situation that made him angry. When he lost his temper, he could be verbally abusive. Sometimes he lashed out physically.

The thought caused her stomach to clench. Calondir never lashed out at her, not after she had threatened to cut off his hands and had left him. That had happened many years ago. For a very long time now, they had existed in two separate spheres emotionally, and they only came together to work on demesne issues.

Ferion was a different matter. Throughout his childhood, she had worked to protect him from his father, but now that he was an adult, she could no longer be present every time he met with Calondir. All she could do was try to keep Calondir from finding out.

*You can't make Ferion quit, Bel,* Graydon told her gently. *I've seen it with people who can't stop drinking. Ferion is the only person who can make him quit. He has to hit bottom, whatever that might mean to him, and he has to choose at a fundamental level to change.*

Her gaze dampened. She said, *One step at a time. For tonight, I'll just be glad to get him out of here.*

The Orc guards watched but did nothing as they reached the door. When Graydon opened it, heat, light and noise poured out. Squaring her shoulders, Bel stepped inside and he followed.

In contrast to the air of general decay outside, the interior was decorated with plush carpets and paintings. A variety of scents assaulted her nose—liquors, a clash of perfumes, the grease from cooked meats, and unwashed bodies.

Smoke hung in the air, both tobacco and hashish. Music played somewhere, competing with shouts, loud conversation and coarse laughter.

The place was packed with both humans and those of the Elder Races. While some women were scattered throughout, the majority of the clientele was male.

Most stayed focused on the game they played, but several glanced at them curiously. In direct contrast to what had happened in the street, the males' attention lingered on her cloaked, hooded figure.

Graydon moved so close, she could feel the brush of his muscular body at her side. His energy had grown darker and bristled with aggression.

The only way to get through this was, well, to get through it. Squaring her shoulders, she strode through the first room.

Soon, she was sweltering. The loud sights and sounds assaulted her senses, and the confinement of the heavy cloak became intensely uncomfortable.

She couldn't seem to draw in a deep breath, and the thick, overly scented air caught at the back of her throat. Her heart pounded in hard, heavy slugs, and she longed to shove the hood away from her face.

Ferion wasn't in the first room they searched. Nor was he in the second, or the third.

She picked up her pace, shouldering between people as her gaze darted everywhere. From time to time, Graydon's muscled arm shot out to block someone from approaching her.

*He's not here.* Distress flooded her. *He's not here.*

*Take a deep breath, Bel.* Graydon put a hand on her shoulder in a solid, reassuring grip. He drew her to the nearest wall, shielding her from curious stares with his body.

With the fingers of one hand, she lifted the edge of her hood so that she could peer up at him. His rough face was grim, his eyes hard. He looked entirely different from the gentle, easygoing man she had seen earlier at the masque.

*Ferion might not be here now, but he was recently,* he told her. *I can catch hints of his scent, even through the stink in this place. We need to check upstairs, and in the back rooms.* He paused. *Will you allow me to do that for you?*

There was something about how he phrased the question, along with the expression in his eyes, that sent her back to their earlier conversation.

They had walked through all the public gaming rooms,

but Malfeasance pandered to more than just the gambling vice. There were drugs here, and somewhere, there would be rooms for sex.

Graydon was trying to spare her, in case Ferion might still be here after all.

Within the span of a moment, her imagination ran riot. Images of Ferion drugged or naked crowded her mind.

Abruptly, she shoved them away and decided to let Graydon help her. If Ferion really was still here, she didn't need to see her son in such a state.

She nodded. *I would appreciate it if you would.*

He hesitated, looking down at her. *I don't like to leave you here alone.*

She touched his hand as it rested on her shoulder. *Remember, I can take care of myself.*

*I'm quite sure you can, but I still don't have to like it.* His fingers tightened. *The sooner I go, the sooner I can return. I'll be as quick as I can.*

*Thank you.*

She watched him leave. For such a massively built man, he was remarkably quick and light on his feet. His powerful frame was thick with muscle, yet his movements were as lithe and sinuous as the cat in his Wyr form.

As he disappeared, the atmosphere in the crowded room underwent an almost unidentifiable change. The room felt colder without his presence.

Repressing a shudder, she turned on her heel to scan the area. She took note of the number of males who began to watch her, some slyly, while others perused her with open assessment, even avid curiosity.

Opening herself partially to the psychic currents, she caught snatches of thought and intention. Some wondered why she kept her identity hidden. One or two took note of the unremarkable quality of her cloak and dismissed her as a potential mark. Others fantasized about the body her cloak hid.

A few contemplated rape.

She regarded them all coldly. *If you wandered into my Wood*, she thought, *not a single one of you would escape alive.*

One of the men approached her with an unsteady gait.

"Ooh, you looks like you might be a tasty bird underneaf all that," he said. A strong scent of brandy washed over her. "'Ow much d'you charge for the night?"

She scanned him, but he wasn't one of the would-be rapists. Dismissing him as innocuous, she pulled a gentle swath of Power between them.

An expression of confusion crossed his face, and his eyebrows drew together. He turned away, muttering to himself. After wandering along the edge of the room, he shouldered his way into a game of dice.

She sent a second glance over the room. Her small spell of misdirection had shaken off the attention of several of the others, but she hadn't rid herself of all of them.

That was the problem with such spells. They worked on some people, but not everybody. Someone with a strong enough, determined mind could break through them.

She couldn't stand and do nothing while she waited for Graydon to return. Focusing her attention on the games, she tried to imagine what Ferion might do.

Or at least what she thought Ferion might do. It was painful to admit that she was no longer quite sure.

She did know he favored games of both dice and cards. As she considered the various tables, she noticed the presence of several more armed Orcs standing at attention at regular intervals along the walls.

While she studied the Orcs, a well-dressed Vampyre male gave her a long assessing glance before he turned back to watching the tables.

He was so clearly not like any of the other males who were watching her, she opened her mind again to sense his intentions and got the impression of a cold, businesslike mind. The Vampyre wasn't at Malfeasance to gamble. He was working.

Coming to a decision, she strode toward him. While he did not appear to notice her approach, he swiveled to face her as she grew near.

The Vampyre bowed. He was not a young one. He had

some strength of presence and an aura of accomplished Power.

"My lady." His smooth smile contained a hint of sharp tooth. "We are honored that you would grace us with your presence. Are you interested in joining a game? Perhaps a discreet one, in a private room."

So much for trying to keep her identity a secret. Still, one person recognizing her was not the same level of disaster as it would be if the whole room had.

She told him telepathically, *I am not here to play any of your games, but I would appreciate a few answers to some questions.*

He cocked his head and switched to telepathy. *Please, do tell me more. It would be my pleasure to service you in any way you desire.*

His oily manner ran along the surface of her skin. Repressing a shudder, she snapped, *Ferion Thalinil. He was here at some point in the recent past. Do you know where he is?*

*Ferion is your son, is he not?* The Vampyre prowled close, eyes flickering with a predatory gleam. *How heartwarming to see such familial concern. It speaks well of you, my lady.*

Disliking his overly familiar attitude and how close he came, she held herself stiffly. She refused to let this creature see how he affected her. *Have you seen him today?* she persisted. *Do you know where he might have gone?*

The Vampyre inclined his head and assumed a mournful expression. *My deepest regrets, but we at Malfeasance consider the privacy of our patrons to be one of our highest priorities. Whether or not the Elven heir mentioned where he might go upon taking his leave here is not for me to s—*

The insincerity in his voice was as abrasive as his oily manner. Bel did not often feel the urge to violence, but as she considered him, she imagined taking his head in both hands and twisting it off his shoulders.

She interrupted. *I'll make it worth your while.*

His dark gaze flickered, and the corners of his mouth

indented as he repressed a satisfied smile. *How might you do that?*

Lifting the edge of the hood again with one hand, she met his gaze and said softly, *I'll let you live.*

The Vampyre froze, and all hint of a smile vanished. *Ma'am,* he said, his attitude stripped of pretension. *I'm not supposed to divulge that information. Please understand, this isn't personal. My employer is—he's not a man to be crossed.*

After the traits he had exhibited, she had no pity for him.

*It will be much worse for you to make an enemy of me,* she said softly. *I know your face. I will find out your name, and where you live. Whereas, if you tell me what I want to know, your employer need never know that the information came from you, or that I was even here. You have an opportunity right now to make an intelligent choice.*

Breathing heavily, a sure telltale sign of stress in a Vampyre, he glanced sideways with just his eyes at the nearest Orc standing against the wall. *Your son was invited to attend an exclusive game at my employer's country estate. He left shortly after arriving here.*

She felt another pang that Ferion would have chosen to leave without letting her know. What kind of grip did this need to gamble have on him?

Perhaps he had left a note at the house. Even as she thought it, she knew she was grasping at straws.

While the Vampyre did not mention his employer by name, she knew he meant Malfeasance's owner, the pariah Djinn Malphas. A Djinn had no need of a physical residence, unless he chose to entertain creatures of other Races.

She asked, *Where is this place?*

*I—I've never been to his country estate, personally.* The Vampyre loosened his cravat with pale fingers. *From listening to other patrons talk when they'd been issued an invitation, I do know that it's a day's ride out toward Wembley.*

*Wembley,* she repeated, searching her memory of the geography of the outlying areas. *That's west.*

*Yes, my lady.*

*What else can you tell me of this estate's location?*

*The patrons complained about one of the inns on the highway, close to the estate. They said the food was terrible and it took forever to get service for their horses.* A touch of desperation entered his mental voice. *Truly, that's everything I know.*

All he had offered were minuscule bits of information, but she could hear the sincerity in his voice. In a clench of despair, she turned away, just as a volcano of fury entered the room.

For a moment, she almost didn't recognize the towering figure. While she stared, she heard everyone in the room take a collective breath as they moved away.

Only then did she realize it was Graydon who stalked toward her, his face pale and set while his Power boiled in a chaotic, hot corona around his clenched body.

She felt the blood leave her face and forgot to telepathize. "What is it?"

His white, taut lips barely moved. He said in a low voice, "He's not here. We need to leave before I start murdering people."

In the background, to his right, a couple of men slipped out a doorway. They were inconsequential. As soon as she saw them, she put them out of her mind. She took one of Graydon's hands. It was bunched into a rigid fist. Even his skin was hot to the touch.

She could not imagine what had happened to fill him with such rage. As soon as she touched him, his hand loosened, and he curled his fingers around hers.

"Come on," she whispered.

Together they strode for the front door. She noticed that the Orcs standing against the wall wouldn't look at them any longer.

Once outside, she gratefully took deep breaths of the chill night air. Not even the whiff of stench from the street rubbish could dampen her relief at leaving the stifling smells inside Malfeasance.

Graydon strode down the street so fast, she had to trot to keep up. His anger was still palpable, and his expression so dark, she bit her lip and kept silent for several blocks, until they had left all the activity behind them and reached a quiet, dark section of street.

With immense relief, she shoved back the confining hood. A slight, cold breeze, still damp from the recent rain, brushed against her overheated cheeks.

"I'm going to burn that place to the ground." His whisper was so forceful, it came out as a hiss. "I didn't do it because you were there. I know how much you need to find your son, but I'm going back to level that building."

"Dear gods," she said. She stopped walking, which meant he had to let go of her hand, drag her along behind him, or stop walking too.

He stopped. As she gently tugged, he spun around to face her. He had clenched her fingers so tightly, they had gone numb, but she didn't protest. Overhead, the cloud cover had broken, and a pale spray of stars arced across the clear night, silhouetting his tawny head.

Even though his rough features were in shadow, she still tried to search his expression as she asked, "What happened?"

He blew out a forceful breath and rubbed the back of his neck with his free hand. Then he rubbed his face as well. Through her palm, she could sense when the furious rigidity in his body eased.

"No," he said. "I won't saddle you with that information. I'm handling it."

She rejected that, categorically. "How on earth could you be handling whatever is back there, when we just walked out? I should know what the cost of rescuing my son is. *He* should know what his actions cost."

"That's not fair or accurate." He stepped closer. The heat from his body warmed her. "Ferion has nothing to do with this. I caught no hint of his scent throughout the rest of the place. It's likely he has no idea what happens beyond the gaming rooms."

Again, her imagination ran riot. She had seen the gambling for herself. What was left?

Drugs and sex. She thought of how several of the men had considered her figure. Even when there was virtually nothing for them to see, other than the fact that she was feminine, they had assessed the possibilities in what lay hidden underneath the cloak. How a few had contemplated rape.

A sudden wash of emotion brought tears to her eyes. She pointed back in the direction of Malfeasance. "Whatever is back there—you would stop it right now if it wasn't for him, wouldn't you?"

No, she thought. If it wasn't for me.

This has nothing to do with Ferion. Graydon checked his behavior for me.

Slowly, his grip on her fingers loosened. He raised both hands to cup her jaw. His hands were so big, she felt completely nestled within the warmth of his hold.

"Beluviel, listen to me," he said. His voice had gentled. "Normally I do a much better job with my temper. I shouldn't have lost control like that, or said anything that I did."

She gripped his thick, strong wrists. "Don't apologize. Just explain."

"You've done me a great honor by trusting me tonight." He touched her lips with his callused thumbs, as if he would read her expression in the darkness by touch. "I want you to trust me a little further. Let me handle what I found at Malfeasance. Trust that I *am* handling it. And trust me when I also say this doesn't need to concern you."

He had said before that he was handling it. Whatever it was. What could he have possibly done to handle anything in the short amount of time he had left her alone?

But she trusted him. Didn't she?

Poking at herself, she realized that, yes, she did trust him, substantially more than she had at the beginning of this gods awful evening, and even more than she had realized.

"You'll tell me if I need to know?" she asked.

"I swear, I'll tell you if you need to know," he said. "But you don't need to know. Stay focused on your son. This does not have to become your battle."

She thought about that. Then she gave him a little nod. "Very well."

He bent his head.

For a crazy, heart-stopping moment, she thought he might actually kiss her.

On the lips, no less.

If he did, it would turn this whole evening completely upside down.

As it turned out, he *did* kiss her, but not on the mouth. He pressed his lips to her forehead, almost as if he thought she might need comfort, which was stupid, of course, because nobody had offered her comfort in a donkey's age.

People always came to Bel with their problems and expected her to fix them, and she did. Somehow, she always did, no matter how difficult the problem or how long it took.

The press of his mouth against her sensitive skin evoked the wildest upsurge of longing she had felt in a winter's eternity. It mingled with the earlier yearning she had felt to fling herself against his chest, to pat his waistcoat, to nestle against the warm, friendly blaze of his aura.

Closing her eyes, she pretended to drift into his caress, as if she had every right to enjoy his touch and they had all the time in the world.

And every single part of that was wrong.

He murmured, "I'm so sorry we didn't get any information about Ferion."

His words jolted her back to reality.

Reluctantly, she pulled away, and his hands fell from her face. With the same kind of wildness that had gripped her several times already that evening, she missed his touch so desperately, she almost reached for him again, except she didn't have the right.

She forced herself to be relevant. "We did get some information," she said. "The Vampyre I was questioning when you showed up—he said that 'his employer' had invited Ferion to an exclusive game at a country estate, a day's ride west of London toward Wembley. He claimed Ferion left right after he had arrived."

"Did he, now?" Graydon said thoughtfully.

She chewed at her lip. "It's not much to go on, but it will have to do. I didn't think to ask how long ago that happened.

Since Ferion didn't attend the masque, I had assumed he arrived at Malfeasance sometime this evening, but that isn't necessarily true. The only thing I know for sure is that I saw him at breakfast. If he went to Malfeasance directly afterward, he's had almost a day to travel already. I don't have a moment to lose."

The gods only knew how much financial damage Ferion might do before she found him, let alone how much time she might be gone.

Her absence would be noted, and the chances that she could keep this from Calondir were growing terribly thin. Lianne and Alanna were in her confidence, but none of their other guards and retainers were.

"What do you mean?" Graydon asked.

"A carriage will take too much time," she muttered. "I'll need to travel by horseback, and take either Lianne or Alanna with me. The other one will fuss, but someone needs to stay behind and try to run interference."

Big hands settled onto her shoulders, startling her out of her preoccupation. Graydon said, "I said, what do you mean, you don't have a moment to lose?"

Looking up into his shadowed face, she said, "Thank you so much for what you've done. Can you possibly do me one more favor and take me to Grosvenor Square before we part for the night?"

His hands flexed, and for some reason, his body tightened again.

He said, "No."

## ⇒ FIVE ⇒

He hadn't meant to sound so abrupt.

He hadn't meant anything at all. As he had gathered her meaning, denial had rolled over him, and the word had leaped out before he realized it.

Looking into Beluviel's beautiful, upturned face in the uncertain light of the moon, he saw that his answer had taken her aback. She blinked and straightened her spine. He could feel the rigidity of her shoulders through the palms of his hands.

He was beginning to recognize her reaction. Whenever adversity struck, she straightened and readied herself to meet it.

He needed to unclench and think of something more coherent to say. Unfortunately, that would require understanding himself more than he did at the moment. Realizing he gripped her too tightly, he forced his fingers to relax.

She said with obvious constraint, "If you need to leave right away, I'm sure I can hire a hansom from Malfeasance."

Violence flashed through him at the thought of her walking back to that filthy hellhole. He swore under his breath and reined himself in. "I apologize. I meant, no, I'm not going to just drop you off at Grosvenor Square. I will take you to Wembley, if you'll let me."

She drew in a breath. Sensing she was about to deny him, he rushed on. "Before you say anything, think about it. I can get you there much faster than anybody other than a Djinn, only I won't demand a favor from you in return. We can stop at the posting houses along the way to make inquiries. You'll locate Ferion and Malphas's estate much faster with me, and besides—"

Besides, I don't want to leave you just yet.

He caught himself before he said it. He had no business feeling that way, let alone confessing such a thing to her.

Aside from the fact that it was inappropriate in the extreme, a part of him—the part that was all cunning and no conscience—realized that if he said it, she might feel forced to turn down his offer.

He wasn't prepared to let that happen.

"Besides what?" Her gentle question brought him back to himself.

"It might be best if you had extra protection," he finished, feeling lame. Then he gained more surety as he thought about it. He told her, "Malphas will not be happy to have us arrive uninvited, but with representatives of two different demesnes, not just one, on his doorstep, it might check his behavior."

"Are you certain you can leave your sentinel duties for that long?" she asked. "You traveled all the way from New York to attend the masque. I'm sure you must have meetings and social functions on your schedule. Won't Dragos have need of you?"

He brushed that aside. "Constantine and I have very light duties while we're here. I won't be leaving any task that I can't pick up again once you and I are done."

"If you do take me, this must be a private arrangement," she said. "Something just between you and me, not between the Elven and the Wyr demesnes. We must maintain absolute secrecy."

"Of course," he replied. "I already promised my discretion on this matter. That extends to the trip to Malphas's estate."

"We really could travel so much faster," she said slowly. "We could return to London faster too. Perhaps I can still find a way to keep this from Calondir's attention."

Now that he had said his piece, he waited for her to make her decision.

She gave him a tentative smile. "Yes, thank you. I would be most grateful for your help. I still need to return to the house, so I can change into travel clothes. I want to see if Ferion has left a note. If he did, we might be able to glean information from it. Also, I need to leave further instructions for Alanna and Lianne."

"I must return to Vauxhall to let Dragos and Constantine know I'll be leaving London for a short while," he said. He had another piece of business to attend to, but he would not mention that to her. "I can take you to Grosvenor Square. Then I'll go to Vauxhall. I'll need to stop at our rooms at our hotel so I can change, but afterward, I can return for you."

"That would be marvelous," she said with such evident relief, he wanted to smile. "In fact, that would be beyond marvelous. Graydon, I don't know how to convey my deep gratitude."

"There's no need, my lady," he told her. "The fact that I've been able to help you is thanks enough."

He meant it sincerely. He truly did, but the cunning part of him, the conscienceless part, whispered other, less altruistic reasons for what he did.

*Getting the chance to spend more time with you, to ease your path, to share a smile or two . . . To touch you in small ways, your hand, your shoulder, perhaps kiss you again, on the forehead or the cheek. Or the mouth.*

No, he did not say it. He shouldn't have even thought it. But he did.

He did, and he realized that he was not only fine with keeping all manner of things from Calondir. He began to understand that he was willing to keep any number of things from the rest of the world as well.

He had arrived at a dangerous place. Constantine had been right. Beluviel was the very definition of unattainable, for so very many reasons that Graydon didn't think he could count that high.

Yet in spite of all of that, he was beginning to develop deep feelings for her. Deeper than mere respect or affection.

Fortunately, this adventure of theirs would be brief, and it had a built-in conclusion. Beluviel would go back to her life, and he would return to his. Perhaps that was why he felt the need to grab onto this experience. This might be the only chance he ever got to share any time with her.

After glancing around at the darkened, deserted street to make sure they were unobserved, he shapeshifted and crouched to assist her in mounting onto his back. Once she had settled firmly at his shoulders, he launched. Lifting his head as he sliced through the air, he relished leaving the heavy urban smell of London below. Her soft, delighted laugh made his soul smile.

The flight was another short one. Soon, he spiraled down toward the park at Grosvenor Square. It was one of the most affluent and fashionable areas of the city. Telltale sparks of Power dotted the neighborhood. Several magic users were in the vicinity.

Taking care to keep a good distance from them, he landed near a large old oak tree. She slid from his back. He told her telepathically, *I'll be quick.*

*Thank you.* Her gaze flashed up to his. *I will too.*

*Meet me in this spot when you're ready,* he said.

*Yes.* She paused and unexpectedly stroked her fingers down the feathers of his neck.

He froze. She couldn't know how intimate that seemed, or how sensitive he was to her touch even through the sleek covering of eagle feathers. Pleasure at being petted ran down his spine.

He should say something or step away. He did neither. Instead, ever so slightly, he leaned into her touch.

It was wrong of him, but his wrong button seemed to be broken, and he didn't care.

When she stepped away, for a moment, he felt bereft. He lingered long enough to watch her stride toward one of the houses that contained several sparks of Power.

As she left, it became harder for him to see her. Within a few more steps, she disappeared completely from sight, and he realized she had a serious talent of her own for cloaking.

With no further excuse to linger, he turned away and launched again, heading back to Vauxhall and the masque.

This time, without Beluviel, he didn't care if he was observed. He landed inside the Gardens, shapeshifted and took a main path that led to the dancing area.

Midnight had come, and everyone had removed their masks. Quickly, he strode past several groups of drunken partygoers as he searched for Weston.

He found the earl in close conversation with a striking redheaded woman dressed as Athena, the Greek goddess of wisdom. Walking past the couple, he said telepathically, *Weston, forgive me for interrupting. May I have a word?*

*Of course,* replied the other male. *Give me one moment.*

While Weston made his excuses to his companion, Graydon wandered over to the refreshment area. The cocktail fountains were still flowing with brandy and champagne, and plentiful heaps of food remained on the tables.

Helping himself to a large plate of sausages, he ate with quick economy.

From behind his shoulder, Weston said, "You look like you're eating to store energy for a flight, not for enjoyment."

Weston was an avian Wyr. Graydon shouldn't have been surprised that the other man was so astute.

He chose not to respond to that observation. Turning away from the table, he said, "What do you know about Malfeasance?"

Weston's mild expression never flickered. He was a tall man, although not as tall as Graydon, with chestnut brown hair, aquiline features, deep-set eyes, and a mouth that was tilted, more often than not, in a slight, ironic smile.

Known as a private man, Weston held a quiet Power. Graydon liked and respected him. He also knew that a number of people feared Weston. But a number of people feared him too.

As Graydon watched, the other man took a plate and helped himself to a meringue and a savory jelly, and then he turned to face the crowd.

Weston said, "I doubt very much you would enjoy what Malfeasance has to offer, my friend."

Graydon switched back to telepathy. *Are you aware that they hold women against their will and sell children for sex?*

The earl's aquiline features remained impenetrable, but instead of taking a bite of his meringue, he set it carefully on his plate. Nothing about the man revealed what he was thinking. Not even his pulse had increased.

One might almost have thought Weston truly indifferent to the news, or that he already knew, but Graydon had been acquainted with the earl for a very long time. He didn't believe that Weston had known, because if he had, he would have already done something to stop it.

No, this was news of a most tragic, revolting sort, and yet still Weston never exposed his reaction. Graydon admired his iron self-control.

With one forefinger, Weston nudged his meringue a minuscule distance on the plate. He said, *I was not aware of this. You have been to Malfeasance? You've seen this for yourself?*

*Yes. I've just come from there. I was pursuing a private matter. Because of that, I refrained from doing . . . a lot of things. I paid for the children for the night. They're being fed supper.* Rage flared up again, and he clamped down on it. With dogged determination, he finished the last of the food on his plate then set it aside carefully. *I'm fully prepared to go back, but your government may have a serious problem with the Wyr of New York if I take the kind of action I feel needs to be taken.*

Weston set his plate aside as well and met his gaze. *Thank you for coming to me instead. I can only imagine how difficult it must have been to leave. You have my word, I will have the children in my custody within the hour and make sure they will be returned to their families or acquire good homes. I will also ensure the women receive the care they need, including respectable employment, if necessary.*

*And Malfeasance?* Graydon growled.

The falcon's eyes flashed. The difference between his feral gaze and impassive expression was jolting. *Rest assured, in a very short while, Malfeasance will no longer be in existence.*

He blew out a breath. *Thank you.*

*If you'll excuse me.* Weston gave him a slight bow. *The evening has grown late, and I have just discovered I have much work to do.*

Watching Weston stride away, he recognized the liquid shift in the earl's body. Civilization had receded, and the man's predator had come to the fore.

The tightness in Graydon's muscles eased somewhat. The earl was a man of his word. Graydon had no doubt that Weston would do what needed to be done.

Glancing over the crowd, he located Dragos easily enough. The dragon was surrounded by people, and he stood head and shoulders over almost everyone in his vicinity.

Graydon shouldered his way through the crowd, exchanging pleasantries with those who greeted him. When he had approached close enough to come to Dragos's attention, the dragon gave him a nod.

He said to Dragos, *A matter of some personal urgency has arisen.*

One of Dragos's inky eyebrows rose. *You have a personal urgent matter? Here, in London?*

*I'm afraid I can't say anything more,* Graydon said. *But I need to leave for a day or two.*

*I don't like secrets, unless they're mine,* Dragos said, giving him a piercing look.

*I understand,* Graydon replied. *Unfortunately this one is not mine to tell.*

Over the crowd, Dragos's gold eyes narrowed on him. *This has nothing to do with me, or the Wyr demesne?*

*Absolutely nothing,* he said.

After several moments, the dragon said, *If I don't hear from you in two days' time, I'll come looking for you.*

Graydon gave him a lopsided smile. *You'll hear from me.*

Dragos nodded. Without any further word on the matter, he turned his attention back to the people conversing around him, releasing Graydon from his sentinel duties.

Pivoting, Graydon left the crowd behind in swift, long strides. The further he got away from the party, the faster he walked, until the wild, untamed creature living inside pressed him into a run.

As he ran, he shapeshifted and left the earth behind.

After a brief stop at his hotel, where he changed out of his evening attire and donned sturdy traveling clothes and weapons, he winged toward Grosvenor Square.

He loved being a sentinel. He loved the responsibility and the challenge, the sense of justice and satisfaction he got from a job well done. The predator in him gained huge satisfaction from hunting down criminals, and the possessive side of him loved claiming the Wyr demesne in New York as his own.

He shared that fierce pride with the other sentinels. They were more than family; they were a nation. He had a place that he had fought for, that he bled for, and that he worked hard to keep.

He shouldn't be feeling this riotous upsurge of emotion. He shouldn't be so eager to get back to the woman who defined *unobtainable.*

The concepts of family, justice and nation ran deep in him, but the gryphon lived in a place deeper still.

It reached for the sky with the same passion as it flew toward Grosvenor Square, toward the impossible, the unobtainable, and it did so because the need to return to her was like the need to fly, like an arrow in the heart.

It did so, because it couldn't do otherwise.

He plummeted down to earth in the park where he and Bel had parted. As he landed beside the large oak tree, he thought he was alone with nothing but the deep green of the rich grass for company.

Then the shadow underneath the oak moved. Whipping around, he held his impulse to violence in check because part of him was still convinced the moving shadow *was* the tree. They carried the same signature energy, the same scent.

The shadow became a tall female Elven warrior. A thrill ran over his muscles as he recognized Bel.

The pure, inviolate maiden from the masque had vanished, along with her simple, feminine gown. The starlight overhead was dimmer than the light that shone in her large, dark eyes.

She had braided her long hair and dressed in leather, sturdy and more suitable for quick travel than Elven armor, and she had strapped a sword to her back. Over it all, she wore a cloak. Instead of the plain black cloak from earlier, this one was more subtle as it took on the colors of the night around her.

This was the Lady of the Wood. She knew the wild spaces of the world. She had given birth to many of the oldest of them. People of the Elder Races from all over the world revered her, and not least among them were the Wyr.

Most times, it was easy to set aside ancient memories and knowledge, to make way for the prosaic living of the day to day. Looking at her now, the gryphon knew fully who she was. He remembered, and, proud though he could sometimes be, he felt an almost overwhelming urge to kneel.

He didn't, but he did bow his head deeply. *My lady.*

She touched the long, pure line of his beak. *Beautiful gryphon. Thank you for carrying me on this journey.*

*I will carry you anywhere you need to go,* the gryphon told her. He crouched. She leaped onto his back, and the place at his shoulders that had begun to feel empty in her absence felt complete again.

He launched into the night air and climbed until they had left civilization behind.

Only then did he wheel in a great arc and fly west.

# ═ SIX ═

Even though Bel had experienced the gryphon's flight once already, they hurtled through the air much faster than she had believed possible. Her heart soared as, within minutes, they left London behind.

They would find Ferion. She knew it. They would find him before he could do too much financial damage. If Graydon would consent to carrying both of them back to Grosvenor Square, they might even be able to return before daybreak, or at the very least by noon.

With any luck, Calondir might not have even returned from the masque. Or perhaps he might linger over an assignation and not return until later that day. Either way, for the first time that evening, she was filled with hope.

Briefly, Graydon slowed his speed. Even as she began to question it, he surged forward again with an adjustment in direction, until she realized that he had started to follow the path of a shadowed road below.

Soon they came to a cluster of buildings. As the gryphon decreased his altitude and wheeled, Bel studied the area.

While most of the buildings were dark, the biggest one

was clearly a posting house and inn. Even though the hour was late, lamplight still shone in the windows.

*Would you like to stop and inquire, or do you want to travel onward?* Graydon asked.

After a moment, she replied, *I think we should travel onward. This place is too close to London. I don't believe Ferion would have stopped so soon.*

*Very well.* Once again, the gryphon surged upward. As he picked up speed, she thought she would never tire of the experience. The cold, fitful wind sliced away her tiredness and discouragement, until her mind felt keen and blade sharp.

She asked, *How long will it take us to reach Wembley, do you think?*

*I doubt it can be more than an hour's flight,* he told her. *Locating a country estate without specific directions will take longer.*

*Perhaps, if we can find the astonishingly terrible inn, we'll be able to get directions from there,* she said dryly.

*I hope so,* he replied.

Curious, she asked him, *How do you suggest we search?*

He paused. *I don't suppose Ferion left you a note?*

She shook her head before remembering he couldn't see it. *No, he didn't, so we don't know when he actually left.*

*In that case, I don't think we need to stop until we reach Wembley. Once we're there, we can work backward along the road. With any luck, we might run into Ferion himself, but if we're too late to catch him, at the very least, we can hope to get directions to Malphas's estate. It's owned by a Djinn. Any visitors Malphas has will be much more distinctive than the average traveler. Someone will know of the place.*

*That makes sense,* she said. His logical thinking gave her a sense of deep relief. He was a mature predator. He knew the strategies for how to hunt better than she did.

*How are you?* he asked. His deep mental voice had gentled again. *Not too cold, I hope?*

Her relief metamorphosed into a warmer emotion. Not only had he volunteered to help her, but his concern for her well-being was genuine.

He was a good man, a kind man, and he had gone significantly out of his way for her without ever hinting at payment or recompense.

Dragos doesn't deserve him, she thought. She trailed her fingers lightly over the sleek, strong line of the gryphon's neck. If he were in his human form, it would be unthinkable to let herself be so familiar, but letting herself touch him while he was in his Wyr form was immensely comforting.

*I'm fine,* she told him. *Thank you for asking.*

His mental voice turned gruff. *Just wanted to make sure. Let me know if you need to stop. I can build a fire so you can warm up.*

His offer brought to mind an image of sitting together by a campfire, Graydon's rough, suntanned features highlighted by bright, leaping flames. The firelight would reflect in his dark gray, attentive gaze, and the surrounding forest would be blanketed by the dark blue of night.

They could talk together. They could just talk, about anything and everything.

Oh gods, she wanted that so much.

More disturbed than she could say, she yanked her mind away from the image. Her normally well-ordered emotions careened all over the place. She didn't know this person she was becoming, with the riotous impulses and wayward desires.

Forcing her reply to sound steady and calm, she assured him, *I don't need that right now, thank you, but I'll let you know if I do.*

She had any number of good people in her life. Alanna and Lianne loved her, and she loved them. She had a rich life, filled with many pleasures and pastimes. She had people who cared about her. Calondir might be Lord of the Elven demesne, but she was its Lady.

She believed in the Elven demesne. She worked and cared for it, just as she nourished the Wood and the extensive gardens that surrounded their public home just outside of Charleston. Calondir might rule by law, but she was the one that people came to for advice, problem solving, or comfort.

She was almost never alone, so why did Graydon's

concern and attention touch such a deeply lonely spot inside? The distant ache in her chest grew closer and sharper the longer she spent time with him.

Troubled, she closed her eyes and turned her focus inward. He didn't speak again. They traveled the rest of the way to Wembley in silence.

When the rhythm of the gryphon's flight changed, she opened her eyes. They flew over a large town. One or two lights flickered, but most of the buildings were shadowed and dark. As Graydon banked and turned, she saw the signature wheel of a mill by a glimmer of water.

They had reached Wembley.

After flying in a circle, the gryphon arrowed back along the road.

The first cluster of buildings they came to on the outskirts of the town was as dark as the rest of the town. It was unsurprising, given the lateness of the hour.

Bel noted the distinctive layout of a roadside inn, complete with substantially sized stables in the back. In a few short hours, the inn staff would be bustling to prepare breakfast.

The gryphon drifted down to land in the front courtyard. Once he had touched ground, Bel slid from his back, and he shapeshifted. Somewhere close by, a dog barked then fell silent. The rain hadn't fallen this far west, and the night sparkled with a hard frost.

"I don't suppose you can scent whether or not Ferion might have stopped here?" She kept her voice very low.

"Not here, sorry. Mostly all I can smell are horses and manure." Graydon placed a large hand at her back. He kept his voice as quiet as hers. "Shall I inquire inside?"

She smiled up into his shadowed face. "Thank you for offering, but no, I can ask. We're far enough outside the city, word of my presence won't travel back to Calondir. If by chance he discovers something, it will be from some other source."

He nodded and let her precede him to the front doors. Halfway there, she paused. If she roused the innkeeper or his staff, she might wake any number of their guests as well.

She whispered, "Let's check the stables first. Perhaps there's a stable boy or groom who sleeps with the horses. It might be quicker to question them than field complaints from people staying in the inn."

He nodded. "Good thinking."

They made their way around the inn, to the back. She stood to one side as Graydon opened the barn door.

Warmth, along with the smell of horses and hay, wafted against her cold cheeks. A horse nickered sleepily. Something rustled, and a dog's low, menacing growl sounded from the shadows.

A male voice, breaking with youth and nerves, said, "Whoever you are, you better stay back. My dog bites."

Bel laid a hand on Graydon's arm. She replied soothingly, "We mean you no harm. All we want to do is ask you a few questions. I'm sorry we woke you, and I'm willing to pay for your time."

There was more rustling, along with tiny sounds of flint hitting tinder, and then the warm glow of the lamp illuminated the interior of the stable. A boy, lanky and awkward, and a dog of indeterminate breed peered at them warily.

When the boy looked at Bel, his gaze widened. "Don't that beat all," he breathed. "I ain't never spoke to no Elven lady before. Or maybe you're Fae? I seen Fae and Elves on the road from time to time."

"I am Elven," she told him, smiling slightly at his enthusiasm. "May we step inside and close the door? Otherwise your horses might get a chill."

"Yes, my lady, if it pleases you." The boy glanced at Graydon, who also smiled at him reassuringly. It seemed to help him relax, although his dog remained stiff-legged and bristled warningly.

Bel and Graydon stepped inside. As Graydon quietly pulled the door shut and latched it, she said to the boy, "I'm looking for my son, and I wondered if you might have seen him. He would have traveled through this area sometime late yesterday. He's actually my stepson, so he doesn't quite look like me. He has pale blond hair."

The boy shook his head. His nervousness had not decreased, but the more Bel talked, the more his fear clearly ebbed. "No, my lady. There ain't been no Elves travel on this road for some time. I would've heard if there was. Meaning no offense, but we don't see many of you often."

"I see," she murmured. Disappointment weighed on her shoulders, and her sharp, clear thinking from earlier in the flight clouded over.

Rubbing her forehead, she struggled to focus. She had no business feeling so disappointed. They had barely begun to search. This was simply the first place they had stopped to ask questions

Graydon flattened a large hand on her back, his touch silently bracing her.

He asked the boy, "When they do pass by, do people of the Elder Races stop at your inn? Perhaps you've heard of an estate nearby that's owned by one?"

The boy straightened, his tired gaze growing more alert. "You're talking about what used to be Stanton Manor," he said. "That's about a half mile on the other side of the mill, up the big hill. I hear they're an odd sort up there."

"How do you mean?" she asked quickly.

"Sometimes his lordship hires a whole houseful of staff for a week or two, only to send them home afterwards, and the house goes dark and silent for weeks or months on end. And sometimes, when nobody is supposed to be home, I heard that lights shine in the house." The boy's gaze had turned large and solemn. "Once the constable went up to check, and nobody was there. He said the dust in the place was an inch thick, and it weren't disturbed none. He swears the house is haunted."

"Fancy that, a haunted house." Graydon cocked an eyebrow at her. He asked the boy, "If someone came from London, could they travel by another route to reach that house, or must they pass this spot?"

After mulling it over, the boy said, "They could take Old Ferryman's Road. You wouldn't have to go through town if you took that route. It goes directly past the mill."

"Thank you," Graydon told him. "You've been very helpful. I have one last question for you. Could you sneak into the kitchen for some bread and cheese? Perhaps there might be some cold chicken or a roast left over from supper. Anything would do, and it doesn't have to be fancy."

"Yes, sir," said the boy. "I could wake the missus, and she could cook you a hot meal, if you want. She might grumble a bit, though."

"There's no need to wake your mistress," Bel told him. "We came to the stables so we could avoid disrupting people unnecessarily."

The boy bobbed his head. He promised, "I'll be right back."

Leaving the lantern, he slipped out, and the dog slunk past Graydon, close on his heels.

Bell scrubbed her face with both hands. "I feel uneasy about stopping. Ferion might have taken the other route and gone straight to the manor. He could be there right now."

"That's true," Graydon said. "But you know, if he has arrived, he's most likely asleep. He's had a long day of travel, and it *is* after three in the morning." He paused, studying her. "You've clearly begun to struggle, and I don't like how pale you've become. When was the last time you've rested or eaten anything?"

She peered at him over the tips of her fingers, thinking back. "I suppose it must have been breakfast. I didn't bother to eat any lunch, since I knew there would be so much food at the masque. Then I got preoccupied with other things."

As she spoke, she realized this was the first time she had laid eyes on his human form since they had gone their separate ways, and she was struck by the change in his appearance.

No longer dressed in evening clothes, he wore sturdy clothes in huntsman's colors. A long winter coat brushed the tops of his dark boots. He carried a hunting knife in the belt at his waist, and a sword strapped to his wide back.

The brown and green of his clothes highlighted the tawny, sun-kissed sheen of his hair and added depth to his dark gray eyes.

No wonder the dog couldn't stop growling, she thought. Unlike earlier, when he had been dressed in formal evening attire, now he looked comfortable, dangerous. If it weren't for the kindness in his expression, she could very easily be frightened by this man too.

He gave her a small smile. "It's been a long day and evening. It would be a mistake to show up at the manor in the middle of the night, feeling exhausted and out of focus. Neither Ferion nor Malphas are going to welcome our arrival. In fact, the exchange will probably get heated and unpleasant. As hard as it might be, we'll take the time to eat, and if you think you might be able to sleep, I suggest we find a place that's comfortable enough that you might be able to nap for an hour or so, or at the very least relax, until dawn."

What he said made so much sense, and the prosaic, calm way in which he said it was even more compelling.

Dropping her hands, she grimaced. "You're thinking about this much more clearly than I am. And you're right, of course. Even if we take an hour or two, we've still arrived so much faster than I would have if I'd traveled here without you."

"Shall I wake the innkeeper after all?" he asked. "Would you rest more comfortably in a bed?"

Searching his expression, she hesitated. It had been a long night for doing things she shouldn't have done. She shouldn't ask this of him either, but she wanted it so badly. Maybe she even needed it. It was too hard for her to tell, when the ache in her chest had become so sharp, so sweet.

She met his gaze. "I would feel better in the woods. If you would build me that campfire, I'd rather doze outside. Would you mind?"

All hint of a smile left his expression. If anything, his gaze grew deeper, more intent. "Never. I would love that too."

The stable door creaked open just wide enough to let the boy and the dog slip inside. Hauling the door closed again, he turned to hand Graydon a parcel of food wrapped in a large handkerchief.

Graydon didn't bother to check the contents. He could

smell bread, cheese and chicken. Accepting the parcel, he gave the boy a nod in thanks.

When Bel opened a small, black leather purse and pulled out a few coins, the boy's eyes widened and began to shine.

"Thank you for everything." She handed him the money.

"Yes, my lady. Thank you, my lady." Falling silent, he stared at the coins in his palm.

One corner of Graydon's mouth lifted. He murmured to her, "I believe that's our cue to leave."

He held the door open, and she slipped out into the cold, crisp air. In silence, they walked away from the inn.

She had no idea where they were going. Matching her stride to his, she veered when he veered, following his lead in a daze.

All she knew was that they were going to someplace entirely new, entirely strange. It was the sweetest place with the sharpest pain, and she did not quite know how she could bear it, yet she didn't know how she could survive without it.

When he handed her the food and shapeshifted, she leapt onto his back, and they flew over the town and past the mill. Graydon followed the river and didn't land again until he had reached a tangled clump of woods, some distance upstream from any property.

As she dismounted, she took in the place. A thick blanket of winter leaves covered the ground, while the dark outline of the trees overhead was spiky from bare branches. Evergreens dotted the area, giving the scene a sharp pine scent, while the quiet, rejuvenating sounds of the nearby river played at the edge of her hearing.

It was a clean, undomesticated place. The difference between it and all the other places they had visited in that long night couldn't have been more dramatic.

Some unrecognized burden fell from her, and without realizing it, she breathed, "Oh, this."

She barely sounded coherent, but he seemed to know exactly what she had meant.

"Yes," he said, very low. "This."

Together, they gathered wood. She had countless years of experience to draw upon, and he did too. They didn't even need to speak as they coordinated everything they did with quick, neat economy.

As she cleared leaves from an area, he collected stones to make a fire ring. She walked down to the river to wash her face and hands, relishing the biting cold water. When she returned, he had a fire started and had even found a fallen log to use as a seat.

"Thank you," she said fervently.

His smile lit up his rough face. "My pleasure."

Rolling her tired shoulders, she slipped out of her sword harness, set it aside and sat. Echoing her movement, he joined her on the log. The fire quickly took hold, and flames began to leap, throwing off bright, intense heat.

She heaved a sigh. "Cities are hard."

He had begun to unwrap the food. The glance he gave her was brief and heartfelt. "Don't I know it."

"How can you stand to live right in the middle of one?" she asked, curious.

"I guess it's necessary," he said. He lifted one wide shoulder in a self-deprecating shrug. "New York isn't nearly as big or as intensely urban as London, and after a time, one gets used to it. There are so many challenges to face every day, which helps, and between all the sentinels, we make sure that we get plenty of time to roam. I've felt more cooped up since I've been in London than I do at home."

The handkerchief held a large chunk of bread, several uneven slices of cheese, and part of a roasted chicken. He offered her the food, and she took the bread, breaking it into two pieces, one much larger than the other.

Keeping the smaller piece, she gave him the large one, while he set the food cloth on the ground between them and handed her a slice of cheese.

She took a bite of the bread and cheese. The crust of the bread was golden brown and crunchy, while the softer inside was yeasty rich, and the cheese had a sharp, creamy tang. It was delicious.

She said around her mouthful, "I don't think that was the horrible inn."

His deep, quiet chuckle vibrated the log. "I don't either."

The fire heated her face and hands, while the cold evening air brushed the nape of her neck. The warmth of Graydon's steady male presence enveloped her, and the combination was more delicious than the food.

After a few moments, she grew so warm, she shrugged out of her cloak and draped it on the log beside her. Whenever either one of them moved, his arm or thigh would brush against hers, and the simple, visceral pleasure of his nearness washed over her all over again.

I'm happy, she realized with surprise. In spite of everything going on, at this point in time I'm actually happy. It's not that I was unhappy before—but before, I lived with an absence of this intense new feeling.

And none of it would last past sunrise. This deeply peaceful, nourishing experience was as fleeting as any other, and that was the sharpest, sweetest pain of all.

After he took the last mouthful of his bread and cheese, he began to pull the roast chicken off the bone and offer her the choicest tidbits.

She accepted a few bites then declined any more, content to watch him finish the meal, which he did with relish. He had been right. Eating had steadied her.

His head bent, he kept his gaze on his task. The firelight picked up bright glints in his hair. His hair had a tendency to an unruly wave, and he kept it short and no-nonsense, no doubt, she thought, in some effort to tame it.

When he finished the chicken, he tossed the bones onto the fire, shook out the handkerchief and wiped his hands on the cloth.

She had gotten so used to the silence that when he spoke, she startled. He asked, "Do you mind if I ask you a question about something that is really none of my business?"

She should say no.

She should politely, gently erect proper social barriers between them.

She should do a lot of things, but some renegade part of her was growing greedy for any excuse to relate to him, any opportunity to extend and deepen the sense of companionship.

"Please do," she said. A tiny, tattered remnant of caution caused her to add, "I may not be able to answer, but you may certainly ask."

With that, he looked up, spearing her with his gaze. "Why are you with Calondir? It's quite clear that you and he do not live in accord."

The heat and intensity in his eyes was searing. She could only hold his gaze for a few moments. Jerking her head away, she stared blindly at the fire. She felt shaken to her bones.

She told him, with difficulty, "That's a long, very old story."

"I have time," he said quietly.

She swallowed hard. "We don't live as husband and wife, and we haven't since—well, since too many years to count. We're business partners. Our business is running the Elven demesne, and we do that very well."

"You were with him, then you lived apart for some years," he said. "When you got back together, he had his son, Ferion. That's really all I know."

"Yes, that's right," she murmured. Ancient memories played through her mind. "Originally, we did live together as husband and wife. In the beginning, I thought I loved him. He could be so charming and charismatic when he wanted to be, but I think he married me to acquire a prize. At any rate, for me it was a disastrous mistake. After a brief time, I left him. I had no intention of ever speaking to him again. Then he came to me one day with Ferion." She sighed and rubbed her eyes. "Ferion's mother had died giving birth to him, and he was so tiny, so completely innocent and new, I could almost hold his entire little body in one hand."

"I didn't realize he was so young," Graydon said. His gaze never strayed from her face.

She didn't mind his scrutiny. It was as warm as a physical caress. "He was only a few days old. Calondir put him in my arms and said, 'My son needs a mother. If you want him, you may have him to raise as your own. But if you do, you must return to me. I will not let any son of mine live away from me.'"

He let out a long sigh.

It sounded so heartfelt, she gave him a sidelong, wry smile. "Well, you can imagine how I felt. I had wanted a child for so long, and you know how rare that blessing is for us. As soon as I held that sweet baby boy, I couldn't let him go. He became my whole world, and I adored him completely."

She had twisted her fingers together in her lap. One large hand came down over both of hers. Graydon said softly, "That happened a long time ago, Bel."

"Yes, it did." She turned her hands over to cup his. He had thick, long fingers and a broad callused palm. His skin was warm. "A very long time ago. Meanwhile other things happened, and tensions grew in various factions among us. None of it is relevant today, except that creating the Elven demesne outside of Charleston was actually my idea."

"I didn't know that, either," he murmured.

She shrugged. "The thing was, I had been gone from that particular group—the kernel of what became our demesne—long enough that people looked to Calondir for leadership, not to me. So, we created a charter and set sail, and established our demesne outside of Charleston. It was all very forward thinking and exciting, in its own way."

His mouth took on a sour slant. "Calondir became Lord, and you became consort."

She nodded. "Ferion grew up, and I planted the seeds for my Wood and nourished it into growing, and it's been my home ever since. Usually, Calondir and I don't get in each other's way, except when it comes to Ferion. Often I go weeks without seeing him, as either one of us might be either in the Wood or in residence in the Charleston home."

His fingers tightened. "It's a business arrangement."

"Yes. Except for Ferion, it is." She sighed. Calondir was actually not that bad as Elven High Lord. He just made a rotten husband and father.

"That doesn't bother you?" he asked. "Have you never wished for anything else—for something more?"

She lifted her eyes to meet Graydon's dark, steady gaze and whispered, "For the most part, our personal arrangement has never really mattered, before now."

He turned toward her, leaning forward. She shifted as well, her face turned up to his.

Her gaze dropped to his rough-cut, sensitive mouth, and her body pulsed as she remembered the warm caress of his lips on her forehead.

What would it be like to have those lips cover hers? While everything she had told him was true, no Elven male would dream of trying to touch or kiss the consort.

For the most part, that arrangement had never really mattered before now either. She could hardly remember what it was like to kiss a man, let alone imagine what it might be like to kiss someone with Graydon's combination of gentleness and virility.

The sense of connection she felt to him was becoming almost unbearable, as deep and wild as the wood that sheltered them.

Of course, she had to go and do something to destroy the moment.

Before she fully realized what was coming out of her mouth, she said, "Now, it's my turn to ask you a question. How can you stand to work for Dragos?"

# ⇒ SEVEN ⇐

The loathing in Bel's voice was so evident, Graydon shifted position, subtly pulling back.

He needed to put some physical distance between them. Somehow, he needed to calm the riot of feelings her question roused.

He couldn't blame her for how she felt about Dragos. She was, after all, only one of many who felt that way.

Once, very long ago when the world was new, all of the ancient Wyr had been feral. Dragos had been the most feral of them all, a gigantic predator that did not distinguish between the natures of the creatures he hunted.

Graydon kept his voice measured as he told her, "Once, we were all more beast than human, but that, too, was a very long time ago. Dragos is not what he used to be. None of us are. He is the one who originally had the vision for the Wyr demesne. He approached each of the sentinels to get our support. He created the laws, and he and the sentinels work together to uphold them."

She shook her head. "It's hard to fathom we're talking about the same creature."

"In a very real sense, I don't think we are." He paused. "Yes, he can be a challenge, but I believe in everything he has accomplished. Just as you feel with the Elven demesne, I believe in our demesne and what it stands for. So much so, I've dedicated my life to protecting it and upholding its laws."

The delicate skin around her eyes tightened. She said, "With my head, I can understand what you're saying. But my heart remembers the terror of watching the Great Beast fly overhead, and the anguish of loss I felt at the people he slaughtered. I'll always remember that he is a killer."

Her words felt like a slap. He turned his face away. As the evening had progressed, his feelings for her had grown richer and more complicated. They shared such a deep love for the woods, and he understood how passionate she felt for her son, but now he felt chilled with the realization of what real distance lay between them.

He said, "Bel, *I* am a killer."

After a moment, she touched his averted face, her warm, slender fingers cupping his chin and urging him to turn back to her. With reluctance, he complied.

"I see what you are, gryphon," she told him. "You're proud, and incredibly strong, and courageous, and you're very dangerous, precisely because you are also so good and kind that people might forget the reality of everything about your nature. Even considering all that, you could never be like him, not in a million years."

As he looked into her eyes, her large gaze was so full of warmth it banished the chill almost completely.

Almost, except for the knowledge of the distance lying between them.

The wild part of him that fought against any kind of restraint rebelled against the awareness. Just as it had driven him through the air to her, it drove him forward now.

Moving with gentle care, he took hold of her hands, holding her so lightly, she could pull away from him with a single easy gesture. Like the rest of her, her hands were beautifully formed, the bones slender and graceful.

She didn't pull away.

Bowing his head, he pressed his mouth to her fingers.

They were on a runaway coach, hurtling nowhere.

She would never be able to live in New York, so close to the dragon.

He would never be able to live in the Elven demesne, so close to Calondir. Even if Graydon would consider leaving his duties, the Elves would never accept a former Wyr sentinel in their midst.

As Constantine had said, she was the very definition of unobtainable.

Yet he still reached for her.

"Look at us," he said against her fingers. "You with your commitments, and me with mine. We live a world apart from each other."

A tremor ran through her. "Graydon," she murmured. "What are we doing?"

He lifted his head. He could drown in eyes such as hers, so wide and dark, yet so full of light. "Bel, tell me not to kiss you, before I do something we might both regret."

"I can't," she whispered. "I want it too much."

Her unsteady confession struck away the last of his resistance. Holding his breath, he lowered his head to the pure, plump arc of her lips.

Then he was touching her mouth with his.

He was kissing Beluviel, the unique woman who personified that first, unique breath of spring, while the warmth and giving softness of her lips shaped to his, and oh my gods, she was kissing him back.

That single caress was so damn *shocking*, he nearly came in his pants, and *that* shocked him with a raw pulse of adrenaline that ran like fiery liquor over his skin.

Slowly, not believing his remarkable fortune, he let go of her hands and slid his arms around her long, supple torso. She nestled closer, and the way her muscles relaxed and curved into him was downright miraculous.

She was so far above him, so far beyond his reach, he wasn't entirely sure any of it was real, except his body knew differently. His muscles grew tight and his heart pounded as if he were racing, while his starving lungs forced him to suck in air, and the desperate ache in his hardened cock felt like a mortal wound.

He had crossed so many boundaries in himself, he had no idea what this new, foreign place held for him.

Stroking his fingers down her long, silken braid, he eased away to look down at her. A dark rose color flushed her cheeks, and her eyes shimmered. At the sight, a thread of alarm streaked through him. She wasn't teary, was she?

She made a soft, urgent sound at the back of her throat, took his head in both hands, and reached up to kiss him a second time.

This time, she slanted her mouth over his and touched his lower lip with her tongue. The caress was so intimate, so needy, shock washed over him again.

It was all the invitation he needed. Crushing her against his chest, he ravaged her mouth, plunging into her with his tongue over and over.

Her fingers worked against the back of his skull, threading through his short hair, while she matched his kiss eagerly. Only half aware of his actions, he took hold of her long braid and wound it around one hand until he made a fist at the nape of her neck.

He was burning, burning. He felt too big for his clothes, on fire for her. Every goddamn breath he took was filled with her luscious, feminine, unique scent. Suddenly starving for every new sensation, he pulled away from her mouth and ran his lips along the petal soft skin of her cheek.

Either he was shaking, or she was, or perhaps they both were. He held her tighter.

"Bel," he whispered, drunk on the delight of saying her beautiful name. "Beluviel."

She shuddered and sobbed out something in his ear. What she said, he didn't know, but the sound of her trembling voice snapped him back into himself.

He could have pretended it hadn't. Clearly she wasn't rejecting him, so he could have pressed on. He didn't want to stop, but he lifted his head anyway.

The golden firelight gilded her rosy skin. Her lips were slightly swollen from his kisses, and the long, graceful arch of her throat as she bent her head back in willing acquiescence of his grip in her hair was utterly perfect.

With a quick glance, he committed the sight to memory, and then he focused on the expression in her gaze. She gazed at him with a combination of such pleasure and pain, conflicting impulses threatened to tear him apart.

He whispered, "I shouldn't want you so desperately, but I do."

"I shouldn't delight so much in hearing you admit it," she whispered in reply. "But I do, and I want you too."

He tightened his fist in her hair. "Tell me we shouldn't be together, just once."

He watched as her trembling mouth shaped a stunning reply. She whispered, "I can't think of a single reason why we shouldn't be together, just once."

"We can steal this hour for ourselves," he said slowly, watching every telltale, tiny shift in her expression for any sign of refusal. He couldn't bear the thought she might think of him with regret. If she showed a single hint of remorse or reluctance, he would stop.

There was none.

Stroking her fingers through his hair, she murmured, "There's no reason why we can't. No harm will be done."

There was something wrong in what they said to each other, but his fevered brain couldn't quite puzzle it out. His growing hunger for her was louder than any other instinct or doubt.

"No harm," he agreed hoarsely. "We can take this time together. Just until dawn, just you and me."

"And we don't tell anybody about this," she whispered, searching his gaze. "Afterward, we go on living our lives, just like before? You'll go back to your demesne, and I'll return to mine?"

"Yes."

Loosening his grip on her hair, he pulled her braid apart. The long, dark strands cascaded over his fingers. Against his callused skin, it felt incredibly soft, like water or silk.

Obeying an impulse, he buried his face in a handful of her hair.

That was when he began to realize where they had gone wrong. There was no way he could make love to this incredible woman and go back to his life as if nothing had ever happened. The very fact of her threatened to change him at a fundamental level.

He was beginning to think she might be everything he could ever want or need. She certainly embodied far more than he had ever thought he might find in a woman.

And she was nothing he could ever have for himself.

Not truly, not past dawn.

Just as he couldn't turn away from her earlier at the masque, he couldn't turn away from her now. It would be a terrible thing to close the door on spring and never venture forth to experience all the wonder that living his life to the fullest could bring, even if he could only have an hour with her.

Easing out of his arms, she undid the fastenings of her leather vest, pulled it off and set it aside. The jacket was heavy, he noted, and stitched with a thick lining, a good solid understated piece of armor. Underneath, she wore a white silk shirt, embroidered along the neckline and wrists with a curling green vine.

Touching the vine with one forefinger, he murmured, "Pretty."

She gave him a luminous smile. "I stitched it last month. I like to remind myself that winter is temporary, and spring always comes."

"You're not too cold?" he asked her again, stroking her cheek. She shook her head, leaning into his touch. "We can spread my coat on the ground."

"And we can use my cloak as a blanket," she murmured.

"You deserve a much finer bed than this." Unable to resist, he leaned forward to caress her lips with his.

She said against his mouth, "This is the best bed I could hope for."

He shrugged out of his coat and laid it out on the ground. The fire was beginning to die down, so he took a moment to add the last of the wood to the blaze. As it flared up, he turned back in time to see her pull off her leather boots and pants.

Her long, bare legs were flawless. Muscles flexed over narrow, graceful bones as she bent to scoop up her pants and drape them over the log. Her hair fell longer than her shirt, the feathery ends brushing against her thighs. As she bent her head, the tip of one pointed, elegant ear peeked out of the dark, shining strands.

Transfixed, he stared at her.

Sex, for him, had always been rowdy and affectionate, and an altogether temporary condition. It was damn fine physical exercise, and an excellent way to release tension and get a comfy cuddle or two.

The next morning, he would feel fit as a fiddle. With a whistle and a spring in his step, he was ready to get on with his day. He honestly didn't mind paying someone generously for a good time, as long as she wanted to do it, was happy to be paid and enjoyed her work.

In contrast, he was stricken by the depth of emotion he felt when he looked at Beluviel.

With a silent roar, hunger banished his soul to live inside his skin. It became the raw, feral force that drove the beat of his heart, the pulse of his blood. In all the countless ages in which the gryphon had taken flight, this was the first time he left himself behind.

Tearing off his shirt, he rolled it into a bundle, so she would have a pillow on which to rest her head. As she took note of what he did, she gave him a smile that softened and lit her beautiful features.

Rising swiftly to his feet, he pulled her against his bare chest and took her mouth again. Kissing her drove the hunger to a fever pitch. He felt more than a little mad from it, as he dug his fingers into her hair and plundered the soft, secret recesses of her mouth.

A shudder rippled through her body. Protectively, he nestled her closer and murmured against her lips, "You *are* cold."

She shook her head. "Not when I'm near you. You throw

off heat like a furnace." She ran her hands over the bare expanse of his chest. He had a deep suntan, and his pectorals were liberally sprinkled with hair that was a darker shade than the hair on his head. It narrowed to a sleek arrow that shot down his abdomen.

Pleasure washed over him at her caress, along with a hint of self-consciousness. He muttered, "I'm a lot hairier than most Elves."

"I love it," she breathed, looking down his length. She leaned forward to rub her face against his chest, a gesture not only affectionate but so sensual and animal-like, it touched a deep, atavistic part of him.

His hunger sharpened to an uncontrollable spike of need. Bending, he scooped her into his arms and laid her on the ground. As she settled back onto his coat, she flung out a hand, snagged a corner of her cloak and dragged it close.

He wasn't cold either. The heat from the fire and the chill night air felt invigorating to him, but still he allowed her to shake out the cloak and drape it over his back. She was taking care of him, and he *loved* that.

He needed to see all of her. With shaking fingers, he unbuttoned the front of her shirt, until the edges fell to either side, and she lay exposed to his scrutiny.

Absolutely, without a doubt, the most important and lovely part of her was her spirit. Feminine and quietly strong at the same time, she drew him in like a lodestone. Even knowing and believing that, the physical sight of her overwhelmed him.

She was exquisitely shaped everywhere, with the same narrow, long bone structure. Her flat stomach was punctuated by the graceful arch of hipbones, and her pelvis, which was sprinkled with a small tuft of dark, silken hair. In contrast to her slim rib cage, her breasts swelled in generous curves, tipped by jutting, pale pink nipples. As he watched, they crinkled and stiffened in the night air.

At the sight, a guttural croon broke out of him. Bending down, he took one nipple in his mouth ravenously and sucked.

Arching, she cried out, the silvery sound spearing

through the quiet predawn. Astonishment overcame him at the intense pleasure he found at flicking the delicate, plump morsel of flesh with his tongue.

While he suckled, he ran a greedy hand all over her body. His hunger for her had become a driving need, and he was fast losing any sense of finesse he might otherwise have had.

While he stroked and petted her, he was vaguely aware of her hands working at the fastening of his pants at his waist. She yanked his clothes open, and, once freed, his erection spilled into her hands. Her fingers closed somewhat clumsily over his cock, and he felt as massive and hard as an oak tree in her grip.

He was losing control, losing it. Arching his back, he pushed his cock into her hands, while he suckled at her breast and thrust one hand between her legs.

As he discovered the satiny, soft petals of her private flesh, he found her deliciously wet. Caressing her deeply, stroking into the entrance of her passage, he drew more of her moisture out, until her arousal coated his fingers.

She groaned, or he did. They might be eternally separate but they moved as one. His lungs worked like a bellows, the breath sawing in his throat as he switched from suckling on one nipple to the other, drawing on her deeply while he rubbed and explored her, until he encountered a tiny, precious nubbin of stiffened flesh.

Sharing this kind of raw, carnal intimacy with her was incredible. He would be more awed if he wasn't so immersed in her.

As his fingers connected with her clitoris, she cried out and lifted her head off the ground. Enchanted, he rubbed her rhythmically, while her hands roamed his body with a frantic urgency. With one hand, she cupped his balls and stroked his erection, while with the other, she stroked and caressed his chest, plucking at his nipples.

Then she stiffened, her lips parting on a gasp, and her wide, dark gaze flew to his. He looked deeply into her eyes as he stroked her, transfixed by the way she shivered and groaned as she climaxed.

Events cascaded, and suddenly, they were moving too fast. The urge to be inside her was too strong. Growling, he moved between her legs, covering her body with his, and she guided the broad, thick head of his cock into place.

Gazing into her eyes, he entered her, and she was so hot, so wet.

Her inner muscles tightened on him as she wrapped both legs around his waist, and he couldn't help but move. He couldn't stop. He pinned her down, hips flexing, and she cradled his entire body as she tilted up for every thrust.

Making love vanished into animal rut. He needed to get deeper, to dominate. Fire overtook his body. Gripping her by the hip, he increased his tempo until he was pistoning into her. She cried out, winding an arm around his neck.

His own climax slammed up the base of his spine, and it was all too fast. It came on too strong, sank invisible teeth into him, and it wouldn't let go. Groaning, he spurted into her. He was so blinded by the extreme pleasure, he was only vaguely aware of how she rocked with him, encouraging every last ripple.

It wasn't enough. It couldn't ever be nearly enough.

He needed to continue, to go deeper, spill more of himself into her, until there was nothing left of him to give. Until there was no turning back.

A shock of realization slapped him.

What he needed to do—it was absolutely the one thing he shouldn't.

Gasping, he withdrew. It was the hardest thing he had ever done. His cock was still so stiff and aching, he couldn't bear to touch himself, while he buried his face in the extravagant dark pool of her hair.

I can't fall in love with you, he thought.

But it was too late for that. He was already in love with her.

It had been too late from that moment at the masque when he took her hand and tucked it gently into the crook of his arm.

He had always been a little in love with her. How could he not be? Falling the rest of the way had felt so effortless, so right. All it had taken was spending a little time with her, talking to her, holding her in his arms.

*I can't mate with you and leave you. And I can't stay with you either. There's too much distance lying between us, too many impossible barriers.*

She cupped his cheek and tried to meet his eyes.

"It's not you," he said. He sounded too harsh, and concern darkened her expression. "It's not this. It's me."

"What can I do?" she whispered.

"Nothing. I just want this too much." He yanked her cloak off his back and shoved it into her hands. Everything he did was too rough, but he couldn't control himself. He realized he had been so on fire to get inside her, he hadn't even gotten fully undressed.

Tearing off his clothes, he stood when he was entirely nude. His cock ached fiercely. So did his soul.

He realized he could see more of the clearing than he could earlier, and he looked up at the eastern sky. The pale gray of predawn crowned the neighboring trees. It was almost dawn. They had run out of time.

Striding away, he headed for the river. When he reached the bank, he dove in. Icy water closed over his head.

It was the only way he could think to quench the fire that ran in his veins.

*I can't mate with you and hope to live.*

# ⇒ EIGHT ⇐

Left alone by the fire, Bel curled on her side and drew her knees to her chest. She stared sightlessly at the dying flames.

Making love with Graydon had been more raw and elemental than she could have imagined. It had also been over much too quickly. Sharing that sense of closeness and pleasure, the urgent need for each other. His body was so powerful, and he used it so gently. She fingered one of her nipples, still sensitized and swollen from his mouth.

She loved sensuality, and she enjoyed making love. She'd had other lovers besides Calondir, both before marrying him and after they had decided to reunite for the sake of the baby.

But the community they had established in South Carolina was a close-knit one, and she hadn't taken a lover since they had created the Elven demesne, so long ago. She had set that part of herself aside and focused on the many other aspects of her life.

She felt as if she had drifted into a state where she had been only half-alive, partially awake, but now her sexuality had flared to life again, opening all her senses.

The ground felt harder, the air cooler, the fire warmer. Her skin was hypersensitive to the weight of her cloak and the uneven folds of his coats underneath. Unaccustomed to being with a man, the private place between her legs throbbed.

The look on his face as he left her. Her emotions felt heightened too, and the pleasure she had felt turned to ashes. Her eyes filled.

Blinking back the wetness, she searched for the handkerchief from the parcel of food. When she found it, she used it to clean the inside of her thighs. Then, as the clearing lightened with dawn, she dressed.

Funny. She had been so warm before, she had felt like she was burning up. Now she felt so cold, her bones ached.

She kicked apart the dying fire and began to toss dirt onto the most stubborn of the embers. As she worked, Graydon returned in silence.

He was naked, of course, and dripping wet, and completely unself-conscious about his nudity. He moved fluidly, without affectation or hesitation, like an animal.

Staring at him, she forgot what she was doing. They had coupled together in such an uncontrolled, heated rush, this was the first time she had truly seen all of him.

Unclothed, his masculine body was lethal in its perfection. He was the same golden tan all over, his tall broad bone structure wrapped with heavy, powerful muscles. The sprinkle of dark brown hair on his chest arrowed down his long, rippling abdomen to his groin.

No longer erect, his penis was still large and heavy. It lay in a thick arc over round, tight testicles. She swallowed as she looked at him. No wonder she was so sore.

She dragged her eyes up to his closed expression. His jaw was tight, and he held the firm lines of his mouth in an uncharacteristically stern line.

"I'm sorry," she told him. "If I had been thinking more clearly, I wouldn't have started dousing the fire before you'd had a chance to dry off and dress."

With the back of one hand, he swiped at a droplet of water on the end of his nose. "It's all right. I needed the cold."

He wasn't deliberately being mean or cruel. She didn't believe he could ever be that with her. He had simply closed himself off emotionally, in a way that he hadn't been since he had stepped into her path at the masque.

Ducking her head, she went back to her task, not stopping until she was certain the fire had been extinguished. Out of the corner of her eye, she watched as he dragged on his clothes. It couldn't be pleasant to dress while still wet, but he didn't complain.

She couldn't blame him for erecting an emotional wall. In fact, the wisest thing she could do was follow suit, but she missed that magical sense of connection they had shared. She missed it desperately.

As she looked at the strong lines of his throat where his shirt lay open, she had to swallow again. And oh gods, the desire she felt for him was stronger than ever.

*I want this too much.*

The quiet force behind his words ripped through her memory. She should respect the closed wall she saw in his face and leave him alone. She had to let go of him. Their brief time was over. The sun would be up in a matter of minutes, and she needed to find her son.

Her feet didn't understand any of that reasoning. Acquiring a will of their own, they carried her over to him. He watched her approach with a dark, brooding gaze. She thought of half a dozen things she might say, but everything seemed to run the gamut between needy and banal.

In the end, she simply shook her head at him. Her mouth twisting, she walked forward and put her arms around his waist, hugging him tightly. He stood rigid, neither denying her embrace nor responding to it.

The sweetness had left her heart, until all that remained was pain. She buried her face in his chest, muffling a sob.

Finally he moved. His arms closing around her, he bowed his head over hers.

Her voice thick, she managed to say, "I am experiencing a great deal of difficulty at the thought of letting you go. I probably shouldn't tell you that, but I can't seem to help myself, because among other things, over the course of this night you've become my dear friend, and I've cherished confiding in you. And I want this too much, too."

He held her tightly with his whole body.

"I shouldn't have left you so abruptly like that," he said into her hair. "Bel, I don't want to let you go. Because I can't control my emotions, I've spoiled the last few minutes we had together. I'm sorry."

She ran her hands along the broad expanse of his back. "You have nothing to be sorry for. I understood."

She hadn't yet rebraided her hair, and he ran his fingers through the length compulsively.

He muttered, "Maybe this doesn't have to be over. You said that you and Calondir often spend weeks apart, and you don't always reside in the Wood, right?"

The world stilled. She nodded.

"When I take leave from my position, I could fly down to South Carolina," he whispered. "I could meet you anywhere you like."

As she listened, her heart began to pound. His words sent her across another boundary, to a place where the pain might become manageable, and the sweetness might return.

She shouldn't agree. She should make a clean, complete break, but the thought of trying to deny the part of her that had come back to life was unendurable. She would do almost anything to hold onto it.

To hold onto him.

"Do you really think it's possible?" she whispered.

"We'll make it possible." His warm breath stirred the tiny hairs at her temple. "We may have run out of time right now, but I'm not ready for this to end. It's no use telling myself I should walk away from you—I can't. I won't."

His words banished the chill that had crept into her. Hardly daring to hope they could work something out, she said slowly, "Perhaps I could rent a place in Charleston."

Sinking his hand deep into the hair at the back of her head, he tilted her face up and kissed her, quick and hard.

"Don't misunderstand, I'm not ashamed to be with you," he

said against her lips. "If our lives were even marginally different, I would shout about this from the rooftops. But as things stand, I'm not sure Charleston would be the best idea. If word got out, frankly, I believe the world would put a great deal of pressure on us to stop seeing each other, and I don't ever want to give you the slightest reason to turn me away."

"No, I could never be ashamed of being with you either." She stroked his rough face as her mind raced over options. "And you're right. While Calondir might have no interest in the fact that I may be sleeping with someone else, he would hate to know that I had developed a liaison with one of Dragos's sentinels, let alone . . . oh lord and lady, let alone how everybody else would react. Perhaps I could buy property a short distance outside the city, a small house with enough of a garden so that you could land or launch in privacy."

His gaze seemed to turn inward. "I might be able to live with that," he murmured. "This might give us a solution that we can both live with."

The way he had phrased that first sentence seemed odd. Her brows drew together, but before she could puzzle at it too deeply, he kissed her again, slanting his mouth over hers and driving deep into her mouth with a rapidly escalating hunger.

His kiss was so scorching, it burned away coherent thought. Clinging to his shoulders, she kissed him back wildly, causing him to growl low in his throat. Instead of cradling her head, he gripped her neck, a gesture so possessive, it thrilled through her.

He pulled away just far enough so that he could talk, nose to nose with her and staring deep into her eyes with a fierceness that set her heart to pounding. "I don't want to wait to see you again. You'll be in London at least for the next couple of days, correct?"

She nodded, as much as his hold would let her. "I have engagements for at least the next week," she told him unsteadily. "When we return to London, I'll look at my commitments and cancel everything I possibly can."

"I will, too. And as soon as you return to South Carolina, you'll begin looking for that house."

"Absolutely."

"I'll pay for the house."

"Thank you, but there's no need."

He frowned. "I don't like for you to assume all the financial burden."

"It won't be a hardship," she assured him. As he continued to frown, she stroked his hair with a smile. Gentle though he might be with her, he did have his share of masculine pride. She promised, "I'll start searching the day I return. With any luck, I'll find something suitable very soon."

Dismissing the subject of finances, his face creased with an answering smile, and he kissed her forehead. "I can arrange things so that I get at least a couple of days together, every month. We can plan for that. It will be difficult to wait, but as long as I know that I will be able to see you, I can manage."

The sweetness returned, spreading through her limbs. It felt remarkably like joy. She breathed, "Think of it—we'll see each other every month. That sounds almost too good to be true."

"Well, it's far from perfect, and realistically, my life as a sentinel can get unpredictable. There will probably be times when I can't make it, and I won't be able to notify you. If I sent you a letter or a note, it would take weeks to reach you." His mouth twisted wryly.

"I don't care." She laughed under her breath. "That's not true. I do care, but I understand, I promise. No doubt sometimes I'm going to feel horribly disappointed when you don't show up as planned. But right now, I'm just so happy I don't know what to do with myself."

"I know how you feel. I feel the same way, and believe me, I'll do everything in my power to make it happen—" He broke off abruptly. As he looked around, his expression changed.

Suddenly he appeared so different, his features hard and edged, and completely unlike the tender man who had smiled down at her a moment ago. This time, when her heart started to pound, it wasn't in delight but in alarm.

"What is it?" She looked around the clearing as well.

As they had talked, the light had grown much brighter, and dawn had arrived in earnest. The rose-gold color caught on the dark bare branches of the trees surrounding them.

"I don't know. I could have sworn something brushed past us, but I don't scent any other creature. I don't hear anything either." Releasing her, he prowled around the edge of the clearing, sharp-eyed and cat-footed. "Do you sense anything?"

Frowning, she pivoted in a circle, searching the scene as he had.

Everything appeared as it should. Their things lay scattered where they had left them—her cloak, his coat that they had used for a bed, and both their swords lay beside the log they had used as a seat. She cast her awareness into the woods, but the only creatures she sensed were small, furry animals, tucked deep into winter nests.

Just when she had convinced herself they were alone, something invisible brushed past her cheek, carrying with it a sense of ill will.

A figure solidified in front of her. It took on the appearance of a handsome man, with a face like an angel, with golden hair and eyes that shone like sparkling diamonds, but the appearance was a lie. He was no physical man, but a Djinn.

Fear crawled through her body. Normally, when the Djinn appeared, they did so in a whirl of Power like a tornado. This Djinn had masked his Power to creep up on them like a predator stalking its prey.

Movement blurred at the corner of her vision as, with a gigantic spring, Graydon leaped to her side.

"What an interesting scenario I have stumbled upon," said the Djinn. "One of the Wyr sentinels having a tender moment with an Elven lady who is not his." He gave them both a glittering, hard smile that vanished in the next moment. "If I am not mistaken, it is the very same sentinel and lady who visited my establishment late last night. An establishment, I might add, that I had grown quite fond of, and that, as of this morning, is no longer in existence. Coincidence? I do wonder."

"You're Malphas," Graydon growled. He stood so close to her, their shoulders touched, and his energy bristled with protectiveness and aggression.

"Indeed, I am," said Malphas. "I believe I'm in possession of something you want."

She bit out, "Where is my son?"

The look he gave them was so hostile and full of rage, Bel controlled an entirely useless impulse to lunge for her sword. Swords were useless in a battle against the Djinn. "He is up at the manor, but then you already knew that, or you wouldn't be here. He's had a rough night, and he's sleeping it off."

Rage washed over her, obliterating the fear. As she lunged forward, Graydon's arm snaked around her waist, and he held her back. She cried, *"What did you do to him?"*

"You'll have to come see for yourself," said Malphas. "No doubt you can find your own way up the hill to the manor. Don't expect breakfast, and be prepared to beg when you arrive."

The Djinn vanished.

She whirled to face Graydon. "What was he talking about? Malfeasance no longer exists?"

He had paled until he looked bone white. "Get your things. Hurry."

She didn't need any further urging and leaped for her sword and cloak, while beside her, Graydon did the same. Shrugging into his coat and sword harness, he shapeshifted. She leaped onto his back.

Only when he had lunged into the air did he speak. *They were selling children.*

*What?* She felt so crazed with worry, what he said didn't make any sense.

*At Malfeasance,* he said. *They were selling children.*

It took a moment longer for his words to sink in. When they did, she rocked as if he had physically struck her. *Oh GODS.*

*I didn't want you to know.* His telepathic voice sounded more bestial than human. *I'm from the New York demesne. If I had destroyed any establishment here, it could have been interpreted as an act of war, yet I couldn't stand aside and do nothing. I paid for the children before we left. When I went back to the Gardens, I approached Weston and told him—not about you. Weston said he would rescue the children and shut down the business. That was when I left.*

The more she heard, the more ill she felt. *I don't have any words.*

While he'd been talking, he had climbed so steeply into the air, within a matter of a few moments she could see for miles. Any other time, she would have been enchanted by the view of the picturesque English countryside crowned with the new light of day. Winter colors wreathed the land in browns, golds and oranges, and trees rose out of a low hanging mist.

Almost immediately, a manor came into view. Just as the stable boy had described, it sat on top of the hill overlooking the town's mill. She noted bitterly that it was a sprawling, palatial-looking residence. Owning a gambling hell appeared to have paid high dividends for the Djinn.

*We're almost out of time,* Graydon said as he descended. *Listen—Malphas can't be certain that we were behind whatever happened to Malfeasance.*

*You paid for the children,* she said numbly. *Then Weston came to take them away.*

*Yes, but he can't know anything for sure. Weston and I spoke telepathically. I didn't say a word to anyone else. Remember that. Let's not give him more fuel for his anger. We'll get Ferion, and then we'll get out.*

*I understand. Just get me down there!*

She leaped from his back before all the gryphon's paws fully touched the earth. As she ran to the front doors, Graydon shapeshifted and raced after her. His Power roiled as it had back at the gaming hell, with a towering fury.

The large, double oak doors stood open. Neither she nor Graydon hesitated. They plunged inside and paused in the great hall.

To her right, through an open doorway, a fire blazed in the fireplace of the front receiving room. Turning by instinct toward the heat and light, she started to sprint forward, only to be brought to an abrupt halt when Graydon gripped her arm. He gave her a grim look of warning.

Her spirit raged at the restraint, even as she recognized the wisdom in his caution. She gave him a curt nod. Together they stepped forward, looking around warily.

The room was decorated with colors that had been in fashion a decade ago. A blue velvet armchair had been positioned strategically by the fireplace, facing the front hall.

Malphas sat in the armchair, legs crossed. His demeanor was as regal as if he sat on a throne. He rested his elbows on the arms of the chair, fingers steepled in front of his mouth, eyelids lowered over piercing, starlike eyes.

Ferion sat cross-legged on the floor in front of him. He was beautiful in the way that Elves could be, his lean and graceful frame holding a tensile strength. Long blond hair fell past his shoulders, pulled back from his temples and tied with a strip of leather.

His lean, handsome face was blank, while dark purple shadows like bruises ringed his eyes.

As soon as Bel's gaze fell on her son, renewed rage and worry swept common sense aside. She tried to rush forward, but Graydon still gripped her arm. His fingers tightened, halting her in midstep.

"Look who has come to visit this morning," said Malphas. "The adulterers have arrived. Ferion, did you realize your mother has been unfaithful to your father? Faithful . . . unfaithful . . . Those words don't mean anything to me, but I know they matter a great deal to some people."

"You have no idea what you're talking about," Ferion whispered. His dull gaze met hers. "Mother, I am so sorry—"

"Shut up," Malphas ordered.

Ferion's words cut off, as abruptly as if Malphas had stuffed a gag in his mouth.

"You lied," Graydon growled. "There was no exclusive game here. Nobody's here except for you and Ferion."

What did he mean? She glanced around the room again. This time, she noticed other details.

Cobwebs draped in corners of the ceiling. The armchair in which the Djinn sat looked bright and fresh, but the other furniture was dull with dust. On the floor, footsteps clearly showed on the worn, faded carpet.

"Don't mistake me," Malphas said. "I *can* and *do* lie when it suits me, but I didn't lie about this. There was an exclusive game. It was with me. Yes, we could have played it in London, or anywhere else, for that matter. I just like to see how hard people will work for it." He shrugged. "Of course the only people I invite here are the ones who can't resist the game."

She gave the Djinn a look filled with loathing, and then dismissed him to concentrate on her son.

"Ferion, never mind what has happened," she said, struggling to keep the anger from her voice. "We need to leave. We also need to talk, but we can do that away from here."

"I don't believe you understand yet why you need to beg," Malphas said. "So, I'll show you. Ferion, go to your mother."

Graydon said telepathically, *Bel, be careful. I don't know what he's doing.*

His words didn't hold any real meaning for her. They fell far outside the urgency in her mind. As Ferion pushed to his feet and approached, she pulled her arm from Graydon's grasp and rushed forward.

Malphas said, "Put your hands around her neck and squeeze."

She had already moved to throw her arms around Ferion when she heard those words. Before she could recoil, Ferion's hands snaked around her neck. He began to choke her.

Suddenly, she couldn't breathe. Pressure pounded in her eyes.

Instinct took over. She tried to yank back, but Ferion was extremely strong, and she couldn't dislodge his hard fingers.

Even as she arched away and attempted to twist out of his hold, snarling filled her ears. A powerful blow slammed into her chest. Graydon drove his big body between them like a battering ram, and through sheer force, he shoved them apart.

Gasping for air, she stumbled back, fell over one end of

the sofa and sprawled on the floor. Ferion slammed into the nearby wall.

Two booted feet planted themselves on either side of her head, as Graydon straddled her prone body.

Coughing, she rubbed her throat as she stared up at his towering figure. The angles of his face and hands seemed strange and wrong, his fingers tipped with talons and his mouth distorted with fangs.

She had heard of such a thing, but she had only witnessed it from a distance. When they were under extreme duress, sometimes Wyr shapeshifted partially.

Even as she stared, he bared his fangs at Malphas and roared. The sound blasted through the house and shook the floorboards. She felt it vibrate in her chest.

It sounded like a lion's roar, but it was more than mere physical sound. As he roared, his Power boiled out from him in a raw blast toward the Djinn sitting in the armchair. Malphas's figure dissipated under the force of it.

This confrontation had dissolved into catastrophe so fast, it sent her reeling. Flipping over to her hands and knees, she pulled into a crouch at Graydon's feet. Across the room, she saw Ferion do the same.

His expression was filled with the same look of horror she felt twist across her own face. He said telepathically, *I would never—I could never—*

*I know,* she told him.

The Djinn's energy coalesced in the doorway leading to the front hall.

"Now you begin to understand," Malphas said. "But not, I think, fully enough. Ferion, stop breathing."

Slumping back against the wall, Ferion's gaze met hers. His shoulders hunched and his face darkened, as his body struggled.

In a complete panic, she sprang across the room. He clawed at his own neck. She flung her arms around him as she frantically searched for some way to help him. She could find nothing, nothing.

Nothing except an odd frisson buried deep in his body.

To her mind's eye, it felt like a darkened smear across the brightness of his soul.

Graydon roared at Malphas, *"Release your hold on him!"*

*I love you,* Ferion said in her head. His eyes reddened as blood vessels burst in the whites.

If she could strike a blow at the Djinn, she would, with all the terrified fury raging in her heart. But while she could fight very well in a physical battle, at his essence, Malphas was not a physical creature. She was considered one of the most Powerful of her kind, but most often, Elven Power was connected to the elements of the earth.

Her Power connected her to wild, living things. It was the kind that ran slow and deep, and took years to build. By working with natural forces like vines, trees and other foliage, given enough time, she could destroy a city. She had an array of other specific spells, like misdirection and cloaking, but she had no real Power to use against a creature of spirit.

The only weapons she had of worth in any conflict against the Djinn were things like connections and political influence. Those, too, were weapons that could be wielded very effectively, but only over time.

In that moment, though, there was only one thing she could think to do that might work quickly enough to save Ferion's life.

"You want begging." She didn't even recognize her own voice. "Fine, I'm begging you. Please stop this. Do you need to see me on my hands and knees? Look, I'm already here."

Cold satisfaction settled into Malphas's face. He said to Ferion, "Breathe."

Instantly, Ferion's body arched as he sucked in a huge breath of air. Wheezing, he closed his arms around her.

Graydon strode across the room to stand protectively over them. Staring at the Djinn with open hatred, he snarled, "You've made a massive mistake."

"Have I?" said Malphas. He strolled into the room. "Pray tell, how did I do that? Did I force Ferion to come into my establishment to gamble? Did I make him accrue the kind of debt that he cannot repay?" He looked down at her son.

"Ferion, did I compel you to ride out here to take part in a game? Answer."

As she stared down into her son's face, shame darkened his features. He kept his gaze downcast as he whispered, "No."

"There you have it." The Djinn shrugged. "By making a series of choices—not just one—he created a situation where he cannot keep his side of a bargain. I might be a pariah, but that single fact adheres to the very heart of Djinn culture. By Djinn law, I am well within my rights to force a satisfactory conclusion to the bargain by taking some kind of recompense."

"You preyed on him," she said hoarsely. "He's a good man with a bad weakness, but instead of recognizing that, you gave him credit to continue to gamble, when you knew he couldn't pay."

"Irrelevant," Malphas told her. "At any point, he could have said no and walked away, paid his debt and been done with the exchange. Now I've called in my markers, his debt has come due, and he cannot pay it."

The situation had gone so far beyond disastrous, implications reverberated in her mind. Malphas knew about her and Graydon. Of all the creatures to discover them, he was the one who actively wished them harm. And Ferion had accrued a debt so significant, Calondir was sure to hear of it. Life as she knew it began to crumble around her ears.

Maybe I can still fix this, she thought. If it's more than I can pay, I might be able to borrow money in secret. I have friends who might help.

"How much does he owe?" She looked down at Ferion. "How much debt are you in?"

Pushing out of her arms, he sat, moving quite unlike himself, as if he were an aged, frail human. While he was breathing easily again, his face remained gray, his eyes despairing.

He said, "Too much."

"I believe you still misunderstand," Malphas said. "You can't pay his debt for him. Only Ferion can keep his side of the bargain—and he's done so the only way he can, with the one thing he owns that is of any worth to me. I've placed a lien on his soul."

# ⇒ NINE ⇒

What do you mean, you've placed 'a lien on his soul'?" Graydon repeated.

Blood pounded through his veins as his body demanded a fight. He held onto his self-control by a thread.

He couldn't hope to win in a fight against Malphas, not alone. At best, he could hold his own. He could even probably drive the Djinn away, but Bel and Ferion were much more vulnerable. If it came to outright battle, they might become casualties, and that possibility was unacceptable.

So he did the only thing he could. He held himself in check. By the glitter in Malphas's diamond eyes, he could tell that the Djinn knew he held the upper hand.

Malphas smiled. "The Djinn make connections to those people with whom they strike bargains."

Bel rose to her feet, her posture tense and defensive, and her beautiful features drawn. All her tentative happiness from earlier had vanished. "You're not talking about social connections. You mean something more literal."

"Yes, I mean real, psychic connections. Normally what a Djinn creates is nothing more than a sensitivity, or an awareness, so that the Djinn can hear if that person summons them. Or they might need to check to make sure a bargain is being fulfilled." Malphas watched as Ferion thrust to his feet. His expression was almost sensual with satisfaction. "I've learned how to manipulate connections into something stronger and deeper."

Bel gripped Graydon's arm. She said telepathically, *There's something buried deep in Ferion. It's smudged and dark like a shadow. I saw it a few moments ago when I scanned him to try to see why he had stopped breathing.*

*Do you think you can remove it?* he asked.

She shook her head. *It's completely foreign to me. I'm not even sure what it is, or how much damage it might do to him if I tried anything.*

Ferion said, "He can force me to do things. I can't control myself."

"Precisely." Malphas crossed over the room to sit in the armchair again. "In order to pay his debt, Ferion has sold himself to me."

Bel rounded on the Djinn with such a feral expression on her face, she could have been a match for any Wyr. *"Remove it."*

"Not on your life." Malphas's voice had turned soft and deadly. "For a very long time now, I've wanted to have a lien on the soul of a highly placed individual in a powerful demesne. Having one on the heir of the High Elven Lord is a dream come true."

"None of the demesnes will tolerate this kind of assault," Graydon snarled. "When word gets out, it won't matter if you're abiding by Djinn law. *Dragos* won't tolerate it."

"Now we come to the heart of the matter." Malphas laced his fingers together and crossed his legs. "Here are the cards that I hold—I own one beloved son and Elven heir, and a certain knowledge of an affair between two people that would never be sanctioned if it became public."

Here it comes, Graydon thought. He met Bel's gaze again. He could see in her darkening expression the knowledge of a gulf widening between them.

The Djinn continued, "Here are the cards that you

hold—you know what can happen if somebody gambles with me and gets in over his head, and what I can do to them in retaliation. Also, let's face it, if you drum up enough outrage over Ferion, you could very well gather a hunting party of sufficient strength to kill me. Does this accurately sum up the situation?"

"You can remove any uncertainty in that," Graydon bit out. "We *will* hunt you down and destroy you."

The Djinn heaved a sigh. "Oh, very well, I'll grant you that. But could you locate and destroy me before I kill Ferion?"

Bel's face went chalk white. She whispered, "No."

"That's correct." Malphas's reply was filled with false gentleness. "No, you couldn't. So then the real question becomes, how much is Ferion's life worth to you? What will you pay in order to keep him safe? Because I will tell you right now, owning the lien on one eternal Elven soul—and the heir to the South Carolina demesne at that—means a very great deal to me."

"He can't hold me hostage if I'm not alive," Ferion whispered. He stared at Bel, clenched and unpredictable, his gaze burning in the dark sockets of his white face.

A quiet sound came out of Bel, as if her own soul were being wrenched out of her.

"You will not commit suicide," Malphas told him. "Neither by direct action, nor passively by searching for a way to be killed in battle."

Graydon turned his entire focus on the Djinn. He growled, "What do you want?"

The Djinn had been leading them to this very place, because as soon as he heard Graydon's question, he nodded.

"I propose a bargain," he said. "A life for a life. I will not force Ferion to do anything against his will, and much as I am tempted to, I will say nothing about your touching scene in the woods. In return, you will leave me and my business interests alone. You'll say nothing to anyone about what has occurred, nor will you do anything about what you've learned here." Malice crept back into his handsome features. "And you and Beluviel will never tryst again."

Renewed rage and denial exploded in Graydon's body. He started forward. This time it was Bel who grabbed at his arm.

He growled, "Like hell we won't."

Malphas lifted one shoulder. "I understand we live in a small world. You'll see each other at masques and meetings. You might converse at soirees, or share a dance, and if you really must, you can always gaze soulfully into each other's eyes. But you will never *be* together again. Not as lovers. Not as a partnership. Those are my terms."

Ferion snapped, "This is between you and me. As you so eloquently pointed out, I'm the one who created this mess—and I'm responsible for the debt. Leave them out of this!"

"Oh, no," Malphas replied. Without appearing to move he was suddenly standing on his feet. While he faced the three of them, his unblinking, shining diamond eyes remained fixed on Graydon. "You took it upon yourself to meddle in my affairs. Now Malfeasance has been shut down. The building has been razed to the ground."

"When did this happen?" Graydon fisted his hands.

"An hour before dawn."

The need to rend the other male into pieces caused his fingers to lengthen into talons. "While Beluviel and I were looking for Ferion."

"You might not have destroyed the building yourself, but you were involved." The Djinn hissed, "I know it!"

Suddenly Bel screamed, *"You monster, there were children in that hellhole!"*

Malphas's face began to look like the mask it was. Power blazed through the handsome features, and he forgot to move his mouth when he spoke. "What the flesh peddlers did with that part of the business was of no concern of mine. I care nothing for matters of the flesh. All that matters is the game."

At that, Graydon realized Malphas was as much of an addict as Ferion. He turned the realization over in his mind, as if assessing a new weapon.

Somehow, he might find a way to make use of the real-

ization, except at the moment he was having trouble concentrating.

Just the thought of never being able to touch Beluviel
again, kiss her lips, stroke her hair was making him more
than a little mad. Easing his arm out of her hold, he stalked
toward the Djinn.

"You're a pariah," he snarled. "You don't keep your word."

He had no idea what showed on his expression. Whatever
it was, Malphas retreated in the face of it. "I know how to
keep a pact when my life is at stake."

Suddenly Bel stood beside Graydon. She said between
her teeth, "I don't believe you. You won't really give up your
leverage on Ferion."

Malphas's physical form dissipated. His disembodied voice
resonated in the room. "Do you really have a choice? Think
about it. Besides, Ferion is only Calondir's heir. Likely, he will
never become the Elven High Lord himself. He'll continue to
live a half life, with no real power or purpose. While I'm happy
to have gotten my claws into him, there's no guarantee my
time and trouble will amount to anything."

Instinct more than anything caused Graydon to whirl.
Malphas had reformed and stood behind Ferion, one hand
on the Elf's shoulder. Ferion stared at them fixedly, a muscle
leaping in his rigid jaw.

"Make your choice," Malphas said. "Throw the dice."

Graydon stared at the Djinn's hand on Ferion's shoulder.
Then he looked at Bel.

Tears streamed down her cheeks. Graydon didn't think
she was even aware of it. There was so much love and
anguish in her expression when she looked at Ferion, something inside Graydon broke.

Maybe it was the hope they had created when they talked
of meeting every month. The small house with a large, private yard had sounded so perfect to him, and it was never
going to happen.

Ferion was the child of her heart. She had spent so many
years loving, protecting and nurturing him, hoping for the
best in his future and feeling pain at his struggles.

*I will keep looking for a way to get out of this,* Graydon told her telepathically. *No matter how long it takes, no matter what I have to do. I will not stop until we're all freed.*

*Graydon, no,* Bel said. *There must be something we haven't thought of, something we can still negotiate.*

*Can you think of any angle to use?* he asked. *Because my God, I'm more than ready to hear it.*

Her face clenched. She remained silent.

Aloud, he said, "We'll take your deal, Djinn—except for one codicil."

Malphas arched one golden eyebrow. "What's that?"

Sometimes in life you had to draw a hard line and say this will not happen, no matter what the cost, not as long as I am alive to stop it.

He said between his teeth, "If you ever again even passively support child prostitution in any form, holding a lien on Ferion's life won't protect you. Nobody will be able to protect you. I won't stop hunting you until you are nothing more than a bad memory scattered on the wind."

The room throbbed as his Power boiled over. In the silence, he heard Bel's distressed breathing, but even though he had just laid her son's life on the line, she never uttered a word of protest.

Ferion said with quiet force, "I support that codicil."

Malphas made a quick, slicing gesture. "Of course. I'll make certain of it."

Bel said softly, "You do realize that if anything happens to Ferion, my first thought will be of you. If he dies, all your leverage fades away. That card you think you hold over me and Graydon, and what happened between us—it means nothing. So it would be prudent of you to make sure nothing happens to my son."

*Means nothing.*

The two words beat against Graydon's temples.

What did she mean by that? Everything she said held a ring of truth. Did their time together mean nothing? Or did she mean keeping it secret meant nothing?

Don't react, he thought. Don't show this predator any hint of blood.

Malphas lowered his head while he assessed Bel with a calculating gaze. "Understood."

"Now, get your hand off him." Bel's voice was sharp enough to slice steel.

Smiling, Malphas lifted his hand away. "From your hostility, I take it there'll be no invitation for me to join you for the holidays. No? Oh well, one does endure. In any case, I'm needed elsewhere. I have a new gaming hell to establish. Do shut the door on your way out." He leaned forward to say in Ferion's ear, "I'll check in with you frequently."

Ferion's gaze cut sideways, his expression filled with such loathing that if Malphas had been a physical creature, Graydon felt sure he would not have survived the next few moments.

The Djinn's form blew into a whirlwind that dissipated almost at once. Graydon cast out his awareness, seeking for any hint that the Djinn lingered in stealth, but Malphas was truly gone.

He felt as if he had just wallowed in manure. As he rubbed his face hard, Ferion bolted out of the house. Bel's gaze shot to his in a brief, surprised flash. She strode after her son.

Graydon didn't follow them. He could already hear the sounds of retching outside and knew Ferion hadn't gone far. No doubt, they needed a few moments in private. In any case, he knew he needed a moment.

He couldn't stand to be in the confines of the dust-filled room any longer. In fact, he would be doing the world a favor if he destroyed the room altogether.

Striding over to the armchair, with one vicious kick he booted it toward the fireplace. It shot across the room, crashing into the flames and knocking logs and embers everywhere.

Following the glowing constellation scattered across the floor, he kicked embers toward the heavy velvet curtains shrouding the front windows. Then he upended the sofa on the rest of the coals.

Malphas would still prey on foolish gamblers, but he wouldn't be taking anybody's life in this place again.

When Graydon was through, he walked into the hall to sit on the bottom stairs of the wide marble staircase, elbows on knees and head in his hands while he waited to make sure the fire spread.

It wasn't enough destruction to suit him. He wanted to rip apart the countryside, set fire to the world. What a wretched, fucked-up day.

After a few moments, quick, light footsteps approached. He didn't have to look up to know it was Bel. He would recognize her footsteps anywhere, now.

She sat down on the stairs beside him. "The curtains in the receiving room are going up in flames. You set fire to the house?"

He rubbed at his dry eyes. "Not burning the house wasn't part of the bargain."

"If this were any other day that would make me laugh." She sighed. "I suppose you've thought of the surrounding countryside."

"I surveyed the area as we flew in. There may be dust all over the furniture, but sometime in the past growing season, the grounds were well tended. The immediate area is clear of trees and shrubs. Whoever originally built the place set the stables well away from the house." He looked over his hands at her. "Where's Ferion?"

"He's gone to tend to his horse." In the strong morning light that streamed in through the open front doors, she looked almost as bad as Ferion had, her skin a chalky white, and dark shadows like bruises ringed her large, lovely eyes. "He says that he can feel the lien. It's like a shackle on him."

He told her, "I don't want you to take this the wrong way, but I could throttle him right now."

She leaned forward to rest her elbows on her knees as he did. She had taken a moment to braid her hair, rather haphazardly, and the long dark silken rope slid forward over her shoulder.

"I'm so angry, I can barely speak to him in a civil tone,"

she replied. "It's incomprehensible to me how he could create such an overwhelming trap, not only for him but for us as well. Can't he see how his actions have affected others—how they've affected me, and now you?" Her eyes filled with sudden liquid. "Does he think so little of his life?"

He needed to touch her so badly it clenched in his stomach like sickness. Malphas mentioned dancing. The Djinn had allowed for them to touch, and that might have been the cruelest part of the bargain.

Slowly, Graydon reached out. When she placed her hand in his, his fingers tightened around hers.

He said, very low, "I can understand wanting and needing something so badly you're ready to gamble your life away for a chance to have it."

Her gaze slid sideways at him, and he caught a glimpse of the anguish he had seen in her expression earlier. "This is my fault. I should never have taken your offer of help. I should never have paid his debt the second time, or the third. If I'd only—"

A different kind of pain cut through him. Taking her hand, he held it to his chest, committing the feel and the weight of it to memory, the sensation of her slender fingers curling around his, the softness of her skin. Then he released her, and stood.

"That's where you and I differ. I could never wish away making love to you." Despite himself, a note of bitterness entered his voice. "No matter what else happened, or what the cost."

"Gray," she said softly, "that wasn't what I meant."

"I know what you meant." If he looked at her, he would kiss her. He closed his eyes. "Can you sense the connections Malphas attached to us?"

She hesitated. "Not really. I felt his Power shimmer when we agreed to the bargain, but now . . . I can't feel anything. It's not anything like what I felt in Ferion."

He knew better than to entertain any foolish hope that Malphas wouldn't be able to sense if he and Bel made love. The Djinn would not have demanded terms he couldn't enforce.

He strode to the doorway of the receiving room. The fire had taken hold with a vengeance. It was small satisfaction. When the blaze grew large enough the smoke would attract people from the nearby town, but they had several minutes before that happened.

Outside, the country air was clean and sharp like a knife. He went around the back to find Ferion emerging from the stable, leading a saddled roan. As he approached the Elven male, he noted how terrible Ferion looked, his normally youthful-looking face lined as if with age.

Graydon wanted nothing more than to unleash his rage on the other man, but the thought of what he had said to Bel remained with him. Need for her ran through his veins, turning part of him into a traitor with ugly thoughts, urging him to do anything it took, just so that he could be with her again.

The predator in him had taken note: nowhere in the Djinn's bargain had it said Graydon couldn't kill Ferion and be done with Malphas once and for all.

That same predator took note of Ferion's inattention and relative fragility, the vein pounding at the side of his neck, the way his hands shook as he handled the reins.

Graydon would do almost anything to be with Bel again, except take from her what she loved the most.

Turning and crossing his arms, he faced the house. Silently, Ferion led the horse over to him and stood by his side.

After a moment, Ferion said, "I'm appalled at my own actions and offer you my most heartfelt apologies. I make no excuses for what I've done."

"That would be wise of you." Graydon used the most neutral tone he could manage. At the moment, his control was fragile at best. If the Elf had started down that path, he didn't know what he would have done. He said, "If this hasn't made you hit bottom so you realize you've got to change, I don't know what will."

"It did." Ferion's voice was so quiet, even Graydon almost didn't hear him. "It happened when Malphas confronted me. When I truly realized I had no other way to pay my debt. Nobody else could take my fate from me, and he—fixed the lien inside of me. I—I didn't realize such a low point could exist."

As he listened, unwilling sympathy took hold of him, dissipating his rage.

Ferion whispered, "Always before, this voice inside my head compelled me on and on. I convinced myself that when I won, I could pay any debt I accumulated. I could even pay back my mother everything she had spent on my behalf. Once I won that big, I could quit whenever I wished." His raw gaze cut sideways to Graydon. "I knew that voice was crazy. I just couldn't seem to stop listening to it."

Graydon rubbed the back of his neck, trying to ease the knot of tension that had taken residence between his shoulder blades. He acknowledged, "I reckon I have a version of that voice in my head too."

Only his voice had urged him to make plans to fly down to South Carolina once a month. It whispered to him that somehow the arrangement would have made it acceptable for him to mate with her, that he would survive each interminable month, as long he knew he would get to see her again.

Even as part of him had known better—that eventually something about the arrangement would have crumbled—it hadn't stopped him from trying because he would have done almost anything to be with her again, including mating in silence and giving her a kind of devotion she had not asked for, and likely wouldn't have welcomed had she known.

"Whatever happened between you and my mother," Ferion said, "I'm doubly sorry about that."

"We're not going to talk about that," Graydon said between his teeth.

Off to one side of the house, Beluviel came into view. She walked toward them.

Ferion whispered, "I saw how you looked at each other. I also know she hasn't chosen to be with anybody in a very long time, so while we might not talk of it, I wanted you to know—I'm so sorry for that too. More than anyone else I know, she deserves to be happy."

As soon as Bel had come into sight, Graydon's attention fixed on her. Hungrily, he soaked in every aspect of her appearance.

She looked composed and calm, her dark gaze focused. As he took in her settled demeanor, he recognized the distance that had been growing between them was now complete.

He told her telepathically, *You realize Ferion can no longer be trusted. Malphas might not be able to resist compelling him to do small, sneaky things. Whatever he thinks he might be able to get away with, he'll do.*

The full, generous curve of her lips tightened. She replied, *I know. I'll have to keep watch.*

*If there is anything I can do to help, don't hesitate to send for me.*

Giving him a steady look, she shook her head and told him in a gentle voice, *You are good-hearted and generous to the very end. I will not send for you, Graydon. It would hurt too much to see you.*

A violent pain flared. How sensible she sounded, how emotionally honest and yet dismissive at the same time.

In one corner of his mind he knew he wasn't being fair, but the uncivilized beast he fought to hold in check wasn't interested in fairness. It wanted to snatch at her and rage against the world.

But she was not Wyr. She couldn't know how his beast rebelled at the thought of being sensible. Of leaving her.

He made himself breathe evenly and loosen the fists he had pressed against his sides. "So, we hold our ground."

"And Malphas wins," said Ferion bitterly.

Bel gave her son a look of rebuke. "Holding one's ground is not passivity. It takes its own kind of strength. Sometimes the hardest part of a battle is holding one's ground. At most Malphas has gained a standoff. He has not won anything yet."

"Nor will he," said Graydon. "Although this may turn into a very long war. Have patience." He looked up. Dark smoke was beginning to billow out of the manor's windows and chimneys. "We should leave. I can take you both back to London."

"I can't abandon the horse," Ferion said.

That small, selfless statement helped Graydon feel a little more kindly disposed toward the other male.

"It's a hired horse, yes?" When Ferion nodded, he said, "Tie the reins to the hitching post beside the stable doors. It's far enough from the house, it'll be safe from the fire, and you can be certain that Wembley's constable will be up here momentarily, along with many other people. They'll make sure it gets returned to the stable where it belongs."

Ferion did so. Within moments, both he and Bel settled astride on the gryphon's back.

The return flight to London was mostly made in silence, each one of them wrapped up in thought. When Graydon landed in Grosvenor Square, it had just turned midmorning. The sun had begun to take the chill out of the frigid air.

Tradesmen crowded the streets, conducting business, although many who had attended masques the night before would still be abed. Graydon maintained his cloak. He sensed Bel's cloaking spell as she did the same.

She and Ferion slipped from his back. Together, they both moved to face the gryphon. He would not even get the chance to say good-bye to her in private. Pride made the gryphon hold his head high.

"Thank you for everything," Ferion said. "I will never forget what you've done for my mother and me."

"Make something good come out of this," Graydon told him. "Stay away from gaming tables."

A harsh breath escaped the other male. "The thought of gambling again makes me feel ill."

Well. At least there was that.

Bel stepped forward, looking up at him. Her expression caused his chest to ache. Telepathically, she said, *I will miss you with all my heart.*

The pain in her mental voice was so apparent, every imagined rebuff or slight he had felt over the last several hours vanished in an instant.

Slowly, the gryphon lowered his head until he rested his beak against her chest. He breathed deeply, filling his lungs with her scent one last time. She stroked his head.

*This isn't over,* he told her. *Don't ever forget it.*

Nodding, she stood back and wiped at her eyes. He felt the physical separation like a knife cut along his skin. Ferion put his arm around her shoulders. Graydon watched as they walked to their house.

Once she had disappeared from sight, he launched again and stayed aloft for hours, hurtling through the air as fast as he could in a crazed flight going nowhere.

Malphas couldn't kill Ferion without also freeing them to hunt him down, but that did not defang the Djinn, not while he held the lien on Ferion's soul. If they broke the bargain, Malphas could control or torture Ferion with impunity.

That meant Graydon couldn't hunt for Malphas, or say anything to anyone based on what he had learned that morning.

But, like setting fire to the house, there was nothing in the bargain to keep Graydon from watching and waiting for other leverage that may come his way.

And nothing whatsoever in the bargain that could keep him from using it.

# ≡ TEN ≡

## *South Carolina, December 2015*

As Graydon flew south along the coast, he left the snowfall behind in New York.

Gradually the air warmed. The cloud cover cleared enough to reveal the glow of the moon. He watched the shadowy ocean and the glowing lattice of the coastal cities while he considered the challenges that lay ahead.

The biggest challenge was figuring out how to speak with Beluviel in private. If Linwe refused to tell Bel he was coming, and if, as Linwe had said, she was secluding herself, trying to talk to her would not only be difficult, it could very well be dangerous.

The Elves had been through one hell of a year. Earlier in January, their numbers had been decimated. Their Lord Calondir had been killed, and for a brief time, Beluviel herself had been controlled by a Powerful madman, Amras Gaeleval.

Graydon's muscles clenched as he remembered carrying her from the battlefield. She had been bloody and suffering from exposure to the cold. An atavistic, primitive part of him had wanted to lash out at the world, to keep her from any harm.

But she wasn't his to protect. Giving her over to the care of the healers and walking away had been one of the hardest things he had ever done.

Aside from the loss of so many Elves, for Bel, one of the most devastating losses had to have been the death of her Wood, which had been destroyed when a fire swept through it.

And the most dangerous consequence of all—Ferion had inherited the power and title from his deceased father.

Now Malphas held the lien on the soul of the Lord of the Elven demesne. Any hope Graydon had entertained of finding some way to renegotiate the terms of their bargain had died along with Calondir. Malphas would never give up the possibility of control over a demesne ruler.

In fact, in Graydon's jaded opinion, it would be downright miraculous if Malphas hadn't already forced Ferion to commit stealthy, nefarious acts that furthered the Djinn's own interests without giving him away.

If they could only catch him reneging on the bargain, they would have enough to take to the Djinn, who could forcibly sever Malphas's connections on Graydon and Beluviel, and might even be able to lift the lien on Ferion. But it would be foolish to hope Malphas would make a mistake that catastrophic.

It didn't matter how sharp an eye Bel tried to keep on Ferion's actions. Nobody could watch someone else all day, every day for years on end. With the power shift that had occurred earlier this year, Ferion could set any number of obstacles in her path to keep her from getting too close to him.

One grim consolation lay buried in the midst of tragedy. The Elven demesne had faced so many challenges in recovering that Ferion—and through him, Malphas—hadn't had time to do more than pick up the pieces.

Also, throughout the summer months, the Elder tribunal had maintained a constant physical presence in the demesne, erecting Quonset huts as temporary medical and psychiatric hospitals to aid the recovering wounded.

Large quantities of other kinds of aid had poured in from all over the world in the form of food, clothing, temporary propane-powered generators, and tents to house the Elves who had recovered enough to leave the hospital. Even a cell tower had been built a few miles away to facilitate in coordinating the relief efforts.

The tribunal had only removed its presence when autumn came, and the surviving Numenlaur Elves had been ready to travel home again. Still, as a community, the Elves who remained in South Carolina would be raw and jumpy.

Linwe had exaggerated on the phone, but only a little. Like all the other demesnes in the United States, the Elven demesne covered a large area, including Charleston, and Graydon could enter it quite easily.

What he couldn't do as easily is approach the main Elven home, the nucleus of their society, without permission.

While he considered recent events, the gryphon stole over the South Carolina Elven border in the early hours of the morning.

Because he had been part of the events in January, he was familiar with the geography. He knew exactly the moment when he flew over the Wood.

He had been expecting to find the area still mostly deadened by fire damage. Instead, to his surprise, he saw that much of the debris had been cleared away. In its place, he sensed a new wild Woodland presence.

The new growth covered a massive area. It wasn't nearly as large as the previous Wood had been, and he didn't think it was sentient.

At least, not yet. It was too young for that.

But it was burgeoning with rich, abundant life, and it was indisputable evidence of a strong, positive, restorative force.

The Lady of the Wood had in no way been idle or incapacitated over the last six months.

The gryphon did not know how to cry, but the man who lived inside the Wyr beast felt inexpressibly moved and fiercely relieved.

Passing over the heart of the Elven home at high altitude, he saw firelight dotting the area. Even though it was the early hours of the morning, a few people were awake.

The old, sentient Wood no longer acted as guardian over the Elven home. They would feel that vulnerability keenly and keep watch through the night. At least, he knew he would if he were in their shoes.

He arrowed away until he reached a bluff beside the shoreline. There, he landed, changed into his human form once again and walked along the edge of the Wood. Locating a likely spot on the beach, he descended to lean his back against a boulder, and stare over the dark ocean at foam-capped waves.

Where was she sleeping? Had she taken other lovers?

Something deep in his chest twisted at the thought, although he couldn't blame her if she had. Two hundred years was a long time, even for those as long lived as the Elder Races.

He had burned for her, but that didn't mean she had burned for him.

He had lain awake countless nights, reliving over and over every detail of their too-brief lovemaking. The scent of her hair. The taste of her soft nipple against his tongue. The look in her eyes and arch of her body as she orgasmed.

But that didn't mean she had.

He had longed to talk to her, many times over the years, just simply talk, as one would to a treasured friend.

And yet, that didn't mean she had.

At times, he thought falling in love must be the loneliest experience in the world.

Truthfully, he no longer knew if he was in love with her, or if he was merely ensnared by the luminous memory of that long ago experience. Part of him felt frozen in time, trapped by a cruel enchanter.

Yet, if he had truly mated with her, he would have died long ago. They hadn't had time for his instinct to mate to solidify irrevocably in his bones.

He needed to find out what he still felt for her, but more than that, he was grimly set to endure whatever might come. Life was complicated and messy. Often it didn't offer resolutions or answers to questions.

Restlessly, he shifted, digging the heel of one boot in the

sand. He would wait until dawn, and then he would call Linwe again.

He couldn't fault the young Elf for her dogged protectiveness of her mistress, but Linwe was not yet forty—she was very young for an Elf, and hotheaded, and at the moment, he couldn't help but wish that Alanna and Lianne were still Bel's attendants.

While they only knew a small fraction of what had occurred in 1815, it would have been enough for them to find ways to connect him to Bel, not erect barriers. But last he heard, Alanna had been killed in March, and Lianne had moved to a position of command in the Elven warriors.

He pinched the bridge of his nose and sighed. Having time to brood was never a good thing. The most effective coping mechanism he had found over the last two centuries was to keep so busy he didn't have time to dwell on matters he couldn't change.

Right now, the most important objective was to kill Malphas and release Ferion from the shackle of the Djinn's control once and for all—for Ferion's sake, for Beluviel's, and for the sake of the Elven demesne itself.

Otherwise, the Djinn's poison would seep slowly through the Elven demesne until his corrupt influence spread out to darken the rest of the world.

B el woke from a sound sleep.
    She stared at the dark ceiling of her bedroom while listening to the quiet sounds of the Elven demesne at night. Her rooms were located in one of the most attractive areas of the main Elven abode, overlooking the river.

Just outside her living area, a spacious balcony hung over the river itself, where she often sat to gaze at the water, or watch the trees as they changed through the seasons. Sitting on the balcony and immersing herself in the scene was the only thing that gave her peace anymore.

The soft, soothing sounds of the outside waterfall played constantly along the edge of her awareness.

That wasn't what had awakened her.

Her sensitive hearing picked up other sounds, as the few people who were awake moved and talked quietly in the area.

She couldn't hear what they said. Their murmuring voices were too faint and ran along the background of her consciousness, rather like the sound of the river.

Everything sounded just as it should, completely normal.

Shoving back the bedcovers, she pulled on her robe and went out on the balcony. The cool night air brushed the last cobwebs of sleep from her mind.

Something had awakened her. She cast her awareness out, searching for a hint of the malevolent presence that had preyed on her son so long ago. She never stopped watching or listening for Malphas.

She couldn't find any evidence of the Djinn, but someone or something had walked in her young, vulnerable Wood. Someone who was not Elven, or human. She was quite familiar with the noisy psychic footprint of humans.

The tiny, rudimentary spirit of her new Wood was convinced that nothing was untoward. The only creatures that had passed through it were wild ones, both small and very large . . .

Hmm. A very large, wild creature might bear some investigating.

The Wood didn't speak to her in a language that anyone else would recognize. None of the Woods that she had nurtured to maturity had.

Rather, it shared impressions with her and on occasion images, and a boundless sense of vitality. Over time it would deepen in spirit and awareness.

It gave shelter and sustenance to the creatures that lived in it, and watched the play of nature within its borders— mating, birth, the scavenging for food, the hunt of prey, eventual death.

Eventually, it would grow to recognize the natural rhythm of life in the wild, and become sensitive to occurrences that did not fit the pattern. It would welcome friends, acquire the ability to shield its borders from most intruders, and actively work to expel what it recognized as enemies.

Most of that lay in the future. For now, this Wood was young and inexperienced, and at times, she had to admit, somewhat silly. There was no telling what it considered a very large wild creature, except it would never have reacted in such a way to a herd of wild deer.

No, this, whatever it was, was something unusual. Something strange and . . . not alarming, not quite that.

Something exciting?

Any number of Wyr could be very large. If they were in their Wyr form, the Wood might consider them wild.

Dragos was indeed very large.

So was Graydon.

It was impossible to quell the irrational hope that surged as soon as the thought occurred to her. She could not imagine Graydon would come. Ever since Wembley, they had seen each other only in public. Even after the battle with Gaeleval, he had carried her away from the scene, straight to a team of healers and then he had disappeared.

Gazing at him at political functions, watching his shuttered expression from a distance, nodding and smiling as though there were nothing at all between them, no history of intimacy, no empty ache deep inside of her . . .

Malphas had seen how to get revenge on them with a particular kind of cruelty.

With a discipline born of long practice, she set the thought aside.

Since she was considering the possibility of the Wyr, she could think of no reason for Dragos to have come south either. While he had invaded the Elven demesne before, he must be busy in New York with the business meetings and preparations that surrounded the masque.

Shaking her head at her own foolishness, she stepped back indoors to dress in trousers, boots, a loose, comfortable shirt and a quilted jacket. Hesitating over the thought of carrying weapons, the thought of the Wood's youth and inexperience caused her to slip into her sword harness, just in case.

She considered waking Linwe, or taking one of the night guards with her, but after studying the Wood's alert, calm interest, she decided not to. She could always raise an alarm later, if necessary. For now, she trusted her ability in cloaking her presence.

Her rooms were located at one end of the building. A private stairway led from the balcony to the river's edge below. The guards on duty were much younger than she. None of them noticed as she strolled from the clearing.

*What do you have to show me?* she asked the Wood, only not quite in so many words. Her question was more of a nudge and a sense of inquiry.

The Wood tugged her along narrow paths, toward the coast. Other races might have had difficulty following the nearly invisible paths, but they were her design. She knew them like she knew the back of her hand.

As she hiked, a sense of peace and freedom came over her, two things she no longer felt when she resided at the Elven home.

Soon, she realized the Wood was taking her further than she had expected. Her old Wood had covered miles. This new one would be no smaller by the time it finished growing.

She began to run. Her Elven nature gave her tremendous stamina. If necessary, she could run for days, although if the Wood continued to urge her in the current direction, she would run out of land.

She ran out of land.

When she neared the shoreline, a sense of freshness brushed against her cheek, damp with the breeze that blew off the ocean. Breathing deep, she scented the water, refreshing and brisk, and carrying a hint of brine.

The path curved, taking her out of a sparse line of new saplings that would soon, with her encouragement, take on the aspect of a large, old-growth forest.

The path followed the top of a long bluff. Favored by the

Elven guards, it provided a good vantage place to look out over the shoreline and water.

At the highest point on the bluff, she paused to scrutinize the view. Moonlight cascaded over the scene, gilding the water and the edge of shadowed clouds with ivory and silver.

Below, at the edge of the beach, a half-hidden figure of a very large man reclined against a large boulder.

Her heart began to pound. Her stupid, stupid heart.

She couldn't be right. The man was too far away. The lighting was too uncertain for her to recognize his identity at such a distance.

Still, she wanted it so badly to be true. Keeping her cloaking spell tight around her body, she made her way down the side of the bluff to the beach below.

Walking toward the relaxed figure, she stared without blinking, until details became clear.

The man wore jeans and a jean jacket. A battered pack rested beside him. His arms were crossed, as were his legs at the ankles. The cascade of moonlight glinted off wavy, tawny hair. He had let it grow some years ago.

With his chin tucked to his chest, his face remained in shadow, but every line of his rough, sun-kissed features was stamped indelibly in her memory.

*"Graydon,"* she whispered, disbelieving and, for one moment, deliriously, unutterably happy.

When he whipped to his feet with catlike speed, she let go of her cloaking spell.

He walked toward her, stepping out of the boulder's shadow. The ivory moonlight touched his cheekbones, his jaw, the masculine curve of his lips.

As he grew near, the Power of his presence enveloped her. She felt nourished again by a warm, friendly blaze. Just as she had in the Vauxhall Gardens, all those years ago, the same crazed desire to fling herself into his arms and nestle against his chest washed over her.

At the same moment, she felt the impulse to back away. What could Malphas sense down that mysterious, ephemeral connection he had established with them?

All this time, while she couldn't fully trust Ferion, she also knew she couldn't fully trust herself.

"Hi, Bel." Graydon stopped a few feet away and made no attempt to touch her. Silence fell between them and stretched into something intolerable. Finally, he asked, "How are you?"

She lifted one hand and let it drop, at a loss as to what to say.

I miss you.

I want you.

I think about you every day, and when I roll over half asleep in bed, my hand reaches for yours, but you're not there. You're never there.

You never were.

Every word of Malphas's bargain was emblazoned in her memory. As she ran over the words in her mind, she remembered. She could touch him. The terms of the bargain allowed for it. What a hateful thing.

She didn't even know if Graydon would welcome her touch. She was painfully aware that he had not reached out to touch her.

She asked, "What are you doing here? What's wrong?"

Even in the uncertain light of the moon, the intensity of his gaze seared her. "What if I wanted to see you?"

Where had pleasantries gone? Those social niceties one said when encountering an acquaintance one hadn't seen in a long time. Without the trappings of a political function or public gathering to stop them, they had plunged immediately into a raw, intimate place.

Her breathing turned ragged. "You wouldn't come here just to see me. Not after all this time."

"I wouldn't?" His hands tightened into fists. "One of the hardest things I ever did was leave you with the healers, back in January. I couldn't stay by your side—none of them would have let me, so I had to completely leave the demesne. The only thing I could stand to do was go back to the Other land and help from that end. Since then, I've scoured every online news source for how you were doing, and how hard you've worked to help the recovery effort."

She had done everything she could think to do for the demesne. From the moment she had left her sickbed, she had worked every day for the last six months until she dropped from exhaustion.

Now, when people came to her for help or advice, she gave it to them by rote, because part of her couldn't help but answer, even as she wondered if she really had anything left to give.

Wrapping her arms around her middle, she confessed, "I read everything I can about New York and the Wyr demesne, just so that I can see your name."

His voice lowered. "From time to time, I've slipped down to Charleston. I look at the houses for sale. The ones with a big, private yard."

His words were quiet, even gentle. They devastated her completely. Before she quite realized what she was doing, she flung herself at him in an uncontrolled lunge, blindly trusting him to catch her.

As she collided against his body, his arms slammed around her. He gripped her so tightly, she knew his hold would leave bruises, and she welcomed it. She didn't care.

He was breathing as heavily as she, as if he had been running for a very long time. Burying his face in her hair, he muttered, "I would walk from room to room in those empty houses and wonder if you still thought of me."

*"Oh gods."* The words felt wrenched out of her. She couldn't hold him any tighter than she already did, but she still wasn't close enough. She wanted to climb up his body, open his skin, crawl inside and never leave. "I've wondered if you thought of me too. I've wondered if you moved on, or if you've been with someone else. I didn't have the right to ask. I still don't."

"I haven't been with anyone else," he murmured, cradling her. "Have you?"

Her arms tightened around his neck. "No," she whispered. "I haven't found anybody who can replace the memory of being with you. What am I saying? That makes it sound like I've been looking, and I haven't. I . . . I'm unbalanced and obsessive. I wouldn't recommend living this way to anyone, and yet, I still can't give up the thought of you."

*"Good,"* he said between his teeth. He gripped her head in both hands, holding her with such tense care, she could feel the tension vibrating through his big body.

Tilting her face up to his, he held his mouth just over hers. Not quite touching or kissing, but so close she could feel the heat from his lips. She shook with the desire to cross that tiny distance and kiss him.

How could this have happened between them so long ago? It felt as if it had been yesterday. Her voice wobbled. "This is why I've never tried to see you alone. One look at you, one touch, five minutes, and it all spills out."

He growled, "Don't be balanced, Bel. Don't turn away or find someone else. Wait for me. Wait to see what we can have together. You said it once, don't you remember? Holding your ground is not passivity. Work for this. Stay the course."

She touched his mouth with shaking fingers. "What course is there? We've been living in a trap for two hundred years. Now Ferion is Lord of the demesne, and I—I don't know him anymore."

"What do you mean?" He massaged her temples with both callused thumbs.

"Once I knew he was a good man who made a few bad mistakes. Now, mostly he says and does the right thing, but sometimes I find him watching me. I don't know who's looking out of his eyes, or what he's thinking, or how much Malphas might have twisted him."

When emotion clogged her throat, she had to stop. Memories from very long ago played through her mind. As a towheaded, Elven boy, Ferion had been intelligent, loving and mischievous. How she missed that boy, with a deep, specific pain that only a parent who has become estranged from her child could truly understand.

Graydon stroked wisps of hair off her face. "Does he gamble anymore?"

His words pulled her back to the present. She paused, thinking. "No, not to my knowledge. Not since England."

"Then don't lose hope, not yet."

She drew back so she could search his shadowed expression. "Gray, why *did* you come? Has something happened?"

Gently, he laid a large, broad hand over her mouth, stopping her flow of words. *We should talk telepathically,* he told her. *We haven't done anything to trigger the connection, and I don't sense Malphas anywhere, but he has slipped up on us before, remember?*

*I could never forget.* She gripped his thick, strong wrist, staring up into his dark, shadowed gaze. *You* do *know something!*

A slow smile widened his mouth and crinkled the corners of his eyes.

*A few months ago, information came into my possession,* he told her. *I didn't go looking for it, and it also has nothing to do with what happened to us and Ferion two hundred years ago, so it doesn't violate the terms of our bargain. I sent investigators into the field to verify the details and gather more evidence.*

The thought of the risk he had taken made her stomach clench. Her fingers tightened on his wrist.

Before she could say anything, he added quickly, *They're very good investigators and experienced professionals, thorough and careful to hide their tracks. I took great care.*

Her breath shuddered. *Of course you did.*

*I also went outside both our demesnes. They're not even Wyr. Well, one of them isn't. The other who is Wyr has no ties to the Wyr demesne—in fact, he used to be an Elder tribunal Peacekeeper. He's young, but he's respected for the impartiality and quality of his work.*

*What did they find?* she asked.

*Exactly what you would expect.* His gaze turned fierce and eagle-sharp. *What happened to Ferion was no isolated incident. Malphas has enslaved others, Bel. Humans, Dark and Light Fae, Vampyres. His reach crosses over multiple demesnes.*

Disappointment began to darken her hopes. *None of that goes against Djinn law, just as Ferion's debt didn't.*

*I have several things to say to that.* Just as he had so long ago, he pressed his lips to her forehead. Closing her eyes, she leaned into his kiss. *Since Malphas has enslaved them, their behavior has changed.*

She sucked in a breath. That sounded like her worst nightmare about Ferion. *What do you mean?*

*Bank statements show them funneling money to accounts that can be traced back to his casino. In itself, that isn't alarming, since supposedly they owed him money anyway, but some have switched political parties. A couple are committing fraud, even though the investigators could find no history of criminal behavior in their past. A few months back, there was a senator's son who died in a boating accident—do you remember?*

Her eyebrows drew together. *You mean a human senator in the federal government?*

*Yes.*

She searched her memory but came up blank. *No, I'm sorry. I don't remember. Usually, I take note of that sort of thing, and I send a message of condolence.*

He stroked the back of her neck gently. *You've been preoccupied with your own problems here.*

That was true enough. *What happened?*

*Before he was killed in the boating accident, the senator's son spent a great deal of time at Malphas's casino in Las Vegas. Senator Jackson, his father, arrived, paid off a debt totaling close to two million dollars and took his son home.*

He couldn't seem to stop touching her, and his small caresses were drugging her with pleasure. She rubbed her face, forcing herself to concentrate as she digested his words. *Unlike us, he was able to get to his son in time.*

*Also, unlike us, the debt was in the official casino records. The Senator could pay it off, and Malphas couldn't claim that only his son could clear the debt.* Graydon paused. She realized he was standing on the balls of his feet, his big body poised for action. *Shortly after, the son died in a freak squall.*

Her mind raced over possible consequences. *Is there proof that Malphas murdered him?*

*No. But we don't need conclusive proof of a murder.* He framed her face with his hands. His gaze had turned fierce. *We have enough proof of everything else, along with what happened to the other victims he enslaved, that we can now establish a clear, documented pattern of behavior without ever mentioning what happened to Ferion.*

She repeated, *Documented behavior.*

The reality of what he was saying began to sink in. Over the last several months, while she had been fighting to recover along with rest of her people, Graydon had been patiently, carefully collecting proof to use against Malphas.

Along with everything else, she remembered what he had said, as if it had happened yesterday.

I will keep looking for a way to get out of this. No matter how long it takes, no matter what I have to do. I will not stop until we're all freed.

He had kept to his word. Looked at houses in Charleston. All this time, when she had been fighting despair and discouragement, he had been quietly fighting.

Her heart filled with a powerful, unnamed emotion. Wetness spilled from the corners of her eyes.

He said, *This is no longer about whether Malphas broke Djinn law. This is about crimes against other Elder Races. Crimes against humanity.*

*You're saying it's a matter of tribunal law,* she breathed.

He nodded. *After all the victims from Devil's Gate, and the human casualties in the Nightkind demesne, along with other problematic events, like the bombing of the Oracle's home in Louisville, the human government is acting very spooked right now. Senator Jackson is heading a federal subcommittee to look into what they claim are abuses committed by the Elder Races. His appointment can't be an accident. Relations between humans and Elder Races have never been so strained before. The tribunal will not be able to set this aside.*

She moistened dry lips. *You mean we can get enough support to kill Malphas.*

*I really believe we can.* He watched her expression closely.

Her hands were shaking. She pressed them together. *But if we attack him, we're putting Ferion's life on the line.*

*I didn't say it would be easy or without risk, and we couldn't attempt anything without some serious planning. The one thing I know for sure is we can't let Ferion rule the Elven demesne while Malphas controls him. We have to free him, and free ourselves.*

Slowly he bent and angled his head. She froze, waiting to see what he would do next.

He put his lips on her cheek. They were warm against her chilled skin. The sensation caused her trembling to increase.

In the barest thread of sound, hardly more than his lips moving against her skin, he whispered, "Come to New York. We can figure out what we need to do then."

# ⊰ ELEVEN ⊱

Instead of lifting his head afterward, he kept his lips pressed against her cheek, resting against her, breathing her in.

The sensation ran along her nerves, causing the private place between her legs to throb.

Heated images ran through her mind.

The way his gentle fingers had probed at her sensitive flesh, discovering exactly the right way to give her the most pleasure, the urgent need with which he had suckled at her breasts.

The way his powerful body had moved to cover hers as together they positioned his cock at her entrance, and he had pressed inside her. Even though it had been years, it felt as powerful as if it had happened yesterday.

It grew harder to stand on her own. She needed to pull away from him, to let the cold fresh breeze clear her mind, but she was so hungry for his touch, she found herself leaning into him instead. She gripped the edges of his jean jacket for support, while she tried to think.

She whispered, "I told everyone I wouldn't go to the masque this year."

"Say you changed your mind," he murmured. He touched the delicate skin at her throat, stroking his fingers along her skin. "Say you need a break. That's valid, Bel, especially since you've worked just as hard, if not harder, than anybody else to get your demesne back on its feet. And think about it—there's no better time for you to come to New York without rousing suspicion. The masque is next week. Is Ferion attending?"

She shook her head. "No, he said he would stay home as well."

"If you came right away, that would give us several days to figure out a plan of action. We can talk everything over, free from his scrutiny."

Indecision gripped her. She held herself tense, trying to see her way clear to the best decision.

She felt as if she were surrounded by a wall of thorn bushes, and everywhere she turned, wicked, needlelike thorns were ready to tear into her flesh. Her mind spun in circles, looking for a way out of the trap.

If she did nothing, Ferion might very well remain under Malphas's control, which would be disastrous for both him and the Elven demesne.

Things couldn't continue the way they were, but moving forward felt full of danger and uncertainty. Graydon was talking about going to war against one of the most dangerous creatures on earth, a first-generation Djinn.

Yet if she went to New York, Graydon would be there.

Opening her eyes, she looked up at him. The expression in his shadowed gaze made all her uncertainty vanish.

She said, "I'll come."

His body tightened. "When?"

She lifted her shoulders in an uncertain shrug. "As soon as I possibly can. The flight itself is a short one. Perhaps by tomorrow night? It will look too strange if I try to come by myself, so I'll have to bring at least one guard. I can say that since I'm the only one going, with probably Linwe, there won't be any need to send staff to open up the Elven residence in the city."

That strategy would also prevent Ferion from keeping watch on her through house attendants. She hated that she had thought of that, or that it was a realistic danger.

Her plan solidified in her mind. She told him, "I'll stay at a hotel, if I can get a room or a suite at this late date."

"I'll make sure you get a suite," he promised. "New York gets so crowded around the time of the masque, we always keep a few suites in reserve at some of the best hotels, to cover unexpected contingencies. I can send you an email with the reservation."

That made things significantly easier. "And I'll contact you once I arrive."

He took a deep breath. "Okay. I'll expect to hear from you by tomorrow night." He put his hands on her shoulders. "I don't want to say good-bye," he muttered. "As stupid as it sounds, I feel superstitious about letting you out of my sight right now."

"I know what you mean. I feel the same way." She threw her arms around his neck.

He hugged her tight. *Bel,* he said telepathically. *I want you to know, I would be doing this for Ferion's sake, regardless of anything else.*

For some reason, that brought tears to her eyes. He really was such a good man. Stroking his hair, she told him, *I believe you.*

*A lot has changed over the last two hundred years. When we find our way free of this, all I want is the chance for you and me to figure out what we might mean to each other.* His arms tightened. *Okay?*

*I would really love that, Graydon,* she told him wistfully.

With obvious reluctance, he released her. *Until tomorrow night.*

She rested her hand on his chest and promised, *See you soon.*

Watching her, he backed up a few steps. Then he turned, shapeshifted into the gryphon and leaped into the air. He was only visible for a few moments, then his form rippled and faded from sight as his cloaking spell took hold.

Gods. To see the gryphon again, after all these years. He was glorious. Watching him soar like that, with such power and grace . . . She felt unbelievably heavy, like a lump of clay forever trapped on earth, and she longed to ride in the air with him again.

Holding her breath, she stared up at the night sky for long moments after he had disappeared.

Finally accepting that he was truly gone, she turned and climbed the bluff. As she walked along the path on the journey home, she braced herself for the next steps.

She had to sell this story like it was really true, and that wouldn't be easy. Ferion's truthsense was enhanced by the fact that he had known her for a very long time.

Graydon kept his speed strong all the way back to New York. He had a lot to do in a short amount of time. As he traveled north, he entered the winter storm system again.

Snow swirled around him for the last half hour of his flight. By the time he landed, he had flown well over a thousand miles, and a good portion of that had been in inclement weather. He was tired and more than ready for a bucket of hot coffee and a hot, filling meal.

If he showed up at the Tower, he could help himself to the copious amounts of food in the cafeteria, but he would never get a moment's peace. People would approach him with their problems, and he would spend all his time explaining that he was on personal leave.

Instead of going to the Tower, he stopped at Ruby's Diner, a local restaurant that had been a favorite of his for the last thirty years. He ordered two steaks, half a dozen eggs, and a double helping of biscuits and gravy, along with coffee. The food was hearty, and the coffee was so strong it could put a dead man back on his feet again.

Outside the diner's plate-glass windows, large, fluffy flakes of snow swirled. Several of the customers were either Christmas shoppers or masquegoers. The snowstorm seemed to foster a sense of camaraderie. Laughter and cheerful conversation filled the diner.

He was such a long-standing customer, and they knew him so well, they always kept the barstool at one end of the counter available for him.

Other than giving him a permanent seat, they didn't make any fuss or call him by his title. He enjoyed the sense of anonymity and the chance to eat his meal in peace while he watched the ebb and flow of the other diners.

*I'm unbalanced and obsessive. I wouldn't recommend living this way to anyone, and yet, I still can't give up the thought of you.*

She had said that to him only a few short hours ago, but in the bright, bustling light of a New York morning, the words already began to feel distant and unreal.

He had lied to her, and she hadn't even noticed.

He had said, all I want is the chance for you and me to figure out what we might mean to each other.

Because that was what a normal, healthy person might say. He had been faking it in the hopes that the rest of him would fall in line, and it hadn't worked.

He wasn't normal or healthy. He was every bit as unbalanced and obsessive as she claimed to be. They really were trapped in much the same place as they had been two hundred years ago.

Only, if they managed to break free of Malphas, he thought likely that she would move on to a new, different life, while he would still be in the same place, wanting her yet unable to have her. He didn't know how to protect himself while still fighting for a chance to be with her.

In the cold light of morning it didn't seem very realistic to hold out hope.

He was still Wyr. She was still Elven.

He had made promises to Dragos, to the other sentinels— Pia and Liam—and he intended to keep them. Bel had already proven over the centuries how devoted she was to the Elven demesne.

While the world had changed and Calondir was dead, Bel's feelings for Dragos ran deep and bitter, and with good reason. Dragos's help in January might have mitigated some of that bitterness, but it couldn't have erased all of it.

As he considered the obstacles that lay between them, he looked around the diner.

The most generous way to describe the restaurant would be to call it retro. Still sporting much of the original décor from the 1970s, it was worn, outdated and definitely working class.

Faded green linoleum covered the floor, while the booths and barstools were covered in orange vinyl. The cracked seat on his own barstool had been patched with a strip of duct tape.

The tables were covered with a layer of faux wood, which was nearly as worn as the floor. The food was hearty, not designer cuisine, but it was well cooked and savory. He felt comfortable in this place, at home. It wasn't fancy, but neither was he.

He tried to imagine Bel enjoying the diner.

It wasn't that she was stuck-up. She was the exact opposite. She was attentive to others, and genuine, and her graciousness caused people from all walks of life to gravitate toward her.

She also wore clothes that were handsewn—jackets covered with a fortune in delicate embroidery and seed pearls, along with handcrafted boots, and silk shirts. Everything about her screamed money and class.

He looked down at himself. His jean jacket, jeans and boots had certainly seen better days, and his plain gray T-shirt had come from a plastic multipack of shirts he had bought at a superstore.

As he rubbed his tired face, he encountered stubble on his chin. The catlike part of his nature was obsessed with cleanliness, but he wasn't sure when he had last shaved.

Wednesday? Maybe Tuesday?

Resting his elbows on the bar, he propped his head in his hands. He didn't know who he was trying to fool. If you took away the extraordinary events that had thrown them together so long ago, in real, ordinary life, he and Bel were pretty much like oil and water.

"Job getting you down, Gray?"

He looked up at Ruby, the owner of the diner. She was an elderly human woman, around seventy years old. Slim and energetic, with dyed red hair and tortoiseshell glasses, she stayed active in the daily running of her business, claiming her customers kept her young at heart.

He told her, "My job's a piece of cake."

She snorted as she filled his coffee cup. "Pull the other one, why don't you?"

One corner of his mouth tilted up. "Well, some days it's a piece of cake. Other days . . . hey, it's why they pay me the big bucks, right?"

"You need a good woman to make your life easier." Ruby rested her coffee carafe on the counter beside him.

Over the years, they had bantered many times like this before. His smile turned genuine. "You applying for the job?"

"Oh, sweet cheeks, if I was about forty-five years younger and a whole lot more stupid, I would hog-tie you and fight off all comers." She gave him a wink. "But you would always be leaving in the middle of the night. Or you would come home scratched up and bloody, and not say a word about what happened. Some people can handle being the spouse of a cop or a soldier, yet I never was one of them. But we woulda had a lot of fun, you and me, before it all went to hell."

Laughing, he pulled out his wallet. "We sure would have."

"Put that away." She tapped him on the shoulder with a gnarled finger. "You know better than that. Your money's no good here."

"I've always gotta offer, Ruby," he said, although he tucked his wallet back into the pocket of his jeans.

She nodded with a grin. "That's one of the many reasons why I would have hog-tied you. My ex? I had to take him to court for child support, and he always waits for somebody else to pay in a restaurant."

"That's not right." He shook his head. "If I had a wife and child, I would do everything in my power to make their lives good, and they would never want for anything."

I would fight for them, live for them.

Die for them, if need be.

The words sounded melodramatic over morning coffee, so while he thought them, he didn't say them aloud.

"That's another reason why I would have hog-tied you." Smiling, Ruby looked at him over the rim of her glasses. "I don't hafta tell you that people get crazy around masque-time. Be careful out there, and come back to see me real soon."

"I will," he promised.

Predictable as it had been, the exchange had lightened his mood, while the food had given him a surge of much-needed energy. Stepping out, he walked down the street, watching his surroundings carefully until he was certain he was a good half block away from anyone else, and he could sense no nearby magic.

Only then did he take out his cell phone and scroll through his contacts until he found the right one. He punched Call.

Voicemail kicked in. It was a robo-message, giving only the number, no name or any other identifier. He hung up without leaving a message and dialed again.

This time, the Vampyre Julian Regillus, the Nightkind King, picked up. "Graydon. Let's save some energy and pretend you and I have already had a conversation about what time it is."

In the background, Graydon heard a familiar feminine voice. Melisande, the Light Fae heir and Julian's lover, said, "Did you say that was Graydon calling? Tell him hi for me."

"Melly says hi," Julian said into the phone. "We're about to go to bed."

"Don't be mean!" Melly exclaimed.

Graydon bit back a smile. In New York, it was only eight in the morning, which meant that in Lake Tahoe, it had just turned five. For most people, depending on their race and personal habits, it was either too early or too late to be calling, unless the reason was urgent.

"Are you in New York for next week's masque?" Graydon asked. "Or are you coming?"

"No," Julian replied. "I haven't talked to Xavier for a couple of weeks, but I think he's planning to attend as regent. I meant it when I said I'm taking a year off. Melly and I are at home."

Graydon leaned back against the brick wall of a building so he could watch the street in both directions. "Sorry to interrupt your vacation."

"What's going on?"

"Do you remember the conversation you and I had a couple of months ago in San Francisco?" He ran one hand through his hair. The snow had already damped the ends. "We talked about a mutual acquaintance. You shared sensitive intel."

Earlier, in the spring, Melly had been kidnapped by one of the Nightkind council, and her mother Tatiana, the Light Fae Queen, had asked Graydon for help in finding her. Julian had actually been the one who found Melly.

Afterward, he had shared with Graydon confidential information about Malphas. Names of victims. Dates. Graydon's entire investigation had been prompted by that small, vital list.

"I'm not likely to forget." Julian's voice had gone very alert and crisp. "Have there been new developments?"

"Yes, significant ones." Graydon paused as he watched an elderly male cross at the nearest intersection. When the male turned the corner and disappeared from sight, he said, "Do you want to have a say in what comes next?"

"You're damn right I do," Julian growled.

Graydon nodded, unsurprised. "Things may happen quickly. How soon can you get to New York?"

"I'll be there by the end of the day," Julian told him.

Melly said, "You're not going without me." Something rustled. Suddenly she sounded much closer and clearer than she had before, almost as if she had climbed into Julian's lap. "While we're on our way, you're going to explain how this fits into your concept of 'vacation.'"

Julian said, "That's complicated."

"It's always complicated." Melly sounded amused.

Julian said, "Graydon, I'll call you when we're in town."

"Sounds good. Talk to you later."

Once he had disconnected, he continued down the street. In Wembley on that last morning, he had said the war might be a very long one. But not even he had conceived of just how long it would be.

He had never lain in wait for so long, or hunted with such extreme care. His prey had never been quite as dangerous as it was now, nor had the stakes ever been quite as high.

The part of him that was a predator had to admit it felt good to take action, good to be moving toward some kind of resolution. Now that he had begun his play, events would escalate. The pace of the hunt would take on its own life.

Cloaking himself, he changed into the gryphon and launched into a short flight that took him into the heart of Manhattan. Circling down upon an exclusive boutique hotel, he changed back into the man and strode into the lobby.

His destination was a three-bedroom suite several flights up. He rapped on the door and waited.

There was the soft sound of muffled movement, then the door opened. The woman who answered it was human, rather tall, dressed in jeans and a black turtleneck, with an athletic build and blond, shoulder length hair.

She was around thirty-eight or forty, Graydon guessed, or at least she had been when she had become a Vampyre attendant. She was attractive in a clean, spare way, with the sharp, intelligent gaze of an experienced soldier.

"You must be Claudia Hunter," he said.

The woman smiled. "I am, and of course you're Graydon. It's nice to finally meet you in person. Come on in." Turning, she raised her voice. "Precious, our visitor has arrived."

Noting with approval the businesslike Glock she wore in a holster at the waist of her jeans, Graydon followed her into the living room area of the suite just as another male unfolded his long body off the couch.

The male was Wyr and young, perhaps mid- to late-twenties, and he carried a canine scent. He had a kind of handsomeness that smoldered, with dark burnished skin, bitter chocolate eyes and rather overlong black hair.

He was also very large, easily as big as Graydon, and that was not something Graydon was used to running into very often.

"Luis Alvarez," said the young Wyr, holding out one hand.

"Nice to meet you." Graydon shook hands with him, grinning. "Your partner calls you 'Precious'?"

Luis's dark gaze cut over to Claudia, and his face changed. The difference was at once both subtle and, to Graydon's experienced gaze, remarkably telling. Inwardly troubled, he kept his own expression neutral.

Luis said softly, "Inside joke. The first time Claudia and I met, I was injured and in my Wyr form. I couldn't shift back into a human for a while."

Claudia chuckled, her own affection for Luis obvious. She said to Graydon, "He is one big-ass, mean-looking dog. I had to name him Precious."

If Graydon was not mistaken, that big-ass, mean-looking dog had mated with his non-Wyr, human partner.

And Wyr mated for life. Luis would never leave Claudia, never stop in his devotion to her, yet she had a different nature entirely.

If she ever felt the need, she could leave Luis, and eventually that decision would kill him. Their lifespans were also quite different. She would age quicker than he. When she died, he would too. It was a hell of a thing for a member of another race to take a Wyr as a lover.

Of course, it was a hell of a thing for the Wyr, as well.

Belatedly, Graydon caught up with what they had said. He put two and two together.

"Wait," he said. "Are you the two that discovered the magic-sensitive silver mine in Nirvana, Nevada? The one where the owner kept slaves in a small pocket of Other land to mine the silver?"

Both Luis and Claudia sobered, their smiles dying. Luis replied, "Yes."

"I'll get everybody a cup of coffee," Claudia said. She walked out of the living room.

Graydon said to Luis, "That explains your Peacekeeper background."

Luis nodded. "I was an investigator for the Elder tribunal and met Claudia in Nevada. I was close to death when she found me. She saved my life. After the case was concluded, we took time off. When we decided to look for a job, we had some very specific requirements."

"One of my requirements was I needed to become a Vampyre attendant," Claudia said, as she walked back into the room, carrying coffee mugs. "Short of becoming a Vampyre myself, which I don't want to do, being an attendant is the only way for a human to significantly improve their health and lengthen their life."

Ah. So she knew that Luis had mated with her.

She handed a mug filled with coffee to Graydon, meeting his eyes with a direct, steady gaze, and he realized she had seen how troubled he had become. He murmured a thanks and sipped the hot, black brew.

She said, "Working for Carling will extend my lifespan significantly. It still won't bring me to anything near what Luis's life would have been before he met me, but instead of having thirty or forty years together, we'll now have eighty. Maybe even a hundred, if we're lucky, and I'll be fit and healthy to the end."

"You fuss too much," Luis told her. He accepted a mug too. "Things have turned out better than I could have hoped. I like fieldwork and being independent, so those were my requirements. Long story short, we ended up in Florida, applying for positions at Carling and Rune's agency. We've been working for them ever since."

"Well, you know I wouldn't have trusted you with an investigation as sensitive or dangerous as this if Rune hadn't recommended you so highly," said Graydon. "I want to go over everything to make sure it's in order."

"Of course," said Luis. "Since we didn't know what you

might choose to do, I've created files that meet Elder tribunal litigation requirements. It's kind of my thing."

Graydon glanced at Claudia again. The twinkle had returned in her eyes. She said in a gentle voice to Luis, "I get all hot and bothered when you talk about files and litigation requirements."

The younger Wyr laughed a little under his breath, and his skin darkened.

Watching them, Graydon's sense of discouragement turned to hope. If anybody looked mismatched at first glance, it had to be Luis and Claudia, yet they appeared to have found a solution that allowed them to be together in the best way possible.

Maybe he and Bel really could find a way to be together. Of course, they might not, but at least it looked more possible than it had earlier at Ruby's Diner.

"I want to have a meeting on this sometime later tonight," he told them. "I would like for you both to attend, if you would."

"Of course," Claudia said. "Rune and Carling are in town, and they wanted to be kept updated. Is it all right if they attend too?"

"I would prefer it." Rune was one of the most formidable fighters Graydon had ever known, and as a Powerful witch and Vampyre, Carling had once fought in a war against a first-generation Djinn—and won. Her input would be invaluable.

"I'll let them know," Claudia promised.

Luis led him to the dining table and logged him onto a laptop. Once Graydon had taken a seat, Luis handed him something square and black. It was an external hard drive.

"The laptop's Wi-Fi capability has been disabled," Luis told him. "The only record of the files is on that hard drive. This is as secure as we could possibly make it."

"That's terrific."

Plugging in the drive, Graydon explored the contents.

The files were massive. Neatly labeled, each folder contained copies of financial records, photos, and extensive notes, each document logged with the date and time. There were also interviews in audio files.

The other two left him to his reading. It took him several hours, but he reviewed each file thoroughly. He worked through lunch.

Silently, without interrupting him, Luis set a plate stacked with roast beef sandwiches beside his elbow. Graydon nodded his thanks and, without taking a break from reading, plowed through the food.

Finally he closed the hard drive, unplugged it from the laptop and slipped it into his pocket. Looking for Claudia and Luis, he followed the sound of a TV and found them in one of the bedrooms.

They hadn't bothered to close the bedroom door. On one side of the bed, Claudia had propped her back against some pillows. She was reading a thriller. Luis lounged beside her, watching ESPN. They looked relaxed, like a dangerous pair of cougars stretched out after a long hunt, and just about as domestic.

"Damn fine, meticulous work," Graydon told them. "I'd offer you a job—I can match or beat whatever dollar amount Carling and Rune are paying you—except I can't help you with the Vampyre attendant issue."

Both Claudia and Luis's expressions lightened with pleasure at his praise. "Thank you," Luis said. "Is there anything else you want us to do before this evening's meeting?"

"Can't think of a thing," Graydon said. "Get some rest. I'm going to go home, shower and take a nap myself." He hefted the external hard drive in one hand. "Again, you've done a great job, and it's not that I don't trust you, but I'm gonna keep this with me now."

"Sounds good," Claudia said. She swung her legs off the edge of the bed, stood and walked with him to the door of the suite.

"Until tonight, then," he said. He met her gaze. "Be careful. Lay low."

She smiled. "Don't worry about us. We're good at laying low."

He returned her smile, but it died quickly as he stepped into the hall.

They *were* good. They appeared to be competent warriors, and were some of the best investigators he had worked with in a long time, but going to war against a first-generation Djinn was one of the most dangerous things anyone could do. The casualty count was invariably high.

People were going to die due to the decisions he made over the next several hours. One way or another, he had been in command of other soldiers for a very long time, so he was no stranger to seeing it happen. He had experienced that particular kind of loss before.

That never made it any easier.

# ≈ TWELVE ≈

After Graydon left the hotel, he shapeshifted and flew back to Cuelebre Tower.

It had stopped snowing, but the snow hadn't yet lost its newness. The city looked pristine and sugarcoated. Even in the daylight, Christmas and masque lights twinkled along the streets.

He arrived at Cuelebre Tower quickly enough. His apartment was on the seventy-eighth floor of one of the most stringently guarded buildings in the city, so he never bothered to lock his balcony doors. That meant he could come and go with a decent amount of freedom.

Aiming carefully, he executed his shapeshift as he landed, with a sense of timing built on years of experience. Once he strode inside, he went into his bedroom, stripped and stepped into the shower.

Call him obsessive, but he set the portable hard drive on the bathroom sink where he could keep a visual on it, and he stayed under the jet of the showerhead for a long time, letting the hot water ease cold, tired muscles.

A sound came from his living room. He lifted his head out of the jetspray. He had company.

Grabbing a towel as he stepped out, he took a quick swipe at his dripping hair, then wrapped the towel around his waist and went to see who had invaded his apartment.

As he entered the living room, Constantine closed his refrigerator door. The other gryphon looked a little wind-blown, and his color was high underneath his tanned skin. His handsome face wore lines of tiredness.

All four gryphons were some version of tawny and brawny. Rune and Constantine were the two most handsome, and while Bayne had a certain ruggedness to his good looks, Graydon had always been comfortably aware that he would only be considered handsome through the gaze of someone who looked at him with true love.

Constantine said, "You've got no food in your fridge. What's the matter with you?"

Graydon suppressed a sigh. Leaving his balcony door unlocked meant, of course, that other avian Wyr who had security clearance could enter his apartment too.

He replied, "Since I didn't know when I would be coming or going over the next few days, I threw things out. What are you doing here, Con? I've been up all night and I'm tired."

"I've been up all night too." The other gryphon inspected the Keurig on Graydon's counter, selected a cup and started the machine. After giving Graydon a quick once-over, Constantine said, "From the look of things, I probably had more fun with my night than you did with yours."

"I'm not available to talk about work stuff. You'll have heard I'm on leave right now."

"Why, yes. I did hear that. I thought it was interesting, since you never ask for a leave of absence. I mean, sure, you take your vacations when it's your turn, but you don't ask for time off. Like, literally almost never, which makes it memorable when you do."

He stared pointedly at the mug Constantine pulled from the machine. Not that Constantine chose to pick up on it.

The other man blew on the hot liquid in his mug. Then he took the bottle of scotch Graydon had left on the counter and splashed some liquor into his drink. "In fact," Con said, "I'm pretty sure this is the first time you've asked for a leave in, oh, let me think . . ."

Graydon watched the other man without moving. Damn him, Constantine was sharp as a whip, stubborn as a bulldog, and he had a memory like a computer—he just wouldn't give up or stop piecing things together. His personal life was a mess. He catted around compulsively, and he was always wrecked and hungover, but he was a vicious, talented fighter, and his mind never, ever shut off.

Constantine gave him a gentle smile. "If memory serves, wasn't the last time you took a leave of absence when we went to London all those years ago? And wasn't that right after you'd had a private conversation with the Lady of the Elven demesne, at the Vauxhall masque?"

Exasperated, Graydon said, "Now, why the fuck would you remember something like that?"

"I watched you walk away with her, and you didn't reappear until the next day. I remember it so clearly because afterwards, you were uncommunicative and withdrawn for weeks. Gray, that's not like you. You're usually a laid-back, friendly, cheerful kind of an SOB."

Sighing, Graydon pinched the bridge of his nose. "You're not going to go away, are you?"

"Nope, I don't think I am." The other man turned back to the Keurig machine. "Why don't I make you a cup of hot chocolate or coffee while you get dressed? Then we'll chat."

Spinning on his heel, he stalked into his bedroom, dragged on black sweatpants and a sweatshirt with a hood and pockets. Tucking the hard drive into one of the pockets, he strode back into the living room to face his tenacious friend.

Constantine had stretched out on the couch, boots propped on the coffee table, balancing his hot drink on a flat stomach. He had set another full, steaming mug on a coaster in front of a nearby chair and had put the bottle of scotch beside it.

Growling underneath his breath, Graydon sat in the chair.

He inspected the mug. Constantine had made him a cup of coffee. After having drunk so much coffee already, he almost set it aside. On second thought, he grabbed the neck of the scotch bottle to splash some into the drink.

He took a swallow. The hot coffee-liquor mixture burned all the way down.

He said, "I'm giving you fifteen minutes. Not a second more. After that, I'm booting you out and going to bed."

"Fair enough, fair enough." Constantine narrowed one eye at him. After a moment, he said abruptly, "It was Beluviel, wasn't it? Back then. Even though I *said* to you at the time that she was the definition of unobtainable, something caused you to fly straight at her like a moth to the flame."

Graydon drank his hot drink and said nothing.

"She was married. She was the Lady of the Elven demesne. She was all kinds of inappropriate." The other man paused. "Is it Beluviel this time too?"

Graydon finished his drink.

"You're not going to say, are you?" Constantine looked half-admiring and half-annoyed. "What the fuck, Gray? You said you'd give me fifteen minutes."

He cocked an eyebrow. "Didn't say I was going to talk. Just said I'd give you that much time."

The other man's wry smile faded. Constantine said, "While I can respect your level of discretion, I'm trying to help you, man."

The other gryphon didn't sound like his feelings had been hurt, but still, his direct, quiet words shook Graydon's resolve. Shoulders slumping, he rubbed his face.

Con was one of his oldest friends and coworkers. To say they had a friendship was a misnomer. He was more like a somewhat irritating, good-hearted brother. He was also loyal to the point of death, and while currently he was being intrusive, he didn't deserve a cold shoulder.

"Con," he said, setting aside his mug and leaning his elbows on his knees, "I appreciate you poking your nose into my business." To make sure his words didn't carry any sting, he gave the other man a sidelong look and a smile.

"I'm trying to keep a strong separation between all this"—he made a vague, all-encompassing gesture that included Constantine and his surroundings—"and a long-standing issue that is really, mostly not mine to tell."

Silence fell between them. Then Con shifted his boots off the table, took the scotch bottle and poured more into his empty mug.

He said, "You know what I think?"

One corner of Graydon's mouth lifted reluctantly. "I have a feeling you're about to tell me."

Constantine didn't even blink. He pointed the top of the bottle at Graydon. "Maybe this has to do with Beluviel, and maybe it doesn't. After all, whatever happened in London was a long time ago. But I do believe you wouldn't be trying so hard to compartmentalize if you weren't involved in something dangerous."

Like Graydon had said. Smart as a whip.

Constantine said softly, "You're trying to protect everybody, aren't you?"

Oh, fuck it. He reached for the bottle again, and the other gryphon surrendered it to his grasp. He muttered, "I'm trying to keep the Wyr demesne from getting involved in any fallout, but I can't protect everybody."

And people were going to die. Closing his eyes, he took a pull straight from the bottle.

"You're such a stupid shit," Constantine told him affectionately. "Every single one of us, including Dragos, Pia *and* Liam, would go to the mat for you."

"But I don't want you to," he said in a very quiet voice. "I want you all to thrive and be happy, and totally ignorant of any trouble. I don't want any of you to get hurt because of something I got involved in a long time ago."

"Well, you know what? You don't get to choose that." Con tilted back his head and tossed off the last of his drink. "Okay, here it is. It's true enough that some of us have had more than enough shit hit their fans over the last eighteen months. But I'm not one of them. So you cut me in on the secret, and as long as I can help watch your back, I'll also help you keep it quiet."

Moved, he said, "Con, there's no need for you to get invo—"

"On the other hand," said Constantine, cutting him off with a charming, ruthless smile, "if you don't cut me in, I'll tell Dragos and the other sentinels everything that I know, or at least everything I've surmised thus far. Then you can try fighting your way out of the pile all of us will make as we sit on you until you spill everything."

"You wouldn't," growled Graydon.

Con rolled his eyes. "Do you even know me?"

Anger, affection and worry caused conflicting impulses that held him frozen for a moment. Finally, he snapped, "Are you working tonight?"

"Nope, I've got a date," Constantine said. His blue eyes were unrepentant. "Actually, I've got two dates, back-to-back. I'll cancel them."

"Fine. I'll let you know when and where," he said. "Now, get out of here so I can take a nap, will you?"

"Sure, no problem. Didn't mean to interrupt." When he started to growl, the other gryphon gave him a limpid smile as he stood. "What, was that too much?"

He stood too. Setting aside all his other emotions, he looked into the other man's eyes. "Thanks, Con."

A small smile creased Constantine's features. He slapped Graydon on the back lightly and left the apartment by way of the hall door.

Once alone, Graydon rotated his stiff, sore shoulders and went to crash in his bedroom. He was going to be no good to anybody if he didn't get some rest.

Plugging his phone in to charge, he stretched out. The hard drive dug into his ribs. He shifted the sweatshirt, stuck his hand in his pocket and fell asleep holding onto the evidence.

When he woke again, his bedroom had gone dark.

Rolling over, he snatched his phone off the bedside table. He checked the time. It was much later than he had expected, nearly seven o'clock. This close to the winter solstice, sunset had been over two hours ago.

Quickly, he scrolled through his messages. While he had tons of emails and several voicemail and text messages, he ignored most of them.

The latest text he had received had been from Julian, almost ten minutes ago.

> We've checked in at the Four Seasons. Let me know where we're meeting.

Landing a room or suite at the Four Seasons at this time of year was no small feat. Apparently Julian still had plenty of clout, even if he was on hiatus as Nightkind King.

He double-checked his messages again. No word from Bel. No response to the email he had sent with a hotel reservation. If anything, he should have heard from her first, not Julian, who had flown in from California.

Equal parts dread and anger coursed through him as he tore off his sweats and dressed. He should never have left her.

He could feel it in his bones.

Something had gone wrong.

After a long, stressful day, tension tied Bel's body in knots.

Linwe chattered as she pulled clothes out of suitcases and hung them in the closet.

"I'm so glad you decided to do this," said the younger woman. "Really, I think getting away for a few days will be wonderfully refreshing. I know you want to keep this visit low-key, but maybe we can slip out to your favorite museums, and attend one or two parties along with the masque. Nothing elaborate. You know, just saying hi to some of your old friends."

When tragedy had struck the Elves in the spring, Linwe had stripped the cheerful blue color off the tips of her short, layered hair.

Then sometime in November, the color had come back. Now the tips of her hair were neon pink. Bel's gaze followed the pink as it traveled in and out of her closet.

Since she had said good-bye to Graydon and made her way back to the Elven abode, she hadn't been left alone for a moment.

She had walked into the main hall to get some breakfast, where she almost immediately ran into Ferion with two of his senior advisors, Gerend and Imrathon. They invited her to join them for breakfast. Shortly after, Linwe appeared.

With an instinct born of long experience, Bel took her time, pretended she had an appetite and joined in the general conversation. In a natural lull, she said, "I think I've changed my mind about attending the masque this year."

Naturally, that got everyone's attention, but everything else fell away as she raised her eyes from her meal to meet Ferion's. His gray gaze rested on her thoughtfully, while his face remained impenetrably neutral.

As she regarded him, she thought, I have no idea what you're thinking. I have no idea who you are any longer.

Only this time, instead of the thought causing her mere pain, she had felt a pulse of fear.

The memory from that morning made her swallow hard. Walking over to the phone on the antique desk, she lifted the receiver.

"Yes, my lady?" a pleasant Elven voice said.

She recognized the voice immediately. "Vilael, please send up tea."

"Right away, my lady," Vilael promised.

Vilael was one of Ferion's people, and Linwe—Linwe was affectionate and loyal. She was supposed to be Beluviel's, but with the way the younger woman was acting, Bel was almost convinced that Ferion had said something to her.

He could have said something innocuous-sounding, like: I'm worried about her. Keep an eye on her. Let me know what she does and where she goes. We all want my mother to be happy and healthy.

It wouldn't have taken much. And Linwe, the gods love

her passionate heart, would have thrown herself at the assignment wholeheartedly.

When the tea tray arrived, Vilael set it on the antique desk. He gave her a small bow. "I put a few small cakes on the tray, in case you might be hungry, my lady. I know you didn't have any supper, but I thought you might like something to nibble on."

"Thank you." She waited for him to leave. Then she turned to Linwe. "You've been with me all day, and you must be tired too. Don't bother with the rest of the clothes."

"It's no trouble," Linwe said with a quick smile.

"It is for me," Bel said quietly. "I'm tired and ready to be alone. Just because I chose not to go down to supper doesn't mean you should skip a meal. Go get a bite to eat, and unpack your own suitcase. I'll take care of the rest of my things, and I'll see you in the morning."

Linwe's shoulders drooped. "Yes, ma'am."

She knew the younger Elf loved her and meant no harm. Bel touched her shoulder as she walked past, and the small gesture lifted Linwe's head. Giving Bel a grateful look, she slipped out and shut the door quietly behind her.

Finally, finally Bel was alone. She stretched the stiff muscles in her neck and surreptitiously looked around her bedroom.

Handpicked antiques from all over the world decorated the room, and luxurious bedding adorned her bed. Everything about the room was designed to bring the occupant pleasure and relaxation, but for once, she couldn't enjoy the décor.

She looked carefully at the wainscoting and crown molding in the corners of the ceiling.

Are there any hidden cameras? she wondered. How am I being watched?

Because she knew she was being watched. Somehow.

Since she didn't know how, or from what angle, she still didn't feel secure enough to pull out her cell phone to text Graydon. Perhaps she could slip outside to the gardens and text from there, but she needed for everything she did, every move she made, every expression on her face, to appear entirely normal.

She looked at the tray of food. Could she eat the food? How paranoid should she be?

It wouldn't be poisoned. She was certain of that. Not with anything lethal.

But what if a sedative had been slipped into the tea, or baked into the delicious cakes?

Again, it wouldn't take much, just something innocuous. And it could have been presented in such a way to well-meaning attendants that it would help her relax . . . while the drug would also keep her docile and compliant.

She felt like she was building a conspiracy from nothing. There was no basis for any of her fears, and yet, it was all entirely possible. It could all be true.

*Bel,* Graydon's deep, gentle voice sounded in her head. *Are you all right?*

Despite her best intentions to remain as normal-looking as possible, she startled. There was no way to recover from that, so she didn't even try.

She walked into her bathroom to splash water on her face and drink fresh water from the running faucet.

She said to Graydon, *You nearly gave me a heart attack. What are you doing here? Where on earth are you?*

*I'm in the air, circling your building.*

She couldn't imagine the kind of tight maneuvering he had to be doing in order to fly close enough so that he could telepathize with her without setting foot on either the roof or the grounds.

Leaning her elbows on the edges of the sink, she hung her head. *I hope you're cloaking yourself hard.*

*I am, don't worry. Why are you here at the Elven residence? Why didn't you go to the hotel like we had planned, and why haven't you gotten in touch?*

*Things didn't go quite the way we planned.* Taking her time, she dried her face and hands on a towel. The possibility that she was being surveilled even in her own bathroom sent a burst of rage through her. Her hands clenched in the towel. *Ferion insisted on coming with me to New York, and this is literally the first moment I've had to myself since I got back*

*to the Elven abode this morning. Graydon, I feel like I'm
going crazy. I think I'm being watched, but I'm not sure.
Everybody has been hovering around me.*

There was a pause. Just when she had started to think
that he had left telepathic range, he said, *You should trust
your gut. If you think you're being watched, you probably
are. This is going to be more complicated than we had
expected.*

*Yes. I don't know if Ferion is acting out of concern, or
if something else—someone else—is driving him to do all
this. Gray, I can't read him anymore, and it might have been
out of character enough for me to want to come to New York
to spark some kind of trigger.*

It didn't help that she hadn't gotten any sleep since she
had first awakened in the early hours of the morning. She
was exhausted and not at all convinced she was thinking
clearly.

*He might be acting out of concern,* Graydon said. *But we
have to assume otherwise. Do you feel unsafe?*

Going back into her bedroom, she pulled the rest of her
clothes out of her suitcases and hung them in the walk-in
closet. *No, not quite that. I don't think. I don't believe for a
moment that Linwe, or almost any of the others, would do
anything to hurt me.*

But one or two might.

If Ferion ordered them to, they really might.

For the first time, she weighed the value of her life against
the value of Ferion's, and she realized that she came up
wanting.

Yes, she was prominent in the Elven demesne. Yes, she
had social standing outside in the inter-demesne community.
None of that came close to holding the power to shape new
law and strike inter-demesne agreements, and to carve out
policy in the international arena.

How much would it mean to Malphas to maintain control
of the Elven High Lord? Would he kill to maintain it?

If both she and Graydon died, their bargain disappeared,

and Malphas could do anything he wanted with Ferion. Anything at all.

She shuddered.

*You said "almost,"* Graydon said softly. *You didn't say nobody would hurt you. You said almost nobody would.*

*There are some Elves who would do anything their Lord commanded.* She added wryly, *Normally, that's a good thing.*

*I want you out of there,* he growled.

Her suite in the New York Elven residence had a balcony that overlooked a half acre garden, surrounded by a high stone wall. She had insisted upon it. Every opportunity to get into the fresh, open air was important to her.

Abandoning her wardrobe, she went to the balcony doors to throw them open. Snow covered the floor of the balcony, and the bitter December wind whipped into the rooms. The icy shock was like a welcome tonic, shaking loose the tired fog that had begun to take over her thinking.

She stepped outside and looked up at the heavy, overcast sky. She wanted to do so much more than merely talk with Graydon. She needed to look into his eyes, touch his face, wrap her arms around him and hold him tight again.

She said, *Gray, I think you and I might be in danger. Now that Ferion's become Lord of the demesne, his value to Malphas has increased exponentially.*

A rush of wind blasted her. She fell back a step, staring as Graydon's cloaking spell fell away, and the boiling air in front of her transformed into his massive human form.

He wore black fatigues, a black long-sleeved shirt, and a black vest. His rough features were set and hard. He looked as he had that terrible morning so long ago, full of icy, unpredictable rage.

"Dear gods," she breathed. He wasn't supposed to be here. He had just triggered every alarm the Elves had on the property. They had less than a minute before any number of guards burst in on them.

"Come with me now," he said. His stormy gray eyes were intent, fierce. He held his hand out to her.

Her heart hammered. She couldn't do something so simple and revolutionary, could she?

Just take his hand.

Leap with him into the night.

It would break every expectation anyone had ever had of her, and a wild, desperate part of her wanted to smash every one of them.

Holding his gaze, she put her fingers into his.

"I can't," she whispered. "We shouldn't."

"Fuck what we should or shouldn't do," he told her.

Even as he said it, he started to smile. She could see that he knew how insane he sounded. She stepped closer to him so she could feel the warmth of his presence again wrapping around her like a hug.

"Thank you for coming to check on me," she said. "But we need to ride this out. Remember, standing your ground is not passivity. We might discover something useful." She looked up at him. "We might save lives."

He heaved an aggrieved-sounding sigh, but his hand tightened on hers. "I broke your rules," he said. "I'm sorry."

A smile broke over her face. He stared at her, his expression arrested. "I am so glad you did," she told him.

The door to her bedroom slammed open. Linwe, two guards and Ferion burst inside. They all carried weapons. Ferion and one of the guards pointed handguns at Graydon as they strode across the room to the open balcony doors.

Unhurriedly, Graydon folded her hand against his chest. His gentle smile widened, his eyes steady. How could she not want to gaze at him forever?

But she didn't. Instead, she turned as unhurriedly as Graydon to face the quartet of unsettled, angry Elves in the doorway.

"There's no need for alarm," she said in a quiet, calm voice. It was one of the hardest things she had ever done, since she felt anything but quiet and calm. "Please put your weapons down. I'm only getting a visit from an old friend."

Ferion's and the guard's guns lowered a little.

But, she noticed, they didn't lower the guns very much.

Linwe stared at Ferion, and the other guard's eyes widened with consternation.

"What are you doing here?" Ferion asked Graydon. His voice sounded flat and expressionless, almost as if he were an automaton.

"I'm saying hello to Bel," Graydon replied. Like Bel, he spoke quietly, without undue aggression, although standing so close to him, she could feel his Power bristle with unseen spikes. She knew he was on a hair trigger, holding his own instincts barely in check. "Do you always bring loaded weapons into your mother's bedroom?"

Ferion bared his teeth in a smile. "I do when there is an intruder. You're trespassing on Elven territory, Wyr."

"Don't be ridiculous," Bel said. Her fingers tightened on Graydon's. "There's no intruder here. Graydon was passing by, and I invited him to stop for a few minutes."

"You didn't inform any of the guards this was going to happen." Ferion gestured, and the guard holstered his gun. He lowered his own Glock but continued to hold it. She might not be able to read him any longer, but his body language was tense.

"It was an impulse decision," she said gently. "Graydon had only just landed. You showed up more quickly than I could think to call down. I had no idea I was being watched with such care. Thank you for looking out for me."

Now both guards turned to watch Ferion, while Linwe regarded her with a troubled, baffled expression. Bel could tell that the younger Elf sensed that something was seriously wrong.

Linwe said brightly, "Graydon, it's great to see you! You should have said you were stopping by."

Bel bit back a smile as Linwe rushed over to throw her arms around Graydon. Smiling, he hugged her back. "Like Bel said, it was an impulse visit."

"Step out of the room," Ferion said to the guards. As Linwe gave him an uncertain look, he added, "You too."

Linwe looked to Bel for confirmation. In that moment, any hint of doubt Bel might have had about the younger woman vanished. Linwe was clearly on her side.

Bel told her, "Go on, do as you're told. Have a good night."

"Yes, ma'am."

The three Elves left the room, although Linwe trailed behind the two guards and looked distinctly unhappy about it.

As soon as they had left, Ferion turned to confront Bel and Graydon.

He demanded, "What the hell are you two doing?"

# ≈ THIRTEEN ≈

She couldn't hold back asking any longer. "Who is asking, you or Malphas?"

When at first he didn't answer, her widened gaze flew to Graydon's in alarm.

Even as Graydon started to speak, Ferion said, "Your question is not quite accurate. Malphas can't possess me like some bodiless demon."

Graydon's eyes narrowed. "But he can give you orders and compel you to obey. Is he compelling you right now?"

"He's always had that ability." The blood had left Ferion's face, and his lips were white.

"That isn't an answer." Bel stepped toward him, her fists clenched.

Ferion didn't respond. Instead, he looked at her steadily.

All of a sudden, she saw her son again in his gaze, her good, loving, flawed son. Her eyes filled with moisture, and she strode over to throw her arms around him. He held her tightly.

Graydon asked, "Has Malphas compelled you to do things in the past?"

The muscles in Ferion's arms grew rigid. He put his face in her hair and didn't answer.

After suspecting for so long, both relief and fury swept through her. She said over her shoulder to Graydon, "Silence is its own answer."

"Yes, it is," Graydon growled. "So he has already broken the bargain, and it's up to us to prove it and hold him accountable."

Her breathing had turned ragged with her emotions. This was the kind of risk one suffered when one bargained with a pariah. For law-abiding Djinn, if a bargain was not upheld, one could present a case to the Demonkind council. If the case was proven, the Djinn would need to make reparation.

No such strictures bound a pariah. They had already been judged by the Djinn and found wanting, and had been barred from society. The only way to stir others to action was by proving that the pariah was doing too much damage to tolerate—because going against a Djinn came at such a high cost.

Everything was stacked in Malphas's favor. He could cheat while knowing the cost to hold him accountable was too expensive, whereas if she and Graydon broke their side of the bargain, he would . . .

What would he do? Tell the world that they had slept together two hundred years ago? Other than a mild titillation and perhaps a tabloid headline, the world would yawn in his face.

Would he kill the High Lord of the Elven demesne? If he did, he would be signing his own death warrant, because nobody—nobody in all the Elder Races—would allow him to commit such a crime and get away with it.

But if he was pushed into a corner, he could torture Ferion with more extreme acts of control—and that was the one possibility that was so unendurable. She simply couldn't bear to watch it happen.

Hold steady, she thought. Stay the course. Play the long game.

"Ferion," Graydon said. "What if Malphas ordered you to hurt Beluviel?"

Ferion's arms loosened from around her, and he stepped back. His expression turned tender and trapped at once. He whispered, "I would do everything in my power to fight it."

"Yet, you can't swear for certain that you wouldn't do it. Just like the first time."

The first time, when he had choked Bel because Malphas had ordered him to. Silence again, weighted and toxic with everything left unsaid.

Ferion turned away. "I would have to fight anyone who tried to stop me from doing what I was ordered to do, but then I'm sure you remember that. It doesn't mean I would have to win. I can always be killed."

"Don't say that," she said between her teeth.

When he glanced at her, the frozen, tight lines of his face softened.

He said, "I've been living for two hundred years as both hostage and slave, all because I couldn't control myself when I really needed to. It doesn't matter if I'm sorry. It doesn't matter if I grew up a hell of a lot and learned my lesson, or if I would die before I ever did it again. Every time I think this situation can't go on or get any worse, somehow it does. So far Malphas hasn't forced me to do anything catastrophic. It's been the small things, the mean, sneaky things that keep me from sleeping and eat at my soul."

"You never said anything," she murmured, stricken.

His gaze turned wry. "What could I have said? Anything would have made you feel worse, more trapped. I love you too much to put you through that. But now that I've become the High Lord, and the Elven demesne has stabilized, we all know the situation has changed."

"What do you suggest we do?" Graydon asked.

Ferion's reply was immediate. "I take responsibility. Because of my addiction, people have been hurt, and I would pay any price to bring this hell to an end. So I want you both to do what you have to do to end this, and I will have no choice but to do what I must. And I want you to know that whatever happens, you have my blessing."

Graydon's immobility caught her attention. He watched Ferion, his face expressionless, and somehow that frightened her more than anything.

As she watched, his demeanor shifted. His expression became mild and innocuous. Even his body language changed.

"I don't really catch your drift, buddy," he said. He rolled his broad shoulders in an easygoing shrug. "I just stopped by to say hey to Bel. You know, two old friends taking a few minutes to play catch-up."

As Ferion turned to stare at him, Graydon told him in a quiet voice, "We haven't abandoned you, son, and we haven't broken any bargains. We won't, either. Aside from the fact that you know you can trust your mother, you have my word on that."

An expression crossed Ferion's face, one that Bel hadn't seen in a very long time. It was vulnerable, even hopeful. He whispered, "Thank you. Please don't let me do anything to hurt the Elven demesne or my mother."

"Like I said, there's no reason for us to go there." Graydon gave him an easy smile. Even to Bel's hypersensitive hearing, every word he said sounded sincere. She could fudge and tell a certain number of untruths while sounding sincere, but Graydon's talent for lying had hers beat. "Even if you've been ordered to keep an eye on her, she's not doing anything but normal activities. Seeing friends and attending parties. You know, getting a breath of fresh air after a hard six months of work. Isn't that right, Bel?"

Halfway through, she realized what Graydon was doing. He was feeding Ferion the kind of information that the other man could give to Malphas.

It didn't matter what Ferion personally thought of what Graydon was telling him. If pressed, he would be able to repeat exactly what Graydon had said, and he would be able to claim it sounded like the truth.

She could tell when Ferion realized it as well. A slight

smile spread across his features. "With that kind of reassurance, perhaps I can ease up on the number of guards I've set to watch over her." He met her gaze. "Linwe can report to me."

"Of course she can," said Bel. She could tell the younger woman to report only simple, innocent activities and to cover for her when she might disappear. Poor Linwe would be very confused, but she would comply. "It will be a remarkably boring task, I assure you."

Her son inclined his head. "Very well."

"Ferion," said Graydon, "do you know what Malphas can sense? How closely does he watch you?"

The younger male rubbed the back of his neck, frustration evident in his tight body language. "I think he can't sense my activities unless I can sense him. I've become attuned to his presence, maybe because of the bond between us. But he doesn't have to spy on me. He knows I have to follow his orders—or at least the letter of his orders. While he's slipped up once or twice, usually he's very detailed at giving orders that don't allow much wiggle room, no doubt because of his Djinn nature and bargaining experience."

Graydon raised his eyebrows. "If you're more attuned to his presence, perhaps Bel and I are too."

Ferion shrugged. "You might be. He said once that he would feel it if you broke the bargain. Something to do with the connection he established with you. Other than that, he can't spy on us all the time." He paused, and his expression turned uncertain, searching. Hesitantly, he continued, "If I were to guess, I think he's spread very thin."

Satisfaction flashed through her. He was trying to figure out the boundaries of his confinement and help them any way he could.

Graydon said in her head, *That would make sense, if Malphas's network of slaves has grown. But even so, Ferion would remain one of his highest priorities.*

She said quickly, "I think we've talked enough about this." She added privately to Graydon, *If Malphas thinks to ask him what we've discussed, Ferion will have to tell him.*

*Agreed.*

Clearly, Ferion thought of that as well, because he said, "I believe we have, too."

She turned back to him. "What are you going to tell Malphas about this, if he asks?"

Out of the corner of her eye, she saw Graydon nod in approval.

"I will say that Graydon stopped by for a brief visit." Ferion smiled. "And that my mother is doing exactly what she does on every trip to New York, and the reports from my guard confirms it. Normal activities. Seeing friends, attending parties." He said to Graydon, "You should leave now."

Graydon said comfortably, "Sure, no problem." He didn't move.

Bel said in a firm voice, "Good night, Ferion."

The Elven male hesitated. Then he said, "Good night."

As he stepped out of the bedroom, she took a deep breath and let the tension leave her spine. What a strange, heartbreaking yet hopeful conversation.

Taking her by the elbow, Graydon gently nudged her out onto the snowy balcony again. As she complied, he pulled the doors closed behind them.

Silently, he told her, *It's late at night, in December. I doubt there are any surveillance cameras out here. Even if there are, they can't hear what we say telepathically.* He pulled her into his arms, and she went willingly, burying her face in his warm, strong neck. As he cupped the back of her head, he asked, *How do you think it went?*

*As well as can be expected, and better than I had feared.* She sighed, losing herself in his clean, male scent and the warm strength of his large body. *We were all as careful as we could be. I think Ferion will try his hardest to do what he said he would—but we still can't trust him.*

Much as she wanted to. Much as, she now believed, he truly deserved.

*I agree.* Graydon rubbed his face in her hair.

She could feel every finger as he spread his hand against her and rubbed her back. The sensation was soothing and arousing at once. Warmth spread through her, and an ache grew in the private place between her thighs. She bit her lips, wanting so badly to act on her feelings and yet not daring.

He added, *When it comes to Ferion, we need to think in probabilities, not assurances. And we need to think of how to get you out of here without triggering any response from him, or Malphas.*

*Both you and Ferion opened that door,* she told him. *Now I'm going to walk through it. You're going to leave, and I'll call Linwe in here and tell her we're going for a walk. I like to walk in Central Park. For me, it's a perfectly normal activity.*

*Good gods, Bel. Tell me you don't go walking in Central Park at night.* He sounded concerned and amused at once.

She pulled back to tilt an eyebrow at him. *Do you really think anyone would see me, if I chose for them not to?*

A smile creased his face. *You have a point.* He sobered. *As soon as you're out, I'll come get you. We can still have that meeting tonight after all.*

Her pulse quickened at the thought. *Yes. I'll be a half an hour—no later than an hour at the most, I promise.*

His gaze darkening, he laid a big hand along the side of her cheek. For a moment, he didn't say anything, and neither did she. Promise though she might to meet him, it was still not a certainty.

She would probably meet him in no later than an hour.

Ferion would probably keep his word. At least, now she knew he wanted to.

Graydon muttered, *You could still come with me now.*

*Just take your hand and fly into the night,* she whispered back, smiling at him. How she wanted to. She couldn't think of anything more perfect.

*Yes.* He took her hand to his mouth and pressed a kiss into her palm. At the sensation of his lips against her sensitive skin, hot pleasure weakened the muscles in her legs.

She forced herself to remain coherent. *I can't just go with you. I don't think we dare be that overt. We need to try to give at least the illusion of some normality, in order to support the lie. It isn't only Ferion we need to be mindful of. Malphas might actually have other spies in the Elven household. If he's spread thin, as Ferion's surmised, what more logical way to keep an eye on one of his most valuable investments? That's what I would do.*

Air hissed between his teeth as he sucked in a breath. *I hadn't considered that possibility.*

*You've been busy,* she told him. Unable to keep from touching him, she pressed one hand over his, at her cheek, smiling up at him.

His gaze grew heavy-lidded, piercing. Slowly, he lowered his head. He gave her plenty of time to realize his intent and pull away.

Even as she noticed it with one part of her mind, the rest of her grew fevered. She felt crazed by desire. She needed to feel his lips against hers so badly, she couldn't stand it. Raising up on her tiptoes, she met his open mouth with hers.

The breath left his body in a shudder, as if he had slammed into a wall. Suddenly he crushed her against his chest, kissing her with the same kind of rampant hunger that swept through her like wildfire.

Slanting his lips over hers, he pierced her over and over with his tongue, fucking her mouth, while he gripped the back of her neck and held her in place.

A whimper escaped her. It was such a needy, sexual sound, it sent a thrill of shock through her.

It didn't sound like her at all. She was usually so careful and considered. Her first instinct was to reach for diplomacy, to speak the quiet path and measure every action she took.

This sounded like a husky, impetuous stranger driven wild by her feelings, like someone who might do anything to be with the person she needed—including lying. Cheating. Killing. Her body caught fire.

In that moment, she forgot everything else. The bargain, the danger. Graydon could have done anything to her, and she would have welcomed it.

She needed him to do everything to her.

He growled softly. It wasn't a nice, safe sound, full of affection or play. He sounded feral and dangerous. He sounded like she felt.

The beat of her pulse filled with urgent need. The rhythm became the entire world. She existed in the rushing flow of life in her veins.

Then he went taut, his massive body clenched in protest even as he dragged his mouth away from hers. His pulse hammered too, fast and hard, while his breathing had turned harsh and ragged.

She moaned, "You're going to kill me."

She hadn't meant anything by it, but for some reason, he reacted poorly. He recoiled. Then, closing his eyes, he leaned his forehead against hers.

He whispered, "Not if I have anything to say about it, I won't."

She stared at him in perplexity. What an odd thing to say. She wanted to tell him, no, of course not. *That wasn't what I meant.*

But before she could say anything, he gave her one more brief, swift kiss. He told her, *I'll see you outside in an hour or less.*

*Yes.*

His arms fell away. She had a moment to mourn the loss, and for the first time, she felt the cold December wind. He turned, jumped onto the railing and leaped into the air. Just as he had on the beach, he shapeshifted into the gryphon and then disappeared in the next moment.

Staring after him, she sighed in equal parts pleasure and frustration. Then she turned to go back inside. Part of her wanted to worry at Graydon's odd reaction, like a dog with a bone, but that would have to wait until later.

For now, she needed to change into sturdy walking clothes, summon Linwe and get out of the house.

Graydon exploded into the night sky with the kind of fury that came out of desperate longing.

Leaving her.

He was always leaving her.

That fact had been all but unendurable from the very

beginning. Now it tore at him like harpy's claws. The memory of her soft mouth moving under his, her slender body aligning against him, the small, sexy sound that had come out of her. His soul felt lacerated, his skin raw.

He needed to stay with her, but he shouldn't. He needed to protect her from what came next, but he couldn't. People were going to die, and it was always possible that one of them would be Ferion.

Or her.

Everything inside of him rebelled at the thought.

Not bloody likely. Not if he had anything to say about it.

This time, when his vision came, it slipped into him with the stealth of an assassin. White snow. Black rocks. The red of heart's blood.

Ah, at long last, the vision felt close, very close.

He felt a fierce kind of satisfaction that he wouldn't have been able to explain to any other person. One way or another, he was going to get this fucker off his fucking back.

As soon as he had cleared the Elven residence, he flew a few more blocks then landed and shapeshifted again. Digging out his phone, he texted Claudia and Luis, Julian, and Constantine to meet in ninety minutes at the suite in the hotel. Claudia and Luis could contact Rune and Carling.

Then, unable to wait passively, he changed back to the gryphon. Flying back to the Elven residence, he circled it, watching everything. He felt obsessed, like some lunatic stalker, but he couldn't stop himself.

The Elven residence was a three-story detached brownstone mansion in the fashionable Flatiron District. Despite the lateness of the hour, lights shone in several different parts of the house. In the back, the walled garden lay mostly in shadow, with a few security lights shining along the walls.

As he circled, he watched the balcony doors and windows that led to Bel's suite. Lights shone there too, until suddenly they went dark. His adrenaline spiked. At last, she was on the move.

Swinging around to pass over the front of the mansion,

he kept his flight pattern tight and small, until he saw the front door open.

Bel and Linwe slipped outside. They walked down the street, Bel's dark head close to Linwe's bright pink one.

Graydon felt the impulse to follow them, but he stayed on task, watching the mansion.

A few moments after they had left, another Elf slipped out the front door. For a moment, the front porch lights illuminated the Elf's face.

It was a male, the same guard that had pulled his weapon along with Ferion earlier in Bel's room. After the Elf checked both directions, he started down the street after Linwe and Bel.

As he left the mansion, he became harder to detect. He had started to cloak himself.

The Elf had one major disadvantage. He wasn't nearly as good at cloaking as Graydon was at stalking.

Coasting silently around forty yards in the air above the Elf, Graydon watched him for a few blocks until he was quite sure. The male was, indeed, following the two women.

His predatory instincts roused.

It would be so easy to kill him. All the gryphon would have to do was plummet down. His paws flexed as he considered. His long claws would pierce the guard's body before the Elf had a chance to draw breath and scream. He could carry the body away to dispose of somewhere else.

The decision shook through his taut body, but one thought held him back. He didn't know if the guard was Ferion's and innocent, or Malphas's spy.

Even then, the guard could be innocent, and simply suffering from the same kind of coercion as Malphas's many other victims.

At the last thought, sanity intervened. He pulled himself up and shot ahead to the women. Swooping down, he glided over their heads.

*You're being followed,* he said in Bel's head. *Two blocks back.*

She tilted her head back. He caught a glimpse of her face before his trajectory took him past the women. Pulling up, he swept around and glided over them again.

*Gray?* Bel said. *I've explained things—partially—to Linwe. There's a taxi rank up ahead, in front of a block of restaurants. Linwe will take a taxi to Times Square, find an all-night restaurant and wait to hear from me. Can you pick me up?*

*Absolutely,* he told her.

As they turned a corner, they walked out of sight of their stalker. Graydon plummeted. He landed beside Bel and let his own cloaking spell fall away.

At the same moment, she said to Linwe, "Run."

Giving him one spooked glance, Linwe darted toward the nearby restaurants and taxis. He noted in satisfaction that she was a fast sprinter. Despite the snow and ice, she flew surefooted down the sidewalk.

As Linwe raced away, Bel leaped onto his back.

At long last, the space between his shoulders, that spot which had been empty for so long, felt complete again.

*Hold on,* he said.

Cloaking himself again, he launched and drove into the air as high and fast as he could. Wheeling, he flew back the way they had come.

Below, on the street, the Elven guard raced around the corner. After looking around, he sprinted toward the restaurants and the taxi rank.

"Linwe got away!" Bel said. "Even if he gets a taxi too, all they need is a head start of a few moments, and she'll lose him."

*Good enough,* the gryphon growled. *Feel free to praise me for not killing the guard.* He felt rather than heard the soft laugh that rippled through her body. She stroked the back of the gryphon's neck. "You did such an excellent job," she told him. "Thank you for restraining yourself."

*It was not easy,* he told her, even as the pleasure of her touch rippled down his body. *I'm feeling particularly growly and predatory right now.*

"With good reason," she said. The smile had died from her voice.

*Everything will be okay,* he told her.

He willed that he was right, with every ounce of strength he had inside him. He would make sure that it was okay.

If he was only strong enough, fast enough, smart enough.

If he could hold the course, find the right actions to take, he knew they could win through, despite what the vision warned.

He would make it happen. He would.

In short order, they reached the hotel. After landing and shapeshifting, he put his hand to Bel's back and walked with her through the revolving door.

He could tell she was working her subtle magic, deflecting others from noticing them, because despite their fast pace, and despite the fact that Graydon was well known in New York and Bel's face was internationally famous, no one turned to look at them or remarked on their presence.

They made it through the lobby without fuss, and took the elevator up to the suite. As he knocked on the door, she stood beside him, to all appearances looking calm and composed, but he noticed how she twisted her hands together until the knuckles showed white.

He covered her hands with one of his and squeezed. Her large, dark gaze lifted to his, and she gave him a grateful smile.

This time, Luis answered the door. The younger Wyr nodded a greeting to Graydon, while his gaze lingered on Bel.

Almost imperceptibly, Luis's expression lightened, and despite the fact that the younger Wyr had mated with another woman, and the fact that Bel was not Graydon's, he felt a possessive snarl build at the back of his throat and an almost uncontrollable urge to get violent.

The impulse knocked him back into himself. He was getting perilously close to mating behavior again. He had to find some way to throttle back emotionally, but the only way he knew to do that was to have a complete cutoff from her—and after enduring the last two hundred years, he didn't know if he could make himself do it again.

As Luis stood back from the door, Graydon let Bel enter first. When he stepped inside, the younger Wyr murmured, "You okay?"

He shot Luis a glance. It shouldn't come as a surprise that Luis was so perceptive. "Don't worry about it."

Bel lingered and glanced over her shoulder at them. Smoothly, Luis switched to telepathy. *Does she know how you feel?*

He sounded concerned. Graydon shook his head at the younger man.

*It's complicated,* he said shortly. *And how I feel is not the focal point right now.*

*Understood.* Luis said aloud, "The living room is pretty crowded, but this was the best place we could think of to maintain privacy."

Graydon followed Bel down the short hallway. The younger Wyr hadn't exaggerated. Counting Luis, nine other people awaited them. A couple of opened bottles of wine sat on the coffee table, along with Diet Cokes, and several glasses.

Graydon took a quick sweep of the room. Claudia sat in a yoga position, cross-legged on the floor, her spine straight and posture relaxed. She looked like she could maintain the position all night if needed. Luis joined her, sprawling on the floor beside her.

Carling and Rune occupied one comfortable armchair. Rune lounged in the chair, while Carling perched on one arm and draped her shapely torso along the back, curling around his shoulders like a cat.

Slightly disconnected from the others, Constantine stood by the window. He leaned against the wall in a casual pose, arms crossed and one ankle kicked over the other. His posture was relaxed, but his sharp, curious gaze took in everything.

Julian sat at one end of the large couch, while Melly sat on the floor at his feet and leaned against his legs.

There was another couple present, which came as a surprise to Graydon. Bel responded to a flurry of greetings as

Graydon frowned at the new, unexpected pair. A human woman sat at the other end of the couch. She was young, with pretty features and strawberry blond hair.

Graydon recognized her easily. She was Grace Andreas, the most recent in a long line of Oracles that led back to ancient Greece. Standing beside her, arms crossed, stood a tall, imperious-looking Djinn male with raven hair, white skin and diamondlike eyes.

He was Grace's lover Khalil, a second-generation Djinn. Graydon's mind clicked through a mental Rolodex, until he had placed the Djinn's connections. The most important one stood out. Khalil's father was Soren, the head of the Elder tribunal.

Rune had followed the direction of his gaze and said telepathically, *You do know they work for us too, right?*

*I know,* Graydon said. He didn't like any surprises at this late point in the game. *I just wasn't expecting them.*

*Trust me,* Rune told him. *Khalil has valuable experience to bring to the discussion. And both Khalil and Grace are every bit as reliable as Claudia and Luis.*

Graydon relaxed slightly. He had known Rune for as long as he had known any of the other sentinels. Rune had been Dragos's First sentinel for centuries, before he met and mated with Carling. Graydon did trust the other gryphon—with his life, if necessary.

With several people's lives, if it came to that.

Claudia nudged Luis, who rose to step into the kitchenette. Returning, he carried two dining chairs, which he placed opposite the couch. Murmuring a thanks, Bel sat.

Choosing to stand, Graydon reached for one of the Diet Cokes and popped the tab. He had a feeling the caffeine would come in handy.

"I guess that's everybody," he said. "Thanks for coming."

By the window, Constantine stirred. "Now that we're all here, why don't you tell us what the hell is going on?"

Graydon took a deep pull from his Diet Coke before he answered. "Some of you already know, or at least, I'm pretty sure you must suspect," he said. "We're here to discuss how to kill a Djinn."

The atmosphere in the room shifted, as if everyone had drawn in a collective breath.

"No shit?" said Constantine. The other sentinel coughed out a laugh. "Now things have gotten really fucking interesting."

# ⇒ FOURTEEN ⇐

Khalil spoke. His voice was deep and pure, like a bell. "I want to be clear from the beginning about Grace's and my involvement. We might attend this discussion, but I will not take part in a war against another Djinn again. Small children rely on me. Grace relies on me."

Grace turned to look up at Khalil, and the expression of love on her face turned her into a luminous beauty. Khalil rested a large hand on her slim, tanned shoulder.

Out of the corner of Graydon's eye, he noticed Constantine turning thoughtful. While Khalil held his Power in tight control, it was still evident in the nearly invisible shimmer surrounding his physical form that he held a great deal of it. If Khalil wouldn't participate in any action against Malphas, it underscored just how dangerous an undertaking killing the Djinn was going to be.

"Khalil brings up a good point," Graydon said, as he met the gaze of each person in the room. "Just because you're here right now in this room doesn't mean you've committed to doing anything—and going against this particular Djinn will be hard. He's a first-generation pariah." He paused a moment to let that sink in. "We have a lot of information to share. If anybody needs to see documentation, we've got it. Just remember, this is only a discussion, okay?"

"Let's hear what you've got," Julian said. He looked sharp and totally engaged. At his feet, Melly nodded to herself. Shifting, she reached up and back, and laced the fingers of one hand with his.

Graydon didn't have to overhear any telepathic conversation they may have had. Her body language said it all—whatever Julian might choose to do, she would support him.

Graydon started talking. He used the kind of format that sentinels used in meetings.

Subject: Malphas, first generation pariah Djinn.

Issue: Trafficking and enslavement. Collusion, fraud. Suspected murder. Documented crimes against the Elder Races, along with crimes against humanity.

Danger level: Extreme.

After he had summarized, the silence in the room was so deep, he could hear each individual's breathing. Then came the questions, and almost everybody had several.

With a nod to Luis and Claudia, Graydon gave the floor over to them, and instead of leading the conversation, he became an observer.

Khalil's expression remained so studiously impassive, Graydon suspected he was cloaking strong emotion. The Djinn's hand never left Grace's shoulder. She had shifted so that she could lean against his hip.

Julian, Melly and Constantine had the most questions, while Rune asked a few and interspersed the conversation with his own observations.

Of the group, Carling and Bel remained silent. The quality of Carling's stillness was entirely different from Khalil's. She was like a river rock that had been worn smooth over time.

Bel's attentiveness showed subtle engagement. The skin around her eyes tightened at some of the information, and her lips compressed, a quiet sign of inner turmoil.

He wanted to reach out and touch her, like so many of the couples who were present did with each other. Instead, he adopted a pose much like Constantine's, leaning against a wall with arms crossed.

While he maintained a physical distance, he couldn't stop himself from watching her profile. He felt like he could never get enough of simply looking at her and feeling a sense of her presence.

Eventually the questions over the details of the investigation slowed, and that was when the conversation turned challenging.

Graydon asked Carling, "You were a member of the Elder tribunal. What do you think of the case as we've presented it?"

She lifted a shoulder in a liquidly graceful movement. "It's much more solid than many cases the tribunal approves. But the outcome of acting on this one will also be much more costly than many other cases. I believe you'll get approval for taking some kind of action, but what this current tribunal will commit to doing itself is something I'm no longer qualified to answer."

"Can you take a guess?" he asked.

"At the very least, I would guess you'll get Peacekeeper troops to back up any independent action you may be prepared to take. It's not sufficient, but it may be all they offer, although how they could justify that in light of what transpired with Senator Jackson's son and the current unrest in the human Congress, I don't know. At most . . ." She shook her head and shrugged again. "Personally, I will be very interested to hear what Soren is going to offer."

Rune looked at Graydon. "I've been meaning to ask, what led you to investigate this?"

Graydon had been expecting that very question. He said simply, "I received an anonymous tip."

"You've put in a significant investment in time and money over an anonymous tip," Constantine observed. "Since you've been so careful to keep this separate from the Wyr demesne, I assume you've paid for the whole investigation out of your own pocket."

Bel's gaze widened and flew to meet his. He could tell by her disturbed expression she hadn't thought of that before.

Small though her reaction had been, the room was full of smart, observant people, and her consternation did not go unnoted.

Constantine's attention fixed on Bel. He said, "I find the compilation of this group fascinating. For example, I know I'm only here because I pestered you until you didn't have any other choice. How did everyone else end up here, and why?"

At that, Rune spoke up. "Graydon came to us originally to have our agency handle the investigation. We put Luis and Claudia on the case, and we wanted to be part of the concluding consultation, which is why we're here. Since we had some idea of what was going on, we brought in Khalil and Grace for their input."

With that, everyone focused on Julian, Melly and Bel.

Melly said simply, "I'm here because Julian is. I had no idea any of this was going on."

"I'm not going to lie, Graydon knew I'd have a dog in this fight," said Julian. "Earlier in the year, I helped block Malphas from harming someone in my demesne. Since then, he has nurtured a grudge. He helped to trap me when Justine kidnapped Melly."

Rune looked at Graydon. "Sounds like you can add another count of collusion to that list."

Julian nodded and continued. "I have every reason to believe he would act with malice again, if an opportunity presented itself." He cupped Melly's shoulders. "I won't have him coming after me, or anyone else I care about. I want him dead, and I'm willing to help do whatever it takes to make it happen."

Carling turned to Beluviel. "And you, Bel? What brings you here?"

Bel replied readily enough. "I am interested in the outcome of this conversation."

Julian shifted, an uncharacteristic sign of restlessness from a Vampyre. From his position by the window, Constantine's eyes narrowed, and Graydon knew Bel wasn't going to get away with that nonanswer.

"Why is that, and how did you learn of it?" Carling pressed. "Has Malphas harmed you in some way?"

Bel met Graydon's gaze. She gave him a small, sober smile and said nothing.

She was experienced at diplomacy. She could have replied in any number of ways to continue deflecting Carling's questions, but as Bel had said earlier, silence can be its own answer.

As everyone waited for her to respond, the natural pause in the conversation grew prolonged. On the couch, Grace shifted, looking unsettled. Both Rune and Constantine leaned forward, their predatory instincts engaged.

"Graydon, you've spearheaded this whole thing," Rune said, turning to him. "Why did you invite Bel?"

Graydon returned Bel's smile and said nothing.

Remain steady. Hold the course.

After all this time, don't falter now.

Constantine remarked, "It appears that either they can't answer, or they won't." Telepathically, he asked Graydon, *Is she here because of something that happened when we were in London?*

Graydon glanced at Constantine, but he didn't answer.

*Daaaamn,* Constantine whispered. *Whatever it is, you and she have been carrying that around for a hell of a long time.*

Julian said, "Graydon, what you've told us is very detailed, but it's quite clear you're not giving us all the information. You want to kill Malphas, and you've presented an excellent case for doing so, but why do *you* want to kill him?"

No answer.

Rune had tensed. He asked, "Gray, are you able to fulfill your duties as First sentinel?"

That was one of the right questions to ask. Without hesitation, Graydon said, "Absolutely, I can do the job."

"Truth," Carling said. She put an arm around Rune's shoulders, and he relaxed against her. "At least as far as I can tell."

"So you are not personally being controlled by Malphas," Rune persisted.

"No," he replied. "I am not."

"That's not quite true, though, is it?" said Constantine. "Your behavior right now is constricted by something."

For the first time, Grace spoke up, her quiet voice hesitant. "I see connections, you know."

The focus of the whole room snapped to her, and her demeanor turned self-conscious. Rune suggested, "Why don't you explain what you mean by that?"

"My Power as Oracle has become attuned to the Djinn, for a number of reasons," she offered. "I've discovered a way to help injured Djinn heal, and I can see the connections they make, with each other and with other races. Most of the time, I don't pay attention, but sometimes they become too obvious to ignore."

Graydon asked, "Can you remove connections?"

At Grace's side, Khalil's eyebrows rose, and the expression in his diamondlike eyes grew piercing and fierce. "Connections are made when Djinn strike bargains. You did not just ask my Gracie to break Djinn law, did you?"

"I didn't ask her to break any laws," said Graydon, keeping his reply mild and nonthreatening. "I just asked if she could. There's a difference."

"I don't know," Grace told him. "I might be able to, but I couldn't swear to it. I don't think I could do it without alerting the Djinn who made the connection to begin with, so I guess it would be a pretty useless thing to try."

"It could be hugely important, if you could break the bond Malphas has put on the souls of his victims," Graydon said. His mind raced to the possible implications. Planning an attack on Malphas would be much simpler if they could free Ferion first.

The Oracle shook her head quickly, dampening his newfound hope. "That kind of bond sounds much more dangerous. I'd be afraid to try anything. For one thing, nobody knows how the victims would respond. If the bond is parasitical in nature, removing it the wrong way could kill them, and I'd be worried that anything I might try would alert Malphas."

Carling asked, "Could you identify someone who has one of those bonds?"

Grace lifted her shoulders. "I don't know. I've never seen anything like it before. I guess, maybe?"

"Why don't you have a look at each one of us?" suggested Carling. "Tell us if you think anyone here has a lien on their soul."

Instantly, Khalil's physical form melted. He flowed over Grace, covering her body completely.

Grace's voice came from the shadowy cloak, sounding slightly distorted. "Now look what you made him do. Khalil, get off me."

"Gracie, there are dangerous people here," Khalil said. "What if someone does carry a soul bond? You might trigger a violent response. While you may carry the Power of the Oracle, you are also quite human and fragile. And too precious to lose."

"Why did you ask her to check everyone?" Julian asked Carling, his eyes narrowed.

"Just humor me," Carling said. "Graydon and Bel aren't answering certain questions, so some influence is at work on them. I'd like to know for sure the room is clear of that particular taint. Khalil, let Grace work."

"I am not preventing her from working," Khalil said. "I am preventing anyone from harming her."

Grace's sigh sounded clearly from within the cloak, and she looked around the room. After a few moments, she shook her head again. "I don't sense any unusually strong connections, and that's the only way I would know to look for it. Khalil, will you please get off me now?"

Silently the Djinn flowed away from her body and solidified into a man again. He resumed his former position, arms crossed and unrepentant.

Grace told Graydon, "The reason I mentioned it is because we were talking about whether or not Malphas was controlling you. Constantine said your behavior was constricted in some way, and I can see that you have a connection with a Djinn. Although that in itself isn't unusual. Several of us have connections with Djinn. A couple of us have quite a few. I've accrued quite a few, myself—I'm now considered quite wealthy by Djinn standards, as a lot of them owe me favors."

Rune angled his face toward Graydon again. "Don't tell me you made a bargain with a pariah Djinn. Did you? Is that restricting you from answering certain questions?"

When Graydon didn't reply, Rune swore under his breath.

From his slouching position by the window, Constantine remarked, "You know, I've been racking my brains, trying to figure this puzzle out. What could it possibly be? You've presented us with several cases where Malphas clearly preys on gambling addicts, yet you can't or won't say how you got the information, or why you're pursuing it."

Nearby, Bel shifted in her seat. It was another tiny tell that didn't go unnoticed. Graydon swept the room with his gaze. Julian's attention hadn't shifted from Bel for quite some time. Both Claudia and Carling watched her too.

Restlessly, Constantine pushed away from the wall, wagging one finger. "Wait a minute. Two hundred years ago, when we went to London—there was a gaming hell that Weston razed to the ground. I remember since it had been so notorious. The news was all over the city the next morning. It especially caught my attention because we had just been visiting with Weston at the Vauxhall masque. At the time, he had seemed perfectly relaxed. He hadn't given any indication of what he was about to do. Of course, he always did have a hell of a game face."

Come on, Constantine, Graydon thought. Piece it together.

Aloud, he said, "The case I've presented to you stands on its own merits. Anything else is speculating outside the boundary of this investigation."

"Did Malphas own that gaming hell?" Rune asked Graydon.

Could he answer that? Ownership of Malfeasance had to be a matter of historical fact, but acknowledging Rune's question with a direct answer might be too leading. It could trigger the bargain, and he and Bel had already skated such a fine line tonight.

So far, he had essentially said just two things. The first was that he wanted to kill Malphas.

The second thing he had said was: here are the facts of an investigation. It was entirely based on other people. None of it touched on Ferion, or stemmed from what had happened in Wembley.

He glanced over at Bel. This time, she gave no hint of what she was thinking or feeling. She kept her gaze on her hands, folded in her lap. She held so still that to an outside observer, she might look like an exquisite Elven statue.

Graydon had seen her many times throughout the years in movement. Normally, her beautiful face, and every gesture and word, were alive with expression. Now, her very stillness was as loud as a shout, for anyone who knew how to hear it.

Carling studied Bel with a heavy-lidded glance. If there was anyone else present who might have the capacity to hear Bel's silent language, it would be Carling.

Constantine looked from him to Bel, and back to him again. *Malphas. You. Beluviel. London. Weston. Gambling addicts. Gaming hell. It's all connected somehow, isn't it? How is it connected? I've never heard of Beluviel having a gambling problem. If she gambles, that has sure been one hell of a well-kept secret. Calondir's dead, so he doesn't matter anymore. Ferion, though—once upon a time I remember he had a wild streak, before he settled down.*

Graydon fought to keep his face stony, unrevealing.

Suddenly Constantine breathed, "God damn. Goddammit. It's Ferion, isn't it? Malphas has a soul lien on the Elven High Lord."

And that, of course, broke the whole thing wide open.

Hearing one of the other sentinels utter the truth out loud sent a thrill of terror through Bel's muscles. Inwardly panicking, she forced herself to remain immobile, while she ran through everything in her head.

Had they played it carefully enough? She couldn't feel Malphas's presence, but at the moment, she couldn't feel anything beyond her own chaotic emotions.

When Carling squatted in front of her, she startled violently.

She had a long acquaintance with Carling that spanned centuries. Over time, she had watched the other woman rise in political influence and magical Power, but always from a distance. They had been pleasant to each other at public gatherings, but they weren't close.

Now, Carling's dark eyes were warm with concern. She put a slim brown hand over both of Bel's and squeezed lightly.

Carling asked in a gentle voice, "Bel, is your son under Malphas's control?"

Bel dropped her gaze to their hands.

Don't say a word. Don't acknowledge the question. Don't betray anything.

Gods, let it be enough.

Carling said, "She's shaking like a leaf."

"Leave her." Graydon's voice sounded unexpectedly harsh, and close.

Carling pulled back as he shouldered in front of Bel.

"I'm all right," Bel told him. "It's okay. It's . . ." At the last moment, she remembered to switch to telepathy. *After so many years, it sounds incredibly dangerous to hear other people talking about this.*

*That's because it is dangerous,* he replied. His dark gray eyes held so much understanding, the expression in them highlighted just how alone and isolated she had felt for so many years, despite being surrounded by loved ones.

She gripped his hands as he knelt in front of her.

There was something so poignant about the moment, surrounded as they were by a sharp, rapid conversation. They remained wrapped in silence, existing on the edge of other people's reality yet entirely immersed in the gigantic landscape they had shared together.

That, to a large extent, they had created together, a

landscape filled with too many secrets, too-brief laughter, warmth, sensuality, and a quiet, enormous determination.

Out of the corner of her eye, she saw the concerned, wary glances that the others gave them. She didn't care what they saw when they looked at her, but she couldn't help wondering what they saw when they looked at Graydon.

Did they only notice the big, kindly, somewhat rough man dressed in plain workman clothes? Did any of them recognize his large heart and true nobility?

She whispered to him, "Please tell me the people in your life value you as much as you deserve."

A look of vulnerability flashed across his face. Gently, he captured her hand again and pressed her knuckles against his lips.

Behind his shoulder, Constantine came into her focus. He was watching them, looking worried, fascinated and surprisingly wistful.

"Graydon and Beluviel," Khalil said in such a strong voice, they turned to him. "No one will ask you any more questions you cannot answer. Do not acknowledge what I say next—just listen. We believe that Malphas has control over the Elven High Lord. And we believe that you must remain silent about that, because he has threatened to hurt Ferion in some way, or perhaps he has threatened to harm either or both of you."

"Graydon wouldn't let the threat to him stop him from taking action, if he thought it was needed," Rune said.

"Acknowledged," said the Djinn with an imperious tilt of his head. "Still, a threat in some form is present. Grace has determined you both have a single connection to a Djinn. I believe it stems from a bargain with Malphas. Otherwise, you would not need to be so circumspect in what you say—or don't say. While some of this conjecture may be wrong, enough of it is true to guarantee one thing. Now my father will have no choice but to take the strongest measures possible."

Graydon blew out a breath. *There it is,* he said softly to her. *There's our war. The genie is out of the bottle now, and there's nothing we can do to stuff it back in.*

*You were leading to this all along,* she said. *That's why you investigated so carefully, why you built such a comprehensive case, and it's why you wanted to have a group meeting. You hoped the others would put things together and come to the right conclusions.*

*More or less,* he said. Ducking his head, he gave her a sidelong, wry glance. *Frankly, I didn't have things that well planned. For example, Con really did push his way into this—and he was the one who had all the right pieces. If I hadn't been so focused on keeping this separate from the Wyr demesne, I would have seen that and included him sooner.*

How could he be so adorable and dangerous at the same time?

Leaning forward, she put her arms around his neck. He leaned into her embrace and wrapped his arms around her, hugging her tight.

She hid her face in his neck. He put his face in her hair. For one more magical moment they stayed alone, in their intimate landscape.

Then his arms loosened. When he pulled back, she had no choice but to let him go, although she resented every inch of physical space that grew between them as he sat back on his heels.

He asked, "I think we're ready to call Soren now, don't you?"

She nodded and stood along with him. "We need to move quickly. The longer I'm gone, the more unpredictable everything feels."

As she turned to the group, she found everyone staring at them in varying degrees of surprise.

They might have separated physically, but Graydon took a protective stance at her shoulder, turned partially to face her. All she had to do was shift her weight to her left foot, and she could lean against his broad chest. Knowing that comforted her immeasurably.

Graydon asked the group, "Who has a connection with Soren?"

Carling, Grace and Khalil all said at the same time, "I do."

"Please, do allow me," Khalil said. Despite Bel's concern

over what came next, the Djinn's satisfied expression caught her attention. He was clearly looking forward to holding his father accountable.

In a quiet yet strong voice that reverberated with Power, Khalil said, "Soren."

Silence fell, as everyone stilled, bracing themselves for the Djinn's arrival. For a few moments, nothing happened.

Carling raised one eyebrow. She murmured, "He must still be miffed at you for getting together with Grace."

"He can bite me," Khalil said between his teeth.

The modern slang, combined with the particular viciousness with which he had said it, spoke volumes about his own feelings toward his father.

A surprised sound, something between a snort and a cough, escaped Melly.

Grace had turned tense. "You haven't talked to your father since he tried to imprison you," she muttered. "Just wait. He'll be curious enough to come."

The young Oracle was right.

Before Bel could do anything more than wonder at why Soren would have tried to imprison Khalil, a comet of Power arched toward them from an uncounted distance, approaching impossibly fast.

A whirlwind entered the room, spinning faster as it coalesced into the figure of a tall man with craggy features, white hair and the piercing diamond eyes of a Djinn.

Soren, Khalil's estranged father and the head of the Elder tribunal, had arrived.

# ⇒ FIFTEEN ⇐

K halil might be dangerous and Powerful, but his father was a first generation Djinn. Born at the beginning of the world, Soren shone with a fierce white Power.

Bel was also one of the eldest of her kind. While her Power was connected to the earth, she could still look on Soren without flinching, but she saw that those who were much younger—Melly, Claudia, Grace and Luis, and even Julian—had to brace themselves for the onslaught of Soren's presence.

Soren had coalesced on the opposite side of the room from Khalil. Once he arrived, neither Djinn's human form appeared to move, but the air bristled between them.

Stirring, Constantine muttered, "They're like beta fighting fish."

"What an interesting gathering," said Soren. "Which of you is going to tell me why my son has summoned me here?"

"I am," Graydon said. "Although I'll leave the others to tell you the details. You and I, along with anyone else we can get to fight along with us, are going to kill Malphas."

Soren lifted one white eyebrow so imperiously that,

despite their differences in physical form and temperament, for one moment he looked remarkably like his son.

He drawled icily, "Please explain what brings you to such a remarkable and presumptuous conclusion."

Bel didn't think Soren was prepared for all the reasons that bombarded him from every direction. The Djinn stood immobile in silence, absorbing every comment.

Wrapping her arms tightly around her middle, Bel looked down at her shoes and refused to react or respond as Constantine, Khalil and Carling launched into why they had concluded that Malphas had placed a lien on the Elven High Lord's soul.

Smoothly, Graydon slipped his big body in front of her, putting his back to everyone else in the room. When he took hold of her upper arms, she raised her gaze to his.

Just like that, they fell into their intimate landscape. Everyone else existed outside the borders. All their noise, all their strenuous argument.

Inside the boundary, Graydon's eyes were warm, calm and clear, lit by a slight smile and free from fear.

She held her hands out to him. In a long, light caress, he slid his fingers down the length of her arms and clasped her fingers. With that gesture alone, he made her feel remarkably precious and incredibly valued.

He was so unlike Calondir's stern, cold personality, she found it hard to believe that the two males had occupied the same universe.

Calondir had been obsessed with the letter of the law, but he'd had no real sense of compassion or the ability to make deep emotional connections to others. She hadn't truly seen that until after they had married. It made many of his decisions harsh and unyielding. She suspected it had also made it easier for him to lash out when he grew angry.

Calondir's son and heir had been his most prized possession. For too many years, she had watched Ferion as a boy try time and again to win his father's love, until eventually he had stopped trying, which was the most heartbreaking thing of all, while Calondir never comprehended what he had lost.

Whereas Graydon . . . He would make an incredible father, if he were only given the chance.

His warmth, patience and affection appeared to be boundless. He would love his child with all of his big, generous heart, and do everything in his power to ensure the child felt safe, wanted and loved. Graydon would always be faithful and welcoming, always be a steady touchstone for a young, vulnerable mind.

The part of her that had gone cold and distant so very long ago, the part that he had resurrected with a touch, resonated to the realization with an immense internal vibration.

He was everything she could possibly want—everything she had always wanted. Among other things, his very loyalty had made him Dragos's First sentinel. It was also why he would never walk away from his obligations.

She was horribly jealous of that stupid, arrogant dragon. Stinking, raving jealous.

Tightening her fingers on his, she said softly, "Now that you've forced Soren's hand, you don't have to go to war against Malphas. You can step away from all of this and go back to your life."

He gave her a smile that was so remarkably sweet, she felt as if she had lived for hundreds of years just so that she could see it one more time. "No, I can't, Bel."

"Why not?" she whispered.

He tilted his head. "Would you walk away?"

Her response came from her gut. Walk away to leave her son's fate in the hands of others? "Never."

His thumbs stroked over the backs of her hands. "Why not?"

Involuntarily, the answers ran through her mind.

Love and commitment. She would die before she let go of fighting for her son.

While his father had viewed him as a possession, *she* had been his only touchstone.

*Hers* had been the hands that small towheaded toddler had reached for when he had taken his first steps.

*Her* lap was where the young boy had buried his head when he had sobbed out his hurts and disappointments.

*She* was the one the proud young man had looked to when he had achieved an accomplishment.

*She* had been the one to tell him with fierce, passionate pride, "Well done."

The only thing that could make her turn on Ferion would be to find out that he had become unsalvageable, as corrupt as Malphas, and a danger to others.

Because, the simple fact was, she was not built to do anything else.

You did not walk away from those you loved. You fought for them, always, with everything you had, even if it meant fighting the long fight, and staying on the hardest, quietest, most difficult course.

No matter how long it took, no matter what needed to be done.

Her lips parted on a soundless intake of breath. That couldn't possibly be what Graydon meant by asking.

Could it?

It was a hell of a logical leap for her to make, from what he had *actually* said, which was *let's see where we might take this* to love.

And now wasn't the time to ask what he had meant. Not with ten other people with super sharp hearing and an abundance of curiosity overcrowding the room, not to mention an impending war with a Djinn.

Words fell out of her mouth anyway. She, who was respected for her sense of diplomacy and discretion, had no control over herself. The last twenty-four hours had obliterated any filters she might otherwise have had.

"What are you saying?" she demanded, yanking his hands.

At her vehemence, he looked quietly astonished. Then his expression shifted to something very male, and so intense it rocked her foundation.

He yanked her hands in return, only his grip was so strong, he pulled her forward until she collided with his chest.

She had to tilt her head back to keep staring at him. The front of her torso, everywhere they touched, felt seared by his hard body. Oh gods, she had *never* forgotten how hungry she had been for him, back in England, but this felt entirely new, deeper and more raw than anything she could remember or imagine.

"Intense though your conversation may be," Soren snapped, "you will have to set it aside for later."

The Djinn's acid tone splintered the bubble that surrounded Bel. Flinching, she realized Soren had moved across the room and stood right beside them. The Djinn looked furious.

Moving so fast he blurred, Graydon snatched at Bel, clamping her against his side, away from the Djinn. At the same time, he snarled at Soren wordlessly.

Oh, dear gods.

Graydon's normal features, that had become so beautiful and dear to her, had vanished.

In his place stood a huge monster, with a feral, distorted face, fangs and claws. In an instant, he had gone from gentle, even sensual, to barbaric and half animal.

Bel's mouth fell open, and she goggled at him.

"Whoa, okay," Constantine said sharply. "Back up, Soren. Back up, now. How the hell do you get a Djinn to back the fuck up? Like right now!"

"I told you he was close to flipping his shit," Luis said.

Rune ordered, "Everybody else, leave the suite! Go out into the hall!"

Carling's calm, telepathic voice flowed into Bel's mind. *Bel, you need to talk to Graydon and get him to calm down. Do it now.*

*I don't understand,* Bel stammered. Funny, she didn't feel the slightest bit afraid. Simply astonished and confused. She hadn't sensed any threat in the room, yet Graydon was clearly primed for battle.

Soren backed away, looking astonished and thoughtful.

*I've seen this behavior before, and I know what it is,* Carling said. *We'll talk about it later. Don't be afraid, honey.*

*I'm not afraid.* Bel switched to verbal speech. She said as calmly as she could, "Graydon, my love. All is well. There's nothing dangerous here at all. Can you look at me?"

The monster had not stopped glaring at Soren. His long fangs were exposed in warning. The massive muscles in the arm that held her clamped to his side were hard as iron.

Where had her gentle giant gone? This was the same monster who had faced down Malphas in the Djinn's country manor house in Wembley.

Something about Soren's antagonistic attitude had triggered Graydon's fight instinct.

The monster didn't appear to pay any attention to her, but she noticed the sound of his growling subsided.

Hoping he quieted so he could hear the sound of her voice, she continued softly. "I need for you to pay attention, Gray. Are you listening to me? I need for you to pay attention to me *right now.*"

She injected all the urgency she could into her voice.

The monster's gaze snapped to her.

Relief caused her muscles to turn shaky. He could listen to her. He could respond.

She laid a palm against his cheek. "Watch only me," she whispered. "Never mind anything else that happens. Pay attention only to me."

As people quietly slipped out of the room, the monster turned his head toward the movement and hissed.

Bel felt her eyebrows shoot up. He seemed to be protecting her? His behavior was beyond irrational. It was . . . it was . . .

When the answer finally came to her, she felt her world undergo an irrevocable shift.

It was Wyr mating behavior.

In an instant, everything she knew and read about Wyr mating flashed through her mind.

When the Wyr began to mate, they turned violent, irrational and possessive. Fascinated by the idea, she had once read everything she could about it.

Not that she had found much definitive information.

Wyr mated for life, but no one fully understood how or why it happened, not even the Wyr themselves. It was a complex occurrence involving sex, personality, emotion, timing and instinct.

She had read first-person accounts where Wyr had described falling in love, and even coping with a broken heart after a love affair had ended, yet they hadn't experienced the mating frenzy.

As one Wyr female had said, she had fully believed she was in love, and thought she understood the full range of what that meant in terms of emotion, but it was only some years later, after she had mated, that she finally understood the depth of fulfillment, completion and even the edge of despair that mating gave to her.

If the mating Wyr weren't handled with understanding and care, they could turn on lifelong friends and family. For even the gentlest among them, a time of mating could be unpredictable and dangerous.

Just as quickly as realization hit, Bel felt overcome by a huge tidal wave of reaction. Everything in her soul cried out in hunger and gladness, and reached greedily for the immense, precious gift that seemed to appear as if by magic in front of her.

If it had been another man, the possibility might have frightened or disturbed her, but this was *Graydon*.

This was everything she had ever wanted for herself, everything she could have hoped for. His warmth, his gentleness and constancy, and yes, this fierce, frightening creature as well. There was nothing cold or distant about him.

All other considerations fell away. The other people in the group, their lack of privacy, the challenge that lay before them, even the danger to her son.

This time, she put both hands to the monster's face and turned him toward her.

He could have easily resisted her touch. Physically, he was much stronger than she was. But he obeyed the urging of her hands. The snarl that had distorted his lips eased.

Stroking his hair, she thought, I have never seen anything more beautiful than this.

"Come here," she whispered. "Come here."

The monster's eyes narrowed. For a moment he looked uncertain and so filled with yearning, it caused a deep ache to fill her chest.

Watching her closely, again he obeyed. He bowed his head.

As he did, she stood on tiptoe and kissed that adorable, dangerous monster on his snarly, fang-filled mouth.

He froze. She could tell he wasn't even breathing. Where she leaned against his chest, the powerful engine of his heart hammered too fast against her breasts.

Then the shape of his body and the contour of his mouth changed. His bruising, iron-hard hold on her gentled.

He gathered her close, slanted his mouth over hers and kissed her with such passionate tenderness, tears spilled out of the corners of her eyes and streaked down her cheeks. She kissed him in return, holding onto him fiercely. For that one moment nothing else existed.

When he eased away, he looked sober and self-contained. His expression was so unlike what she had expected, she shivered.

After a quick glance around the empty room, he muttered, "I lost control."

"Yes, you did," she told him gently. "Do you remember what happened?"

His mouth tightened. He passed a hand over her hair in a fleeting caress, then let her go and stepped away. "I remember enough. Soren was angry and aggressive. He came at us too close, too fast. He's such a dangerous Djinn, it threw me—back to the manor house." His dark gray eyes met hers briefly before he turned away. "I apologize. It won't happen again."

Thrown off-balance, she stared at his broad, powerful back. She thought she had understood what was happening, but this wasn't anything like she imagined. After such ferocity, and a kiss so devastatingly tender she could still feel his lips on hers, he now acted almost as if he was embarrassed.

Could she have read the situation wrong? Had he really just been thrown back to the confrontation in Wembley?

She felt as if a whole shining future had been snatched away from her. Just as fierce and overwhelming as the joy that had swept through her only moments ago, disappointment crashed down on her so heavily she felt a crushing weight on her chest.

She wanted that future. She wanted it desperately. She wanted him, and the kind of love she sensed that he was capable of giving.

I love him, she thought. Somehow, at some point in time, I fell in love with him.

I want him, more than anything I've ever wanted in my life.

If nothing else, admitting the truth to herself was an immense relief.

She stepped toward him, one hand outstretched, not that he could see it, since he still had his back turned toward her. "It's all right, Graydon. I don't want you to apologize. I want . . ."

I want my monster back. The words sounded so raw and needy, she caught herself before she could say them.

His shoulders had stiffened. With an unpleasant shock, she realized that he didn't welcome anything she might have to say. His silent, rigid posture stopped her words as effectively as if he had stuffed a gag in her mouth.

Breathing hard, she pulled the ragged pieces of herself together. After a moment, she said, "Since you've recovered, we should ask the others to return."

"Yes," he said. He strode toward the door that led to the outside hall. "We have a lot to do, and as you pointed out, time is slipping away from us."

His too-quick response shoved her over some kind of edge. She felt as if she had been heading toward that place for a very long time.

After running a gamut of emotions over the last twenty-four hours, she jammed on the emergency brake and came to a full stop. Angling her jaw, she put her hands on her hips.

Maybe it was unwise. But she was tired of trying to be wise. Of trying to think only of the greater good or taking the best course of action.

She was fed up with taking the long view, holding the course. Always looking out for other people.

And fuck diplomacy. Really, just kick that shit to the curb.

This, she thought, is about what I want. No one else.

Telepathically, she said, *We have a lot to do, and a lot to decide. None of it is going to be easy. I get that now is not the time to talk. Even so, I still want you to know I love you. Graydon, I'm in love with you. I think I have been ever since that night we spent in the forest.*

Quick as a cat, he spun around to face her. His gaze had turned raw, and a muscle leaped in the tense line of his jaw.

Whatever barrier he had erected between them seemed to be gone. In the face of his intensity, the fierce focus she had acquired splintered completely.

She stumbled on. *So . . . either you'll welcome that, or you won't. But I'm not going to be silent about it. And . . . and well, that's all I had to say. Oh, except—after we get done killing Malphas and fighting to free Ferion, I'm going to fight for you too. Unless . . . unless of course you don't want me to.*

Aaaggghh.

As a rousing declaration of love, that foolish speech left a lot to be desired. She felt stupid and naked, and completely out of her depth.

After they stared at each other for a pulsing moment, she threw up her hands and charged for the door. Someone, anyone needed to come back into this blasted suite. In fact, right now would be a good time.

"I love you too," Graydon said aloud. His voice had gone hoarse. "For two hundred years, I've been waiting for you, hoping for you. Fighting for you any way I could. I never dared let myself hope you might feel the same way, or I couldn't have walked away from you."

He strode across the room toward her.

Before she fully realized what she was doing, she leaped at him and crashed into his chest.

He didn't even stagger as he snatched her out of the air and crushed her to him. Blindly, hungrily, she wrapped her arms around his neck, her legs around his waist and held onto him with everything she had.

"Are you mating with me?" she whispered, burying her face in his hair.

"I'm beginning to, yes," he said very low into her neck. "I haven't gone too far. Not yet, so if you're not sure about this in any way, there's still time to back away."

Back away from the warmth of that friendly blaze? From his kindness, constancy and faithfulness? Turn away from the smile in his beautiful gray eyes, or the way the proud gryphon seemed self-conscious whenever she praised or petted him? Stop flying?

Let go of this adorable, dangerous man?

Not on your life, she thought. Never again in his life, or in hers.

She went nose-to-nose with him. "That goes for you too," she whispered. "Would you back away?"

"Never." His response was immediate and adamant, and his gaze was as steady as bedrock. "Not unless you needed me to."

Pressing her lips tightly together, she nodded, for a moment too overcome to speak. The whole conversation felt as necessary as breathing, yet it was also precipitous, immensely inconvenient.

Issues piled up in her head. Malphas, Ferion, and oh gods, if they both survived this coming confrontation, she was going to have to find some way to come to terms with that blasted dragon.

If they both survived.

Once her mind started thinking along that path, it couldn't stop.

If Graydon went too far mating and something happened to her, neither one of them would survive. The realization sank some serious teeth into her and shook her harder than anything else had.

She had to let him go for now. She had to, until this whole nightmare was over, because she couldn't do anything else. The thought of him mating with her, only to die if she did was unthinkable.

"We'll have time," she said. She hugged him again with all her strength. "Later—afterward. We'll *make* time to figure this out. We'll take all the time we need. We'll have all the time in the world."

He pressed his lips to her temple and told her, "Of course we will."

Of all the conversations they'd had, that was the only thing she had ever heard him say to her that sounded like a lie.

Her legs loosened from around his hips. As he let her slide to her feet, she frowned up at him.

What the hell?

Something felt . . . incredibly off. She didn't know what it could be. Everything was fraught with too much tension, driven by a lack of time and extremely limited privacy. Even though they had hardly begun to talk, they had to focus on other concerns.

If it was just a matter of pressing a pause button until they could talk at a later time, she could handle that. Her life had been filled with countless moments just like this one, where her personal concerns had to go on hold because of some other, more pressing matters.

What she didn't think she could handle was the thought that everything she wanted, everything she had begun to dream about and hope for, might vanish again like an illusion.

"We will," she insisted.

His expression hardened. "If I have anything to say about it, we will," he promised. "We just need to fight hard enough, cleverly enough. There is a way to win though."

Truth had come back into his voice. Relieved, she grabbed onto that thought and didn't let go.

"I couldn't have held on for so long if I didn't believe that," she said. She had to believe it. It was the only thing she had to hang on to.

He pressed his lips against her forehead. "Let's call the others back in. We have a war to plan."

She straightened her shoulders. Enough people in the group had such sensitive hearing that everything she and Graydon had said aloud to each other had been said virtually in public.

She wasn't embarrassed, and she certainly wasn't ashamed.

Still, as Graydon rapped his knuckles on the door of the suite and the others returned, she felt heat touch her cheeks.

It was hard to bare one's soul to someone else. She had also just bared her soul to ten other people. The sense of exposure was unsettling to say the least.

Most avoided meeting her gaze, except for Constantine. He stared at her with the same mixture of curiosity and wistfulness that she had noticed before.

Her self-consciousness vaporized as Soren entered the room. He studied both her and Graydon with a piercing frown.

Soren said, "I have heard everything that the others had to say. Now I want to hear it from you."

Biting her lip, she stared at the floor. Graydon said carefully, "If you've heard everything, you know there's only so much we can say."

"Not true," replied Soren. "I can remove any connection you may have with another Djinn."

Astonishment and hope flared. Her gaze flashed up and collided with Graydon's.

She asked, "Can you do it without alerting the other Djinn?"

"I believe so. If you will allow me to do so, that is." Soren raised his eyebrows pointedly at Graydon. "May I approach?"

# ≈ SIXTEEN ≈

The surge of relief Graydon felt at Soren's words was painful in the extreme.

Imperceptible though his connection to Malphas was, it had become unbearable, as heavy as the shackle Ferion had said he carried.

Starting to nod, he forced himself to pause and consider every angle. He said tensely, "What if you try and fail?"

Bel twisted her hands together, her expression mirroring his feelings. They had come too far, and had gone too long, to screw this up now.

Soren's brusque manner softened as he regarded Bel. He told them, "I will not fail. If I cannot remove the connection from you without alerting the other Djinn, I will not do it. But I am one of the oldest and strongest of my kind. I am also one of the most adept. I have removed connections before that have been deemed invalid, when I've acted as either a member of the Djinn assembly or as head of the Elder tribunal."

"Yes," Bel said suddenly. "I believe you. Please, do it."

Soren inclined his head. He glanced at Graydon, and instead of approaching Bel, he held out his hand.

She strode over to him, slipping her fingers in his. Graydon tensed. He *hated* how close the other male was to her, and he fought the urge to knock them apart. Violent thoughts flashed through his mind, and his body knotted, muscles leaping with tension.

Vaguely he was aware that the other Wyr, Luis, Rune and Constantine, were all watching him closely. He knotted his hands into fists in an effort to maintain control.

Bel and Soren stood looking into each other's eyes. Something happened, some tiny shift, that was too subtle for Graydon to fully assess.

Soren said quietly, "It's gone."

"You're sure?" Graydon demanded.

Soren gave him a wary glance. "Yes, I'm quite sure."

Bel's composure splintered, painfully and completely.

Her face twisted. Bending over at the waist, she cried out, "We've got to stop Malphas! We have to kill him! He trapped and enslaved my son. Oh gods, he's enslaved him for two hundred years. *I need him dead!*"

Her raw, anguished fury rocketed around the room. In response, Grace's eyes filled, and Claudia and Luis flinched. Carling angled her face away, while Constantine and Julian stared at Bel, their eyes burning.

Soren turned to him. "Come, gryphon. Take your freedom."

Graydon had to fight an almost overwhelming urge to step forward. The need to be free came close to eclipsing everything else. He shook his head and said harshly, "No."

"Dude," said Constantine.

Bel straightened to stare at him. "No?"

"We need to get Malphas onto a battlefield," Graydon told her. "That means I need to be able to summon him. Then we have to hit him as hard and as fast as we can, so he can't get away."

"He's right," Khalil said. "Setting a trap will give you the highest probability of success. If Malphas goes on the run, waging war against him will be drawn out, miserable, and twice as dangerous. That's what happened when we fought and killed Lethe." When Khalil and Carling looked at each other, a shadow fell over both their faces. He finished quietly, "The damage from that war was very great."

"I can help with that," said Julian.

Graydon's eyes narrowed. "How?"

"As Vampyres age, our attributes get stronger, just like any of the other Elder Races." After returning to the suite Julian hadn't bothered to sit again. He stood, arms crossed, with Melly at his side.

"Exactly what does that mean for you?" Soren asked. "What attribute do you bring to this confrontation?"

"I can hold onto my prey," Julian told them. "If I can get my hands on Malphas, he won't be going anywhere. Not unless he either frees himself, or I'm dead."

Beside Julian, Melly's face turned bone white. She whispered, "That's ridiculously suicidal."

"I figure it'll get intense." Julian jerked his head in a short acknowledgment. "Which means everybody else is going to have to kill him quick."

Julian and Melly's dialogue faded into silence, as they had an obviously tense and quick telepathic exchange. Melly gestured, her movements jerky and uncontrolled, and Julian hauled her into a tight hug.

Rune's attention had remained fixed on Graydon. He said, "You might summon Malphas, but that doesn't necessarily mean he'll show up."

He acknowledged that with a nod. "I've thought of that too. I haven't called on Malphas in two hundred years. He'll come. He'll be too curious not to. The most critical thing we'll need to do is make sure our attacking forces are cloaked so completely, Malphas doesn't sense them. He'll need to believe I'm alone."

Bel came to his side. She touched his arm, watching his face. "Do you think you can get him to stay long enough to solidify, so that Julian can get hold of him?"

"I think so," he told her. "Especially since I'm going to offer him the one thing he can't resist."

"Not another bargain, I hope," Constantine said.

"Oh, no."

"What do you have in mind?" Rune asked, narrow-eyed.

The predator in Graydon came to the forefront. The savagery of his anticipation for the upcoming confrontation filled him completely.

Until they finished this, Malphas could still discover what had happened. He could still torture or control Ferion, and if the Djinn saw that his connection to Bel had been removed, she would be in even more danger than before.

Finally, finally, the waiting, the calculation, and planning were over.

They had to end this quickly, before they lost the element of surprise.

He bared his teeth in a hard smile. "I'm going to offer Malphas a wager. Who's in?"

"Me," said Julian. Beside him, Melly's eyes filled, but she folded her lips tight and didn't object.

Rune and Carling glanced at each other and nodded. Rune said, "We're both in."

"Fuck, yeah," said Constantine. "I wouldn't miss this for the world."

"And I," said Soren heavily. "I'll also ensure we have Peacekeeper troops. They can maintain a perimeter, provide a backup assault, and help with—the aftermath."

Soren meant they could help with the wounded and casualties. The room fell silent, as everyone absorbed his true message.

Claudia said, "Much as I hate to say it, Luis and I are outclassed and outgunned for the main fight, but we're very willing to help with any backup you might need."

"I'm afraid I can't offer anything further, either," Grace told them. "None of my skill set is suitable for this battle, and as Khalil has already said, I'm the guardian of two small children. I can't put myself in danger. I'm out."

"I can offer help," Khalil said unexpectedly. As the others turned to stare at him in surprise, he added, "I won't go into battle. That much is still true, but I can provide quick transportation if needed."

Melly said between her teeth, "Goddammit."

In a gentle voice, Julian told her, "You're out."

"I know." Tears glittered in her eyes. "I *know*. Goddammit!"

The only one in the room who hadn't spoken yet was Bel. Turning to her, Graydon saw that she was composed and calm again. A wave of tenderness washed over him. She didn't have the skill set to fight a Djinn either.

When she spoke, she didn't do as he expected and acknowledge that she was not suited for the upcoming battle.

Instead, she said, "Unquestionably, the fight with Malphas is going to be the most dangerous part of this whole venture. But there's still another war to be fought, and that's keeping Ferion alive and protected. As we don't have any idea if Malphas has spies in the Elven household, or how many, that's my battleground."

He flexed his hands, fiercely willing himself to not shapeshift. By sheer force of will, he kept his rigid expression from transforming and his talons from emerging.

He had gotten too focused on his hunt and had stopped thinking about anything else. A sneaky part of him had been too relieved that Bel wasn't suited to a fight with Malphas, and he'd stopped considering anything further.

She would still be in danger, and he couldn't be with her, or protect her.

As Melly had said, goddammit.

*Goddammit.*

While he struggled to maintain control, everyone seemed to speak at once as they laid plans. After the most brutally long, difficult wait of his life, events hurtled forward, faster than he could control.

The team that would attack Malphas needed a site where they could lay the trap. Rune and Constantine drew close to Graydon while they batted ideas back and forth. Their conversation snagged his attention. Focusing, he joined in.

On the one hand, it felt good to plot strategy with the other two gryphons. It felt right in a way that had everything to do with the centuries they had worked together in countless similar situations.

On the other hand, Graydon's muscles jumped underneath his skin. He couldn't stop staring at Bel as she was surrounded by the others, immersed in her own strategy meeting.

Once or twice, she looked toward him too. When their eyes met, it was with a shock of connection that knocked everything and everyone else aside.

He had to force himself to turn away and concentrate on the task at hand.

"Finding the right kind of venue is going to be tough," Rune said, rubbing his jaw.

"It's got to be in New York," Graydon said. "Otherwise, with the masque so close, I don't think Malphas will buy it."

Constantine frowned, crossing his arms. "But it's got to be away from other people. There has to be room for the fight, and no room for collateral damage."

Rune released a frustrated sigh. "I agree, but that's a very narrow set of requirements. If you want an abandoned warehouse area, there are a few places in Queens or in Brooklyn along the East River that might work."

"No," Graydon said. "That feels too risky."

"What about the FDR Four Freedom memorial?" Constantine asked. "It's on the tip of Roosevelt Island, and it closes overnight."

"That's a possibility," Graydon said slowly.

But he didn't like it, and he could see the same dissatisfaction on the other two men's faces. Not only did the memorial close at night, but it was also winter—yet those factors only lessened the risk of possible harm to others. They didn't negate it.

None of them really knew what kind of area the battle would cover. So much of that would hinge on whether or not Julian could maintain his hold and truly keep the Djinn grounded.

Constantine said, without much conviction, "Governors Island. Again, it's closed to the public at night."

Rubbing his neck, Graydon shook his head. "I don't know, man. I don't like it."

Rune snapped his fingers. "I've got it. Hart Island."

Graydon blew out a slow breath, as he thought about it.

Hart Island was at the western end of the Long Island Sound. He could reach the island quickly and easily by air, so it was close enough to allay any suspicion.

Roughly a mile long, and a quarter of a mile across, Hart Island was also inaccessible to the public. Over a decidedly dark history, it had been a quarantine, an insane asylum, a workhouse for boys, a missile base, a Civil War prison camp, and a potter's field—and now the island was the largest tax-funded cemetery in the world.

Aside from prison burial crews and a ferry that landed at a memorial gazebo once a month, the island lay abandoned, haunted by a dark past and the dead.

It was also warded by prison guards detailing burial crews by day, and with copious *restricted area* and *no trespassing* signs. There were crumbling buildings, along with an uneven landscape along the shore, which would offer plenty of places for Peacekeeper troops to hide as they lay in wait.

Tactically, the island was perfect.

"Yes," he said. Constantine nodded.

"One last thing, which is no longer my call to make," said Rune. He watched the two sentinels' faces closely. "Do we tell Dragos?"

Graydon met Constantine's blue eyes. "You know my feeling about it, but I'm also aware that I'm too close to this issue to be objective."

"I agree with your earlier decision," Con said to him. "Some of us have had more than enough challenges to face over the last eighteen months. If we tell Dragos, he'll be tempted to get involved, and this doesn't have to be his fight. We have a strong enough force as it is. We move ahead on our own."

Rune said, "Your call, guys."

Constantine lifted one broad shoulder. "Hey, it's why he's got sentinels in the first place. Otherwise, we'd be, I dunno, secretaries, or some dumb shit like that."

For the first time in what felt like a long time, Graydon burst out laughing. "Indeed, my man," he said. "We'd be some dumb shit like that."

Rune clapped Graydon on the shoulder. "I'm going to

check in with Carling and see what the other group has decided."

When he left them, Constantine moved closer to Graydon. The two men watched as Rune maneuvered around furniture and people to reach Carling's side. He touched her shoulder, and Carling's face softened as she looked up at him. Rune leaned over to kiss her temple.

Telepathically, Constantine asked, *Do you think he regrets it at all? I mean, leaving his position as First.*

*Maybe, sure,* Graydon said. *Sometimes. In certain moods. Regret's kinda the underbelly of all those "what if" questions we ask ourselves late at night. He didn't stop caring about any of us just because he mated with Carling. Yet, I don't think he ever regretted mating with her. They both enjoy the work they do through their agency. It's challenging and rewarding, and I believe he's happy. Really happy.*

*I wonder what it feels like,* said Con. *To have someone become your whole world, and to have them rely on you. Must be a hell of a thing.*

It felt painful. Necessary.

Hovering on the edge of mating as he was, he couldn't think of any other words to describe it.

Constantine's gaze cut sideways to him. *Would you ever think about leaving your position for a woman?*

The other man's question wasn't an idle one, he knew. Not after what everybody had witnessed happen earlier. He looked at Bel again. She was hugging Grace. As she let go, Khalil swept Grace away in a swirl of Power, no doubt taking her back home to her niece and nephew in Florida.

*I made a promise,* Graydon said. *Not when we became sentinels. I mean recently. And I intend to do everything in my power to keep it.*

Somehow, he would. Never mind that at the moment conflicting needs threatened to tear him into pieces. He would hold the course. All he had to do was figure out how.

*She's your chance, man.* Con gave him a sidelong smile. *You've got to take it.*

Determination hardened his resolve. *We'll see what we have together—after.*

He had calmed enough from the frenzy that had touched him earlier to remember the many tensions and challenges that lay between him and Bel. It was impossible to grapple with any of them properly, to move forward or settle emotionally, until Malphas was dead.

The Djinn may not have killed him yet, but he still had brought Graydon's life to a stop.

One way or another, that ended tonight.

Pivoting, he took stock of everybody, assessing the mood in the room.

Tension pulled the air tight, vibrating like the string on a bow before an arrow is unleashed. People talked faster, fueled by adrenaline, their voices crisp as they laid their plans.

While the three gryphons had talked, Bel must have called Linwe, because at some point the younger Elf had arrived at the suite. Soren had also fetched another Councillor from the Elder tribunal, a tall Elven woman named Sidhiel Raina. Both the newcomers looked shocked and sober, so the others must have filled them in on the news.

Khalil returned as well, and both Djinn left to organize and transport troops of Peacekeepers to Hart Island. And somehow—Graydon hadn't tracked how, exactly—Julian had acquired a rare Elven suit of armor.

He emerged from one of the bedrooms after donning it, carrying a helmet under one arm. The suit molded the contours of his powerful body, the subtle matte of its surface providing a natural camouflage as it reflected the colors of the room. While the camouflage would be effective in any number of scenarios, especially from a distance, this time it wouldn't be adequate to hide him from the Djinn. Once Julian and Graydon had decided their final positions, Carling would have to cast her strongest cloaking spell in order to hide him.

Finally, Graydon couldn't stand it any longer. He strode over to Bel, where she stood in a tight huddle with Sidhiel,

Linwe, Melly, Luis and Claudia. As he approached, she turned to face him. She had been watching him too.

The others retreated. Sidhiel and Linwe lingered the longest, until Luis and Claudia took their arms and pulled them away. Surprise and objection flashed across the Elven women's faces, but they acquiesced to the others' urging.

As Melly left, she said quietly to Bel, "We're ready to go when you are. We'll wait for you outside."

"Thank you," Bel told her.

The door to the suite closed quietly behind the Light Fae princess.

Graydon lifted his eyebrows. "Melly's going with you?"

Bel nodded jerkily, flattening her hands on his chest as he drew her close. Absently, she stroked her palms across his pectorals as she replied, "She said it would be too unbearable to watch and wait while Julian goes into battle." Her dark gaze lifted to his. "I understand how she feels."

Bowing his head, he rested his forehead against hers. "As do I. I hate that you have to confront Ferion without me."

"We don't have a choice," she whispered as she clenched her fingers on his biceps. "Everything has to happen simultaneously. Soren can't try to remove the soul lien until Julian has Malphas trapped, otherwise we'll run the danger of tipping Malphas off. And we have no idea what's going to happen when Soren does remove it, or what kind of attention we may draw from the rest of the household."

He gritted his teeth. "If only there was any other way to do this. Tell me Linwe is going to guard you."

She nodded again. "And Sidhiel. Between Sidhiel and I, we should represent enough authority to try to win some kind of control over the situation, if—if Ferion can't."

Ferion could die when the soul lien was removed. He could be dangerously unstable. Graydon's face tightened as his mind raced through various catastrophic scenarios.

"Letting you go is the hardest thing I've ever done," he gritted.

Just as it had been the last time. As it had been every time.

She threw her arms around his neck. "Absolutely do not worry about me," she told him in a strong, steady voice. "Don't give it a foothold in your thoughts. Not only will Sidhiel and Linwe be accompanying me, but also, Luis, Claudia and Melly will be going too. And Soren, at least until he frees Ferion. It's a good, strong group. We'll be all right."

He needed to believe that. Tightening his arms around her, he concentrated fiercely on the sensation of her long, slender body against his.

She murmured, "You're the one I'm worried about. Gods, Graydon. The risk you're taking. I feel sick thinking about it."

As dark as a raven's wing, the vision brushed along the edge of his mind. White, black and red like heart's blood.

It was so close now, he could almost touch it.

"Don't think about it," he murmured. He passed his hand over her silken hair. "Instead, think about this."

Even as her pretty, plump lips began to form a question, he covered her mouth with his.

For one moment, everything else fell away. He surrendered his soul to it and kissed her with all the passion he had, eating at her plump, soft mouth like it was a banquet he had never eaten before, and would never have again.

Underneath his lips, her mouth came alive, and she kissed him back with such transparent, desperate longing, it tore at him inside.

Cupping her face, he whispered against her lips, "There's nothing else but this. Nothing else but us."

Her mouth trembled. "I—I don't know how I can bear it if . . ."

He kissed her again, hard. "Stop, don't think of it. Be here, right now. We have all the time in the world. We've lived together for years. Picture it . . . Look at how happy we are."

Her eyes flew open. As she stared at him, two tears spilled out of the corners of her eyes and flowed over his fingers. She tried to smile. "We've lived together?"

He nodded, pressing his lips to her forehead. "We've had children. What a handful they've been, growing up, but we've loved every minute of it. And we did buy that house, outside the city. We go there every chance we can."

"The one with the big, private yard," she breathed. Her fingers curled around his wrists, thumbs working over his skin.

Hungry for her mouth again, he kissed her over and over. "We have the most beautiful garden," he told her. "It's a bit wild and secretive, but we like that very much."

A ghost of a laugh came out of her, the tiniest shiver of air against his lips. "I have a vegetable garden in the sunniest part of the yard. You go hunting, and bring home wild game."

"And our friends come to visit." He smiled against her mouth, thinking of it. "We are always happy to see them and yet glad when they leave, so we can have the place to ourselves again."

"It's so beautiful," she breathed. "You're right, I am happy. I'm more happy than I ever dreamed possible."

All the immense number of hours he had experienced throughout countless days, and they counted as nothing against the richness of the life he lived in that one moment.

When the suite door opened, the beast inside him wanted to rage at the interruption. He let the impulse die. There would be plenty of fighting, soon enough.

Constantine said quietly, "Gray, it's time. Everything is set up. We've got to go."

Just like that, with a few quiet words, their happy, rich life together that was built in a single moment faded.

Their eyes met. The brightness that had begun to touch Bel's face darkened.

Dropping his hands, Graydon stepped back.

Leaving her. He was always leaving her.

Turning away was like taking a knife to the gut. Somehow, he managed to speak around the pain. "On my way."

# ═ SEVENTEEN ═

The three gryphons flew to Hart Island together. Rune carried Carling, while Julian rode on Graydon's back.

Aside from Soren, who would join them as fast as he could, they were all the principals who would be spearheading the attack.

Graydon wished they had more Djinn support, but the Djinn made decisions based on consensus. If Soren took this issue to the Djinn assembly, they would talk the subject to death, and he knew somehow word would get back to Malphas. They couldn't afford to risk losing the element of surprise, and they didn't have the time.

The night air felt wet and heavy, like another snowstorm was imminent. Lowering clouds filled the sullen sky. There wasn't a star in sight, only an indirect illumination cast by the hidden moon.

Julian asked, "What kind of wager are you going to offer Malphas?"

*I don't know.* He hadn't had a chance to think that far ahead. *All I know is he won't be able to resist a gamble.*

The Vampyre laughed. "Cutting it a little close to the

bone, aren't you? Well, something had better occur to you quick."

*Don't worry,* he said. *I've got this. Just be ready to grab him when he solidifies, and we'll be good to go.*

As they flew in low to the approach to Hart Island, Julian directed them to the appropriate section of shoreline. "There's thirty Peacekeeper troops hidden in those nearby buildings, mostly war mages and medics. Soren and Khalil brought them in, so there aren't any scents or foot tracks in the outlying areas. For the last half hour, they've been layering deflection spells over the group, along with cloaking spells."

A disembodied, familiar Djinn presence rose up to meet them. It was Khalil. The Djinn informed them, "They're hidden well enough. If I can sense nothing, neither will Malphas."

Graydon's skin began to prickle as he studied the narrow, uneven beach. Nearby, a tall, crumbling chimney stack jutted into the sky.

As he circled the area, the view aligned, until he could look up at the length of the chimney stack as it towered over the land like a behemoth.

Constantine and Rune circled with him, the three gryphons wheeling like gigantic birds of prey.

Julian slapped his shoulder, splintering his preoccupation. "Where do you want me?"

*You don't need to breathe,* he said. *And the cold won't bother you. The best place for you to hide is under water, at the shoreline. The water will cover your scent.*

"Agreed," said Julian. "The water it is."

"We can't land here," Carling shouted to them, "or we'll leave too many footprints in the snow. We need to take cover in the nearby buildings. When Julian makes his move, we'll be out here as fast as we can. Julian, make your drop. I'll cover you with cloaking spells."

*On my count,* said Graydon. He swung around, descended further and spread his wings so that he coasted over the water as he approached the shore. *One, two—drop.*

Rolling off his back, Julian hit the water with a splash. A moment later, Graydon's paws touched down on the cold, rocky ground. He barely noticed when Rune dove, spun and dove again, while Carling layered cloaking spells over the area where Julian had disappeared.

Shapeshifting, Graydon stared around him.

Overhead, the clouds broke apart. As the moonlight grew sharper, he saw white snow covering black rocks on the beach. Whorls of ice banded the rocks where the uneasy ocean rocked and lapped.

White, and black, near a dark, tempestuous shore.

He had never been to this place before, and yet he recognized every detail of it.

*See you soon, buddy,* Constantine said in his head.

The two other gryphons, along with Carling, winged toward the buildings and disappeared.

Khalil said, "This is where I leave you. Good hunting."

The Djinn's presence arced away.

Graydon's heart began a slow, hard pounding, like the deep clanging of a bell. He breathed deeply and evenly to manage the dump of adrenaline plunging through his veins.

Telepathically, he reached out to Julian. *You close enough to hear me?*

*Yes,* said the Vampyre. *I'm a few yards away, just beyond the ice.*

*Okay,* he said.

Okay.

Balancing on slippery, broken rocks, he moved away from the shoreline until he reached the end of the narrow beach, where he turned, putting the chimney stack behind him and facing the ocean.

All his planning fell away. All the talk, the preparations. He had lived the very best of his life in a single moment. The only thing that remained was the sound of his breath as he released it. It vaporized into the endless winter's night.

Injecting Power into his voice, he called out, "Malphas."

The pariah took his time answering the summons.

As Graydon sensed Malphas's leisurely approach, he

realized that for all of their caution and extreme effort in laying the trap, the Djinn wasn't acting like he was suspicious.

He was acting contemptuous.

Angling his jaw out, Graydon crossed his arms as he waited.

The Djinn poured onto the scene without materializing. Like an oil slick, his presence smeared the fresh night air.

"I get no Christmas cards, you don't write." Malphas circled around Graydon. "Now, after all this time, you decide to pick up the phone. One wonders why one even bothers to respond."

Hatred clogged his throat. Curling his lip, he growled, "And yet, I see one does."

"Curiosity does sometimes get the better of me." Like a devil riding his shoulder, Malphas sighed in Graydon's ear. "And oh look at what a dismal setting. You couldn't even invite me to a nice restaurant."

The Djinn was toying with him, like a cat with a mouse.

He refused to flinch, and said between his teeth, "I would rather be caught dead than be seen in public with you."

Truth.

If he stuck to the truth, he couldn't go too far wrong.

Malphas laughed. "My feelings, they are wounded. If I had a heart, it would be broken. What do you want, gryphon?"

"I want to change our agreement."

Come on, asshole. Show your face.

"No, I don't think I want to do that. I'm perfectly content with our bargain as it is." As leisurely as he had arrived, the Djinn's presence began to fade.

Graydon raised his voice, and injected a note of scorn. "Coward. Don't you even want to hear the terms of the wager I want to propose?"

Malphas paused, just as Graydon had felt sure he would. Pouring back, the Djinn said, "*You* want to propose a wager to *me*? You surprise me, gryphon. You're not a gambling man."

He snapped, "I am when I've got nothing left to lose."

Again, truth. He would gamble everything to get a chance at another moment with Bel.

The frigid air around him boiled as Malphas snapped back, like a shark gnashing invisible teeth. "You have no idea what you're talking about. Because believe me, sentinel, you have got a great deal you could lose. Friends. Coworkers. Even a fledgling dragon."

He did not just go there. Renewed rage set Graydon's body on fire.

*Come on, you bastard. Materialize.*

"If you don't want to hear my wager, fine," he whispered. "Fuck off. I'll find some other way to be rid of you."

"And risk the so lovely Beluviel, and her son?" Contemptuous shining eyes appeared in front of Graydon. "You won't get rid of me unless I say you can."

"A wager," said Graydon. His talons had emerged, and he could feel that his teeth had lengthened. He hid his fists underneath his crossed arms. "All or nothing. Or maybe you don't have the balls." He barked out an angry laugh. "Listen to me, what am I saying? Of course you don't have the balls. Not really."

Malphas slammed into his physical form in front of Graydon, wearing, as he always did, the same golden hair and angelically handsome face.

And as he faced Graydon, he set his back to the ocean.

The Djinn told him, "You don't have the damned guts for an all-or-nothing wager."

*Julian,* Graydon said. Aloud, he spat, *"Try me.* I'm sick to death of this arbitrary barrier you shoved between me and Beluviel. Do you hear me—I am fucking done."

"You don't get to say when you're done," Malphas enunciated, stabbing at the air with one finger. *"I own you."*

Behind the furious Djinn, a dark, powerful figure rose out of the water and slipped over the edge of the ice. It crawled toward them, its helmeted head featureless in the moonlight, at once silent and so predatory that, even though he knew it was really a friend, Graydon's hackles rose.

He growled, "You'll never own me, Djinn."

"I own the piece of you that you want the most," Malphas sneered. "The chance to be with Beluviel again. How have the last two hundred years been for you—watching her at public functions, talking to her, never being able to copulate again without killing the one person she loves the most?"

"You are the most vindictive asshole I have ever met," Graydon told him. "And I'm done arguing with you. Do you want to gamble for a bigger piece of me or not?"

"Oh, I will love putting a bigger noose around your thug neck." Malphas gestured angrily.

Crouched on the ground behind his knees, Julian snaked both bare hands around one of the Djinn's ankles and said, *Got him.*

Astonishment bolted across Malphas's face. The Djinn's Power rippled, but his physical form didn't dissipate. He tugged at his leg, but he couldn't dislodge the shackle on his ankle.

Son of a bitch. Part of Graydon had been too skeptical to believe it could happen, but the Vampyre had done it. He had really trapped Malphas.

Everything exploded.

As Malphas whirled to kick at Julian, Graydon leaped on the Djinn, fangs and talons out. While he tore at the Djinn's physical form, he used his Power like a battering ram, bludgeoning Malphas with raw brute force.

It was an inelegant attack, but it was all Graydon had to use against him.

As fast as he tore wounds into Malphas, they closed again. Abandoning his kick, Malphas rounded on him with an inhuman snarl and bludgeoned him back, with a round-house punch fueled and magnified by his own Power.

If the blow had connected, it would have crushed Graydon's face. At the last moment, he jerked to one side, and the blow caught him along the side of his head.

Pain exploded in his skull, and his ear rang. Savagely, he sank his teeth into the side of the Djinn's neck and tore away a chunk of flesh. It melted to nothing as he spat it out, the gaping wound at Malphas's neck healing over.

Vaguely, he was aware of Malphas kicking at the dark, armored figure at his feet.

Then Constantine fell on them from the sky, the weight

of his body slamming them both to the ground. With a harsh eagle's cry, Rune joined them, driving his lethal gryphon's beak into the Djinn's body. Constantine shouted something, but Graydon couldn't make out what. The ringing in his ear was too loud.

Power gathered nearby, a great deal of it. Carling crouched a few yards away, hands up as she whispered an incantation. Graydon caught a glimpse of her face. She looked tense and afraid.

He had just enough time to think, well, shit. This is going to get a whole lot worse.

Malphas howled in rage. The Djinn's body heaved, and erupted.

Julian might have him trapped and embodied, but he never had been human. Like the illusion that it was, his human form melted. His body grew larger, and tentacles with spikes exploded from his center.

Many tentacles, with needle-sharp spikes. Julian flung his legs around one tentacle, keeping a death grip on it. He was a big, heavy man, and he carried an extra forty to fifty pounds in armor, but despite his weight, the tentacle lifted him into the air and slammed him into the rocky ground with a crash that Graydon felt at the back of his teeth.

Rune shouted, "Watch out!"

Constantine curled and twisted at the same time, narrowly escaping the tentacle that drove toward him. He slammed his booted foot repeatedly at the tentacle, until it appeared to snap.

It reformed, flowing back into the monster's body.

They had pissed Malphas off, but they weren't killing him. Graydon wasn't even sure they were hurting him. Djinn were creatures of Power and spirit, not flesh.

"When you tear off pieces of his body, throw them toward me," Carling shouted. "Otherwise, he'll just keep re-forming!"

Throw pieces of the Djinn at the witch. Got it.

With a roar, he tore into Malphas's new monster body, ripped away a tentacle and tossed it at Carling. She flung out one hand, fingers splayed. Power shot out from her palm like a fireball and obliterated the tentacle before it could melt and flow back into the Djinn's body.

*That* hurt him.

Malphas's howling raised in tone, until it sounded like the whistle of a gigantic teakettle. The sound split the air, driving like a spike into Graydon's good ear.

As the sound increased, the monster's body began to heat, until a light poured out that was so bright, Graydon had to squint to endure it. The heat increased until the Djinn felt like a burning flame.

All the while, his immense body boiled and convulsed. The three gryphons tore pieces off the monster, flinging them at Carling. Most of the time, she struck them with a ball of Power, but sometimes she missed, and they flowed back into the Djinn.

Tentacles flailed, driving spikes toward each of the men. One tentacle snaked around Graydon's waist before he could deflect it, lifting him bodily to slam him repeatedly into the rocks. He felt ribs snap and coughed in breathless anguish.

The heat turned unbearable. He felt his skin sear where he came in contact with the Djinn.

Someone shouted. Not the teakettle. One of them.

Julian was bellowing in agony.

How long could the Vampyre bear to hold on?

If he lost his hold, they lost Malphas. He couldn't get away. He couldn't.

The battle hadn't lasted for very long, but it felt like it had been going on forever. With renewed frenzy, Graydon tore at the monster, gouging huge chunks out of his flesh.

The monster heaved, flipping over completely, knocking them all to shit. At the same time it speared Rune high in one thigh. As Rune roared, it flung him with such vicious force so that Rune slammed into a waist-high boulder half submerged in water. His head snapped back, and he slid into the icy water.

Screaming, Carling lunged after him.

Graydon had just torn a tentacle from the monster's body.

The physical shape flowed away from his grasp, back into Malphas's body.

At the same moment, Peacekeeper war mages raced onto the scene while medics jumped into the water to help Carling pull an unconscious Rune to shore.

"Over here!" one of the Peacekeepers shouted, his hands up and beckoning.

Graydon twisted at the waist. His broken ribs ground together: more agony. This nightmarish bastard had to die. Growling, he tore off another tentacle with his teeth and flung it over his shoulder at the Peacekeeper.

Constantine shouted. Even though the other sentinel strained against the monster, so close the two men could have touched, he fought on the side of Graydon's deafened ear. His shout sounded like it came from a great distance.

The world was in motion. Everything happened so fast.

Hard hands clamped onto his shoulders as the other sentinel grabbed him and twisted. Despite the fact that Graydon was the bigger and heavier of the two, Constantine bodily yanked him off his feet, thrusting himself between Graydon and the monster.

Con's mouth was open, forming words. Graydon saw the other man's lips shape: *"LOOK OU—"*

A spike burst out of Constantine's chest, in a starburst of blood. A massive tentacle drove the spike through the other man's body so hard, it knocked Constantine into Graydon and pierced through Graydon's chest wall, biting deep.

Impaled together, the two men's eyes met, horrified dark gray looking into a blue gaze that turned rather wry. Blood poured out of Constantine's mouth. He lifted a hand to his lips, as if to stop the flood.

Then the tentacle shook them off, flinging them both to the ground. Knocked end over end, the rocky ground tore at Graydon's body until he rolled to a stop. His rib cage was shattered to hell. He tried to suck in a breath, fought to get up on his hands and knees.

Shaking uncontrollably, he finally got one knee underneath

him and looked down at the ground. All around him, people were shouting. Chaos surged along the beach.

None of it touched the immense, bottomless silence inside him.

He saw white on black rock. As he pressed a hand to the wound in his chest, his blood mingled with the red of his friend's heart's blood.

It dripped between his fingers, spreading in the snow like the bloom of roses.

Some things in life are axiomatic.

There really is no good way to rip off a bandage. And there was no unobtrusive way to invade the Elven residence in New York City. Even the stealthiest entrance would set off every alarm in the large, tightly guarded house, so they had to be prepared for confusion and violence until they got the situation under control.

Bel and her group had to wait until the battle had started on Hart Island before they could act. They needed to know that Malphas was trapped before they moved on Ferion.

As they waited for word, they gathered again in the living room of the suite. Bel felt physically ill, and from the white, tense expression on Melly's face, the other woman felt the same.

Somehow, Julian would get hold of the Djinn, and somehow, the others would attack. Fueled by her runaway imagination, images played through her mind.

Soren held a cell phone in one hand. When it vibrated, she felt her stomach bottom out.

He glanced at the screen, his face grim. He said, "It has started."

Dread made her muscles tremble. That very moment, Graydon was fighting for his life. So was every one of the others who fought with him.

There were six people in Bel's group, not counting Soren. The more Powerful of the Djinn could transport up to ten or even fifteen people at a time. The one thing they required was that they touch the people they transported.

At his words, everyone gathered close, putting a hand on Soren's arm or shoulder. Bel also put an arm around Melly to give her a quick hug. Giving her a grateful look, the younger woman leaned against her slightly.

The tornado of Soren's Power rose, and swept them away from the hotel.

She closed her eyes, enduring the chaos. Intellectually, she knew what was happening. A friendly Djinn had explained it to her once.

Soren would experience the transport very differently than anyone else. While the others would lose their orientation in time and space, Soren could even slow down as he searched for the right spot before materializing.

He would look for Ferion, wherever Ferion might be. Only when he had found the Elf would he bring the group to the physical location, and even though it was the middle of the night, she realized Ferion could actually be anywhere.

If Ferion had sent the guard tailing Bel and Linwe, the guard might have reported back to him. Even now, he might be hunting for her, because she had been gone for an unusual amount of time.

The world began to reform around her. At first she became aware of the others in her group—Linwe, Sidhiel, Luis, Claudia and Melly. Then the details of their surroundings came into focus. They had landed in the large, richly appointed study in the New York Elven residence.

Bel got a split second—not even enough to draw in a complete breath—to take in the scene.

Ferion slumped in an armchair in front of a fire, a long, lean leg kicked over one arm. His eyes were closed, and he leaned his forehead against a brandy snifter that he held in one hand. He looked so tired and desolate, her heart twisted.

In the next instant, his expression flared and he leaped to his feet. Shouting, he flung his snifter into the flames as he lunged toward the sword that hung on the wall behind his desk.

He was one of the strongest fighters in the Elven demesne, lethally fast, but he was no match for the speed of a first-generation Djinn. Materializing beside Ferion, Soren grabbed him in a headlock.

Two Elven guards were always stationed in the main hall of the residence. They burst into the room, weapons drawn.

As Claudia and Luis strode to the double doors, Claudia punched the first guard. Power glimmered around her. The blow lifted him off the ground and slammed him into the second guard. Both men tumbled several yards, back into the hall.

Luis and Claudia threw themselves at the double doors and slammed them shut. While Claudia flipped the locks, Luis dragged heavy furniture over to block the doors. Shouting sounded in the hall. Heavy pounding boomed on the doors, echoing through the room like a thunderclap.

"What about the windows?" Luis asked.

"They're barred, and the curtains are drawn," Bel called out. "All the windows on the first floor are bullet and magic resistant."

While Claudia and Luis had acted so fast and decisively, Linwe, Sidhiel, Melly and Bel still stood frozen in the center of the room.

Sidhiel strode to the door. "Let me out of here," she ordered. "I'll talk to them."

"Not on your life," said Luis. "As wound up as they are, they'll kill you soon as look at you."

"Do you know who I am?" the Councillor demanded.

"Doesn't matter who you are," Claudia said breathlessly. "To them, right now anybody in this room is a traitor."

"They're right, Sidhiel." The authority in Bel's voice made the other Elven woman pause.

"A little help would be nice," Soren informed them.

Bel spun to look at the Djinn and her son. Ferion fought the hold Soren had on him with a mindless ferocity. It was clear Soren tried to hold onto the male without hurting him, but Ferion acted like a rabid animal.

His torso arched. He went into convulsions, foam flecking his lips.

Soren gritted, "The soul lien was booby-trapped."

Oh, shit, shit.

Bel leaped at them, as did the others. She shouted, "Get him down on the ground! Turn him on his side!"

Soren flipped Ferion in midair and laid him on the ground. Bel gripped Ferion's head. Linwe laid the weight of her torso over Ferion's legs, while Melly wrestled to get his flailing arms pinned. Luis ran at the heaving group, fell to his knees and slid across the floor to help Melly.

Strangled sounds came out of Ferion's twisted lips. Bel shouted, "He's choking on his tongue. Somebody get me a pen or something flat like a stick!"

Sidhiel dove at her, offering a dagger in a leather sheath. Bel ran a frantic gaze down the length of it. She recognized the workmanship. Ferion couldn't bite through the leather to the blade underneath. It would do.

She forced it between his lips. Extreme terror gripped her by the throat. When Ferion stopped breathing, so did she. She whispered on a strangled gasp, "Soren."

"Almost there," the Djinn said. He knelt beside her, both hands flat on Ferion's chest.

A blow hit the double doors so hard, the wood cracked from top to bottom. Claudia had been bracing against the furniture. She skipped back, calling out, "Another blow, maybe two, and they're going to be in."

Soren's Power flared hot and bright.

Bel could sense deep inside Ferion's body that hateful, darkened smear. With a *snap*, it disappeared.

The convulsions stopped. Ferion sucked in a huge, audible breath. His watering gaze flew to hers. She saw sanity in his gaze. The terror eased its grip on her throat. She wiped his face and pulled the dagger from between his teeth.

Another blow at the doors knocked a large hole in the splintered wood. "I don't want to shoot at these people," Claudia called out in warning.

"I have to go to Hart Island," Soren told Bel.

*"Wait!"* she cried out, as the Djinn began to dematerialize.

He paused. Conflicting urges tore at her. She swept the room with a glance. It had all happened so quickly. Claudia had fallen back to the group surrounding Ferion's prone body. In a moment or two, guards would pour into the room.

On the one hand, there was still so much to do here. If she were a betting fool, she would lay money on Malphas having spies in the household.

On the other hand, her heart and soul was on Hart Island, fighting to the death.

There was no real choice. Grabbing her son by his collar, she hauled him up to her face and demanded, "Are you good to go now?"

Still coughing and sucking in air, his eyes widened at the harsh command in her tone. He nodded.

"Then don't just lay there. You're the Elven High Lord." Wild-eyed, she flung out a hand and pointed at the door. *"Get on your feet and clean up this mess, mister!"*

"Yes, ma'am," he wheezed. He reached out, and Sidhiel, Linwe and Luis helped him to his feet.

Bel whirled to Soren. "Take me with you!"

Launching from a crouch, Melly flung herself at them, her pretty face desperate. "Take me too!"

Soren didn't waste time on any more words. He swept the two women together, and whirled them away.

# ═ EIGHTEEN ═

They left one chaotic scene behind, only to plunge into another.

For the first in many long years of travel, Bel experienced a rough landing from a Djinn transport. Soren all but flung the women at a narrow strip of rocky, icy beach. Melly grabbed for Bel, and both women staggered and fell. Landing with both hands splayed, Bel sliced one of her palms on jagged ice.

Too many details—too many sensations—pummeled her. Gasping, she pushed her hair off her face and struggled to make sense of what she saw. Beside her, Melly did the same.

Brutal cold and wind bit at her exposed skin. Peacekeeper troops poured over a hill, onto the beach. Something that looked like a giant, bizarre monster but felt like Malphas's Power, whirled and struck at nearby troops that flung spells at it.

She sought Graydon but didn't see him.

The monster's physical form dissipated into pure, incorporeal Power. Malphas had dematerialized, which meant Julian had fallen. Instead of arcing away with the normal speed of a Djinn, like a shooting star, Malphas lifted into the air with a ragged lurch.

Soren had solidified enough to drop Melly and Bel onto the ground. As Malphas began to retreat, Soren melted into pure Power and launched after him.

The two Djinn collided overhead. A concussion of Power burst out like a bomb blast, exploding nearby trees and knocking everybody to the ground. With a huge, yawning noise, a nearby chimney stack collapsed, throwing billows of snow and dust into the air.

A screaming whirlwind rose as the two Djinn fought. Hurricane force winds lifted a column of water out of the Long Island Sound.

Carling and other Peacekeepers struggled to haul a lax body out of the heaving, foaming water. Once again, Bel's stomach bottomed out. She caught sight of Rune trying to lift his head. He was alive.

Melly grabbed Bel's arm so hard, she left bruises. Her expression agonized, the younger woman shouted something, but Bel couldn't hear the words over the shriek of the noise.

Melly raced away, slipping and sliding over the treacherous ground. Bel followed the trajectory of her sprint. As her perspective shifted, she realized there was a figure prone on the ground. The figure wore Elven armor, which made it blend into its surroundings. Shaking convulsively, it held up blackened hands. Julian.

But where was Graydon? Bel stood on tiptoe, straining to find him.

A Peacekeeper raced past, yelling at her, "Get down! Get down!"

Ignoring him, she stumbled forward, driven by the need to find Graydon. Debris whistled through the air, shards of bricks and trees turning into deadly missiles as the Djinn's battle raged overhead.

Inside, hope had twisted into a despairing cry. If she didn't find Graydon alive, she would lie down right then and there, and die.

Then, as the swirl of running figures parted, she saw two men, sprawled together, covered in blood.

So much blood.

Two tawny heads, so different, and yet so alike. Pain exploded in her chest. Blind to everything else, indifferent to the gargantuan fight tearing apart the night sky, she lunged toward the men.

As she drew close, details struck at her.

Constantine lay on his back. His body was soaked with blood from neck to groin. Graydon crouched over him, cradling the other sentinel's head in his arms and shielding him from the deadly debris.

Bel fell to her knees beside them. In one horrified glance, she took in Constantine's handsome, still face, the rictus of agony that twisted Graydon's. Suddenly there weren't enough tears in the world.

"Oh, my darling," she said brokenly.

She gathered Graydon into her arms. He was too big. She couldn't hold all of him, but, with all the love in the world, she tried.

As soon as she put her hands on him, she sensed his struggle to breathe. It snapped her into knifelike focus. Running a sharp gaze over his hunched figure, she realized that not all of the blood was Constantine's.

She screamed, *"WE NEED A MEDIC HERE!"*

Overhead, another colossal concussion blew out with such force, it split the earth. Peacekeepers fell screaming into huge cracks.

She threw herself over Graydon and Constantine to shelter them both. As the concussion dissipated, she realized— one of the Djinn was gone. Staring skyward, she strained to find Malphas, but she couldn't sense him anywhere.

The overwhelming noise from the howling wind died. She could hear people shouting to each other.

Low, over the water, the ragged presence of a single Djinn drifted, like a ship foundering at sea. It carried a dull, faint thread of Soren's Power.

Across the beach, where medics were working on Rune, Carling stood. Her voice filled with such Power, the words rocketed down the beach. *"Khalil, bring Grace! Your father needs you!"*

Bel's heart pounded. Once. Twice.

It couldn't have been longer than a moment.

But so very much could be lived, and lost, in a single moment.

Even as the signature whirlwind of an approaching Djinn blew onto the beach, Soren's thin, ragged presence dissipated into the night with a final sigh.

A thick layer, like cotton wool, surrounded Graydon, disconnecting him from everything else, except Bel.

Shock. Or lack of air.

The broken bones in his chest shifted as he tried to draw in a breath. He thought maybe one of his lungs had collapsed.

She cupped his face, her beautiful eyes fierce and determined. Her lips formed the words, "Hold on, love. You're going to be okay."

I am, he thought. I'm holding on.

He clenched one hand on her wrist, held onto Constantine with the other.

His vision narrowed as pain tried to turn the world black, but he fought it off. As he snapped back to consciousness, she was lowering him flat on the ground.

Peacekeepers ran up. Someone tried to pry Constantine from his grip. He bared his teeth in a silent snarl, resisting, until Bel bent over him, her face filling his vision.

She told him gently, "They'll take good care of him. The very best care. Please, let them help."

His arms loosened, and they lifted Constantine away. Someone pulled an oxygen mask over his face, while another person cast a spell that took away the grinding pain.

He began to drift again.

"My lady, you need to move away and let us work on him," said one of the Peacekeepers.

That got his attention. Rousing, he growled. Talons sprang out on his hands, and his teeth lengthened. The medics' eyes bulged and they pulled back.

"I'm not leaving him," Bel said. "You're going to have to work around me." She bent over him again. "Graydon, do you understand? I'm not leaving you."

He relaxed, marginally, and nodded. He said in her head, *Never leave.*

*Never again,* she told him, stroking the hair back from his face. *I swear it. I'll stay right here with you every step of the way. Trust me.*

He did. He trusted her completely. His death grip on her wrist eased enough so that she could twist around and thread her fingers through his.

Blurry, disconnected images blew by, like snowflakes driven on a winter storm.

The dragon arrived, along with the other sentinels. They dropped raging out of the sky. After a quick shocked assessment, they threw themselves into helping, their faces stricken. A Djinn's presence raged along the beach, causing Graydon's fight instinct to rouse again until he realized it was Khalil, who also helped, his energy furious and chaotic.

Then somebody said, "One, two . . ."

Why were they counting?

The world shifted, as people lifted him onto a stretcher. He locked his fingers on Bel's. They would have to cut his hand off to separate them. Huddling that thought close, he drifted again.

Then several people wheeled him down a corridor. Dammit, he was in the hospital. Bel strode beside the stretcher, still holding his hand. When he realized she was still with him, he let his eyes close again.

Drifting.

Consciousness returned. Dr. Shaw came into his field of vision. The Wyr falcon's large, golden brown gaze met his steadily. "You're going into surgery," she told him. "Stay calm, Gray. You're going to be all right. Do you understand?"

His gaze cut over to Bel. She was still with him, just as

she had promised, the grip of her slender hand strong on his. She said reassuringly, "I'm going into surgery with you."

He nodded, squeezed her hand, and fell into true darkness.

After a long, formless time, he went into what seemed to be a waking dream. His eyes were closed, or very nearly so. At some point they had put him in another hospital room. Gods, he hated hospitals.

Again, he checked to make sure that Bel was with him, and she was. Still holding his hand, she sat by his hospital bed.

Dragos and Pia were also in the room. Pia's complexion was pale and blotchy, as if she'd been crying. Dragos's hard expression looked jagged enough to cut steel.

"You could take a quick break," Pia said gently. "Just to take a shower while he's still out. The staff would let you borrow a set of hospital scrubs. You could even use the shower here in this room."

"I'm not letting go." Bel sounded calm and decisive. "I made him a promise."

Comfort stole into the cold dark pit of his heart.

Dragos and Pia looked at each other. Pia said to him, "I know Kathryn said he would heal on his own, but I can't bear not helping. What he's been through was hard enough. And anyway, Bel already knows what I am."

Dragos remained silent, his mouth hard and tight. After a moment, he gave her a slight nod.

Pia came on the other side of his bed. Carefully, she lifted away the sheet that covered his bare, bandaged chest. She removed the gauze covering an incision, and then she did something else, he couldn't tell what, but she must have cut or pricked a finger somehow, because the tiny scent of new blood joined the stink of antiseptic.

Then a miracle filled his numb, exhausted body. It flowed, gentle and warm like sunshine, healing and soothing the torn and broken places in him. It felt loving and clean, new like a benediction, and transformative like forgiveness.

*Because I never want you to feel a moment's pain,* Pia

murmured in his head, as she tenderly tucked the edge of the sheet back across his chest.

Aw, cupcake.

For the first time in what seemed like forever, he took a deep, easy breath and sighed with relief.

After Pia had finished, she kissed his forehead.

"I know you didn't do it for me," Bel whispered. "You did it for him. But still, thank you so much."

Pia nodded and wiped her face. She said, "You're right, I didn't do it for you, but both you and he are welcome. And if I can't get you to take a break, at least you need to eat something. I'll get you a hot meal from the cafeteria, okay?"

"Thank you," Bel said softly.

"Do you have any preferences?"

"Soup, or really, anything will be fine."

"Okay, I'll be right back." Pia's quick signature footsteps tapped away.

Silence filled the room, as Pia took away her comfortable ease of manner. Dragos and Bel confronted each other over Graydon's prone figure.

Bel's fingers trembled. He wanted to move, to sit up to break the tension leaping between the other two, but he was so damn tired. The thick barrier of cotton wool wouldn't let him move.

The dragon growled, "You can't have him."

After a long moment, Bel said, "I already have him, and I'm not letting him go." A quiet thread of steel ran through her words. "He's mine now. But I will tell you this much, Beast. I love him too much to make him choose between the people he loves, and the commitments he feels the need to keep. You're going to have to live with the fact that I hold that power . . . and I will not wield it, because what I love most about him is his big, wonderful heart, and I'll do everything I can to protect it."

Even though they sounded like they were fighting, a different kind of warmth and healing stole into him. Squeezing her fingers, he fell deeply asleep.

• • •

The spike burst out of Bel's chest. Her dark gaze turned wry, before the light in them faded.

And there was red, dripping into the white snow. Blooming like roses.

With a muffled shout, he woke in a clench.

He was still in the hospital room. The remains of a dinner tray sat on a nearby table. Bel had climbed into the bed with him, curling against his side, with her head on his chest. She was sound asleep.

As he grabbed her, she woke with a start and rose up on one elbow. Her cheek was lined with creases. "What is it?"

"I dreamed you died," he said from the back of his throat.

Quick compassion flashed across her face. She kissed his neck, the line of his jaw, his mouth. "I'm right here, just as I promised I would be."

He said against her lips, "You're not going anywhere."

"No, never. I swear it."

He drank in her breath that carried the words of that promise, kissing her deeply. She stroked his hair, kissing him back.

When he could bear to say it, he whispered, "Constantine."

Her eyes filled with sadness. Wordlessly, she shook her head.

He had already known, but still, he had hoped against hope. He buried his face in her hair, feeling gut shot. She held him with her whole body.

After a moment, he asked, "Rune? Julian?"

"They're both going to make it. Rune—he took a bad wound to the thigh. It nicked the femoral artery, but when he fell into the icy water, it slowed the bleeding enough. Carling and the medics got to him right away." She ran her fingers along the line of his bare shoulder. "Julian's hands were badly burned. I don't know what his long-term prognosis is. But I know he's alive."

"What about Ferion?" He ran his hands down the long

graceful curve of her back, pressing her closer to wipe away the ugly memory of the dream.

"He's okay. He— For a few minutes, I was afraid he wasn't going to make it. I don't know much, yet, about what happened back at the Elven residence after I left except that I heard Ferion tracked down and killed a few of Malphas's spies. Malphas had fixed the soul lien so that it would kill him if anybody tried to remove the spell, but Soren was able to break it before Ferion choked to death. Soren's—" Through the palms of his hands, he felt her swallow hard. "He's gone too. Malphas was trying to run when Soren stopped him."

Two eternal souls, gone forever.

"I remember," he said in a low voice. He thought of the crashing Power overhead, and the destruction on Hart Island. "Gods, what a high cost. Did anybody else die?"

"No," she told him quickly, kissing him again. "Everybody else is okay."

He nodded, turned his face away and covered his eyes with one hand. Pain tore at him, along with sickened grief.

Silence fell in the room. Bel nuzzled his chin and stroked his hair, offering comfort. After several minutes, he whispered, "I feel like this is all my fault."

Her head had begun to drift down to his chest again. At those words, she straightened back up. "How can you say that? Why would you think this was all your fault?!"

After spending his whole life hiding his visions, it was remarkably hard to break the silence. He forced his way through it, saying through gritted teeth, "I'm—I guess you'd say I'm psychic. I see things before they're about to happen. Sometimes I can change things just enough, so that something else happens instead."

The alarmed concern in her eyes turned to fascination. "You have the second sight?"

He lifted one shoulder in a shrug. "Always have. I . . . saw what happened on the beach a long time ago." Unable to look at her, he averted his face. "Not everything. I never see everything clearly."

"I've had several conversations with previous Oracles over the years," she murmured. "Every one of them said that visions can be terribly difficult to interpret." She asked gently, "What did you see?"

"Blood, dripping from my chest wound. The white snow, the black rocks, the water—some kind of high building. Heart's blood. Hart Island, only I didn't know it was Hart Island until I got there. I'd never been to the place before, outside of my vision."

She laid cool fingers against his cheek. "When did you first see it?"

He pinched the bridge of his nose hard, and whispered, "Two hundred years ago, when I saw you at the Vauxhall masque."

"Two hundred years ago." She sat up so that she could stare down at him, her expression filling with horror mingled with wonder.

He deserved her horror. It would serve him right if she walked out of the hospital room and never came back. He saw Constantine again in his mind, and another wave of pain washed over him.

"Let me get this straight," she said. "All that time ago, you saw what you thought was your own death, and you still offered to help me?"

His jaw tightened. He nodded. "I didn't see anybody else, or any details. If I had only seen Constantine, I would never have agreed to let him come. He died because of me."

She twisted around to face him fully, some kind of extreme reaction tightening her face and body. Whatever her initial reaction was, she held it back until she calmed and looked more balanced. He respected that so much about her, how she found her own ballast and considered her words carefully.

After a moment, she said in a slow, deliberate voice, "First things first. I think you must be the bravest man I've ever known."

That was the last thing he had expected her to say. Frowning, he opened his mouth to reply, but she slipped her hand over his lips to stop him.

"Graydon, you saw what you thought was your own

death, and you still stepped forward without hesitation to offer to help me. You never backed down. Not once. You confronted Malphas at Wembley, you waited all this time." Her voice wobbled until she firmed her lips and continued. "You spearheaded the investigation, you set the trap for Malphas—you drove this whole thing forward, all the while thinking it would probably kill you."

"I had to," he whispered. "I don't back down. I can't live my life that way. And besides, I wanted you so badly."

Her eyes filled with tears. "I think I must be the luckiest woman in the world," she breathed. "Second point. You need to put the blame for this exactly where it belongs, on Malphas."

Breathing raggedly, he closed his eyes. She was only saying to him what he had said to other people before—don't blame the victim. Or, in this case, victims. Yet he had such difficulty internalizing her words.

When she spoke again, her voice had turned very gentle. "Third point. Don't take away from Constantine or Soren the power of their choices. Or Rune and Julian, either, for that matter. Maybe they didn't have the second sight, or a vision from two hundred years ago, but they could still see pretty well. They knew how dangerous it was to fight a first generation Djinn, and they chose to do it anyway, just as you did."

He said quickly, "I wouldn't take anything away from them. That's not what I meant."

Her voice gentled even further. "Are you sure? Can you tell me that what they did was all that different from what you did?"

He ran her words over again in his mind, trying to find some fault with her logic, but he couldn't find any.

"Graydon," she said tenderly.

He looked up at her. There was so much love in her expression, so much compassion, a lump rose in his throat.

"I know how insidious survivor's guilt can feel," she told him. "Why did they die, and not me? There must have been something—anything—I could have done to stop it. Those kinds of thoughts will consume your soul, if you don't stop them."

While he listened, he forced himself to breathe evenly. In and out, the raw, simple effort of living. If anybody knew about survivor's guilt, it must be Bel. What demons had she been forced to confront and exorcise over the last six months?

She pressed her lips to the corner of his mouth in a soft caress. "I'm not trying to take away your feelings. Gods, how could I? You need to feel what you feel, and grieve in your own time, and in your own way. The only thing I'm trying to say is, please, don't carry the weight of this on your shoulders. Not this, not when it doesn't belong there."

Unable to speak, he nodded, and he had to cover his eyes.

As soon as darkness pressed against his eyelids, he saw it again—the spike bursting out of Constantine's chest. Pain burned through his muscles like acid.

He also remembered something else. Con had been shouting something at him. Grabbing him, yanking him around.

Hauling him out of the path of danger.

"I didn't change the vision," he rasped. "Con did."

His words shook her visibly. Even though the battle was over, terror flashed across her face, and her slender dark brows drew together. She breathed, "What did he do?"

"He pulled me out of the way, and pushed between me and Malphas." Grief, like stones grinding together, roughened his voice. Malphas had driven that spike so hard, it had not only torn through Con's body, it had also impaled him— just not deeply enough to puncture his heart. "He took the strike meant for me."

"He saved your life?"

His lips formed a soundless word. "Yes."

Her fingers tightened on his flesh, digging into his arms. She whispered, "Then I'll always be grateful to him."

He thought of how much strength and hatred had gone into Malphas's massive blow, how close he had come to losing his life. He thought of that wry look in Con's eyes at the very end. Con had known, and he had done it anyway. A wordless sound came out of him, as if he had just been struck again.

As the wave of pain passed, he grew aware of other things. Bel had gone nose-to-nose with him. Tears slipped down her cheeks, but she didn't flinch away. Her gaze was so naked, so full of emotion. He did not make this journey alone. Where he went, she went with him, right down into the darkest place. Everything he felt, she felt too.

How could she have lost everything that she had lost, and still have the strength to remain so open and compassionate?

"If I didn't have you to hold onto right now, I think I would be going more than a little crazy," he whispered.

"If I didn't have you, I *know* I would be more than a little crazy." Reaching up, she kissed his forehead. "What can I do for you, my love?"

A wave of tenderness washed over him. "You're doing everything." As he took a deep breath, he remembered something else. "Did I . . . dream that you and Dragos argued?"

With a snort, she buried her face in the pillow by his head. "No, you didn't dream it. He was here, and we—we sort of did."

He slipped his fingers underneath her chin, urging her face up. His voice deepening, he whispered, "You said I'm yours."

Color darkened her cheeks. "Yes, and I-I might have told him that I'm moving in with you. Pretty much. Essentially." She bit her lip. "Unless you have a problem with that?"

"Gods, no." He locked his arms around her. "I'm never going to let you out of my sight again."

It was a ridiculous thing to say, but she didn't contradict him. Instead, she clung to him, arms around his neck, drawing one slender leg over his hips. The reality of her presence pounded into him.

She was here, really here with him. For the first time in two hundred years, they were free from all constraint.

Free.

His hot burn of grief turned into raw need. His cock stiffened so hard, it felt agonizing.

Struggling with so many powerful emotions, he rasped, "I need you so much, and yet after what happened, it feels almost wrong."

"Reaffirming love and life can never be wrong," she told him softly. "That's survivor guilt. This is a gift, Graydon. An incredible, precious gift. Everything you do—everything we do—from here on out is a gift. It would be so terrible to waste it."

When everything inside him threatened to shut down, somehow she opened doors, and she made it okay for him to walk through them.

Yes, this was a gift. And if events had happened the other way around, he knew for damn sure Constantine wouldn't waste it. In fact, Con would be the first to shove him forward, back into life.

*She's your chance, man,* Con had said. *You've got to take it.*

His animal surged to the forefront. With a posssessive growl, he rolled her over so that she lay on her back on the hospital bed. So recently healed, his muscles shook with need and strain.

He gritted between his teeth, "Tell me not to do this, and I won't."

If she told him no, somehow he would find a way to stop, if it killed him.

"I would never tell you such a thing," she breathed. "I could never tell you no."

Meeting her gaze, he tore off her clothing with the sharp talons that had grown to tip his fingers. Her gaze filled with fierce light. She looked like the Elven warrior who had once walked out of the shadows toward him.

She took his soul out of his body. He couldn't bear not to give it to her.

Then her clothes were gone, thrown in a ruined pile of fabric to the floor. The sight of her beauty slammed him. Dark, luxuriant hair spread everywhere, and the slender, tensile strength in her body was unutterably lovely.

In an agonized clench, the monster whispered, "I may not be able to be gentle."

"I don't need your gentleness," she said, as she reached up to touch his face. "I need your truth."

Her words rocked him. Truth.

This is truth:

You tear away everything but my essence.

I need the light you carry more than I need air, food or water. I need you more than life.

I treasure the breaths we take together, and I am stricken with envy for them, for they mingle closer and more completely than our bodies can join.

Your beauty makes me fall out of the sky and want to stay tethered to earth. Let me follow you everywhere, my love, through the lightest moments, and the darkest. I can only be happy if we share all our pain.

Don't leave me, I beg of you, for my spirit will go with you, and then I will truly become clay.

He whispered things against her body, the monster. He did not even know what. They were raw and naked, words that came from wounds of the heart, blooming like roses.

She sobbed and twisted underneath the caress of his lips, his deadly hands. He could not make his talons retract, and so he found gentleness after all, for he would die before he could ever mar her delicate beauty.

She tasted exquisite, like every dream he'd ever had of bliss. He tongued her plump lips, plundered the private recesses of her mouth, licked at the slender stalk of her neck where her life beat, strong and sure, underneath the velvet-scented veil of her skin.

While he lost himself in doing to her everything he had ever imagined, squandering the yearning daydreams of centuries, the flow of her body coursed underneath his hands, twisting and turning to match the needs of his body.

Like an enchanted mirror, her gaze told him he was the most beautiful lover in all the land. He had always known he could only be beautiful through the gaze of someone who looked at him with true love.

Passion rose underneath her skin, so that she burned with the kind of luminescence that could only be seen with his soul. He followed the path it showed him, licking along the curves and hollows of her body, suckling at each of her nipples, until the graceful way she touched him grew broken and demanding.

The hunger in her voice as she cried out sounded like music to him, silvery and passionate, like watching the sun glint off a starling's wing. The salt of her aroused scent was earthy, addicting. He rubbed his cheek down the flat, shaking line of her abdomen, drawn inevitably to the most secret part of her.

She parted her legs, granting him access to her most sensitive, fragile flesh. He fell into licking and caressing her with his tongue, tracing the silken, delicate folds with the kind of reverence such treasure deserved. The musk of her arousal slicked his lips.

His own body felt molten hot, his erection so thick and tight, it jutted straight out from his body. As he sprawled on his stomach, pushing down lower on the bed to feast on her, the slight friction of his cock rubbing on the coarse sheets caused him to ejaculate.

Gritting his teeth, he endured the unsatisfying pulse of pleasure/pain. He needed to be inside her *oh gods so badly*, yet he couldn't leave the sensual wealth spread underneath him.

Carefully spreading her plump, ruby-tinted flesh, he found her clitoris. When he put his mouth over it, a breathless cry broke out of her lips. She lifted off the bed, head arched back, while the long, shapely muscles of her inner thighs clenched.

That was what he wanted. He needed to hear her scream. Contentment eased the fire of his own need. It wouldn't last, but he would make it last long enough.

Suckling at her tiny, powerful peak of flesh, he stroked the petals that surrounded her entrance, caressing the dainty folds. More of her liquid arousal coated his fingers. She sank shaking fingers into his hair, sobbing, "I don't know. I don't know."

*What don't you know?* the monster whispered in her head.

"It's so intense, I don't know if I can stand it." The confession tumbled out of her trembling mouth.

*Trust me,* he murmured. *You can take it.*

She was stronger than she knew. She was stronger than almost anybody he knew.

Briefly, deliriously happy, he flicked her clitoris with tense care over the edge of his teeth. Finally he was able to make his talons retract, as he plunged two greedy fingers deep inside of her. With his invasion, he felt her convulse.

The climax rippled out from her core to the rest of her body, and it was so fucking beautiful. So fucking beautiful, suddenly, he could barely wait for her to finish. Somehow, he did, massaging her internal passage to help her through it.

When her pleasure ebbed, he pounced. Crawling up her body, he brought the tip of his cock to her entrance. Her hand collided with his as she reached to help him in.

Savagery returned. As he thrust into her tight, hot sheath, he sank his fingers deep into the mattress, clawing at it from a pleasure so deep, it was like agony.

He needed her so badly, he started ejaculating again with the first thrust. His face twisted, his back arching. Eyes wide, she stared up at him in wonder. As she stroked both hands down his chest, he shot harder into her.

It wasn't enough. It could never be enough.

She's your chance, man.

Take it. Take her.

"You're mine," he growled into her face.

She whispered through lips swollen from his kisses, "Yes."

Almost apologetically, he confessed, "I can't stop. I've got to do it again."

At that, she wound her arms around his neck again. He could never get tired of how passionately she held him. She said against his mouth, "Take everything you need, my love. Everything I've got is yours."

She's your chance, man.

He took everything she had to give.

Such a precious gift.

# ≡ NINETEEN ≡

The day before the masque, they cremated Constantine's remains. Everywhere in New York City, flags were flown at half-mast. Traffic was muted, and many shops closed their doors.

The weather had warmed as well, and a light drizzle fell from the gray sky. It felt as if the whole world mourned his death.

Dragos had ordered a special brazier created, one large enough to hold a man. It was set on the roof of the Tower. The sentinels took Constantine's body, dressed in simple, everyday clothes, and laid him gently on it.

Then everybody who could fit onto the roof of the Tower came. Those who couldn't fit on the roof stood on the stairs, all eighty flights down to the street, where people gathered around the building on the sidewalks. Bel heard later that the crowd extended for several blocks in every direction around the Tower.

She took her place beside Graydon in a circle of the sentinels, holding his hand. Rune and Carling joined the circle. The harpy Aryal wept openly, while her mate Quentin rubbed her back, his jaw tight. Grym and Alexander stared fixedly at Constantine, while the fourth gryphon Bayne bowed his head, covering his face with one hand.

Dragos, Pia and Liam stood nearby. Pia's eyes were puffy and red, and Liam kept wiping at his face. Pia kept her arm around the boy's shoulders. Occasionally she whispered in his ear and tightened her hold, hugging him against her side.

And Dragos . . . Bel did her very best not to stare, but she couldn't help stealing a glance or two at his bleak expression. The fierce gold of his eyes had gone dull, and she thought she saw something hot and smoking on his lean cheeks. It was almost as if the dragon cried tears of fire.

The Great Beast could feel love and loss. He could feel grief. Her understanding of who and what he was metamorphosed into something new. While she could never imagine becoming close to him, she could finally accept he had grown into someone else. He was no longer the animal that had preyed on the Elves so long ago.

Graydon gripped her fingers tight. His expression appeared stony as he clenched down on his grief. He didn't shed tears or speak, but she knew how raw his grief was inside. While she hadn't known Constantine, she grieved for Graydon's loss.

When everybody was assembled, Dragos stepped forward, to the edge of the brazier. Looking down at Constantine's quiet face, he stroked back the tawny hair. He didn't speak any words. Nobody said anything.

The soft murmur of voices stilled, and the rest of the Tower went completely silent, except for the sound of the wind and the rain. While the silence seemed strange to Bel, it also felt somehow fitting, as if the Wyr's grief were too large for words.

Constantine's body disappeared in a great blaze of fire, and he was released forever to the open sky. A column of smoke appeared briefly overhead, signaling to the whole city that he was gone. A few minutes later, when the blaze died down, the brazier was empty. The dragon fire had blazed so hot, nothing remained.

While they held no wake, they had pared work down to a minimum, only to essential personnel. Graydon was still on medical leave, so after the short, silent ceremony, he and Bel walked back to his apartment. Once inside, he didn't release her hand.

Instead, he led her to the shadowed bedroom, and she went willingly. There, he undressed her in silence, while she focused on removing his clothes, injecting all the love and compassion she could into each passing caress, until they stood naked, facing each other.

Graydon's body was as powerful as ever, his massive frame covered with heavy muscles and deeply tanned skin. Vitality poured off him, while inside, she knew his shattered rib cage, breastplate and chest muscles were still strengthening after Pia had healed him.

He could do normal activities, but his surgeon had not yet cleared him for strenuous flights or battle.

A scar like a starburst covered the middle of his broad chest.

She stroked it. The intensity of his silent grief broke her composure. Her face crumpling, she leaned against him and pressed her lips to the shiny scar.

"I'm always going to be grateful to him," she whispered. "Every single day of my life, I'm going to thank him for what he did for you."

A shudder rocked his powerful frame. Breathing raggedly, he gathered her close and kissed her.

Everything he couldn't say poured out of his fingers, his mouth. She felt his pain and need as keenly as if it were her own.

He kissed her so hard and deeply, he bruised her lips. She welcomed the discomfort, kissing him back, meeting his need with her own. His hands roamed her body with restless urgency, cupping her breasts, running down the curve of her spine, gripping her hips.

She pulled away, only to take him by the wrist, fall back on the bed and tug him down with her.

He came eagerly, covering her body with his. His welcome

weight settled on top of her, she parted her legs and wrapped them around his hips until his large, heavy cock pressed against her pelvis.

The need drove them both. As she reached between them to grasp his hard erection he lifted up on his elbows, and she guided him to her opening. This wasn't about sensuality, or taking their time to explore each other's pleasure points. This was something darker and so much more necessary.

Despite the taut urgency in his body, he pushed in gently, rocking deeper with every thrust, until he had seated himself all the way inside her, filling her completely, not just physically but emotionally.

"I don't know how I lived without you," he whispered into her hair, as he moved inside her. "I know I did. There's a full, complete set of memories in my head of a very long, complicated life. But it's almost as if those memories belong to another man. A man very like me, but still someone else."

"I know what you mean," she murmured stroking the back of his head, his shoulders, the broad, long line of his back. "I have been needing and wanting you for so many centuries, before we even met, I just didn't know that what I needed and wanted was you."

He cradled her head in the palm of one large hand, leaning his weight on one elbow as his hips flexed. The hard length of his cock was so big.

He was almost too big, stretching her as far as she could go. It was a deep, good ache that obliterated the cold, empty spot that had existed in the depth of her soul for so long.

She never wanted him to stop. She wanted them to always be joined just like this, moving together, in a rhythm so ancient, so essential it consumed them. They were each among the oldest of their kind, yet this need—this drive—still ruled them.

Gradually, he picked up the pace, and she lifted her hips to meet each thrust gladly. A deep, burning pleasure tightened her body, until it became a high, piercing spike of need.

He reached between them to stroke along the soft petals of flesh at her stretched opening where he penetrated her. Whirls of sensation cascaded through her at each stroke, until he found the tiny bud of her clitoris. When he massaged that small, unbelievably sensitive spot, an explosion rocked her body.

Crying out, she clutched him, shuddering as the ripples of the climax rippled through her nerve endings. He was so beautiful to her—even in the midst of his own grief and need, he gave, he didn't take.

Rocking his hips so that he kept fucking her gently, he didn't stop massaging her, drawing out her pleasure until her sensitivity grew so great, she couldn't bear it any longer.

Pulling his hand away, she pushed at his shoulder and urged him softly, "Roll over, my love. Let me come on top."

Readily, he complied. Keeping them joined by wrapping an arm around her hips and holding her to him, he settled back against the pillows.

Straddling him, she settled into place. With him inside her, this position made him feel even bigger than before. Spreading her hands on his flat, muscular stomach, she braced herself and began to move.

The look in his eyes. His tight, raw expression.

She wanted to cry for him. But that wasn't the kind of release he needed. He needed to break free himself. She picked up her tempo, undulating her torso as she gripped his cock as tightly as she could with her inner muscles. Massaging him, working him, silently urging him to cut loose.

Bowing her head, she held his gaze, and her dark hair fell forward covering him like a silken tent.

As she fucked him, he stroked her breasts and fingered her hair. "I love you," she told him. "I love you."

Her words seemed to break him out of a trance. Gripping her by the hips he thrust up, and up again, until he pistoned inside her. The friction grew unbearable, and while she had wanted to make this about him, her own pleasure skyrocketed again, until another climax slammed into her body. She flung out her hands and cried out from the force of it.

He grabbed her hands, gripping them tightly, as he shoved into her. His careful tenderness splintered and the expression on his face turned feral.

Then he arched his spine and ground his pelvis bone against hers, groaning. She was stretched so tightly inside, she could feel when his cock began to pulse. He spurted inside of her, shaking.

This time, she knew what to expect. Even as his climax slowed, his face twisted. He growled, "It's not enough. It can't ever be enough."

"Come on," she invited softly. "Give it to me. Give everything to me."

He lifted her off his body. Rising up to his knees, with one hand on her back, he urged her onto her hands and knees.

Eagerly, she settled into place, bracing herself for him. It was a frank, carnal position, everything she could possibly want it to be. She had thought he needed to cut loose. She hadn't considered her own needs, or that she needed to cut loose as well.

He came over her from behind, covering her, and before she could reach between her legs to help guide him in again, she felt the broad, thick head of his cock probing at her entrance. This time, when he slid in, she was slick from both of their pleasure, and she felt him enter her in one long, luxurious thrust that shoved her forward onto her elbows.

She groaned, shaking everywhere. The large muscles in her thighs quivered. Everything civilized that she thought she knew about herself fell away, as he wound both big hands into her hair and pinned her down.

"You're mine," he growled. "Say it."

"Yes," she gasped.

"I fought for you. I waited for you. I'll live for you. I'd die for you." With each sentence, he thrust into her again. "You're my heart, my soul. Mine."

"Don't let me go again," she sobbed into the bedspread. "Don't ever let me go."

*"Never."*

He would never give up, never let her go, never stop wanting or needing her. He would always be faithful, always welcoming. The emotional reality of that began to sink in.

Finally, after all the issues that had darkened her life,

this devotion, this adamant dedication, was what lay at shadow's end.

The last of the cold, sharp pain that had haunted her for so long shattered. Tears spilled down her face. She couldn't climax again. She was spent. But still the pressure built, as he kept up such a patient, steady and *oh my gods* relentless pace.

Then her gentle, adorable, dangerous lover came down over her back and bit her at the back of her neck, and it was such a possessive, animalistic thing to do, it shocked her right out of her exhaustion and hurtled her into a third climax.

Sounds came out of her. Sounds that she had never heard herself make. She was no longer in control of her body. He was.

He twisted behind her. With a muffled groan, he began to shudder all over as he climaxed again too. He had barely begun to slow, when he gasped, "Again—I've got to."

She was beyond physical words. She breathed, *Whatever you need. Take me however much you need. I'm yours.*

Totally and completely, devoted to him.

Driven by need, he took her again, and again, until the sun set and the room lay in total darkness. At some point, she felt transformed, existing almost outside of her body, as if she had gone through a crucible to emerge on the other side, a new burnished stranger.

When at last he stopped, he lay on top of her. The weight of his big body anchored her in place, and the heavy beat of his heart slammed into her chest. She could barely muster enough strength to wrap her arms around his neck, but somehow she managed it.

They drifted together, in silence. Unmoored, her mind spun into a lazy journey of disconnected thoughts and images.

Sometimes, when Wyr mated, it enhanced the likelihood of a pregnancy. She managed a slight, exhausted smile. She wouldn't look for such a rare miracle—very, very long ago, she had learned how to be happy with her own life. All the Elder Races, each in their own way, had to come to terms with the same.

But if it did happen, after all these millennia, wouldn't that be something?

Pressing a kiss to Graydon's damp temple, she whispered, "If, by any chance, we are ever lucky enough to have a boy of our own, can we name him Constantine?"

His body went rigid. She had just enough time to think, Oh gods, I've said the wrong thing.

Then, in a strangled, broken whisper, he told her, "I would really love that."

The rigidity in his body fractured in a harsh sob. Shoulders heaving, he buried his face in her neck.

Finally, his grief broke out at last.

Somehow, then, she found all kinds of strength and energy, as she wrapped around him, crooning a wordless comfort, crying with him until neither one of them had any tears left, and together, they took the first steps toward healing.

The next evening was the Masque of the Gods, the huge annual gala event that Dragos held in the banquet hall of the Tower.

Bel had wondered if Dragos would cancel the masque, but he had apparently decided to move forward. Possibly, it would have been too unwieldy to cancel. Dignitaries and tourists had already flooded the city.

More than likely, though, she thought it was a statement of defiance to the rest of the world.

Here we are, the statement said.

We may have been dealt a terrible blow, but we are unbroken.

She didn't see Graydon at all that day. He had returned to light duty, and he wouldn't be able to attend her at the masque. When he apologized, she put her hand over his mouth, stopping him in midsentence.

"I know who you are, and I know what you have to do," she told him. "What's more, I've known it for a very long time. It's part of what I love about you. Don't ever apologize to me for doing your job."

Almost imperceptibly, his expression lightened. He asked, "You're okay with me being a glorified cop?"

He was so much more than that. She had already seen how other people came to him with their problems and questions, and each time, he did his best to help fix them. Over time, maybe she could help him with that. Maybe people would start coming to her, too, once they grew to know and love each other, and they got used to the fact that she was truly part of their world.

She was even beginning to look forward to doing that again, helping people, listening to them and fixing their problems. When the day came, she would be ready for it.

Reaching up on tiptoe, she kissed him, and said against his mouth, "I'm more than okay. I'm proud of you, and I wouldn't have you any other way."

She was far too old and experienced to be under any illusions. There would be hard times, and hard waiting. She knew sometimes she would be scared, and that nothing would make it right again until he walked through the door and came home to her.

She also knew he was more than worth all of it.

When evening came, she went through her clothes, trying to decide what to wear. As a short-term solution to her move to New York, she had ordered her clothes to be shipped from the Elven demesne, and they filled Graydon's walk-in closet to bursting. She would have to decide what to do with her other possessions—furniture, artwork, etc.—but those were decisions that could be made over time.

Finally, she dressed in a simple dark blue dress with a matching domino. She rolled her hair into a twist, pinned it at the back of her head, slipped on a pair of high heels and kept her makeup subtle.

Others would carry on with the masque as normal, but, for her, in the face of the loss that both the Wyr and the Djinn had suffered, she felt anything more elaborate would be wrong.

Linwe met her at the apartment door. The younger woman had dressed soberly as well. She had also dyed her hair black. The color was much starker than her natural dark brown hair.

The black highlighted her elegant bone structure, and the depth and shape of her dark eyes, although Bel knew Linwe hadn't dyed her hair for vain reasons.

"Very appropriate," Bel told her. Gently, she touched the ends of Linwe's short hair. "Although, I must confess, I'll miss the pink."

Linwe ducked her head. "Maybe it can come back someday."

"Is your apartment okay?" she asked.

She had not been able to dissuade Linwe from coming to New York with her, and the younger woman had been so impassioned about the subject, she didn't have the heart to try very hard.

In any case, if she were honest with herself, she found a selfish comfort in Linwe's devotion. While she was ready to make such a deep, overarching change, and she embraced it, leaving the Elven demesne and so many loved ones behind was still hard. It had been her home and her mission for so long.

"This isn't the Wood," Linwe said, with a small shrug. "That's okay. This will be its own thing."

"I'll let you in on a secret," Bel whispered.

A sparkle returned to Linwe's eyes. She whispered back, "What's that?"

Bel smiled to herself. Linwe's sparkle could never be doused for long. She confided, "I'm going to change this Tower for the better."

"Ooohh?" One of Linwe's eyebrows lifted. "How so?"

"I'm going to bring in a touch of the Wood," said Bel. "It'll take some time—and actually quite a lot of money—but you wait and see. The Wyr will thank me for it."

Linwe threw her arms around Bel. "We're going to have such an adventure here!"

She hugged the other woman. "Yes, we are, aren't we?"

Together, they went downstairs. Linwe kept her company as she searched the crowd for Ferion.

Perhaps inevitably, the task threw her back to the Vauxhall masque, two hundred years ago. She had been so anxious and worried that night as she looked for Ferion.

Now, so many things had changed.

In the latter part of the nineteenth century, the Vauxhall Pleasure Gardens had slipped away into the past. Over the years, King Oberon had grown colder and more distant, until he stopped attending public functions.

She had not seen or spoken to him in a long time. Occasionally she glimpsed one of his knights who attended functions in his stead, but they remained secretive and distant. Francis Shaw, the earl of Weston, had been killed in a terrorist bombing attack in London.

This year, along with so many other Elves, Calondir was dead, and now Constantine and Soren were too.

The Djinn were not in attendance at the masque, not even Khalil, nor was the Oracle present. Bel had heard through Graydon, who talked often with Rune, that Khalil mourned his father's passing fiercely, despite how they had fought when Soren had been alive.

It felt odd, in an aching kind of way, to look over the crowded hall and no longer see Soren's tall, Powerful figure, with his distinctive white hair and piercing diamond gaze.

She didn't know how the Djinn mourned as a society, but she had heard that none of them danced in the western deserts. The great plumes of sand and wind had gone still and silent.

And Malphas had finally, finally been killed. She could not help but feel a fierce relief at that particular change.

In the end, she didn't find Ferion. He found her.

A hand closed gently on her wrist. She turned in surprise to discover her son standing behind her. He had dressed soberly as well, and had pulled his long blond hair back into a tight braid.

It lent his handsome features a severity that suited him these days. As a nod to tradition, he had brought a domino, but instead of wearing it, he had tucked it into the breast pocket of his jacket.

Linwe touched her shoulder. "I'll just go . . . Over there somewhere. Text me if you need anything."

"Thank you," she said.

As Linwe disappeared into the crowd, she turned back to Ferion. She couldn't stop herself from putting her hand on his arm and scanning him surreptitiously.

The subtle, corrupt smear of darkness that had been embedded in his soul was completely gone. Finally, her son was free. The Elven High Lord was unfettered, to be whoever he needed to be. Whatever may come of it, only time could tell that tale.

"Mother," he said.

She threw her arms around him, hugging him with everything she had. "It's so good to see you."

"It's good to see you too." His lips widening into a smile, he returned her hug. Too quickly, the smile died and he turned sober. "I'm not staying. I only came because I promised you I would."

Yet another thing that had changed—this time, he had kept his word. Her heart lightened with gladness. "Thank you for coming."

He told her in a low voice, "I also came because I wanted to try one last time to change your mind, if I could. Don't stay here. Come home with me, where you belong."

She shook her head and told him softly, "You know I'm not going to do that."

"You don't have to leave Graydon. Bring him with you. We'll— I'll deal with it." He gestured with one hand. "The Wyr are not our enemies any longer. They've helped us too many times to maintain hostilities. We'll make a place for him. Mom, please."

Unable to help herself, she straightened his lapel, letting her fingers linger as she smoothed the cloth over his hard, lean chest.

"It means so much to me that you said that," she replied. "But you know Graydon could never fit in down there. They are making a place for me here. Not only that, but this is where I want to be." She met his gaze. "I don't belong in South Carolina any longer. Besides, you're not losing me— you could never lose me. We'll come to visit, as often as we can."

His face tightened. "That's not the same, and you know it. And what do you mean, you don't belong in South Carolina? Father was the one who cracked the whip, but for so long, you've been the heart and soul of our demesne."

"If that's true, then it's past time for someone else to fill that role." She touched his face. "My heart is here now. Sidhiel and others will be there to help advise you, and I'll only be a phone call away if you ever need to talk. Think of it, Ferion. You really are free now. The future is yours to take—so take it. Be the wonderful man I know you are, and the kind of leader I know you can be."

He blew out a breath, looking frustrated. "You can be so stubborn sometimes."

For some reason that made her laugh, hard. "It's a good thing I am, don't you think?"

The normally straight line of his shoulder slumped. "This change has really happened, hasn't it? You're not coming home again."

"No, son." Her expression softened at the look of loss that came over his face. "I love you with all of my heart. I'm not coming back, and it will be okay. Let's find a time to talk tomorrow. Give me a call after you get home?"

"Okay, yes." He nodded. "I have several things I need to attend to, but I can call just before supper. How's that?"

"It's wonderful."

Phone calls would be a good bridge. They might talk daily for a while. Then, gradually, as they both adjusted to the change and found their footing in their new lives, those phone calls would start coming twice a week. Then, maybe every other week.

That was as it should be, although she couldn't imagine yet how they were going to coordinate the holidays. Still, one step at a time.

He pulled her into his arms. Bending his head, he whispered in her ear, "Father might have cracked the whip, but you have always been my heart and soul too, you know."

Her heart swelled. Surprised tears sprang to her eyes.

He released her. Even as she opened her mouth to reply, he turned and disappeared into the crowd.

He had barely stepped from her side when Linwe reappeared. The young woman didn't say anything, but her warm expression and companionship provided support as Bel regained her composure.

Soon other people approached, diplomats and representatives from other Elder Races, and she grew so involved in conversation, she didn't have time to dwell on Ferion's departure.

About an hour later, the music stopped.

At one end of the banquet hall, the doors opened, and people moved off the dance floor, making way as the procession of the gods started.

In a masque of any size, seven handpicked actors, dressed as the seven gods of the Elder Races, would walk through the crowd. In smaller gatherings, family members or friends would portray the gods. Legend said that a god attended every masque in secret, but Bel had never known there to be any actual truth to it.

For an elaborate affair like the Tower masque, each of the seven gods was sumptuously costumed. However, unlike previous times, this year, the orchestra did not resume to play a processional.

This year, the gods entered the banquet hall in silence.

A mutter passed over the crowd, then subsided.

Leading the procession was Taliesen, god of the Dance. Part male and part female, Taliesen was first among the Primal Powers because dance is change, and the universe is constantly in motion.

The current Taliesen was portrayed by a slender woman. Following her came Inanna, the goddess of Love; Nadir, the goddess of the Depths or the Oracle; Will, the god of the Gift; Camael, the goddess of the Hearth; and Hyperion, the god of Law.

Last of all came Azrael, god of Death.

Stillness filled the hall as Death walked past. All the

Wyr, including every sentinel, bowed to the elegant figure in black.

Every Wyr, except Dragos. He didn't bow. Bel didn't think he had it in him to bow to anyone. But he did stand rigidly at attention.

The crowd followed the Wyr's lead, bowing to Death and paying homage to the sentinel and the Djinn who had fallen. Bel's gaze filled with moisture, and she bit her lips. As Death came abreast, she bowed as well. The silence remained, deep and profound, until the last of the gods exited the banquet hall at the other end.

The musicians lifted their instruments, music filled the hall once again, and the moment of remembrance was over.

Long after midnight, after everyone had unmasked and the crowd thinned, Graydon came to find her. He looked as tired as she felt. At some point, he had loosened his tie and unbuttoned the first few shirt buttons at his neck.

All of the sentinels, along with Dragos, Pia and Liam, had worn black that evening. While she knew, like Linwe dying the pink out of her hair, that none of them had worn black as a fashion statement, still, the simple formality of Graydon's suit looked good on him.

The black emphasized the long length of his body, along with the power in the breadth of those wide, muscled shoulders. It also highlighted his colors—the healthy burnish of his deep tan, his tawny hair, and the rich depth in his dark gray eyes.

Even though, she did admit to herself, the cut of the suit managed to achieve adequate.

A rush of love for him washed over her. When he came up to her, she opened her arms, and he walked into them, wrapping her in a big hug, while his presence surrounded her with that nourishing, friendly blaze.

She could never get enough of it, never get tired of his companionship. The fact that she was also overcome with desire and deeply, desperately in love with him sealed her fate, and she was content to never leave it.

Nestling against his chest, she lifted her face for his kiss.

He stroked her shoulders. "We're gathering up at the penthouse. It's kinda tradition after the masque, and we'd like for you—*I'd* like for you to come, if you would."

Instantly, she put her own tiredness aside. This was her first invitation to an inner circle gathering. She was frankly surprised that it had come so soon. It was too important for her not to go.

And even if none of that had been true, Graydon wanted her there, and that was all the impetus she needed.

"Of course," she said. As he laced his fingers through hers, and they walked in the direction of the elevators, she asked, "Who will be there?"

"It's just going to be the sentinels. Rune and Carling, and Pia, Liam and Dragos." He paused, giving her a sidelong look. "Fair warning. More than a couple of us might get falling down drunk, including me."

So it would be a very small, select group.

She squeezed his fingers. "Do you need me to stay sober, so that I can get us back to the apartment?"

He shook his head. "I never get so drunk I can't get home."

She told him, "Then I may very well join you, because it's been a hell of a week."

A spark of surprised approval entered his gaze. He said, "It sure has."

Not only was this her first invitation to an inner circle gathering, but it would also be the first occasion she spent any time with the sentinels, or the Cuelebres as a family.

Back in January, before the crisis in the Elven demesne had erupted, she had shared a brief visit and a connection with Pia, but she hadn't spent any time with the other woman since then.

Bel may have been invited, but not necessarily accepted. Not yet. While she had faced countless social challenges before in her long life, this one mattered in a critical way that most of the others had not.

She couldn't pretend that she wasn't afraid. She wanted this to go well so badly, not just for herself, but for Graydon too.

While she couldn't do anything about the fear, what she could do was face the challenge head-on. As she turned to face the elevator doors, she straightened her spine.

When the doors opened with a quiet swoosh, she stepped into the penthouse, Graydon at her side.

# ═ TWENTY ═

Even though nothing showed but calm composure on Bel's beautiful face, in the elevator Graydon had caught a hint of nervousness in her scent.

It highlighted how remarkably good she was at managing the stresses of her own internal reality because as they stepped into the penthouse, her entire attention focused on everyone around her.

It also showed him, up close and personal, that she had a hell of a game face too. He had always known it. He had seen flashes of it in the past, but it was one thing to know and quite another to see that game face in action. He already respected her, but over the next hour, that respect deepened exponentially.

Everyone else was already present. The males had removed suits and ties. Aryal had set aside her formal cut leather jacket. Most of the adults were already drinking, and most of the drinks were the hard stuff. Carling nursed a bottle of bloodwine.

Pia refrained from alcohol. Liam drank Coke, and even though there had been plenty of sumptuous refreshments at the masque, the boy was already eating again. He kept his head down, avoiding other people's gazes.

Like the adults, he had been subdued ever since Constantine's death. Graydon noted the subtle way that Pia kept her attention on him. He had no doubt that she would make sure Liam got what he needed emotionally.

At first, there were small signs of stiffness around Bel, the telltale behaviors of people who had known each other for a long time as they accepted a near stranger into their midst. Within a half an hour, those had melted away entirely.

Bel and Pia spent some time together, tucked into a corner of the large living room, Bel's dark head bent close to Pia's pale blond one. Graydon's gaze slipped over to them several times. He saw he wasn't the only to watch the tête-à-tête. All the sentinels did, Dragos most of all. At the end of their talk, the two women hugged.

There was so much obvious affection between them, it felt good. It felt right, like Bel had somehow managed to slip into a place that filled a hole in their lives, one that Graydon hadn't even been aware that the group had.

Sometime later, somehow, the dam between them all—the one keeping them from talking about Constantine—broke. Graydon didn't catch how it happened. He hadn't felt like drinking hard liquor that night after all, so he had walked into the kitchen for a new six-pack of lager.

When he came back to the large living room, he heard Aryal telling Bel, "He was a total asshole manwhore. He chewed through women the way some people go through Tic Tacs."

"Oh, my." Bel coughed. "That's an image that won't leave my head in a hurry."

As she spoke, she met Graydon's gaze. There was so much compassion in her eyes, he was not surprised that it had touched even Aryal's tempestuous, spiky heart.

Bayne tossed his whiskey back. He said suddenly, "Do you remember that time one of his dates doused his clothes with lighter fluid, set a match to them and threw them out his balcony window?"

"I got a phone call that day," Rune said. "Traffic control from downstairs told me, 'Did you know it's raining men's briefs, and they're on fire?'"

A laugh shook out of Grym. It faded into something close to tears. The gargoyle pinched his nose and expelled a hard sigh. "Nicest asshole you'd ever want to meet. If you weren't a woman."

"Best, most loyal friend," Graydon said. His throat closed, and he couldn't say anymore. Quietly, Bel made her way across the room to put her arm around him. He kissed her forehead, and she leaned against him.

Rune said, "Hell of a fighter. Hell of an investigator too." He tossed a whiskey back.

Alexander offered in a quiet voice, "I didn't get the chance to know him as long or as well as the rest of you, but he had become my brother."

They shared stories about Constantine into the early hours of the morning. No doubt, it wouldn't be the last time they needed to reminisce, but it felt good—good in a way that made the pain of loss more bearable.

*Thank you,* he said in Bel's head.

She looked up at him. *For what, my love?*

*I didn't catch how you started it,* he told her. *But I know you did. We needed to talk about him.*

*The Wyr demesne has never lost a sentinel before,* she said softly. *It's going to take you all a while to heal, but have faith. You will.*

If anyone knew how to survive loss, it was Bel. He wrapped his arms around her, soaking in the comfort of her feminine presence.

Dragos remained silent throughout the reminiscing. He sprawled in one oversized armchair, drinking brandy steadily while his gold gaze watched everyone. It was impossible to tell what he felt or thought. He kept his face impassive.

Pia had kicked off her heels and curled against his side. Absently, he rubbed one hand back and forth along the curve of her hip.

Nearby, Liam sprawled on the floor, playing a game on

a mini tablet. Even though it was almost five in the morning, nobody had suggested that he go to bed. He needed to process the grief as much, if not more, than any of the rest of them.

Eventually, Rune and Carling said good night. They left in a flurry of hugs and good-byes. Rune touched Dragos on the shoulder, and the two men had a brief telepathic exchange. Dragos gave the other man a nod, and the couple left.

Graydon watched, glad that the two men had reconciled enough so that Dragos could accept Rune and Carling as being part of their extended family.

After they had gone, perhaps inevitably, the subject of how to fill Constantine's sentinel position came up. Quentin said to Dragos, "I suppose you've been too busy to give much thought to picking another sentinel."

Hesitantly, Bel said in Graydon's head, *This might be an ignorant question, but do you think he would consider inviting Rune back?*

He shook his head. *Not a chance,* he told her. *They're recovering their friendship, but Dragos would never allow Carling to get that close to the seat of power in the Wyr demesne. In some ways, Dragos and Carling are too much alike. They're both schemers.*

*I guess I should be glad he's been so accepting of me, relatively speaking,* Bel said slowly, her expression pensive. *I've been so preoccupied by working to accept him that I hadn't considered that before.*

He hugged her tight. *Yes, you're Elven, and yes, you were a major force in the Elven demesne. But trust me, you are an entirely different reality from Carling.*

As they shared their private exchange, the others watched Dragos consider Quentin's question. He said, "Yes, I've thought about it."

Graydon met Aryal's frustrated gaze. When Dragos wanted to be inscrutable, sometimes getting any information out of him was like trying to pull giant, dragon-sized teeth.

Aryal said, "You're not going to hold another round of

Sentinel Games, are you? Not only was it a hellish expense, but that week was exhausting."

"No," Dragos replied. "Doing it once was a show of our strength. Holding public games again, especially so soon after the first time and in the wake of Constantine's death, sends another message entirely. I'm thinking of a private event, with a short list of handpicked contestants."

From his position on the floor, Liam said, "It's my spot."

Since it was the first time the boy had spoken that night, it took a few moments for everyone to absorb exactly what he had said.

The sentinels looked at each other. Over by the bar, Aryal pivoted abruptly to put her back to the group. Graydon caught a glimpse of her wide-eyed profile as she mouthed *oh my fucking god* to the wall.

Pia straightened from her position reclining against Dragos's side. Her expression turned guarded, her sharp gaze intent on her son.

"What did you say?" Dragos said, even though Graydon knew the dragon had heard Liam perfectly. "Sit up straight when you're talking, and look at me."

Moving deliberately, Liam did more than sit up straight. He pushed to his feet and turned to face his father.

He didn't seem angry, Graydon noted. Nor did he act defiant. There was something set in his young-looking, handsome expression, as if he had made up his mind, and nothing in the world was going to change it.

For several months now, everyone had been wondering if and how Liam might act out in teenage rebellion.

Here we go, Graydon thought. He braced himself.

Meeting Dragos's gaze, Liam said in a calm, steady voice, "That sentinel position is mine."

"No, it isn't," Dragos said. His relaxed impassivity had vaporized. Now, even though he spoke as calmly as his son did, sharp authority had entered his demeanor. "I will give you a great many things, Liam. I will give you a home, and I will give you my love. I'll give you the best education, and when the time comes, I would be very pleased to give you a strong starting position in my company. But I will not give you this."

"I didn't ask you to," said Liam. His arms hung at his sides, but Graydon noted that his hands had clenched into fists.

Ever since his birth, Liam's Wyr form, the dragon, had strained to reach full-size. In times of stress or crisis, especially, the boy had gone through several growth spurts already.

Now the Wyr demesne faced another challenge that struck at the foundation of its existence. Did the boy stand a little taller than he had the last time Graydon had seen him? Was he broader now across the shoulders, his voice deeper?

Dragos said, "This conversation is over."

"Wait," Pia said unexpectedly. "Dragos, hear him out."

Of all the people present, Graydon had not expected Pia to be the one who spoke up. She had been deeply shaken the first couple of times Liam had gone through a growth spurt.

She wasn't any longer. Now as she watched Liam with a fascinated respect, along with so much love, she reminded him of the tireless devotion Bel had given to Ferion.

Dragos gave his mate a considering glance. As Pia slid out of the chair to perch on the arm of the nearby couch, Dragos leaned forward in his seat, leaning his elbows on his knees and staring up at Liam. Somehow, in those simple adjustments, Dragos's armchair had become a throne.

"All right," Dragos said to his son. "Speak your piece."

Liam glanced around the room. "My dragon is already bigger than any sentinel here," he said. "In fact, my dragon is bigger and stronger than anybody else in this room except for you, and I'm faster than anybody else, except for Mom. The only reason why I don't win in the training sessions now is because I don't have enough experience. Yet."

Dragos raised one sleek black eyebrow. "You are correct on all accounts. And your last point is the essential one."

"Where will I fit in this demesne when I finish growing?" Liam asked. "And you know I'm going to finish growing soon. What job could I possibly take that will satisfy my dragon?" He paused, his body tight. "How do I get experience if I don't do anything to earn it?"

Beside Graydon, Bel stirred. The discomfort in her expression threw him back to what she had once said about Ferion living a half life, never allowed to take too much responsibility in his father's demesne, yet never allowed to roam free either.

Disquieted by the memory, he frowned.

"You ask compelling questions for which we don't have answers, yet." Dragos's voice softened. "We *will* find answers, and you *do* have a place and a home where you're valued and loved, always. *Always*, Liam. But still, I will not give you that sentinel position."

"I'm not asking for you to give it to me," Liam said. "I'll fight for it. I'll take it—just like every other sentinel has taken their position. I'll make it mine. What I want you to do is give me time to get ready for the fight. Dad, don't take this the wrong way, but I don't want to work in your company. And our demesne is so strong, this is the first time a sentinel has ever died, and this chance isn't going to come around again, soon or even ever. The only thing that would be worse than not letting me at least try would be to create an eighth position just because I'm your son."

There was pain in that last sentence, enough pain that when he fell silent, nobody spoke again for long moments.

Finally, Dragos stirred. Telepathically, he asked Graydon, *What do you think?*

Graydon chose his response with care. He said, *I think if you don't let him try, it'll create a rift between you that might take a while to heal.*

The dragon's fierce gold gaze flashed to him. *I'm concerned about that too, but that's not enough of a reason, Gray.*

Pausing a moment to think, he came at it from a different angle. *If he tries and fails, he'll have done what he needed to do, and he'll have answered his own question. If he tries and wins, the demesne won't suffer, and he will have earned a place that I think he needs badly. He doesn't know how he fits in this world, Dragos. Young people don't, and in some ways, his situation is harder than most.*

Dragos's dark brows came together as he listened. Graydon couldn't tell what the other male was thinking, but at least he listened.

He added, *And he's right—if you try to create a position for him, it won't feel real. Give him a chance. That's all he's asking for, just a chance.* He took a deep breath. *It'll be a challenge to keep the position open, but we can hire extra staff. If you'll agree to it, we can somehow make it work.*

Dragos's gaze left Graydon to travel to Pia. After another long pause, she gave him a small nod.

Only then did Dragos turn back to Liam. The boy had never once looked away from his father. As the silence had grown prolonged, he had whitened, and his heart was in his eyes.

Dragos paused, taking in the boy's desperate entreaty.

He said, "I'll give you one year."

Passion leaped into that pale young face, along with an expression of such naked gratitude, Graydon had to drop his gaze.

Liam said fiercely, *"Thank you."*

Dragos cleared his throat. The crisp command in his voice turned husky and gentle. "You're welcome, son."

Graydon told the dragon, *I get that he's not really a child, not in the way that we normally think of children. But still, I don't see how a year can be enough.*

*It's his chance, and that's all he asked for,* said Dragos. *And we don't really know what he can do. I'll be interested to find out.*

T**he** Tower recovered from the aftermath of the masque. Clean-up crews worked overtime to put everything to rights. Dragos, Pia and Liam traveled back home again, to upstate New York.

None of them would be nearly so fast in recovering from losing Constantine, but Bel was a wise woman, and she was right.

It would take them a while to heal, but eventually they would.

For Graydon, he had to fight nightmares of the battle, reliving again and again those last terrible moments when Constantine had leaped at him and spun him around, away from the deadly threat.

Each time, in the dreams, he shouted and struggled, but something always prevented him from dragging them both away, and he had to watch that long, wicked spike burst out of Constantine's chest, followed by the gush of so much blood.

Sometimes, he woke himself up shouting. Other times, Bel shook him awake, and he discovered he had been thrashing around in his sleep.

Once, he woke to the sensation of his fist connecting with soft flesh. Comprehension flashed into his mind immediately.

Sickened by the realization that he had struck her, he lunged to turn on the bedside lamp and whipped around to inspect every inch of her body. Despite her protestations that she was okay, he had to see for himself.

He had caught her arm in a glancing blow, and he was beside himself as he watched the welt appear on the delicate skin of her arm.

At first, she was calm, gentle and supportive, but when he began to drown in self-castigation, she quickly turned stern.

"Snap out of it, my love," she told him, gripping his arm as he sat on the edge of the bed with his head buried in his hands. "It was an accident, nothing more. You couldn't hurt me if you tried. Trust me. The demon of regret that haunts you now will fade."

He did trust her, with his life, but it was still a struggle to accept what she was saying. His breath shuddered in his throat. He whispered, "I don't know how it can. If I had only done something, anything different—"

She came up behind him and leaned against his back, putting her arms around him. Like him, she chose to sleep naked, and the soft press of her breasts against his back was at once soothing and erotic.

"Believe me when I say this," she whispered in his hair. "You can second-guess yourself for the rest of your very long life, and none of it will bring him back. It was battle. Things happen in battle. People we love die in battle. While it's terrible, that's all it is. I may not have been there, but I know this one thing is true—you fought with everything you had. And there was nothing you could have done."

"How can you know for sure?" He turned his head to one side toward the sound of her voice, and she pressed a kiss to his cheek.

"I know it, because I know you," she said. "Because you couldn't have done any differently."

With that, he was able to let go of that particular nightmare. He turned toward her and made love to her with the all-consuming ferocity that gripped him every time they were together.

Dr. Shaw cleared him for active duty and flight. He went back to work, and for some nights afterward, Bel joined the gryphon as he took long, luxurious flights. That place at his shoulders, the place that had been empty for so long, would never feel empty again.

After a few days, Bel turned inexplicably tense and pre-occupied. She became such a nervous wreck, and it was so unlike her, she frankly terrified the shit out of him.

Simple tasks eluded her. She dropped things. Once, she burned a batch of Elven wayfarer bread he had asked her to bake as a special treat. Pulling the pan out of the oven, she burst into tears.

Beside himself, he leaped from the supper table and grabbed her by the arms. "You're a basket case," he told her. "Please, tell me what I can do to help!"

Later he had to admit to himself, it was not his finest, most diplomatic moment.

She cried out, "I know I'm a basket case! I'm a complete wreck, and I can't help myself. Oh gods, Graydon, I think I might be pregnant."

What?

Realizing he had frozen and nothing had actually come out of his mouth, he made a concerted effort to speak.

So he said aloud, stupidly, "What?"

She took him by the ears and enunciated, "I. Think. I'm. Preg. Nant."

"That's impossible," he whispered. His heart hammered in his newly healed chest.

"Well, clearly it's not impossible," she replied. "Just highly—highly—improbable."

"Oh, dear gods," he stammered. "Why are you even on your feet? Here, sit down."

Her pretty mouth fell open. She stared at him as he shoved her into a dining chair, and she sat with a plop.

He told her, "We've got to get you to a healer. *No, wait.*" Even though she hadn't moved from the chair, he threw out both hands. "*You stay put right there.* We'll get a healer to come to you. Have you eaten enough today? Don't you need vitamins?"

Halfway through his disconnected babble, she started to smile. Remarkably, she seemed to calm down. "You're moving a little too fast there, darling."

"What?" He stared at her wildly, kneeling beside her chair. "What about a birthing class? Do you know how to breathe? I've never been in labor before. I don't know anything about breathing."

*"GRAYDON, SHUT UP,"* she shouted.

His flow of words stopped. He snapped his mouth shut and stared at her.

She stroked his hair. "I'm not even sure I'm p-pregnant. I've never been pregnant before, either, so I'm not sure how it would feel. I can just sense something. Something's changed in my energy, and I've been too scared to say anything, in case it might not be true, and oh gods, I want it so badly."

She started to shake again. That pulled him together like nothing else had.

Taking her into his arms, he told her gently, "Ssh, it's all right, Bel. Whatever the answer is, it's going to be okay. We'll get through it together."

She buried her face in his neck. "Promise?"

Cupping the back of her head, he told her in a calm, steady voice, "I swear it."

With his free hand, he pulled out his cell phone. Behind her back, he scrolled through his contacts until he reached the number for the healer on call that evening at the Tower. With one thumb, he typed out a text:

EMERGENCY, MY APT NOW.

Not five minutes later, he heard running footsteps in the hall. Someone pounded on his door. He distinctly heard Aryal say, "Kick it in."

So much for his calm and soothing act.

*Don't kick it in!* he shouted telepathically.

He was too late. The door splintered. Aryal, Quentin, and the on-call healer—Peter—rushed in.

At the crash, Bel startled violently. She lifted her face from Graydon's neck to stare at the three intruders. When she spoke, she was back to enunciating again. "What. On. Earth."

They had upset Bel. He snarled wordlessly at the trio.

Eyes widening, Aryal threw out her hands. "What?! You said it was an emergency!"

"Yes," he snapped. "I'm sorry." He turned to Bel. Her mouth hung open again. "I'm sorry," he told her. Unable to resist her beautiful, astonished face, he kissed her soft mouth quickly. "I'm still calming down. Aryal and Quentin, get out. Peter, come here."

Quentin and Aryal backed out of the apartment.

"Just you wait," the harpy said bitterly to her mate as they left. "Like everything else, somehow this is going to end up being my fault."

Quentin retorted. "Seriously? Somehow, like everything else, this has become all about you?"

"That's what I'm talking about!"

Their arguing voices faded.

Graydon met Bel's brimming gaze. Self-consciously, he told her, "I'll acknowledge I might have overreacted a bit."

Her face shook. Oh gods, she wasn't going to burst into tears again, was she?

Laughter pealed out of her. Bright and silvery, the sound danced around the room, like bubbles floating in a glass of champagne. Hanging on his neck, she laughed so hard tears came to her eyes.

It was such a happy sound, it took him over completely. Entranced, he soaked up every delicious, intoxicating moment.

The healer, Peter, had relaxed. Laconically, he said, "I'm pretty sure someone who laughs that hard is going to make their medical emergency worse. Maybe burst a spleen."

Bel hiccuped and stared at Graydon accusingly.

After a moment, he offered her a small, sheepish grin. "There could have been one. You never know."

She broke into peals of laughter again.

"Looks like my work here is done," Peter said. "You're welcome."

When he started to edge toward the broken door, Graydon told him, "Not so fast, bucko. Come over here."

Sobering, Peter strode over and squatted beside them. "What is it? What's wrong?"

Despite himself, Graydon bristled at the other male's nearness.

Wiping her face, Bel sobered too. Stroking Graydon's arm, she told Peter, "Nothing wrong, exactly. I just think I might be p-pregnant, but I can't tell for sure and we both panicked. Can you help us?"

Like virtually everybody else in the Tower, Peter's expression softened as he looked at her. "Obviously, I'm not an obstetrician. My specialty is acute trauma—all of the Tower's on-call healers are essentially ER doctors. But I might be able to give you a simple yes or no, so you can at least sleep tonight. Then you can follow up with a doctor of your own choice. How does that sound?"

"Okay, yes," she said. "Thank you."

Peter looked at Graydon. "If I'm going to scan her, I'm going to have to touch her. Get in control of yourself, or leave the room."

With an unpleasant shock, he realized he was growling, low in his throat. Bel hooked fingers underneath his chin and turned his face back to her.

"Hey, you've got this," she said softly. "You can do it. Don't drive the nice healer away, especially after *you* were the one to call him here—stop that, don't look at him. Eyes here, Graydon. Look at me."

He concentrated on the sound of her voice, the delicate rose color of her cheeks, the expression of love and lingering laughter in her eyes.

"That's it, I'm done," said Peter. As his head snapped around, the healer stood and backed away rapidly, hands up. "All I did was a quick scan—a peek in and out again." As they stared at him, the healer grinned. "Congratulations to both of you. You are, in fact, pregnant. I couldn't be happier for you."

Pregnant. Or, as Bel had said, Preg. Nant.

"Holy shit," he whispered.

He met her incredulous, joyful gaze. She started shaking again, and burst into tears. As he snatched her close, she started to laugh too. She threw her arms around his neck.

"I'll let myself out, shall I?" Peter muttered. "It's not a big deal, especially since there's just an open doorway to walk through. I'll pull the pieces of the door sort of back into place for you."

Now that the other male was well and truly leaving, Graydon ignored him and concentrated on kissing Bel breathless.

Preg. Nant.

# ═TWENTY-ONE═

Healing did happen, over time. So did happiness.
Graydon would never stop missing Constantine, but over the next several weeks, the nightmares did eventually fade.

He and Bel began to search for a small house outside the city, with a big private yard, where they could go sometimes for weekends and vacations. When they found a charming little Cape Cod cottage, she moved what furniture and artwork she wanted to keep into it.

At her request, he also took her shopping so she could buy several pairs of jeans. He didn't have room to consider that she did it only to humor him. She was too transparently gleeful when she slipped on her first pair of Levi's. As he watched her simple, grinning pleasure, he began to realize Ferion hadn't been the only one who had lived a life constricted by a narrow role to play.

After they went shopping, he took her out to Ruby's Diner for lunch. To his mild surprise, nobody recognized her. She had wound up her distinctive hair into a bun and tucked it into a Yankees' baseball cap. She ordered apple pancakes and coffee, and polished off the meal while she laughed at Ruby's ribald sense of humor, and it was easy.

Loving her, letting her light up his life, was so easy.

As March came and winter relinquished its snowy grip on the city, gradually, life in the Tower began to assume something of a new normal.

He called Lake Tahoe several times to keep in touch with Julian's progress. After surgeries and grafts, along with healing spells and copious amounts of blood, the doctors had managed to save Julian's hands.

He would need several months of physical therapy to gain back the strength and flexibility in his grip, but his long-term prognosis was excellent. Julian himself was not very talkative about the subject, so in order to get any real news, Graydon learned to chat with Melly either before or after he talked to Julian. He was intensely glad to hear the relief and hope in Melly's voice. That old Vampyre was a hard son of a bitch to kill.

Bel stayed in close contact with Ferion. Gradually Graydon watched her relax, releasing the anxiety she had carried for so long. Optimism entered her eyes and voice whenever she talked about the Elven demesne, and her son in particular. He was not only adjusting. After having his soul shackled for so long, he reveled in his freedom.

It appeared he had also learned from his mistakes. Word came to them from a variety of sources that the new Elven High Lord was making considered decisions, marked with temperance and restraint. The news coming out of South Carolina gained a positive forward momentum.

Like Graydon, the Elves would never forget, but after such a dark time in their history, he did believe they had begun to thrive again.

While he and the rest of the sentinels hired new staff, delegated work and generally figured out how to give Dragos the year he had promised Liam, Bel started a massive project of her own.

Architectural drawings and plans took over the dining room table. After approaching Dragos via email, and arguing with him over the course of several days—she swore she would never have followed through with her original inquiry if she'd had to talk to him in person—Dragos allocated a budget for her project that was large enough to make Graydon's eyes widen when she showed him the approval letter.

Stay in budget, the email warned. Or make sure you come in under, because this is all you get.

"We're going to cover the whole rooftop," she told Graydon, eyes sparkling with excitement. "There's such a limited amount of space, we'll have to plant every shrub and tree carefully, but that's okay. The whole roof is going to turn into an oasis."

"Even the helipad area?" he asked, eyebrows up.

"Yes. Helicopters can land perfectly fine on grass. Right now, all the avian Wyr do is launch and land up there anyway. Now people will be able to go up to the roof for picnics too, or to sleep out underneath the stars if they need. And every floor is going to get its own indoor garden. We'll maximize every inch of space—there'll be vertical gardens everywhere. We'll plant ivy and cooking herbs that people can use if they want, and some will be flowering vines." She drew in a deep breath. "This is still a skyscraper. It won't be as wild as a Wood, but it'll be so much more refreshing for everybody."

He loved her passion. He adored her enthusiasm. He was so much in love with her, his body felt like it encased a city of light.

Resting his chin in his hands, he watched her face for hours and listened as she talked over her plans. He helped her pore over résumés as she hired her gardening staff. Some of them would be temporary, while others would become permanent positions. The indoor and rooftop gardens would require ongoing maintenance.

One night, as they curled up in bed, he asked, "I love how happy this has made you, but what are you going to do when you're finished with the project?"

Her head rested on his chest, and he played with long strands of her hair. The need to keep touching her in some way was compulsive.

She was always welcoming, and responded with such pleasure, often their plans for the day flew out the window as they tumbled back into bed, and he was perpetually fifteen minutes late for work. Nobody minded. When he finally showed up, they greeted him with understanding smiles.

"I'll find another project to work on," she told him. She pressed her lips to his pectoral, eyes sparkling. "Maybe I'll take over Central Park. I've always wanted to, you know."

"Now, that would be big enough for a wild Wood." He laughed. She was going to transform the city.

"Wouldn't it just?" Her voice softened. "Besides, silly man, this project isn't what has made me happy. You have. And Constantine has."

Earlier that day, they had found out the baby's sex. It felt a little awkward to start calling such a small entity by such a large name with so much emotional history, but with enough practice they would adjust, and he felt sure that Con would approve if he'd known.

And because of Constantine, their son was alive. There was no better way to honor his sacrifice.

Graydon was learning to be gentle with himself. With care and respect, he set aside those thoughts to concentrate on the wonderful miracle lying beside him.


Bel was entranced with lying in bed alongside Graydon and talking with him about the events in their days. The sensation of his long, powerful frame stretched out beside her, radiating heat like a great lazy hunting cat, preoccupied her utterly.

She couldn't wait to go to bed each night. Yes, the sex was mind-blowing and addictive, exhilarating and exhausting. Yes, her body learned very quickly to hunger for the touch of his mouth, the caress of his fingers, the sensation of his powerful body moving over hers.

Yes, she ached to be filled with him. She needed to be with him so badly, being apart from him for more than a few hours at a time was unbearable.

Apparently he felt the same, for sometimes when she returned from errands, she could barely make it through the apartment door before he pinned her against the wall and tore her clothes off, taking her with an all-consuming hunger.

But every bit as important as the passion they shared was the fact that she loved simply being with him, basking in his vitality, rubbing her foot along the long muscled length of his legs as they talked, the crisp hairs tickling her toes.

Often, she woke out of a sound sleep just to roll over and stare in amazement at his shadowed, relaxed features.

She loved that he couldn't stop touching her. Even as they laughed at the most ridiculous things, he stroked the curve of her shoulder, or danced his fingers along her hip. He would play with her hair, twining it around his hand, or caress the curve of her breasts.

In many different ways, he told her how much he cherished her. Gradually he branded the message into the patterns he drew on her skin, until it revolutionized how she viewed her world.

Now, as their conversation died away, he came up on one elbow and looked down at her. A shadow passed over his expression, a touch of grief and a yearning so strong, it ripped her apart inside. She never wanted him to be in pain. If she could, she would take all of it for him, just so that she could see him smile again.

Closing his eyes, he rested his forehead against her breast. She cradled his head, pressing her mouth to his temple. He whispered, "I can't be apart from you again."

She understood what he meant. He had given his great, noble soul to her without reservation. He had mated with her.

"I can't be apart from you, either," she murmured softly. "You are everything I ever wanted, everything I could ever need. Gray, you're my world."

He lifted his head. The look in his eyes was vulnerable. "No regrets?"

An unamused laugh broke out of her. "Gods, yes. A ton of them. But they all revolve around reaching Ferion sooner, before Malphas had trapped him, so that you and I wouldn't have had to be apart for so long."

And maybe they wouldn't have had to lose Constantine and Soren.

But that path of thought lay in the wrong direction. Asking *what if*s was an insidious pastime, filled with useless pain.

The truth was, eventually, someone would have had to kill Malphas. Somehow, the cost would have been high. Maybe down another road, it would have been Graydon who had been killed.

Firmly, she turned away from that path, to focus on the wealth of what she truly had.

A small smile tugged at his lips. He nuzzled her with his nose. "We would have had that house outside of Charleston."

She shook her head. "That was a pipe dream," she told him. "Or, maybe it would have been a bridge until we got ourselves sorted out emotionally and did what had to be done. If we had ever truly experienced even a smallest part of that dream, I could never have returned to the same dwelling where Calondir lived, no matter how big it was or how separate we lived our lives."

A hint of blade flashed in his eyes. "That's good, because otherwise I would have had to kill him."

"You say the sweetest things," she crooned up at him. When he burst out laughing, she grinned.

As quickly as it started, his laughter died, and hunger took its place.

Oh, she recognized that look. She was beginning to have a physical reaction every time she saw it in his face.

Her heart began to pound, the muscles in her thighs trembled, and desire for him melted through her body in a liquid gush. They grew so sated every time they made love, yet somehow it only fueled the fire.

He bent his head and kissed her, his lips playing softly over hers in such a cherishing caress, tears pricked at the back of her eyes. She kissed him with everything she had, pouring all the love she felt for him through the sensitive barrier of her skin.

Her body was a love letter written just for him. As his fingers stroked along the curves of her breast, the peaks of her nipples tightened. She'd had no idea that she could feel so much pleasure.

Arching her back, she rubbed against his body. Low at the back of his throat, he made a soft, sexy sound, like a growl. But the growl didn't fade. It remained a steady vibration.

With astonishment and delight, she realized her adorable, dangerous lover was purring.

She didn't dare say anything, or he would get self-conscious and stop.

And she never wanted him to stop.

He was so observant. Hiding her face against his shoulder, she decided she needed to take quick action, to keep him from wondering about whatever was happening in her expression.

She began to kiss him all over the broad expanse of his muscled chest. As she gently nibbled, licked and suckled at his nipples, he sucked in his breath.

"I was going to do that," he muttered. "I mean, to you."

"You give me so much pleasure, all the time," she whispered. "This time, let me focus on you."

She ran her mouth down the rippling muscles of his flat stomach. Pulling her hair to one side, she kissed the tip of his large erection. He was beautifully made, his penis thick and full, while underneath, his sac had drawn tight with arousal.

He settled back against the pillows, parting his legs to give her better access, while he stroked her hair and watched her, his look turning heavy-lidded and sensual.

She smiled up the length of his body and told him, "I love you."

As he opened his mouth to respond, she bent her head back to his cock and took him in her mouth.

His whole big body jerked, and he slammed his head back against the pillow. "Holy gods," he gasped. "Your mouth is so fucking hot."

She was too busy licking and sucking along the broad,

thick head of his cock to reply out loud. Telepathically, she murmured, *Is that a good thing?*

"Sweetheart, it's an amazing, amazing thing." Gently, he caressed her cheek, and ran a finger along the edge of her lips where he penetrated her mouth. His hands were shaking. He whispered, "You are so beautiful."

Wordlessly, she crooned. He was beautiful too, everywhere, both inside and out. Opening her throat, she took him all the way in and held the position for one long, luscious moment. When she couldn't sustain it any longer, she pulled back, sucking hard along his length. Then she impaled herself on him again.

She lost herself in sensuality, working him with her mouth, while she cupped and caressed his sac, and spread her hands over the flat expanse of his stomach. When she ran the edge of her fingernails lightly down the inside of his thighs, his body tightened until he was rock hard all over.

"Here it is," he warned on a harsh gasp. "Goddamn."

Ooh. She wanted his climax more than she wanted her own.

Closing her eyes, she reached blindly up to him with one hand, concentrating everything on his pleasure. His hand closed over hers, gripping her tightly, as he groaned and jetted into her mouth.

She found the rhythm of his pulsing, stroking his cock with her tongue. Shaking and swearing, his powerful body jerked underneath her caress, and his warm, salty semen filled her mouth. She swallowed him down eagerly, embracing every last, earthy part of him.

After a few moments, he exploded out of his reclining position. Pulling her head away from his erection, he growled, "I can't take any more of that, but it isn't enough. I've got to get inside you."

He sounded harsh, stripped of everything but need. His compulsion to mate rode him relentlessly, and she surrendered herself to it.

Following his urging, she rolled onto her side, and he lifted one of her legs to spoon her body and enter her from behind. She nestled back against his chest. It was one of their favorite positions, leaving her torso bare so that he could caress her everywhere.

As he fucked her, he pinched her nipples gently between thumb and forefinger, rolling the stiff, peaked flesh between thumb and forefinger. It sent sparks of sensation along her nerve endings, heightening her pleasure. He hooked one arm underneath her waist, reaching around to finger her opening.

When he found her clitoris, she jerked in his hands. He growled into her neck, encasing her in his arms, plucking and rubbing at her pleasure points while his cock slid in and out, in and out.

Making love to him was so unbearably good. So good. As the inner pressure built, her breath came in sobs. She twisted and pushed back against him, trying to find relief.

"I have to come so badly, it hurts," she gasped.

"It's okay, love," he murmured into her ear, the sensation of his voice curling deep into her body. "I'll take you there. I'll always take you there."

He was a man of his word. She could trust in him completely. Whatever he said he would do, he would do.

He kept his promises.

Always faithful, always true.

She had just enough time to think it, before the demands of her body took over completely. The press of his callused fingers moved against her hypersensitive nubbin of flesh, hurtling her forward.

Pleasure cascaded, one peak following the next, as he took her there, just like he said.

He took her home.


Much later, after Bel had fallen asleep, Graydon couldn't turn his mind off. He eased away, tucking the covers around her warm, lax body. After pulling on sweatpants, he scooped something he'd been keeping secret out of his bedside drawer, and stepped outside, onto the balcony.

A moody, fitful wind played with his hair and flowed like

invisible water along the bare skin of his chest. He opened the small box and considered the contents, nestled in dark velvet.

Brilliance sparkled in the shadows. Chewing on his lip, he considered the eternity ring covered in a row of bright, flawless diamonds.

Maybe it was the wrong way to go. He thought the ring was beautiful, and he loved the symbolism of an eternity ring, but perhaps he should have chosen something more traditional to offer as an engagement ring. A diamond solitaire, or better yet, an emerald.

He felt pretty sure she would love an emerald. Maybe he should go back to the jeweler's one more time. And he needed to make a reservation at the right kind of restaurant.

A classy one, with a maître d', cloth napkins, unpronounceable wine names, and too many glasses and forks. Alexander was a classy dude. He would know of the right place.

Or maybe she would prefer something else. A concert? A day cruise out to sea?

Oh hell, he was no good at this kind of traditional shit. It wasn't like he'd ever proposed before.

The balcony door opened, and Bel's sleepy voice sounded behind him. "What are you doing out here?"

Closing the box with a snap, he hid it behind his back as he spun to face her. "Nothing. What are you doing awake?"

"I missed you. It woke me up." She squinted at him. "What was that snapping sound?"

"Nothing!" he insisted.

She stepped outside and drew the door shut behind her. She wore a rose-colored silken wrap that came to midcalf, leaving her lovely ankles and slender feet bare.

"Did you know, you are an excellent liar with everybody except me?" she asked, wagging a finger as she approached.

"What are you talking about?" he muttered, backing away as she advanced. "I don't lie to you."

She chortled. She sounded utterly delighted with life, and with him. "Of course you don't, my love."

The endearment caressed his emotions. It felt almost as if she had stroked her fingers down his chest.

"Never stop calling me that," he whispered.

"Never stop loving me," she whispered back.

At that, he stopped retreating and began to advance. "I'll always love you, always."

As he drew close, she glanced up at him slyly. "Do you love me enough to show me what you're hiding behind your back?"

Oh, damn. This wasn't what he'd had in mind. As he looked around the balcony, he sighed. The ring box was burning a hole in his hand. "Yes, I do."

The sound of her soft laughter wrapped around him again, as warm as a hug. "Gray, I'm sorry for teasing you. If you need to keep what's behind your back a secret, it's okay. Truly."

Now that she had caught him red-handed, as it were, he discovered he couldn't wait a moment longer. Finally, he obeyed the impulse he had felt so very long ago.

He went down on one knee to the Lady of the Wood.

Her eyes went wide. "What are you doing?"

He brought the box around and opened it for her, so that the fire from the diamonds spilled out.

"I never saw myself as a romantic before," he told her in a low voice. "Mostly I'm a simple guy who likes a cold beer and a good steak. You've taught me differently. I want the vows. I want the ceremony. I want dancing, champagne and celebration, and cake. I want a bachelor's night, and for everybody we love to hug us and wish us a happy life, and I want a honeymoon. I had no idea I could want all those things, until you. Beluviel, you are my heart and my home, and the love of my very long life. I don't want to just call you my mate. I want to call you my wife. Please marry me."

Halfway through, she started crying.

Anxiety twisted his insides. Lord, he must have really screwed it up, but if so, he didn't know how proposing in a swanky restaurant could have made it any better.

When he stopped speaking, she fell to her knees in front of him.

"You have given me everything," she whispered. "You've saved my life, my soul. You freed my son, and you've given me another one. I'm so honored you've come into my life, Graydon. I thought I couldn't adore you more than I already do, or be more happy, but I was wrong." Wiping her eyes, she looked into the box. "What a beautiful ring."

He muttered, "I was going to take it back and get you an emerald."

She snatched the box out of his hands. "Oh no, you don't. This is too gorgeous. I think an eternity ring is just perfect."

Pleasure at her obvious delight warmed him to his bones. Bending his head over hers, he whispered, "Here, let me help."

The ring was solidly caught in its nest. Between the two of them, they wiggled it free, and he slipped it onto her finger. The diamonds flashed, lighting up her hand. She splayed her hand, and they admired it together.

"I want cake too," she said. Her dark, smiling gaze turned up to him, and the light in them outshone the diamonds. "And a pretty dress. And vows, and a party."

"And a honeymoon," he insisted. He really didn't want to miss out on that.

"Oh yes, and a honeymoon." She threw back her head and laughed. The sound danced like champagne bubbles in the night. "Who'd have thought it?"

Life had its own kind of rhythm. Shadows might be inevitable, and winter too.

But winter passes. It always does pass.

Bending his head, he kissed her. As he put his heart and soul into the caress, he inhaled her scent.

That first, rare breath of spring washed over him. He knew he would fly at this new life with everything he had.

He, for one, couldn't wait to see what happened next.

"A dark, compelling world. I'm hooked!"

— J. R. Ward, #1 *New York Times* bestselling author

FROM *NEW YORK TIMES* BESTSELLING AUTHOR

# THEA HARRISON

## The Elder Race Novels

## DRAGON BOUND
## STORM'S HEART
## SERPENT'S KISS
## ORACLE'S MOON
## LORD'S FALL
## KINKED
## NIGHT'S HONOR
## MIDNIGHT'S KISS
## SHADOW'S END

TheaHarrison.com
facebook.com/TheaHarrison
facebook.com/ProjectParanormalBooks
penguin.com

BERKLEY SENSATION | Penguin Random House

M1122AS0815

*Centuries ago, two lovers were torn apart by forces beyond their control. Now they have been reunited by destiny and are willing to sacrifice everything again to save a world on the brink of extinction.*

FROM *NEW YORK TIMES* BESTSELLING AUTHOR

# THEA HARRISON

## The Game of Shadows Novels

AVAILABLE NOW

TheaHarrison.com
facebook.com/TheaHarrison
penguin.com

**BERKLEY SENSATION** | Penguin Random House

M1605AS0815